ERIC WH

GRIDLESS

GRIDLESS

a novel by

ERIC WHETSTONE

....

"Luck is what happens when preparation meets opportunity."
– Seneca (Roman philosopher)

"It's just as easy to fill the top half as it is the whole tank."
– My Dad

LIBERTY HILL PRESS

READER'S CHOICE:

GRIDLESS offers the reader a choice in consuming the story. Read the book "cover-to-cover" (as it's presented) or read the parts separately.

"Rachel's Story" follows Rachel, Jake's wife. Flexing her skills and wits, she makes her own way, outsmarting worthy adversaries and overcoming major obstacles. "Rachel's Story" can be read in its entirety before starting "Gridless," or, it can be read afterwards.

Before, during, or after. It's the reader's choice.

Liberty Hill Press
2301 Lucien Way #415
Maitland, FL 32751
407.339.4217
www.libertyhillpublishing.com

Paperback ISBN-13: 978-1-6322-1941-1
eBook ISBN-13: 978-1-6322-1942-8

Printed in the United States of America

Book design by: WhetstoneDesign
Photo illustrations by: Eric Whetstone
(Lightbulb and wind turbine images from ShutterStock, used through enhanced license permission.)

•••••••••••••••

For Trish & Zach, the incredible cheerleaders and supporters of even my wildest dreams. And for my Mom & Dad, the most incredible parents a guy could have. I am blessed. – All my love to all of you.

CHAPTER 1: A NEW DAY

The light on the pole flickered to life. It was almost shocking. In fact, everyone came outside to look at it. There was silence as we stood there, like children in wide-eyed amazement. In the middle of the day, that single 60-watt bulb drew the attention of a midnight fireworks display as it flickered and pulsed and buzzed. After a couple of minutes, it remained at a dim but stable glow. We had long wished for it to illuminate, but it seemed that now, perhaps, we weren't quite so sure.

• • • • •

We've spent a lot of nights out here in "the dark." I've gone through days when I took copious notes, rabidly filling my journal with details and entries of what I'd seen and what I surmised. But paper is a commodity that eventually finds its greater value in a winter night's fire. That is, the good old paper of wood and cotton, the stuff that'll actually burn. Most of what I find blown into the remnant fence rows these days is too plasticized to carry any heat or duration. It goes up like a flash, leaving just an oil spot and an unappealing odor that lingers akin to the aroma of singed hair. Anyway, keeping track of the time seems far less critical than simply understanding the seasons and how to best exploit what they bring.

But last winter was a cold one, and longer than some I've endured. My wife, Rachel, always told me that keeping warm in the north country required an enormous supply of wood or coal. Her plan, in case anything was to upset the daily course of our lives, was always to keep to the south – where the problem was simply a lack of water. Pick your poison: freeze to death or die of thirst. We had joked about it between ourselves on many road trips. Where would we go? What would we do? We talked, and planned... and mostly laughed. It was really just intended to give our minds something to ponder as the miles rolled under the tires. Anyway, it didn't seem as either choice would be necessary for a couple of would-be millionaires who had traveled the world and checked most of the boxes on their bucket list.

Not that long ago, our decisions would have been filet versus New York strip, baked potato or asparagus, and whether my Sleep Number was set to 70 or 75. Ironically, we thought those days carried a lot of stress. But then, we were focused on different goals, in a different place, in an incredibly different time.

Einstein's theory of relativity is based on gravity. The pull of *everything*, including what he determined to be particles of light. He theorized that it bends, shifts, and conforms to the influences of greater mass. I guess all of us do. The speed of a vortex, as you enter deeper into the center, can be insurmountable. I'd seen it myself. Having grown up in the Midwest, I had witnessed more than my share of tornadoes. And, I'd had the childhood pleasure of spending most of one summer cleaning up after a twister hit our family farm. The force was unbelievable, driving blades of grass into wooden siding, exploding the large metal grain bin, and scattering cows and tractors among the trees.

It was utter devastation, and you couldn't see it coming. You could hear the rumblings and feel the uneasiness in the world around you, but that's a hard thing to read. When it's dark, when your communication systems are down, and when there's suddenly a vacuum in the air – you'd best go underground.

So, that's where I am now. Underground. Not in the physical sense of being in a storm cellar beneath five feet of soil, but "underground" in the sense of being out of sight, out of the system. There are things that we all hide from, including guilt, anxiety, and other truths of reality. Everyone disconnects differently from their job, their relationships, their family, or their fear of the unknown. I'm hiding from some uncertainties, some guilt, and from reality. I don't really want to know what life has become for so many. I've begun to get comfortable with myself and what it took to bring me to this place in my life. I was caught in the same vortex as everyone else, but I was prepared to see it through. It was a long rough ride, but I had it easier than most. The darkness we've encountered hasn't been caused solely by a lack of light. It's from an inner emptiness that was realized when suddenly everyone was unplugged, and everyone was off the grid.

As the world spun itself into the beginnings of the vortex, some people, kind of the nouveau hippies of the day, tossed their electronics, their phones and devices, and moved out into the desert or the hills. "Off the grid," they would say. "Gridless." But little did they know that they would find themselves on the new cutting edge.

We had some good laughs at their expense over the years. When we'd travel across states like Colorado and New Mexico, we'd see their beat-up old cars limping into the area Walmart, where they'd come for supplies. I always imagined the historic parallel to this somewhat humorous site as the frontiersmen who made their trek across what became America – guys like Lewis & Clark – breaking from winter camp in the Dakotas to make a Target run for some microfiber towels and a fresh water filter. Maybe it's possible to walk the fine line of rejecting it all while still having it all. What I'm saying is, if you're really going to live off the grid, you'd best know how to make a candle from some beeswax, plant silks, and bark, just in case the solar panels give out. I guess everyone's plan is different.

But planning can only take you so far. Then, it's the execution of the plan. Some of the really serious preppers had the right basis, but most misinterpreted how things would all go down. They wound up being ill-prepared, with too many of the wrong things and not enough of what they really needed. I mean, you can't eat ammo. So you have to convert the ammo into food in some fashion. The ones who stockpiled a ton of weapons and ammo, they were either protecting a solid fortress of food and sustenance, or they were equipped to go out and take it. And for many of the average civilians out there, I'd guess that became pretty scary and perhaps deadly over time.

For the peaceful ones that planted gardens and lived in plastic dome tents, the world was maybe more like they'd hoped, without the whine of airplanes flying overhead and no pressure to maintain a 3-2 split-level ranch with an attached garage – as they used to say. Their existence was likely utopian by their standards, unless their gardens were found by the ammo preppers.

In these parts, that seemed to be two of the more significant factions: the ammo preppers and the nouveau hippies. The rest of the folks were just kind of screwed.

Of course, I'd like to believe that I was a brilliant genius who had it all figured out. But that would be a lie. Mostly, I was lucky enough to be in the right place at the right time, with enough of what was needed and not too much of what wasn't. I believe it was an old Roman philosopher who once said, "Luck is what happens when preparation meets opportunity," or something like that. I've also heard people say they'd take luck over talent. Whatever the appropriate words, I...we...were simply lucky. Fortunate. Blessed.

That's the only reason I'm able to stand in my garden and tell this story today. •

CHAPTER 2: NO APOCALYPSE

I'm still not sure what set all of this in motion or to what extent it has impacted others in the world. I assume that it has become somewhat of a world-scale event, but I don't really know. The fallout for the heartland of our country was certainly devastating, but maybe the coasts have pulled things together. Since I've arrived here, I've tried to avoid most contact with strangers, and folks aren't traveling through here for leisure these days. In some ways, it's been a nice break.

We've all seen the movies, the post-apocalyptic scenes that show animalistic gangs of outlaws, plundering the burnt-out shopping malls and raping the young women who, for some reason, are out near the highway with a torn dress and one high-heeled shoe (credit: *Mad Max* and/or *Book of Eli*). But you know what I mean. It's the standard visual. Hazy, overcast skies, buried in pollution and filth, steeped in violence and chaos. Some of that landed pretty close. I did see glimpses and pieces of that, but it's not what I choose to remember. It's not my biggest takeaway.

Our little group stays busy working the gardens and bringing in fresh water. Most days are more aligned with *Little House on the Prairie* than *Thunderdome*. It's pretty rural and basic around the main camp we've created. In fact, I'd say we've found a new sense of purpose that brings our focus back to the important facets of life: food, shelter, friends, and family. And it really didn't take us long to find our roots in this lifestyle. I've made peace with what it took to get us here.

But the transition was maybe a bit darker than I like to truly remember. The initial understanding of what might be happening, coming to grips with the reality of the situation and making some hard and lasting choices. Sad days, maybe years, for so many. Again, I assume that it's millions, but maybe I've just not roamed far enough or crossed the path of the right messenger. They may tell me different, but it wouldn't change much. We've got what we need, and we're not seeking much more. We keep to ourselves and we stopped trusting the outside reports, as they often contradict each other and seem to promote others' outcome agendas.

I apologize for dragging out my story, maybe trying to forget as well as remember, and while I want to share it all, I really don't want anyone to know the whole story. As I said, some of the choices are pretty hard and they are lasting. •

CHAPTER 3: ONCE UPON A TIME

I was like most guys my age. Comfortable in the career, pleased with my years on the bleachers, watching the kiddo play ball and perform in shows. My teenage dreams of exotic cars and personal jet airplanes weren't coming to fruition, but I can't say I really expected that they would.

My best dreams had come true however, with a loving wife by my side, day and night. Good health had graced our days, and we didn't want for much. If it was within reason, we had it. Plus, we had a stellar kiddo that was, if anything, too talented in far too many areas. Life was good. That was that.

I'd set my own course for success or failure, departing the design studio I had joined shortly out of college. If you needed a logo or a label, I was your guy. What started as a sign-painting hobby as a kid – my friend's lawn mowing service and the local bar's nightly specials – became a full-scale branding operation. Thankfully, everyone knows that a shirt with an embroidered "thing" on it is worth more than a shirt without a "thing" on it. I will say, however, that real honest-to-goodness branding does actually work like we always said it did. It reassures the consumer that there is consistency and quality in the product, due to the continuity and application of the brand identity. It builds trust and solidifies a reputation, which means it's a safe bet.

And, that's why I am still able to, on occasion, grab a Coca-Cola from the vault and know that I'll enjoy that same taste that refreshed me at the movie theatre when I was a kid, or at the ballgame in college, or on my first date with my wife, or wherever I drank the thousands of Cokes I'd tasted over the years. It's still the same. Okay, the cases I've got stored are a little flat now, but opening a mystery bottle and drinking from an unknown source? "No thanks." I'll stick with what I know. That's the value of good branding.

Faith in a product can be worth a lot. And that gets my story back on track. The reason I have a stockpile of red soda cans and bottles in the first place. Spoils of war, some might say. Others would say senseless and disgusting, pathetic and barbaric. But those opinions aren't shared around here much anymore. And I can't say that I agreed with them when they were shared. But some folks always liked to share their opinions regarding how everyone else should behave.

"It's plastic bags that plague the earth," he said. The tall, thin teenager at the craft store where we were buying balloons and plates for a birthday party.

His original question was, "Do you want these bagged?"

"No," I replied. "They're already in bags." I was being both practical and, I thought, humorous. But he saw the opening to toss in a little social critique and enlighten us on his views. I laughed.

Is it really plastic bags that plague the earth?

First, it was the paper bags that had to go. Does everyone remember that? Deforestation was the message then. We were killing all the trees and complete chaos and devastation was certain to come to the human race if we didn't start using thin plastic bags to carry our groceries to the car. Thus, an earlier version of that same kid, 20 years prior, would have been quizzing me on, "Paper or plastic?" followed by, "Paper bags are destroying the earth. You know, plastic recycles!" Again, pick your poison.

You know, maybe it doesn't have anything to do with the bags themselves or what they're made of. Maybe it has everything to do with the trashy humans who tossed their bags to the wind, and littered our roadways and neighborhoods because they were just too frickin' lazy to pick up after themselves. Maybe that was the cause of most of the world's problems, but speaking the truth could be considered a "micro-aggression," and that must be avoided at all costs. The truth isn't what anyone wanted to hear. As you can tell, I still get a bit riled, but there has been so much loss. I do harbor a few soapboxes, so back to what I was saying...

There was even a time when stores gave out woven Tyvec-type bags, with woven nylon straps, in their "green" attempts. They called them "forever bags." The concept they pushed on us, at a couple of bucks per bag, was that we would have one bag for their store, and that we'd use it endlessly – or, until we came the next time and hadn't remembered our forever bag, so they'd sell us another one for another two bucks and we'd add it to our collection of forever bags. But I'm glad they did, as those bags never decay and can't be recycled. Finding a box of them gave us the best herb wall planters I've ever seen. And, they look great. The colors are festive, and the size is perfect!

But again, I've wandered off topic. Too much sun, not enough water. That's why I wanted to go north! •

CHAPTER 4: WHY A PLAN?

My son and I had worked out a plan, in case some catastrophic event would befall us. I had thought it might be some overreach of government, or the public's response to overreach, followed by martial law. It could have been an unlikely alien attack from outer space, but I'm not that whacked. A foreign military attack was always in the cards, however.

Most of the preppers had thought it would be the government. In the old days, my father's days, it would have been concern about nuclear war. Each generation has its ghosts in the closet. That shadow under the bed that just might manifest itself and get you. There are always those who will exploit that fear to the fullest. And then, there are those of us who will just sleep with a baseball bat next to the bed, waiting for the chance to take them out.

I had first faced the monster during a drive to Iowa. Mom and Dad still lived there, and I made somewhat regular trips home to see them, reconnect, and help with some of the to-do lists that need attention as parents grow older. But my realization had nothing to do with the lists back home and everything to do with my lack of planning for the journey. I had done it too many times, and I had become lax in my attention and logic. It would be the last time I let that happen.

Driving up I-35, as I had done too many times to remember, I was about an hour north of Dallas when I realized I hadn't filled with gas before departing. My routine had always been to pull a hundred dollars in cash from the little box on the top shelf in the closet, stop and fill with gas, grab a Coke, a hot dog, and two bags of honey-roasted peanuts. It was 12 hours on the road, so a little preparation was appropriate. But that night, I'd had my mind on other things.

Changing deadlines from clients, a problem with the computer, rushing to FedEx, dropping off a delivery across town, too many irons in the fire. It was also the transitional season that remained fall in Texas but was potentially winter in Iowa. So, the clothes I'd tossed into my bag weren't the best choices, either. Not very well thought out, but hey, it was just another of many two-day, up-and-back treks to clean leaves out of the rain gutters, carry some de-icer into the garage, and bring the Christmas decorations down from the attic. No biggie. I'd make my run halfway across the nation and be back before the neighbors even noticed I was gone.

"Fuel Level Low" was the orange light on the instrument panel. *Damn.* My old truck didn't tell me how many miles I had remaining – ah, the good ole days – but I guessed around 20. That would mean about a gallon remained in the 20-gallon tank. Seemed about right. *Where was I?* My usual method got me through Oklahoma City with about a quarter-tank left, then I'd fill up on the north side of the city. That tankful would get me to Topeka, then up through northern Missouri, and on home to Iowa. It was by rote. Every place I stopped, I knew the fastest pumps, the layout of the bathrooms. Less than 10 minutes – fuel, bathroom, refills, food – back on the road. Smooth and easy.

However, this night would not be smooth and easy. As I looked for the next mile marker, I noticed no lights on the horizon ahead, which I guessed to be around 5 or 6 miles. The next rise would give me a better vantage point, gazing out to maybe 10 or 12 miles. I needed to see something, or my 20-mile reserve of vapors was going to be gone, and I would be walking.

There it was. The red and green glow of the gas price sign on the horizon. Surely within reach, so my heart rate dropped to normal, but I still kicked myself for bringing on the stress. "*Idiot.*" The internal voice from the judgmental side of the brain wanted me to remember this mistake. I would.

I pulled in to what appeared to be a very busy gas station for this time of evening. It was probably around 10 o'clock. So, I would have thought, on a weekday night, this time of year, I would have been one of just a few on the gas side of the pumps, with a parking lot full of truckers nesting down for the night, and maybe a couple of big rigs over at the diesel pumps. But that wasn't the case. Cars and trucks were literally everywhere.

I saw a car pull away from the corner pump and I pulled on in. With my 10-minute timer ticking, I spun out of the seat and swiped my card through the pump's pay slot. Nothing. I swiped again. Likely why the previous car had departed so quickly. Just then, the car in front of me left that pump vacant. I jumped in and pulled up. Another run of the card simply yielded a "See Attendant" instruction. Great.

My mind was not really with me in the moment. I was thinking about the hurried deadlines I'd left behind, forgetting to fill with gas, mostly yelling at myself inside. So, I was kind of blindly walking into the place and really hadn't paid that much attention outside. I was in a bit of a thought bubble, which was about to burst.

"Hey! I said, 'move it!'" It was a short, stocky truck driver in a pair of Carhart overalls and a flannel shirt-jacket, sporting a beard that'd impress any ZZ Top fan.

"Well, I can't move it until I get fuel!" responded another guy, wearing a ball cap, a chained wallet shoved in his back pocket. He appeared to be about my age.

The two truckers arguing at the diesel register drew my focus.

"Look, I don't know what to tell you," said the older gentleman working the cash register. "You've put fuel in your tanks, and we've got to get that paid before you pull out."

"So, how much is it?" asked the second man, his wallet now in hand and open.

"I don't know," said the attendant.

The second trucker chimed in, "I've got less than two hours before my clock runs out, so I've got to get the hell out of here. Move your damn truck so I can get down the road."

"I can't take cash. I don't know how to figure the change," said a younger voice, off to my right.

A young boy was working the checkout for the sandwich shop, and his exclamation brought my mind out of the truckers' ordeal. I turned to see a disgusted man, with apparently his wife and a couple of kids. They tossed their sandwich bags on the counter and stormed out. It added to a pile of bags that were already there. A dozen or so bagged sandwiches, in a pile, on the edge of the counter. The kid was just staring at a blank screen, with no little icons to push.

The language became a bit more edgy. Frustration levels had obviously been simmering for a while.

"Screw 'em, just take it," said the next guy to his group, and they just walked out with their food.

"Hey, you've gotta pay for that!" said an older lady from behind the counter.

"Tried to," another man said, as he took a big suck out of his straw and went out the door.

"C'mon, grab what you want!" said a group of kids my son's age.

It all fell apart pretty fast.

I went back to my truck and backed out into the road. The store was being looted, and the handful of people making sandwiches and working the registers weren't going to be able to stop it. And neither was I.

I thought about it that whole night and many times since. What was my responsibility? What could I have done? Could I have helped? It was an important glimpse inside the dark box of humanity. At the time, though, I needed to find gas and get to Iowa, and that's what concerned me. Logic told me that the power had gone off just prior to my arrival, or maybe their systems were down, some isolated glitch that had shut down their POS systems (what they were probably calling "piece of shit" instead of "point of sale" that night). I assumed that's what it was – *system failure*. Would their systems be satellite or landline? I really didn't know. Up the ramp, back on the road. Not my problem.

How many miles to the next stop? Luckily, not many. I made a quick observation of the place before I pulled in. I was much more aware now, and my intent was to understand the situation before I even pulled into the lot. How many cars? Were people pumping gas? How many inside, in line, standing in a bunch, or shopping throughout the store? It looked more normal. These were all things my eyes had seen at the first stop, but my mind didn't compute.

One exit back, it was a group of people around the checkout, nobody in the aisles, cars with no hoses in the tanks, and trucks lined up around the building but nobody pumping fuel. The vehicles were leaving with frustrated drivers.

That's what I had seen back there, but I wasn't paying attention. All the information I needed, but had failed to process. It was a lesson, one of many, that would prove valuable in the years ahead.

And cash. I had also forgotten to grab any cash from the stash box on the top shelf of the closet. Each year, I received some bonus cash back from my credit card's rewards program. It was a few hundred dollars, and it usually arrived each year in December. I had started collecting it in the little metal box I'd used as my bank when I was a kid mowing lawns. It was my emergency ATM, perfect for spur-of-the-moment date nights with my wife or giving an extra 20 bucks to the kiddo from time to time. But I hadn't followed my routine. So, here I was with eight dollars in my pocket. What if they could have pumped gas, but only accepted cash? Eight dollars worth of gas wasn't going to get me to Iowa, fix a flat tire, or rent a room for the night. You can't expect to travel across half the country with less than 10 bucks on you! I was so mad at myself.

It was a lot of pointless stress. Ultimately, nothing happened and I arrived at my folks' around sunrise. The benefit of being able to stay awake for a couple of days at a time had served me well during final exams in college, and it had its benefits in the adult world as well. For the ever-changing design project it was helpful, but mostly, I used it for road trips.

More recently, I've thought about that night and what was likely an early Internet glitch. In those years, everybody had rushed to connect all of their business sites, cross-reference the inventory data, update the pricing, enact loyalty cards, and add whatever other soft-service gadget they could jam into the works. When I thought about all of that breaking down, I recalled one gas station I had stopped at on my original trips between Texas and Iowa. It was a traditional gas station with two repair bays, bottled sodas and beer, a candy rack, a small assortment of snacks, and two, maybe four pumps. The bathrooms were outside and required a key from the attendant. Those pumps required no satellite feed, no digital access, just some basic electricity and a flip of the handle. You paid after filling, and your approval to pump came in the form of a nod from the guy inside.

I have debated with myself many times about my own actions, and how I helped bring all of this about. Because I, like the thousands of other motorists who travel that highway, eventually chose the bigger, cleaner bathrooms, the vast fountain drink selection, the aisles of snacks, and the two dozen digitally linked pumps that all helped me meet my 10-minute turnaround times.

That old station was still sitting there the last time I drove by, closed for decades now, a sad reminder of a simpler time that we all abandoned. There is always a price to be paid for the gains of technology, but that's a complete departure from my story line, and as you're beginning to learn, I wander enough as it is.

Suffice to say, I always travel with cash and even some extra fuel. I also carry a detailed atlas – that's a road map for you younger readers. And let's just say that I won't be left undefended in the middle of Kansas – regardless of any legislation that may say otherwise. •

CHAPTER 5: GETTING BACK TO THE PLAN

As I said, my son and I had worked out a plan, inspired by my previous story. Actually, I had worked it out. I just sent it to him and said, "We need to have this plan, so review it, and call me." I'm usually not very direct, but on this particular item, I was.

The problem with having a kiddo in college is that, first of all, you miss them. Secondly, you want them to be safe. You want them to spread their wings and fly, yet you are still trying to spread your wings of protection. That's what this plan attempted.

There's a triangle of distance between the Metroplex (Dallas–Fort Worth), Nashville (where Alex was), and hometown Iowa. I had decided that, in the event of disaster, we should try to meet up in northern Missouri. It would be accessible by both him and us in about the same amount of time, and he should be able to make it on one full tank of gas, if that's all he had. My goal was to set a meet point where we could consolidate fuel and resources, assess the situation, and make the final push into Iowa.

Why did I think this plan was necessary? I had felt that, at times, the rumblings of government were louder than they should be, and there seemed to be increasing issues with the overall systems and infrastructures that we all depended upon. Call me a *conspiracy theorist*, call me *cautious*, or call me *crazy*. I'll own any of the titles with pride, and frankly, I don't care what anybody thinks. I know that it's my responsibility to do my best to protect my family, and that's what I'm going to do, regardless of how that appears to the outside world or the neighbors.

Moberly, Missouri, won the dart toss. It has a small airport on the north side of town, just up the road from a Walmart. It's on the very edge of town, and there are some uninhabited farm lots and pull-offs that allow good sight lines. And while I've always been skeptical on technology, I've got to say, Google Maps and Google Earth allowed me to "drive" the whole route and scope it out. Driving there myself later that year, I found it to be just what I'd expected.

So, here's the plan.

In the event of an "event," the plan goes into action. What defines an "event" is anything that causes a disruption in our ability to communicate for more than two days. If it's a tornado or storm, then that's a local event, and I'll know his power is out or lines are down, and he'd know the same about us. The national news would carry the story. The type of event we were talking about is the kind where suddenly we can't get in touch with each other, and we don't know why. Nationwide communications failure, some type of military pulse deployment, foreign or domestic terrorism, etc. Whatever the case, on that level, we depart our homes at the end of the second day. We give it a day to work out, get repaired, etc., but at the end of Day Two, if we don't have an answer and can't communicate with each other, we hit the road with food, fuel, cash, protection, and a plan. We pick up no passengers, and we use mapped routes that we've driven and tested. It doesn't matter if our vehicle is low on gas – although, as my dad always said, "It's just as easy to refill the top half as it is the whole tank." Good advice. In either case, we keep extra gas on hand in our garages. We both store enough fuel to get to Iowa.

At the end of Day Two, we set out for Moberly. We allow each other two more days to get there. When we arrive, we spray paint our logo (remember, branding is important) on the bridge by the airport, along with the date and time. Then we hide. Second to arrive paints their time. The first to arrive is to check the bridge every three hours, at the top of the hour. We meet up and continue onward. By the end of "Event Day +5," we should all be in hometown Iowa.

Obviously there are inherent problems with the plan. An atmosphere-level pulse would toast our vehicle electronics, and a mass military movement would hinder travel. There are downsides to any plan. But having been in the city, both cities – during the Nashville flood of 2010 and any half-inch ice storm in Texas – I know how fragile supermarket inventories are, and I know how panic-stricken the public becomes. In fact, just waiting until Day Two to bug out seems almost too long. That, to me, is the biggest downside possible. So we'll take our chances in the rural areas, which are becoming more and more vacant. Even a bad plan is better than no plan at all.

Once in Iowa, we are among a larger group of relatives. Nothing bonds like blood, they say. Farmers have fuel, and small towns have gas stations with old-fashioned pumps. And if we must, hand pumps and hoses are part of the plan – along with bolt cutters and hacksaws to manage locks and chains. It's not what we prefer, but at that point, we will be a long way from preference. •

CHAPTER 6: A LONG TIME COMING

Humans are interesting animals. We have the greatest intellect of any creature on the planet, with an understanding of science and mathematics that puts your common mule deer or largemouth bass to shame. Yet, we have become so reliant on our intellect that our intuitive reasoning, and certainly our animal instincts, have become almost dormant within us. The deer can physically feel pending changes in the weather, and I've yet to meet a largemouth bass that didn't have enough blankets and canned corn to make it through the winter. As humans, we have shortcomings driven by our need for complex shelter, packaged food, and most unfortunately, our tendency to live in herds that are far too populous for the area of land that they occupy. It is unsustainable with any level of crisis event.

And that is what had been brewing for many, many years. The intellectuals and academics had fostered a belief in urban utopia, where everyone lives in a communal bliss of shared space and harmonious equality. It's a nice idea. As a concept, it can be portrayed as the pinnacle of logic. Efficiency of construction with stacked housing pods, mass transit, and clustered points of access for employment, food, entertainment, and social experiences. It's perfect, as perfect as the pictures that were staged and retouched to portray its existence. And, just as false.

About a year prior to the start of our current situation, the food networks had experienced some dramatic issues. A lot of the crops in Minnesota had been lost. The mass harvests of green beans, sweet corn, peas, and a host of other staple vegetables were cut dramatically as regional power outages, worker uprisings, and transitional legislation caused a trifecta of disaster across America's breadbasket.

New energy rulings and ever-increasing carbon taxes drove the agricultural industry into adopting automated harvesting equipment. Labor cutbacks fueled unemployment and dissension, and an overstressed power grid buckled in the northern Midwest.

Some fields were burned as angry workers lashed out at the farms and companies that left them struggling for jobs as automation displaced their families' means of income. Tens of thousands of acres were destroyed in midsummer when the harvesters learned that the upcoming season would be turned over to the machines. The threat had been there for a while, but the reality sank in, and sank in deep for many of them. Like a gentle dog that is backed into a corner and whipped, eventually the fangs come out and the biting begins. That's basic animal behavior, and we are all capable of it.

Harvest season across the entire Midwest had been powered by diesel fuel for decades. The evolution from horse-drawn implements, and even people-drawn implements, to steam engines, to gasoline tractors, and eventually diesel tractors, had revolutionized the ag industry. And with that, the ability to provide greater amounts of food and nutritional stability to the entire world. The breadbasket of America was the grocery store for Earth. Exports of grain and vegetable oils were shipped worldwide, and to be fair, massive amounts of fruits and vegetables were shipped into the United States, giving consumers an incredible selection of fresh bananas, citrus, peppers, and dry goods. But that level of food distribution infrastructure requires complex logistics and shipping protocols, and transportation had become incredibly expensive.

Again, taxation on the shipping industry had crippled businesses that ran older ships and trucks, and had left consumers – now heavily concentrated in the urban markets – with diminished supplies, no selection, and very marginal inventories. It was becoming a powder keg of stress and frustration.

Refrigeration, the key to extending the shelf life of fresh produce, had become an expense that many shops could no longer afford.

Restrictions on the types of refrigerant that could be used had forced either the purchase of new equipment, or, as profit margins evaporated for many stores, simply the abandonment of the old equipment with no replacement. The local merchants could no longer compete with the Amazons and Walmarts, so they had adapted, selling mostly just high-margin, immediate-need items. Grocery stores had become convenience stores and now they were reduced to being just "critical" stores. Beer, soda, wine, cigarettes, lottery tickets – the true necessities of life.

But the main consideration here is refrigeration. Most of your store-bought vegetables are flash-frozen immediately after harvest. This allows time for packaging, canning, and other meal-prep processing that takes time. The veggies are only ripe for a short period of time, so there needs to be a delay built into the system for these longer, time-consuming processes. Flash-freezing provides that needed delay, but flash-freezing is energy intensive.

Storing frozen food, by the millions of tons, is also energy intensive and expensive. When power systems suffer brownouts and electrical supplies are rerouted to the coast for air conditioning, commuter systems, and data servers, food in the northern Midwest thaws – and spoils. And so it was that summer.

What would normally have been flash frozen was moved to refrigerated storage, and while packing and canning were accelerated, the processes simply couldn't preserve enough of the food for the duration. Plastic bags, which had been a major tool in food preservation for storage and distribution, had become so taboo that brands had been forced to nearly abandon their use altogether. Sourced from fossil fuels, the basic polymer molecules needed to form common plastic bags had been thrown out with the bath water. The intellectuals had perhaps not thought out all of the impacts of their concepts, narratives, and legislation. And that's why I go with the big-mouth bass every time. In the fish's case, no words come out. That's key.

And so it was, that our highly evolved society of superdense population centers and overly educated concept promoters had managed to bring our cities to the edge of malnutrition. That was one of the first shoes to drop in this saga.

And that is one of the reasons that there, in rural Missouri, only two days into the event, I was worried beyond reason about my family and our ability to find each other and endure. The masses were already becoming unruly, frankly desperate to feed themselves and their families.

But I'm getting ahead of myself. •

CHAPTER 7: BAD NEWS / GOOD NEWS

What ultimately saved Rachel and I was the worst news of my career. After almost 30 years of dedicated service to an oil industry giant, my position was terminated, or as they worded it, "taken inside." As an outside consultant, I'd been a part of so many key events, working with numerous presidents of the company and the inner circle to help craft the message and bolster the value of the company. I loved the job, and I loved the people I worked with. The best and the brightest, no doubt. They managed worldwide negotiations and contracts that spanned not only the geopolitical world, but the maze of currencies and taxes and legal red tape that would have strangled all but the best. I had tremendous respect for the titans of industry that I'd seen and had the pleasure to work beside. Anyone I've ever worked with who had amassed a fortune was never intending to sit on a beach and drink martinis while the sun set behind their cabana. No, they were interested in making it work, bringing ideas to life, and employing those who could advance the effort. To those who had real money, it was never about the money.

I had other clientele as well, including some government groups. What a contrast. In the world of energy and engineering, you had to be precise, with volumes, pressures, expansion rates, drilling trajectories, financial components, and on and on. Things could break or explode. Machinery downtime was costly and injuries were worse. Safety at all costs, because being unsafe is simply too expensive. Ultimately, getting a gallon of gasoline to the pump might net you 15 cents a gallon, if you were lucky.

On the other side of the coin, we had the government folks. These reflect a different set of operational standards. The organization is made of those who were often hired to meet a quota or fulfill an arrangement that was politically advantageous. These folks liked to meet and talk and plan and promise. They would always remain pretty vague with their statements and rhetoric, because they produced mostly nothing. At the end of the day, however, their type of organization would reap five times the income per gallon of gas – in taxes. Ah, the government. Bloated and inefficient. If they weren't busy confiscating our incomes to buy our votes, they'd be out of work.

Anyway, times change, directions change. Messages change. And people change. The focus of my beloved energy company had drifted from the real business of the day to playing along with the narrative of the day. We had all watched McDonald's evolve from its former self, chasing salads and lattes, trying to keep up with an imposed purpose of health and fashion. Hey, you're a burger joint. You sell burgers. You're not *supposed* to define the food pyramid for every meal. But they bowed to the pressure, although the pressure never stopped. You can't make "the machine" happy, so you have a choice. You can help load the chambers of your own firing squad, or you can stick to the integrity of your business and your path. You may go down either way, but one way has honor. The other has none.

I actually heard someone outside one of our final meetings say, "They've got to learn. It's not about the damn operations. It's about being on the right side of the narrative!" And that about summed it up.

My beliefs had become outmoded, obsolete, and off-track with the narrative and the ideologies that were being adopted. Out with the old, in with the new. The circle of life. You get the drift. So it was time to move on. •

CHAPTER 8: NO EARLY RISER

Beep, beep, beep, beep... "Ugh." I've never been a morning person, so getting up at 5 a.m. has never been a joy of mine. But I was excited to get underway and put some miles under the tires. If it all came together, I'd meet up with Rachel in just a few days, and life would begin anew.

I'd duped all my data drives, wrapped and stacked my cables in a couple of tubs, and loaded the bubble-wrapped screens in the back of the truck. I didn't need to remember to grab a handful of cash from my metal box in the closet this time, as I had my metal box with me, under the back seat. My clothes, in my typical traveling fashion, were stacked in a laundry basket.

The laundry basket had been my luggage of choice since college, when I used to take a load of dirty clothes home to Mom on occasion. Well, maybe more than "on occasion." But it was easy to take them in the basket, then restack them in the basket. So much easier to work out of than a suitcase, too, when you travel. I had received rolling-eye compliments on my laundry basket in more than a few swanky hotel elevators. And you could almost rate the hotels by the droll stares received from other guests.

"Larry Vuitton...Louis' brother..." I would say, not even making eye contact.

It had become my deadpan response, which usually drew a laugh, even from the most high-brow fashionistas.

I grabbed a quick shower and dried my hair with the towel I'd kept for my trip. I tossed my shaving kit, which resembled a quart-size, zip-seal plastic bag, into my Larry Vuitton. It was so much easier to get ready in the morning when Rachel had Gus, our yellow Lab. I love that dog, but he's an attention hound, pun intended. He prefers to be walked four times a day, which is great for my cardio, but rough on our personal schedules. He's always been her dog, or should I say, she's always been his person. So he was incredibly excited when she asked, "Do you wanna go for a ride?" I'm guessing he hadn't anticipated 40 hours in a truck cab, so we'll see how he reacts the next time that experience is offered.

A flexible cooler held a few Cokes and bottled water, the side pockets stuffed with some snack-sized packets of honey-roasted peanuts and a bag of mostly crushed Doritos.

Riding shotgun was my notebook and planner, as I still kept a duplicate of my calendar on paper, in book form. Old-school methods were sometimes embarrassing, but I had never once said in a meeting, "I'm sorry, I can't confirm that; my phone's dead."

The *actual* shotgun was behind the back seat with a few other things. The ammo cans were deep in the back of the truck – meaning just behind the cab – under some packing blankets, just because. It was also because I'd loaded all of that a few days ago, before our schedules changed. But now it was all set to go. I could just throw in my computer stuff, my clothes, and hit the road.

My spare gas cans were on the carrier, pinned in the trailer hitch mount with our son's old bike strapped down on top of them. Rachel had our trail bikes in the bigger truck. We were going to donate Alex's old bike to Goodwill, but it was in pretty rough shape. And he'd actually sounded a bit sad when we said it was going away. So we kept it. We were thinking of putting it under the Christmas tree again this year, just for humor – 27 years after Santa brought it the first time. A good joke is always worth a little extra effort. •

CHAPTER 9: ON THE ROAD

It was nice to get out on the road and just unplug from everything. So many years of deadlines and emails and texts and calls and...I knew I'd probably miss it, but it was something I always told myself when I'd set out on a road trip. Just the sound of the road for a few hours. It was like a rinse cycle on my thoughts. I just let them spin. Hopes, dreams, wishes, ideas. I'd always wanted to write a book, so I'd play around with concepts. I could always get to the funny part of an idea, then it just seemed too absurd to follow through. Plus, while I like to tell stories, I'm easily diverted off course and my ADD winds the tale around a number of paths before I regain my composure and actually finish. Rachel loved my stories, as did some of our best friends. But I'm likely an acquired taste. Yet I'd covered none of that so far this trip. Just some tire whine and drifting thoughts of life ahead. Moving on to the next chapter of life's real book. Not a midlife crisis, but a later-aged reality. I believed it to be a great opportunity to reset and view life through a more relaxed lens, in an incredibly beautiful environment.

Traffic had been pretty thin getting out of the city. I'd noticed some stoplights out as I passed a usually busy exit ramp, but it wasn't uncommon. You had to pay attention if you drove yourself. The autobots had mostly taken over the roads, and my driver's license required a substantial written test and ride-along assessment. Maybe it was a sign of my age, but I never felt comfortable in autobot mode. And, intersections made me nervous as hell. There had been hundreds of T-bone deaths at intersections since the autobots received clearance to drive. As for the liability, it's difficult to say who's at fault when nobody is driving either vehicle. One lawyer would hang it on the manufacturer, but the manufacturer would put it on the programmers, and they put it on the legislators – and they put it on the owners, who are now dead. "Wow, your family won a million dollars! It's too bad you're dead."

Fortunately, the I-DRAV lobby (Intelligent Drivers Rejecting Automated Vehicles) had put enough pressure on Washington to still let us drive on the interstates if we had the proper licensing. Getting caught "AD" (Actually Driving) in a no-driver zone was nearly as bad as a DWI used to be. Now, you see drunk people out on the road all the time, partying, smoking weed, and just cruisin' down the highway. That's a mind-bender for me.

And getting fuel had seen a major shift. My 10-minute turn times at the convenience store, grabbing fuel, snacks, and the bathroom, had evolved to a whole different scene. Some of the e-plug stations had 50 charging racks or more, lined up in an electric rainbow of colors, shifting from red, to orange, to yellow, to green, glow as the batteries recharged. And the stores had driven the arcade resurgence, as people needed a way to burn 20 or so minutes as their cars recharged, or they could grab a beer at the bar! Who would have seen that one coming?

But it wasn't just the people on the chargers, it was the ones waiting, and the ones waiting on the ones waiting. Some of these places had been converted from old gas stations, becoming a traffic nightmare as dozens of cars waited in the queues. Others had been built with engineered queues to keep everyone orderly, which is great until the third car back goes completely dead and everyone behind him is stuck. Ah, progress.

That's why I carry gas cans for my new hybrid truck. It's a bit of a hassle sometimes, but it's still better than the other route and, in my opinion, well worth the carbon tax they slap on me for every mile I drive. It's basically the fine I'm assessed because my truck has a motor. But with this configuration, I can still stop and grab a soda and some peanuts if I want, fill from my own supply, and I'm back on the road. 10 minutes!

I-35 north of the Dallas–Fort Worth Metroplex is a nice drive. Fifteen minutes outside the city, the vistas reveal wide horizons and rolling hills. I'll take the beauty of any open space over the confines of the city – there's no comparison.

Three hours later, I breezed through Oklahoma City, which had incredibly light traffic as well. I wasn't sure where everybody went, but the freeway was mostly mine. Was it a holiday? It should have been prime rush-hour, so it seemed a bit odd, but I was thinking about life ahead. It was pretty exciting. Maybe I'd finally get a boat.

My kid owed me a boat. At least that's what I'd always told him when we paid for orthodontic work, a car, and college. I counted his debt to me in "boats owed." I wasn't really serious about it, but I did want him to understand the value of what he'd received. It's an easy analogy that made the point while still being lighthearted. At this point, he likely owes me a small navy.

I spent a few more hours enjoying the relaxing scenery, letting the mind wander, and watching the world pass by the windshield. It was going to be a good day.

I turned on the radio just south of Wichita. I hit "scan" to find a local news station, and maybe get some traffic information. It just scanned and scanned and scanned. I flipped it over to FM, just more static. It had been getting more and more overcast, like a storm was coming in. Far on the horizon, I could see the dark bank of clouds. Yesterday, the weather reports had called for a clear day all along my route. Oh well, it wouldn't be the first forecast that had missed the mark.

The storm was moving in fast. Not your typical thunderheads, just a wide wall cloud that spanned the entire horizon. Dark and heavy, it wasn't like anything I'd seen. I sniffed the air. It began to smell like singed hair – my least favorite odor. I turned off the air conditioner to keep the scent outside. Prairie fire, I guessed. There were signs along this route, I'd remembered, warning drivers not to drive into smoke. I knew that they occasionally burned the prairie grass, to help renew it and control unwanted weeds and such. So probably nothing unusual.

Sirius didn't seem to be cutting through the clouds, either. No worries. I preferred to roll along in silence.

A line of patrol cars shot by me, heading north. I hadn't seen any of them along the way. Maybe an accident up ahead? Or maybe related to the prairie fire that was causing the smoke in the sky? It looked like it must be pretty big.

A row of black box trucks passed me, all with government plates. They would have come from Oklahoma City, the closest city to the south. It seemed well beyond what I'd expect for a range fire response. They appeared to be communication vehicles, with antenna arrays and what looked like a folded satellite dish on a rotor. That was odd. I'd seen some weekend National Guard convoys on my Texas-to-Iowa runs, but never rigs like this. And never driving at this speed.

My curiosity was getting the best of me, so I pulled off to the side and dug down deep in the console between the front seats. There it was! My old CB radio. I popped the magnetic antenna up on the roof. The old citizens band radio had come in handy many times, listening to truckers talk to each other about construction delays or accidents.

Way back in the 70s, the CB had become the mobile communication technology of choice. The truckers started the craze, using them at first to warn each other of traffic situations or to talk to dispatchers around the loading docks. Then, they elevated their use to sound the alarm for radar traps and Smokey Bear state troopers on the prowl for speeders. As trends go, eventually everybody got one, and the channels became full of kids yakking, tourists begging directions, and ultimately vile and disgusting language. It was our first look at the voices of the anonymous. Cloaked in a thin veil of static and hum, the opinionated and depraved would curse at the world, spit their blasphemy, and drive away unknown, leaving only their shrill and dark shadow on the conversations of the night. It was a lot like Twitter.

Eventually, the CB airwaves became so obnoxious that everyone gave up on the fad. It was just a noisy, cuss-filled conduit of verbal sewage, so it all went quiet. And once again, a few truckers could actually use it to communicate some important stuff when necessary. Maybe they'd be chattering today. I twisted the dial to "19," the trucker's channel. It was alive with numerous voices, all talking at once.

"...the whole damn thing blew up!"

"No shit!"

"No way!"

"I'm headed home."

"You can't go west."

"They're bringing everybody east...tellin' everybody to stay home, stay put."

"Frickin' mess."

"Probably terrorists," said somebody else, which seemed to be met with some broad approval.

"There'll be more."

"Gonna be bad..."

"Oh, no. Rachel!" I exclaimed. I pulled off to the shoulder and stopped. I'd sent her a text message right before I left Dallas to say I was hitting the road, but I hadn't paid any more attention.

"Where's the damn phone?" I said outloud to myself. She was staying overnight in Salt Lake City, or at least that was her plan.

I found the phone in my backpack, zipped into the center pocket with my calendar and to-do lists. Six missed calls! "Damn it!"

I hit redial. No response. Just a long pause then a fast-busy signal. I touched her face on the screen and hit Send again. Nothing.

"Damn!" I dialed Alex in Nashville, another busy signal.

"Damn. Damn. Damn." This was what *The Plan* had always been for. But not to have us scattered all over the whole damn country. "DAMN!" •

CHAPTER 10: DEEP BREATH

Okay. We all have a plan. We've talked about the plan, the protocols, the logic – all of us. Panic has no value. Worse than that, it wastes time and energy, and it won't change or fix anything. Remain calm. Focus. What's missing here is information and context. I don't have enough of either. In fact, I don't have ANY of either.

"Break 1-9... anybody out there?" I don't think I'd said that since I was a teenager, looking for one of my friends, cruising the neighboring town. It sounded pretty hokey.

"Hey, what 'blew up?' Come back." I listened. No response.

Maybe my mic was broken. I hadn't talked on this thing in years. Usually I just listened, picking up some nuggets of information as I drove. Maybe they were out of range. The CB's only good for a few miles.

Four more patrol cars raced by, full out. I had considered buying a police scanner once upon a time, but I was afraid I was becoming a bit too consumed with gas cans, microwave pasta meals – a cheap MRE, by the way – and my highlighted road atlas. "Preppers" seemed to always come across as a bit unbalanced, and I didn't want to merit that title. But at the moment, I decided it would have been a worthwhile purchase.

So...logic. What's the logic? The logic is that Rachel is west of whatever this is. Salt Lake City is way out there and certainly beyond anything I would be seeing from central Kansas. If it wasn't a big range fire, then it was likely another oil field fire, set by the anti-fossil fuel crowd. They like to wave their blue sky flags while torching jack pumps and pipelines. It seems both the irony and hypocrisy of their protest was lost on them. But they were numerous and evidently well funded, and they liked to burn stuff.

Logic told me that western Kansas, like western Oklahoma, had a lot of capped wells and fields. Some of the fields likely held some natural pressure, having not been pumped in years, and a fire could have started from valve failure. Maintenance was surely lacking, as no investments had been targeted to those fields in forever. That was logical. And, "the whole damn thing blew up" could be an observation of a field or an old storage tank facility. Plus, the main pipelines from Canada ran down through that area as well. Anyway, Rachel would be far beyond that. In fact, she WAS far beyond that area, according to her text message from last night. Salt Lake City was nearly 1,000 miles from here. She was okay. She was safe. Logic told me that.

But "Wichita is on lockdown," one of the truckers had said. Why? That's not where the fire is. And that stray comment, "They're bringing everybody east." What's that mean? East? Due to the threat of terrorism, most likely.

The bombing in downtown Oklahoma City, while it was a long time ago, will always be a hair trigger for taking precautions like this. That had been an attack here in the heartland. It was carried out by Americans, retaliating against what they deemed to be overreaching government. And we'd had a lot of that lately, so people were on edge. The policies and promises weren't panning out. There had been a lot of forced change and the majority of folks, the 90 percent, were feeling pinched. It seemed that anything anybody had was being taken and given to somebody else, no matter what level you were at.

It made sense that the government would be extra cautious.

I turned off the interstate at the next county road and pulled out my road atlas. I was...*here*. There was a farmhouse, maybe a half mile over. It looked like it sat back off the road a ways. Farmers liked to help people. I'd always trusted that.

I ran out of gas once after a date in high school. While the idea was to pretend to "run out of gas" when the girl was with you, I had actually run out of gas shortly after dropping her off. My sports team curfew was 1 a.m., and it didn't look good. After a two-mile walk down a dark gravel road, I came to Watson's Lane. Damn. Old Man Watson was wound a little tight, and he liked to drink. Knocking on his door this time of night, I was likely to get shot at. I wasn't likely to get hit, but I'd need to be careful. *Knock, knock, knock.* It was a pretty timid approach.

Snap! The porch light came on immediately.

"Jesus. What happened?" came a booming voice from inside the screen door.

And while I wanted to say, "I ran out of gas...but I'm not the Son of God," I decided that my sarcasm might choose a better time to present itself.

"I'm so sorry to wake you. I ran out of gas down the..."

"You're Tom's boy." He stood close to the screen looking out into the porch light.

"Yes, sir."

"He and I were in the war together."

"Oh, yes...I think I knew that."

"The last time a group of kids stopped by here in the middle of the night, they'd wrecked. It was just awful...blood...there was a lot of blood..." He seemed to reminisce on that thought for a moment. "Thank God you're okay."

"Yes, sir."

He seemed eager to help. I think he was lonely, kind of a self-made recluse. I never knew the whole story, but he had lived out there by himself since I was a little kid. The old man in the ramshackle house at the end of the dirt lane. In fact, he'd had one of the first "autobots" in our area, so to speak. Every once in a while, when he intended to get completely bombed at the local tavern, he'd harness his horse up to his wagon and bring the whole rig into town. Then, after he'd had his fill, he'd pour himself into the back of the wagon and snap the reins on the horse. She'd pull him back home and into the shed, where he'd sleep it off until morning. He was ahead of his time.

He grabbed a can of gas and drove me back to my car in his pickup, dragging a big fifth-wheel stock trailer as we went. The empty trailer was full of gates and cattle panels that banged and pounded the inside of the trailer at every bump. At nearly 1 o'clock in the morning, you could have heard the ruckus clear across the county. He said he couldn't wait to tell the other farmers at the coffee shop.

"Hell," he said. "You're suppose to run out of gas when she's still with you! Ha, ha, ha!"

"Yes, sir. Thank you, sir." That's the small town. The good news is, everybody knows you. But the bad news is...everybody knows you.

I approached the Kansas farmhouse just as cautiously. No mailbox, but it looked like folks lived there. Mowed lawn, some flowers on the porch, an actual car – the real deal, with a steering wheel. My kind of people.

"Hello?" I announced as I slowly got out of the truck. "Hello. Anybody home?"

I shut the door a little too loudly on purpose, and said, "Oh, hey," just in case somebody had seen me. I walked to the side door, no lights, no sounds. I knocked and opened the screen door. I knocked again on the interior door. Nothing.

The air was beginning to smell ghastly, like sulfur, or the smell of asphalt, or roofing tar. It had to be burning oil. I knocked a little harder and the door swung open.

“Excuse me. I’m sorry. Just need some help here. Fellow farmer. No worries. Need a little help with directions.”

Nothing. I stuck my head in a bit farther. No phone in the kitchen or hallway, which didn’t surprise me. Landlines had gone the way of the fax machine. I retreated back outside.

“HEY! Who the hell are you? What’re you doin’ here? What’re you doin’ in our house?” He was not a happy man, and I couldn’t blame him.

“I’m so sorry, sir.” I had a good 30 years on him, but he still deserved to be called ‘sir’, after he caught me coming out of his house. “I’m sorry, I was looking for a phone...well, I was looking for someone, then a phone...a landline phone. The door was open.”

I held my hands up like I was under arrest. “No harm. No harm.” I continued. “I’m trying to contact my wife, my family...the cells don’t work. I’ve heard that Wichita is on lockdown.”

“Where’d you hear that?” he asked, eyeing me with some curiosity.

“On the radio.”

“The radios are dead.”

“On the CB radio.”

“What the hell’s that?”

“Okay, okay, I’m sorry...I heard some truckers talking on my old walkie-talkie radio. I was trying to get information. They said, “It all blew up.” That’s about all I got.”

He seemed to be calmed by the fact that I'd shared some information. He was evidently at a loss as well. We just stood in a type of standoff, staring at one another. After a moment of awkward silence, he spoke.

"We were headed to get some groceries, in case they started rationing again, you know. When we got up this morning, the power was off and the screens were down. So we went to get some stuff and see what was going on. We got a few things, but we couldn't check out or pay. It was like the systems were down. They wrote our checkout list on paper and made us promise to come back and pay. We've been shoppin' there for years. But, it was crazy. Some people were stealin' stuff! Right there, in front of their faces. Just crazy."

"So what happened?" I asked. "Green goblins setting the world on fire again?"

"It's pretty sketchy," the man answered, pushing back his cap and rubbing his forehead. "Somebody said it was that mountain in Nevada where the Army stockpiles the old nuclear stuff. One guy said it was an asteroid," he chuckled at that one. "Somebody else heard it was Yellowstone National Park...said it's a dormant volcano? It was all guesses. And the screens are down, no surprise."

He caught his breath. I was just listening and thinking. I wasn't sure which option was more likely or which was worse. None of them sounded like good scenarios.

The farmer began to speak again. "Our power comes and goes these days. We never know when it'll be off. But whatever this is, it probably took out some lines."

His wife spoke for the first time. "Great. Another week without power. Last time, we got to the store too late. The shelves were nearly empty, so we thought we'd better stock up early. Get ice for the coolers to save the stuff in the freezer."

She was a cute but strong little thing, with a worker's hands and toned arms. Her hair was cut short and functional, and I guessed that between helping with the farm and taking care of the kids, she didn't spend much time on herself. She had a sweet smile when he talked, nodding as he went along. They seemed like a pretty solid team, but they were both fed up with the cards they were being dealt. Their little daughter stood close to her mom, arms wrapped up around her waist. The lady stroked the girl's long ponytail.

I apologized to the farmer again and wished them well. He had calmed down since he caught me sneaking into their house, and we had a nice brief conversation. I had told them my wife was in Utah, close to Yellowstone, and that's why I was so worried. They empathized with my passion for trying to contact her, understanding why I had gone into their house. They seemed to be taking it all in stride. Their family was trying to adjust to the quirky power failures, working to accept it as just another part of rural life. I wondered why it had to be that way.

It was a bleak and confusing picture. The breadbasket of America, short on food. Massive power lines overhead, but no electricity. Screens in every room, but no credible information. I was looking forward to my new mountain home. It would be a nice escape. •

CHAPTER 11: "RACHEL!"

Back in my truck, I returned to the turnpike and continued northward, not worrying much about speed traps or radar. The state troopers were probably occupied with other duties. I tried Rachel's phone again, anticipating another busy signal.

"Hey! I love you," she said, as if she was in a speed-reading competition. "I don't know how long the cell will hold, so...I'm north of Salt Lake City, I've been on the road a while actually, I-84. The roads north are closed. They'll only let us go west...I'll try to loop over the top, to the lake...if it's okay there."

"Wait...what happened?" I asked excitedly.

"You haven't seen it? Oh Jake, it's awful. Yellowstone erupted...last night, I guess. They're evacuating everybody. They said the dust and ash are moving southeast...Casper, Cheyenne, Denver, all being evacuated. They're making everyone go east. Where are you?"

"I'm at Wichita...almost. Headed to Mom and Dad's to pick up stuff. I should be at the lake in three days. I'll drive straight through."

"How? Oh, Jake, this could be really bad. I was thinking about what we'd talked about. The Power Strip. Will it all go down? What if they won't let you come west?"

"Hey, we always talk about the bad stuff, you know, we probably get too whacked out about that. It'll be okay. I'll check into it and we'll talk. Worst case, I'll take the Dakota route. You've got our maps, right?" I tried to talk with a positive confidence, hiding the real emotion in my voice. Rachel was usually the cheerleader for all of our tasks, but I wanted to keep us positive as well.

"Yes. And I got the last two bottles of water from the hotel's registration desk!" Although she sounded a bit anxious, I could sense the smile when she said that.

"I'm so proud! I love you, babe. Have you talked to Alex?"

"No. I tried but couldn't get through. I'm hoping they're far enough away to be okay. My worst case... if I can't get to the lake... I'll be in Newport. Ha! Don't know where, but I'll find..." and the call dropped.

Even though it was pretty intense, I was so happy to hear her voice. She could always make me smile. And she snuck in a plug for Newport. That was funny. When we were thinking of places to restart, she found a pretty little house on the Pacific Coast, just outside of Newport, Oregon. It was pretty, but neither one of us knew anything about the area, the weather, job possibilities – we had nothing to draw from except the pictures of this one house.

"It's pretty!" she had said, and that was evidently enough for her. So, if she couldn't get to the lake, I guess she was going to find someplace in Newport.

Plus, being very smart, she was also telling me her Plan B. I knew if I didn't find her at the lake, my next stop would be Newport. Everyone would know the beautiful redhead with the yellow Lab, that would be certain.

I immediately called Alex. Again, I got the fast busy signal.

Our plan hadn't included anything about what to do if we could reach each other intermittently. And what Rachel said about The Power Strip was right. That would be a game changer. If the power failure cascaded nationwide, it would be total chaos in just a matter of days, maybe just hours.

Food distribution would be under immediate pressure, especially after the Minnesota fiasco. And most people don't understand the full implications of losing their electricity for the long term. It doesn't just mean no lights. It means no air conditioning, no heat, no refrigeration, no cooking, no communication. And now, for almost everyone, it means no transportation. It's a big problem.

My phone rang. It was Alex. I answered before the end of the first ring. "Hey bud! So glad to hear your voice."

"Hey Dad, just wanted to touch base. I've been trying to call you and Mom all day. We saw the news. Are you on your way to Montana?"

"Mom is in Salt Lake City. She's fine. I'm in Kansas. We're taking different routes, but that's a long story...anyway, I'm going up through Iowa first, then I'll..."

"Salt Lake City? What's she doing there? No! Oh, Dad, she's gonna be trapped!"

"Whoa...hold on. She's on the road, she's on a different route, but she's still headed to the lake."

"But YOU can't get there, Dad. You won't be able to get to Montana from Iowa. Not now. They're pulling everybody east. It's gonna be really bad, Dad."

"Well, let's not get too dramatic. It's some smoke and dust, but it'll settle," I said, wanting to keep myself calm as well. "I haven't found any reliable news about it, just a bunch of opinions."

"Dad, it'll crash the grid. The whole thing depends on the windmills and solar panels across Kansas and Nebraska now. It'll be toast. It's like you said. It's what we've talked about. That's what's going to happen."

"Hey, come on. I'm not always right about that stuff. In fact, I'm almost always WRONG about that stuff. You know how I get!"

"No, we've talked about it out here, too. We're getting out of Nashville, going to Holly's folks. They've always got a ton of food, and we'll take ours, too. And it'll be a house full of doctors. If something happens, everyone will be fine. But if nothing happens...well, then we'll be fine too."

He was going to be fine indeed. I knew Holly's folks, and they were prepared as well. I felt some comfort knowing he'd be around a solid group of people while all of this got sorted out.

"Do you want me to come to Moberly? I'll meet you in Moberly."

I said, "Alex, the plan was to meet in Moberly IF we couldn't communicate for two days. But, we're talking now, so probably not."

"We've got to make sure Mom's okay! She'll be stranded out there. We've gotta find her. It's gonna get really bad, Dad. I'll drop off Holly, then I'm coming to Missouri."

"Alex," I said. "You don't need to..."

"Dad! I'll meet you in Moberly. I'm..." and that was it. The call dropped. I couldn't even get the fast busy signal.

I just stared at my maps and my phone. I found some random radio signals with conflicting news reports. One said a press conference was taking place in a few hours, propping up the president as he worked with "top advisors." Another said government communications were down. Another said the president had been golfing in Colorado and may be missing. How would we know? Each outlet had its own agenda.

I was frozen in time. "Analysis paralysis" is what Rachel called moments like this. "When it hits, you've got to make a decision and move on." She had always said that to me when we were weighing some sort of remodeling scheme or travel plans. And through constant repetition, we'd made it part of Alex's script for "things your parents say all the time" – I'm sure it was a long list.

So I needed to get off the fence and get moving. I needed to get to Iowa, to check on Mom and Dad and get our stuff for Montana. And I needed to get to Montana, or to wherever Rachel was. But, I needed to get to Missouri, because Alex wanted to go with me. I needed to do too many things, and I needed to get started on all of them right now.

But I understood why Alex had said he was coming to Moberly. He wanted to be with us. He wanted to find Mom. He wasn't thinking about his own safety. He was thinking about hers.

Damn! If only I'd said, "No, Alex. Don't come." Then it would be settled. But I hadn't been black and white, cut and dried. I'd been vague, gray, undecided. I really needed to work on that. I asked myself, was he really coming to Moberly, per the plan? It had been the last thing I heard him say. If he drove all the way to Moberly, I'd need to be there. It would slow me down to wait, but I had to be there if he showed up. This damn plan! What good was it? It was just messing things up now. We'd have all been better off without it.

Alex should just stay there, in Tennessee. And Rachel should have been here with me, not on the other side of the country by herself. So there I was, sitting on an exit ramp in the middle of absolutely nowhere. At a true intersection, parked on the off-ramp of life, contemplating the course of our future. The poetic justice was inescapable. •

CHAPTER 12: STICKING WITH THE PLAN

I began to consider all of the grand solutions. I'd meet up with Alex, we'd pass through Iowa and load up on supplies, then we'd head west to meet up with Rachel. Except what about Holly, Alex's girlfriend in Tennessee? He wasn't going to just leave her behind, was he? They'd been together quite a while. What about fuel? How would we even logistically make the trip? Where would we find fuel if we needed it? How would we pump it if we found it? And how would we charge the batteries? Would everyone pillage the stores like they did during the countless epidemics or fringe-induced riots? Maybe Alex was right. Maybe this was really bad.

So, what did I actually know? What facts did I have to make a logical decision?

I began making bullet points in my notepad and marking on my maps. I plotted where Rachel was, based on our call. She was headed west from Salt Lake City. But she had said she was on I-84, so she was already north of Salt Lake. She would have been headed toward Boise. I put a mark on the map, making note of the time that we'd talked. I'd try to guess the timing of her route so I'd have some idea of where she was. I drew a bold line on her most likely path, up Highway 95 and into Kalispell from the west. But what would she do for fuel?

She was smart, she was resourceful, and she was charming. She would either sweet-talk her way through the situation or hold them at gunpoint. Either way, she would have the capability to make it work.

If Alex were coming to Moberly, I needed to get started in that direction. I marked his time and location on the map, too. Then I made a calculation of my fuel and batteries. I needed to top off everything immediately, and I'd already wasted a lot of time sitting here thinking. Another consideration was going to be how we would pay for everything if the systems were down.

But it was decided. We would execute the plan. I needed to get to the nearest stop with fuel and charging. I wanted to get what I could, while I could. And I wanted to check out the attitude and demeanor of the people. Was everyone staying cool and collected, or was the veneer beginning to crack? •

CHAPTER 13: SHOW ME THE MONEY

The payment issue was going to be a big one until the entire network of systems was back online and reintegrated. It was another shoe that would drop amidst the nationwide power outage. Not surprisingly, access to funds and the ability to engage in commerce was going to be "cash only" for quite some time. There would be no swipe of the credit cards, no ATM access, no debit card purchases, no signing on the screen – nothing. What was my account balance at Comerica? Which stocks were in my 401(k)? To most people, those are just more numbers on the screen. Most don't even keep a printed statement for reference.

Luckily, all of our banking and investment records were on paper, in my Critical Box behind the seat of my truck. But what if that were lost? Who else would have records of my accounts, everyone's accounts? And realistically, there was no physical money anywhere anymore. All of it was just account numbers attached to spreadsheets. There was no basis for any of it. It was a hope and a promise, carried on the static in a hard drive, somewhere on a server, plugged into the system, somewhere, hopefully, maybe. For those with sloppy records, this could be cataclysmic.

My Critical Box held all of my most recent bank records, investment records, and important documents. My birth certificate, passport, a power of attorney for my parents, blood type, proof of insurance – all in that box. Along with some DVDs of Alex's achievements: the childhood years, baseball highlights, music videos, live performances, and recordings of his original works. Those things were what I had deemed "critical." With only those things, my life could go on. Each of us had our own Critical Box. Rachel had hers with her, which included copies of our financial records as well, but she carried her own passport, birth certificate, and duplicates of Alex's life package. And, in theory, Alex had his, too. But as with any kiddo, you can sometimes only hope the plan was enacted.

I didn't know exactly how I was going to handle the payment side of this trip. Funding had always been a part of the plan, but the reality of the practice was yet to be seen. Due to our moving, I had pulled a much greater sum of cash than on any other random trip. While we had electronically transferred our accounts to the bank in Montana, I didn't know if there would be delays or possible glitches, and I didn't want to risk that. So both Rachel and I were traveling with sizable sums of cash. In fact, possibly dangerous amounts of cash given this development.

As for Alex, I knew that he had a safety stash of at least $1,000, because I had given it to him years ago. It was stacked in a plastic bag, rolled and wrapped with red plastic tape. It sat, unassuming, under a baseball on his night stand. It looked like a poorly made homespun trophy, as was its intent. Nobody would ever steal it, as it appeared quite worthless. But there it was, always in sight, never to be lost – and easy to grab. I had wrapped it in an entire roll of tape because it would be a pain in the ass to open and use. It was truly "emergency only" money, and the word "emergency" was not to be defined as "need to pay for pizza" or "I can't find my wallet." I knew he had that emergency stash, and it was instilled in him that, if necessary, it could be used to buy him time or safety. We weren't talking about his entertainment budget, and he knew it.

As for me, my most important asset had just become my truck and everything in it. Everything I had to survive this event and bring our family together was in my vehicle. I would defend it with my life, because my life, maybe all of our lives, depended on it. •

INSIDE STORY: WHAT DID I DRIVE?

My fortress, my transport, was a Chevrolet crew cab pickup, the Z71, half-ton model – a Silverado LTZ. It was an all-wheel drive, hybrid diesel, with oversized custom rims and all-terrain tires, a "topper" cover on the back (nicknamed "the fishing hat" by my car friends), and a substantially heavy and mostly unnecessary Ranch Hand front bumper system with a grill guard that could damn near stop a train. As for the color, black-on-black had been the best paint scheme on any car since Henry Ford built his first one, so I saw no need to buck the trend. For its size and weight, I got incredible fuel mileage, plus, with the hybrid system, I could use tankable fuel or plug it into the wall. I liked the flexibility of not being constrained by one source.

Our cross-country runs to Alex's shows, to the cabin in Montana, or back home to Iowa, had given me a lot of experience on how to best use the supply chains. When to fuel, when to charge, when to buy, and when to use my own.

And on this trip, I was indeed carrying my own. My own everything. From my Critical Box to fuel to computers to ammo to my cashbox to Alex's old bike. All contained within or strapped to my truck. Spoiler alert – it got me through. I still have it, although it hasn't seen much use in quite a while.

CHAPTER 14: ALEX, I'M ON MY WAY

I had just reached the Belle Plaine rest area, built as part of the Kansas Turnpike. The stops usually offered some fast food and fuel, as well as charging stations and, with autobots doing most of the driving these days, recently added bars and liquor counters.

The convoy of black government trucks that passed me a ways back had formed a small circle at the north end of the parking lot. The satellite dish was being unfolded and the hydraulic cylinders that controlled its orientation were rotating it slowly toward the sky. A couple of seriously armed guards waved curiosity seekers away from the encampment. One of the trucks had been towing a small trailer, what I figured to be a fuel wagon. I'd seen the big farmers up in Iowa use them during planting and harvest season. This one was just bigger. They were filling it at the commercial truck bay, so it was separated from the others.

Generators beside the main building were humming loudly, and I could see their exhaust rising from behind the picket fence that hid them from view. It would make sense that these "official" stations would be set up to fuel emergency and military vehicles in a crisis. It would have been part of the original concept for the entire interstate system.

I watched as a younger guy worked on top of the fuel trailer. An older guy had been standing beside the rig, but had started to walk back towards the larger group.

I pulled into the second pump behind theirs and began fueling as fast as I could. I swung out of the truck and left the door open to block the view of the hose. I slammed the nozzle in my tank and swiped my card, typing my code with a precision that surprised me. As my tank began to fill, I walked toward the kid on the trailer. I thought it would be best to be overflowing with curiosity about their tank wagon and the radio trucks. My tank needed time to fill.

“Wow, this is quite a rig! Never seen a trailer like this before,” I beamed, like a kid eyeing his first fire truck.

“Right at 600 gallons,” said the young guy holding the nozzle into the top deck of the trailer. He was dressed in a gray cammo shirt and tactical pants, the same as the older guy, and eager to share his knowledge about the equipment. “We can carry enough to...”

“May I help you?” asked the older man, heading back in my direction. He was obviously in charge of the kid. I noted that neither of them were wearing a sidearm.

“Oh, I’m sorry, I was just looking at this trailer of yours...and wondering if you had any information about what’s going on. My wife is out near...”

He interrupted my question and got right to the point, “There’s nothing for you to be concerned about, except to get on home.”

“My wife is up around Yellowstone,” I said, completing my statement. “I’d really like to know what the situation is.”

The kid on the tank wagon began to answer, “We’re heading up to Lincoln. Well, if we...”

“Edwards!” the man barked.

I tried again. I wanted information but I was also stalling for as much time as I could get. My tank needed a couple more minutes to fill and I assumed they’d be cutting me off.

“I’ve heard a lot of different things on the CB,” I said. “Fossil fuel activists setting fire to a pipeline? Terrorist attack on military storage in Nevada? The most credible one said Yellowstone was erupting?”

"Well none of that's an official statement."

I cut him off this time, "So what is the 'official statement'? Where can I get that? My wife could be trapped up there. Aren't you tasked with helping the situation for us civilians? That's what I'm..."

He walked right up to me as he continued, "Do you understand 'need-to-know'? Right now, you civilians don't need to know! So when you do..." He looked over my shoulder towards my truck. "Hey, are you pumping fuel? Those are reserved for us." He pushed past me, but I caught up in one long stride and cut his path.

"So we civilians can't get fuel either? No fuel, no information. As a taxpayer who writes your paycheck, I demand to know what the hell is going on!" And I did want to know. Was this some terrorist act or an act of nature? I thought that'd be something worth knowing, and something that he should tell me.

I stepped right in front of him, blocking him. "Look, I understand that sometimes the truth isn't what people need to hear. If this is a national security issue, I appreciate that, but..." I could hear the pump still spinning, so my tank wasn't full yet.

"Shut it down," barked the man, forcing his way past me.

"Okay, okay. Just tell me what's going on." I was in front of him again, standing by the hose, but not yet taking it out of the tank. He reached around the pump and hit the big red 'stop' button. He glared at me.

The receipt printed out. I tore it from the small slot and made a quick glance. Almost 18 gallons. That would make a full tank. Perfect.

I followed him back toward the fuel wagon, hoping to get some info from the kid, who was more talkative. The old man walked on, toward the circle of trucks at the end of the parking lot.

"So, what's your role? Your Sarg said you guys were a communications group?" Actually, the guy hadn't said a thing about it, but with all of those antennas and a satellite dish, it was pretty obvious they weren't an artillery outfit.

"Tactical communications. Working the edge of evacuation protocol," offered the young guy, again proud to be well informed and doing his best to interact with the public in a positive manner.

The contrast was obvious. The kid had just graduated from training, and the lectures and dictates were fresh. He was excited to put his chops to use, just as he'd been trained. I'm sure he put a lot of effort into it, and he deserved to be proud. I was proud for him. Plus, I was getting some much needed information.

"Edwards!" shouted the older man, walking back toward us again, "Just fill the tank. It's not a press conference." This guy had been in his role for years, I guessed. The rules were different when he went through training. He didn't give a rat's ass what I wanted to know, and I'm sure he didn't care to inform me. That's okay. When it comes to the military, it should probably be more his way.

"Thank you both for your service," I said. The kid nodded, the older guy just looked at me. "Seriously," I said. The older guy stared at me for another second then flipped up his nose in a minimal acknowledgement. He walked away once more. It was the best I was going to get. And I was serious. I appreciate tremendously the work and dedication of those folks. It's a tough job, for them and their families. I hope they've stayed safe through all of this.

"Hey," the kid called out as I started to turn away. "They're saying *Huckleberry Ridg*e. Check it out."

"Thanks. Thank you very much. Stay safe." I was really grateful to have something to work from. I repeated it to myself until I got back into the truck and wrote it on my dash pad. Huckleberry Ridge.

I looked at all of my Wyoming and Colorado maps. I couldn't find it, but maybe it wasn't really a place. Maybe it was a military installation or a code name. The day before, I would have just typed it into Google. Today, I'd have to figure it out for myself.

As soon as I re-entered the highway, I came to a small roadblock. It was just one highway truck with a snowplow mounted to the front. It was a bit out of season, but it was probably just the most handy item for the job. A guy in a yellow vest pointed me toward the exit ramp. Evidently Wichita really was shut down.

I couldn't figure that out. Wichita was so far from Yellowstone, if that's what it really was. I couldn't trust the news to be honest, so I began to ponder other options and wondered if Huckleberry Ridge were maybe somewhere closer to here.

Wichita was home to a number of aviation companies and others with military and government contracts. Aviation, jet propulsion, space works, and probably more offshoots that would be tech heavy with a lot of R&D. Plus, it was geographically dead-center of the United States. What else would be there? How is it connected? Then it hit me.

"The Power Strip!" I surmised, talking out loud to myself. That's where its brain center would be, managing all of the power inputs from Colorado, Nebraska, Kansas, Iowa, Oklahoma – all of the solar and wind and battery feeds would be managed there. Probably deep in some retrofit nuclear missile silo control center. That would be ideal. A location that would already be built to survive a nuclear blast, wired to the coasts, with backup systems, oxygen generators, bunkhouses, the works. That's where I'd put it if I was them. Right in the center. Deep in the ground. Within an urban area that could staff and support it. Wichita.

Yep, that was it. I was sure of it. That lone highway worker, standing by his snowplow, in May. He was the outer perimeter of security for the nation's most complex energy system. I doubted that he knew his importance.

I picked up Highway 54 outside of Eureka, Kansas. My zigzag course had taken me around Wichita, so now I had to decide whether I'd avoid Kansas City or run the gauntlet and stick to the interstates. Those highways would be faster for sure, but I didn't want to get stopped, turned around, or held up in any sense of the word.

I was about 360 miles from Moberly, based on a couple of atlas calculations, which meant it would take all of the fuel I'd just added – all 18 gallons. I could run on just batteries for a while, but with the load I was carrying, I'd be lucky to add 60 miles. But that was better than nothing. So how far would all of it get me? Being conservative, I should have around 500 miles of total range from a full tank of fuel and a fully charged battery set.

Even if I didn't find any more fuel, I should have enough in total, including my portable gas cans, to make it to Moberly, as well as enough to get on to hometown Iowa. Hopefully, Alex would be loaded with fuel as well. That would determine whether or not we abandoned his truck in Missouri. What a concept. To just leave a 40-thousand-dollar vehicle behind because you can't fuel it. •

CHAPTER 15: KANSAS CITY, HERE I COME

My backroad maps for the plan were well thought out, but I decided that my best option was minimizing the drive time and maximizing the efficiency of the truck. Traveling via I-35, I would have the best fuel economy and I'd make the best time. I could be in Moberly in less than six hours if there were no delays. I wouldn't need to stop for anything. I was full on fuel, I hadn't eaten but I had no appetite, and I'd be safer stopping in the middle of nowhere if I needed to pee. I rejoined the interstate just east of Emporia.

I planned to loop around the southern edge of Kansas City, assuming the roads were open. It was getting more and more hazy, and the CB chatter was all about Yellowstone and evacuations that were pulling people east.

There weren't any detailed reports about what had actually happened, the extent of the blast or eruption, or the casualties, not to mention the damage to The Power Strip. But the deaths had to be in the thousands, just in the park alone, not to mention nearby towns, ranches, and farms. At least it wasn't peak tourist season.

I assumed that Kansas City wouldn't be shut down, as it didn't have the infrastructure or assets that I believed led to Wichita's closing. The route from Emporia to the outer loop was uneventful. The only item of note was finding almost nobody headed southwest. All of the traffic seemed to be flowing with me. I did notice the charging stations, however, and only a few were running.

There was a big charging station on the edge of Olathe, sponsored by Tesla and Karman, and maybe a couple of others. The lines stretched around the well-organized lot, with dozens of autobots standing in the queues, perfectly spaced, awaiting their juice. A large tanker truck was parked next to the liquor store, plumbed directly into the generators that converted the diesel into electric power. The doors were open on the generator house and I could see two large yellow Caterpillar engines spinning up the static for the batteries. The fumes from the exhausts made fuzzy ripples in the sky above the tanker. As long as they could get diesel, they could make electricity. Zero emissions? That claim had always perplexed me.

The loop under the south side of Kansas City was the same as any other day. Cars running both directions, it felt normal, just like it had been on many road trips that passed along this same section of road. Maybe all of this would be isolated to Wyoming and a bit of Colorado and Nebraska. That would be bad enough, but at least the rest of the country would be available to help them rebuild. You can't bring back the people who were lost, but you can bring back some normalcy to life. I was looking for the upside.

As I entered I-70, heading straight east toward Columbia, I was greeted by a convoy of state troopers, leading a line of fire trucks and ambulances, all running full out, lights flashing, sirens wailing. The sides of all of them read "St. Louis Fire & Rescue." Another convoy followed. Led by more police cars, this group was full of trailered earth-moving equipment, road graders, and, making another appearance... snowplows. There were literally hundreds of pieces of equipment.

The true scale of this disaster started to sink in, and tears began to well up in my eyes. It was an incredible level of response. In the chaos of all of this, there would be two groups of people who would stand out – the responders and the looters. I wanted to fall into the first group, but I was afraid I was likely to fall in with the second. At least until I got to Rachel. These were the hard choices.

Leaving the interstate, headed north, the impacts were already becoming easy to see. The chatter and occasional radio clips were saying the power was now down nationwide. Everything was running on backup systems and even WLS, the high-powered AM radio station out of Chicago, which could reach Dallas on a clear night, was signing off until they could source enough power to operate.

All of the reports were filled with comments hyping panic and shortages. All the government heads would say is, "Stay home and stay calm." One speaker, I think maybe the mayor of Chicago, was talking to the press while reading his speech for the first time. Perhaps he should have done a run-through prior to taking the microphone. He was in the middle of the speech, trying to calm everyone when he read a line that said "'The Power Strip' should be operational within a few...months? MONTHS! Are you shitting me? How am I..." and they cut his audio feed.

There were no answers, only rhetoric. The purported message was "stay calm," but the real message was all about panic and fear and gaining some political edge. It was the same playbook as always, but this crisis was real. The thing was, they didn't do well with any situation that hadn't been scripted out to the endgame. What was the endgame here? Usually, they already knew. But this time, frankly, they didn't.

The political elites usually had time to sell some stocks, prepare their households, and make plans for the downturn, because they always knew about a crisis in advance. They would call their financial advisor, get some medications or whatever the event demanded, and ride it out, knowing that the speeches were already being written for them to brag about how they were out there working for all of us, fighting to give us what we deserved, and ultimately taking the credit for averting whatever it was. Whatever it was that they had plagued us with in the first place. It was all part of the scripted crisis theatre. But the more I heard, the more I sensed this wasn't from the playbook.

"Just stay at home. Stay calm." That was the only constant I heard across the mix.

But based on the shattered windows at the convenience store in Renick, Missouri, folks were not remaining calm. Nor were they remaining at home. I passed through the small town on my way to Moberly. Home to just a few thousand folks, this was middle America at its core. No Photoshop, no fast edits, no rewrites or slogans. This was the real deal. It was valuable to see.

The winter had been extremely cold, and not much faith remained in the system that was suppose to bring us everything. We were less than 24 hours into whatever this next crisis event was, and society was beginning to lose its grip. The country that had risen to greatness on personal independence and self-reliance had become dependent on sticky-palmed politicians and intellectual idealists, whose only contributions had been programs and regulations, created in some coffee shop or government-funded study. Most of these failed souls couldn't make it in the real world of production and commerce, so they chose this road as their route to power.

Have you ever noticed how so many of them retire from politics as wealthy men and women, when they weren't wealthy before? How can you fail at your business, devote your life to public service, and wind up rich? I think we all know the answer.

And so, as this crisis hit, it was no surprise that with no leadership and no credible information, the people were resorting to their own methods. It would be survival of the fittest. •

CHAPTER 16: ALMOST MOBERLY

I waited until it was completely dark to navigate the streets of Moberly, Missouri. The little city had been our predetermined meeting point for many years, as defined by the plan. But things were beginning to feel very different compared with the last time I drove through town.

My first "trip" to Moberly had actually been via Google Earth, riding along on the camera car via my laptop, checking out the route to see if it met my criteria. It had the things I wanted, and it was well positioned for Alex to meet up with us if he were coming from Nashville. While I will often take the opportunity to rail against the failings of technology, I will say that I, like most all of us, certainly utilize a lot of what it provides. It has its strong points.

As you may recall, Moberly was chosen because of its medium size, the presence of larger box stores that may remain open or accessible during certain events, and the close proximity of rural hiding places in relationship to the stores. If necessary, you could make an actual "run" to the store and return back to your nest in a short time. Also, the farmland would give you longer sight lines for safety. It all made sense on paper, back when I put it together. Bringing it to practice was not something I had ever wanted to do. In fact, part of me felt that working it all out, investing the time and effort into the plan, would somehow tempt fate into making it a complete waste of time. That had really been my hope for this.

Approaching Moberly from the southwest, I wanted to drive through mostly undetected. No lights, slow speed, just rolling quietly to my destination. I had taped over my brake lights with multiple layers of black gaff tape. I didn't want to just break them out, because eventually repairing them could be incredibly costly or nearly impossible.

The city was dark with the exception of a few generator lights, which were sparse. Somewhere near the center of town, a glow rose into the dusty haze. Likely the local hospital, as they would have generators and backup systems still operating. Those would last for a while. Until the tanks ran empty.

Moberly's police force and fire department were stationed at various points, showing a presence and probably hoping to minimize panic, as well as potentially stem some accidents at the larger intersections. Not that there was any traffic. I did my best to avoid all of them, choosing side streets instead. I didn't want to be stopped and questioned. It would simply waste time, but mostly, I didn't want to get turned back.

The north side of town was my target for the night. Out past the airport, there were two specific farm lots with some machine sheds and vegetation to provide a bit of cover. I had originally found them on Google Earth and confirmed them on a drive later that summer. Both were good spots and would meet my needs for the next day or two. I didn't want to stay any longer than that. I'd pick the best place for the night, and that would be my hiding spot until Alex arrived and we continued our trek toward Iowa.

Per our plan, I stopped and spray-painted our family logo on the bridge. I'm not a fan of graffiti, but I rationalized a difference between critical communication that could keep our family together and tagging a train car for the sake of gang art.

Under the logo, I sprayed "23:15, 5/11," using the military time notation. Now, I would wait in my hiding place. I'd check the bridge every three hours at the top of the hour. My wait for Alex began.

I think it was about then that some ash started hitting the windshield. A soft gray powder, almost like talc. As a word of advice, don't hit your windshield washers if this ever happens to you, as it simply turns it into a blurry smear that absolutely does not wash off. And it's sharp, like ground glass, scratching fine lines into my truck when I wiped my hand across it. It was like running steel wool or a fine grit sandpaper across the surface. •

CHAPTER 17: WAITING FOR ALEX

I can't really say that I fell into a deep sleep, but something woke me up around 2 o'clock in the morning. The sound was a loud smack, like when a door gets blown shut by the wind. It was muffled by some distance, but it was enough to bring me to full attention inside the cab of the pickup. It took a couple of seconds for me to gather my wits and remember where I was. My neck was stiff, and I couldn't immediately collect my thoughts on why I was sitting in my truck behind a barn. Suddenly, I remembered all of it – what had happened and why I was there. I would have preferred to remain asleep.

My first look was toward the cattle that had been close to the fence behind me. Cows make great watch dogs, except that they remain silent. Without the added clamor of barking, they're incredibly curious, so they tend to look in the direction of any motion or intruder. I could see three of them in my rearview mirror. They were all looking toward the airport.

I took a long look around, checking my escape routes from behind the building. I put my hand on my pistol, just to be ready. It was all clear here. The sound must have come from the airport or just beyond.

Our binoculars were in the glove box. I pulled up them out and looked in the direction of the noise. I'd never had a quality pair of glasses like these, and they were beauties. I'd complained when Rachel outbid two avid hunters for them at a Safari Club fundraising auction. While they had both consumed a lot of financial lubricant from the open bar, she was stone sober, but she was hell-bent on these binoculars. Spending that kind of money for something you'll seldom use just seemed ridiculous at the time. I'd heard of Bushnell and maybe I'd even had a small pair once upon a time, but that was about all I knew about them. But the girl knows her gear. These were long-range, with some stabilization, and low-light lenses. She said they were worth twice what we paid. I'd have to agree.

My vantage point gave me a view across the airport and over toward the local Walmart. I couldn't see any of the details of the building from my nest behind the barn and trees, but I could see pieces of the property and the parking lot. As good as they were, the binoculars weren't equipped with infrared or night vision, but all I was looking for was a flashlight or a headlight beam. And I wasn't disappointed.

A single flash across a doorway drew my attention. So, now I knew exactly where to look, but I really couldn't tell what was happening with much certainty. Was it someone at a hanger on the airport property? It might be, but it appeared to be further away, toward the back of the store. In the darkness, the two buildings blended together. I saw some headlights jerk around, and in a moment, heard some more of the same noise.

They had pulled the loading dock doors completely off the back of the store. Wow! That gave me two important pieces of information. First, the noise wasn't close to me at all, which meant I was probably safe. Second, it meant that serious looting had begun. People were deciding to get to it early. The stresses of the food shortage, combined with the rhetoric and dissension about power distribution in the rural areas – it was all coming to a critical juncture. There was now too much pressure on the social system. Too much pressure on the people. As store inventories dwindled and electricity went to rations, the only things that were plentiful were uncertainty and anger. And those were abundant. With a complete failure of The Power Strip, it was likely to come unhinged pretty quickly. What had started as a happy day had suddenly become very sad.

I needed to stay sharp. I said a prayer for Alex's safe arrival and for Rachel's well-being. I couldn't let myself believe that they weren't safe. They were safe, they just were not with me. God would keep them safe. I knew it.

As the night went on, more and more people flocked through the back of the store. It was a nonstop line of ants, picking what they could from the tree, carrying the leaves back to their own hills. When it all boils down, it boils down to the essence of what we are. Animals with primitive basic needs. And when we have to, we will behave as animals to obtain necessities. I don't know if that's philosophy or biology or some other science, but it is fact. •

CHAPTER 18: MY BOY

Come on Alex! Where was that kid? I could see the bridge from my lair behind the grain bin and barn. I'd left the can of spray paint at the bottom of the wall, in case he didn't have any, but there was no new marking. No arrival time sprayed next to mine.

Maybe he's not coming at all. That was a strong possibility. We had talked about the plan a few times, and he had maps and notes in the glove compartment of his truck, but that's a long way from certainty. He had his work, his dream, his girlfriend, all there with him. In fact, I felt that the odds were in favor of him staying put, with his life, his plan. But, I had to hold up my end of the deal. I had to give him the opportunity and I had to be there for him if he tried to reach us.

So, I sat in my truck for the next two days, thinking, pondering, planning, and waiting. The time passed slowly, as you might imagine.

The plan called for the first to arrive to wait until four days post-event. Tomorrow would be that day, but I knew in my heart that I'd give him at least one extra day before moving on. The plan had that component as well, and if I left, I would add my departure time to the graffiti wall on the bridge. That would be an incredibly sad moment, I knew. What if he had been delayed by some unknown factor? What if he arrived, out of fuel, out of hope, only to find a set of spray-painted numbers saying he'd missed us by just a few hours? It was too much for me to consider. It was too emotional. I knew that I'd wait at least another day, probably two, but at some point I'd have to move on. I'd need to change my focus to finding Rachel. But I could only focus on one thing at a time. For now, that was Alex.

I had seen some movement around the bridge, but it appeared to be some of the looters, returning that direction from their shopping spree at the Walmart. He'd need to avoid them. Maybe this wasn't the best location. Maybe my plan was wrong on a lot of levels.

BANG! I jumped in my seat and pointed my Glock directly at the passenger window, the laser dot lighting up a face I knew quite well.

"Whoa! Geez. Sorry." Alex was standing there, his hands raised. He looked as strong and handsome as ever.

He'd smacked the window with his hand to surprise me. It was an act of excitement and joy, but it had scared me damn near to his death.

"I knew this is where you'd be," he said. "There were some people walking by the bridge, so I checked the sight lines and figured this is where I'd find you. I saw your tag. You know it's illegal to spray-paint government property, right?"

I jumped out of the truck and met him right in front of the logo on the grill. On video, it would have been a great branding moment for Chevrolet. I hugged him and held him tight. Tears streamed down my face. It was as if all the stress of the past few days was realized and, in that moment, my strong cold shield was dissolved. I was overwhelmed with emotion. My boy was here. •

CHAPTER 19: GOIN' SHOPPIN'

It was just beginning to get light as Alex and I prepared to leave the farmyard. We could clearly see the back of the Walmart. The loading docks had been peeled open like sardine cans, and trash and carts were splayed across the back parking lot en masse. And the carnage didn't stop there, as boxes, packaging, and debris were strung far down the road.

What first caught my attention was one stray cart, rolling as the breeze pushed it across the lot, down a gentle slope, careening from curb to curb. I watched it until the momentum was too much and it tipped over, coming to rest in the intersection. It was a bit haunting. All the signs of civilization, just no people.

"What do you think?" Alex asked, wondering if we should also take advantage of the open box. My gut instinct told me to avoid it, but the availability was obviously enticing.

I could think of only three things we could use, but I guessed the shelves would be depleted. Batteries, a turkey fryer – because they make a great outdoor cooking platform – and firestarter logs. Oh, cigarette lighters for starting a campfire. Just a few things a person could grab and run out with pretty quickly. But it was still theft. Put whatever spin on it you will. Call it necessity, make up an excuse to justify the actions, it's still no different than shoplifting or burglary. Maybe I was just slow to get into the game.

I agreed to check it out. If nothing else, the curiosity had a grip on me. Alex asked me when I'd last been in a Walmart. It had been a few years, actually. I wasn't a fan of how they'd come into the smaller cities across the Midwest and literally killed the main street businesses. I'd seen it too often in towns around home. They'd bring in a million discounted items, undercut the local businesses, and run the mom-and-pop stores out of existence. Then, after the town had lost all of its charm, shoppers would opt to just drive to the bigger city. Whereby, the big company would see their own numbers drop and abandon the location, leaving a vacant warehouse-sized building, usually built from deferred tax funds, to decay with the ruins of the town. Another of my many soapboxes.

Anyway, Alex voted himself as the one to go in and take a look around. He was more familiar with the probable layout of the store, and he was certainly faster if we needed to clear out.

"Two minutes, max," I said. "Just scout it out...I'm not crazy about this."

"Two minutes," he responded.

We stayed behind the small trees that dotted the edge of the airport property. A drainage ditch gave us some cover as we crossed to the retail strip center next door. We dashed across about 20 yards of loading dock, reaching the open gash in the store without any resistance. It was both spooky and exhilarating. But I knew that I wouldn't make a good thief. Just being outside the torn-open doorway was beginning to make me queasy.

My job was to count, out loud, so Alex could hear me. If someone approached, I would go quiet. Silence would be our signal. His goal was to return to the door before I hit 100. Off he ran.

The skylights were letting in just enough glow to see shapes and shadows. During the night, the air had grown more and more dense with haze, almost like the remnants of the smoke generators Alex had used on stage. Putting just a bit of particulate into the air made for a more dramatic light show, as the beams and colors caught the air and reflected out. The best word to describe it would be atmospheric. You could actually see the air.

The interior of the store was in shambles. Racks tipped over, unwanted items tossed to the floor. I could hear Alex kicking cans and boxes as he traced the aisles. It was a good tracking device, as I could tell exactly where he was in the store. I heard a couple of glass bottles shoot across the floor. Evidently a direct hit from his size 12 sneaker.

Then, suddenly it all went quiet. I was still counting, somewhere in the 70's I think. The last thing I heard was the crunch of a plastic bag, then nothing.

I called out a couple more numbers, then hollered, "Hey bud, you OK?" Nothing. Maybe he'd tripped, slipped, fallen. I knew he was on the far side by now. Maybe he'd gone out another door. I stepped onto the sidewalk and scanned the long side of the building. I listened hard. Sometimes, when you really want to hear something, it seems as if you can almost focus your hearing. Like when you want to see something distant, you strain your eyes into a forced optical telephoto mode. I don't know if you can physically do it, but it feels like you can. So I strained my ears and listened as far as possible. There was a faint murmur.

I decided to leave my post and go check on Alex. Trying to build a bit of cover, I called out, "Okay, I'm going to wait right here!" I figured Alex was clever enough to know what that meant. It would be a way of saying that I was on my way. So, I hoped that he and I were both on the same page of "clever." And, I was hoping whoever he was talking with wasn't very clever.

The end aisle of the store ran adjacent to the back wall. As I reached the far end, I could hear their conversation. I wasn't close enough to hear every word, but I was getting the drift of it. Somebody had caught Alex, but it didn't sound like security.

I could hear Alex negotiating.

"Look, I'm just here to check out the store...like you. Maybe I can help you, okay?" He was calm, quiet, deliberate.

I peeked through a toppled shelf and saw the back of a man, shorter than me, but pretty stout with broad shoulders, holding what appeared to be a rifle, pointed at Alex. He was standing behind a makeshift crate, fashioned from pallets and tie-down straps. It was a nice design, built on top of a palette jack from the loading dock. He could haul a lot of stuff in that. Much better than a plain old shopping cart.

"Here," Alex said, "here's an inflatable kids' pool. You could use it to collect water, or as a life raft. This is good stuff. Hey, look up there. There's ONE bike left. You could pull your cart. I'm tall enough to get it...if you let me stand on your cart. You can trust me."

"Okay," the man whispered. But not really whispered. His voice was unsteady, cracking with a tone I hadn't expected. He was overcome with emotion. He was crying. He was just like us. A soul that felt a bit lost, out of place and afraid. He was doing his best, trying to provide for himself and his family, I assumed. I suddenly felt more empathy than fear, even as he swung the end of his rifle around toward my son. I decided my best course was to reveal myself.

"Can I help you, son?" I said in a very steady voice. And I called him son on purpose. I wanted the man to know we were related. We were family.

And I immediately followed up with, "And...may I help *you*, sir?"

He swung around. He was much older than me, maybe early eighties. He was trembling with emotion, clearly out of his element. I raised my hands up. I showed him that I had nothing to hide.

"That's a great idea, Alex. Let's get the bike down. He could use it to pull his cart."

I held Alex as he balanced on the edge of the makeshift cart. He lunged a couple of times and unhooked the bike, which was caught up on a fastener at the top of the rack. It was a low-slung girl's bike with a mermaid on the seat and pink sparkle paint.

We tied the bike to the pallet jack handle with the loose ends of his tie-down straps. Then we stepped back.

The old man was overcome with emotion. He put what turned out to be a BB gun on top of his bounty and collapsed to his knees, weeping.

"I'm sorry," he sobbed. "I'm so sorry..."

"Hey, it's okay. Honestly. We know. We understand. Nobody thinks you're a bad person here. These are incredible times. You're doing your best. You're taking care of someone, right? It's okay."

I was trying to give him some hope and also get us out of the store. We were well beyond our two minutes.

He nodded. We helped him get his rig to the side door and out he went. I'm sure it had been many years since he'd been on a bike, but you know what they say. The first few pumps of the pedals were pretty awkward, and he looked like he might go down in a heap. But it all came flooding back to him, and in a moment he stood up on the pedals and churned away, his crate of goods dragging behind him.

Our adventure had taken us to the Garden Center. My mind tripped back to Alex's comments about the kids' pool. I'd never thought of using anything like that. It was a brilliant idea, and it would require almost no space, uninflated. Maybe there were other things in the store that we could use. Other things I hadn't considered. But I was still wrestling with the concept of stealing. But what if I sent money to them? I could anonymously pay for whatever we took. That would surprise them! Getting an envelope of cash with some price tags from whatever we garnered from our visit. I could do that. That would let me sleep at night.

As I turned to see what we might use, I ran right into a tall, narrow rack. It was a display of seeds. The equivalent of a hundred grocery carts full of vegetables. Just add water... and dirt... and time. We stuffed our shirts and pockets full of seed packets. The rack was untouched before we arrived, but it had become a bare wire skeleton, stripped to its core. I hadn't even thought about having a supply of seeds and I never would have – if it hadn't been for the old guy with the gun, Alex's strange negotiation tactics, and my general clumsiness. I gave a little look to the man upstairs. I said, "Thank you."

We looked around the corners of the deserted store. There were no police cars, no security patrols, nobody even checking on the place. We ran back to our vehicles and pulled out of the farmyard.

I was amazed. Surely the store's management was aware of what was happening, but what could they do? Who would they call? *Call. Call* with what? They could go to the police station, assuming they had some remaining power in their autobot, and verbally file a report. But then what? The police radios would work, at least car-to-car, as long as the cars were working. Just like my old CB radio, the airwaves would be the way to communicate. The cell towers, a necessary component of the cellular phone system, would be down due to the power failure, but two-way radios should be usable in any format. I made a mental note.

That reminded me of the little walkie-talkie radios I kept in my camera bag. We used them for photo shoots and on camping trips. They were only good for a few hundred yards, but they would work car-to-car as well. I dug them out and pulled off on the shoulder of the road. Alex rolled up next to me. •

CHAPTER 20: PAYDAY

"Here's a walkie-talkie for you," I said.

"Hey, I remember these!"

"Keep it off unless I wave to you. Conserve the batteries. If we need to talk, turn it on and immediately call me, so I'll know you're up and running. OK?"

"Roger! 10-4. Over and out."

It didn't matter if the world was coming apart, that kid always had a sense of humor that could bring a smile to the situation. We all need more of that.

I was thinking of so many things, I really can't remember in what order this happened. But, I had been thinking about my most recent project, just completed and sent to the client. Having been "let go" of my position, it was most likely the last job I'd ever do for the oil giant. It had been a good run and my relationship with them was pleasant. The change was just business, more or less.

In the Walmart scenario, I couldn't justify the looting of someone else's property. It was stealing, plain and simple. Taking the seed packets was bothering me. After all, nobody owed me anything. Or did they?

Under the current circumstances, how long would it be before my former client paid me for their last hot-deadline project? They had terminated my contract, putting our move to Montana into motion, then called me in to fix a string of errors made by their internal group. Bottom line, it was like having my chain yanked, plus it's what had actually put Rachel and I in this position, screwing up our departure schedule and separating us across the states. In fact, I hadn't even been able to put together an invoice, my departure was so rushed.

So, I ran through it in my mind, getting more and more upset as I drove. They had fired me, delayed me, summoned me, pressured me, used me, and, if it hadn't been for their last-minute indecision, I would have been with Rachel on this journey. And, if this whole event was as bad as I thought it might be, then I'd probably never be compensated at all. Damn it! If they would have had their act together, my family wouldn't be going through this! It was like a wave that just crashed into my soul, and suddenly I was very upset. I decided that they DID owe me.

And as all of that was washing over me, I looked at my map, taped to the dash, and saw an item I'd marked as a reference years ago. A place I'd been on a photo shoot, taking pictures for one of my client's publications. The article was about the pipeline systems. We had outlined the movement of diesel up across the Midwest in the spring, fueling the agricultural users as the fields were prepped and crops planted. Then, we showed how they made the transition to gasoline for the summer vacation season and Memorial Day traffic. It was amazing how much volume was pushed through this network of pipes, running from the mega-refineries on the Gulf Coast, up through the grain belt, connecting with Canada. The infrastructure that's in place to provide liquid fuels and natural gas took decades to develop and build. It's incredibly safe and reliable, and most of us don't even know it exists. It is simply taken for granted.

I don't know if it was my anger at the situation, my opportunistic dark side, or some deep-seated wisdom that struck me right between the eyes as I looked at that map. But something hit me, and it hit me hard. I knew how I would be paid, and it wouldn't require an invoice.

I waved out the window for Alex to turn on his walkie-talkie. "Hey, good buddy," I heard across the static.

"Turn left, 2 miles up. We're switching trucks," I said.

"Roger...uh, Jake...Bob? Larry." He laughed as he answered.

We jumped out and switched trucks.

As I was passing by Alex, between the trucks, I told him, "Find a place to hide. Meet me right back here in 30 minutes. If you don't see me, turn your walkie-talkie back on." My mind was on autopilot, flying far ahead of me as I developed my idea.

"Wait!" I slammed on the brakes. "We're putting all of your stuff into my truck," I shouted. "Quick – all of it. You can arrange it while you're waiting for me. Everything into my truck. Now." My head was spinning with exactly how this was going to go down. There was a lot of risk, but I had a lot of hope. I knew it would come together.

I grabbed my shotgun and slid it behind the seat of Alex's truck. "I love you," I said. He just looked at me, a bit stunned.

It was about 5 miles over to the mark I'd seen on my map, just off one of the secondary highways that lead to the main arteries for Kansas City, St. Louis, and Des Moines. One of their Midwest distribution centers had been placed perfectly for their supply routes. And today, that was perfect for our needs as well. The pipelines would be running for sure. They would have to be getting backup fuel to the critical users, and they would obviously have a supply for their own generators and pumps. Even with all of the legislated shutdowns, they'd have to be running something today, something to fuel the generators.

I knew the layout of the place, the protocols for coming and going, and the weird little fact that the drivers had to get out and close the gates behind them when leaving the terminal. I had noticed it when I was there a few years ago and thought it was a security glitch.

The large white tanks stood up on the horizon. It wasn't busy, but a number of trucks were sitting under the fill racks. It had come to me like something from a dream, or nightmare, depending on the perspective. My mind spun. Okay, what exactly was the plan?

Alex was surprised to see me pass back by his hideout earlier than expected. It had only been about 15 minutes.

"Okay, here's the plan...and, where were you when I drove by?" I asked, interrupting my own train of thought.

"I was back down there, in that field by an old barn. Hasn't been used in forever. The barn's empty, just some old fencing equipment. An old hay loft. Looks like a good wind would take it down, but it's still standing," he offered. It was a lot of intel for just a few minutes.

"I checked it out in case we needed a place to stay for the night. You just took off without really saying anything, so I didn't know what we were doing. Anyway, we could pull one truck inside, I think. It might be tight, but I think it would fit. The door should swing open with both of us on it." Alex beamed with a sense of accomplishment.

I smiled at him. "Nicely done."

"So, are we staying the night?"

"No, but your truck is." I wasn't intentionally mysterious, I just had a lot on my mind. Adrenaline can do that to you. It heightens the focus but makes for poor communication. "Let's get back there. I'll follow you."

We switched back to our own trucks, and Alex led the way. Just a quarter mile up the road, he turned down through a strip of broken barbed wire fence. The old barn set back off the road a hundred feet or so. I'm not sure why it was still there, as it appeared someone was growing alfalfa all around it. Maybe they used it for storage. Whatever the case, we were glad to have it standing.

It did take both of us to get the doors open, but once we did, Alex's truck fit in nicely. We threw dirt and grass on the truck to dampen any reflections that might draw attention, then lucked across an old tarp, probably used to cover whatever the farmer had stored in there. With that in place, we threw on some more hay. If you peeked in through a crack, you couldn't even tell it was a truck.

Alex crawled in with me, which made me happy, honestly. I still hadn't really said anything, and we crept slowly back up onto the road. Once all four tires were out of the grass and on the pavement, I hit it hard and we sailed back toward the terminal.

"Do you mind telling me what we're doing?" Alex asked, with a degree of calmness that was more sarcastic than it was real.

"We need enough fuel to get to Montana," I said.

"Okay," he replied, with a wide-eyed blankness.

I hesitated for another moment, trying to find some eloquent wording for my next statement, which I couldn't manage.

"I'm going to steal a tanker. That's what we're doing." It seemed pretty logical when I said it. It was very matter of fact. I hoped it would be that easy.

"Alrighty then."

About a mile from the terminal, we slowed to a stop. "You need to be driving," I told him, and I got out and stood next to the door. He closed his door and came around to drive. He slid in behind the wheel. I hopped onto the step bar on the driver's side, holding on to the rearview mirror. As we passed the terminal, I stepped off and slid down into the ditch, opposite the turnout from the lot. I would have taken myself out with a mailbox if Alex hadn't seen it coming and grabbed my shirt through the open window, delaying my jump by a critical second.

I hadn't landed that hard since high school. My Dad had been a solid athlete, earning some scholarship money to play baseball and football back in his day. And Alex was incredibly skilled in sports, also playing some college ball. But I was the proof that some traits skip a generation, and so my lack of coordination and all-around minimal athletic ability had given me a tall, lean machine, with absolutely no control systems in the cab.

At 6 feet, 5 inches, people would often ask "So, did you play ball?"

"I tried to," was my standard response.

And my landing in the weed-lined ditch was as horribly choreographed as you might imagine. I tripped and tumbled through the brush, collecting burrs and thorns and spiderwebs as I rolled to a stop across from the far side of the driveway. I spit out a cocklebur and a few pieces of gravel as I crawled to the deepest part of the ravine.

I knew that every driver stopped, swung open the double gates and pulled through to the road. Once there, they had to get back out of the truck and relock the gates. I'd seen it over and over during my photography visit years ago, and I saw the same thing again on my just-completed intel run.

Like the scene in *Groundhog Day* when the lead character robs the armored car. I just counted the time. And what a great lesson I'd drawn from that silly comedy. Laced through the haphazard adventures of a conceited news reporter caught in a time loop, the underlying message is that you can do anything, make anything of yourself, if you'll just devote the time. It just takes time and the decision to do it. As with most things, we just need to make the decision to do it. To *"go for it"* as they say.

As fate would have it, though, an incoming rig stopped at the gate. That would ruin my plan. If the outbound truck didn't need to stop, I'd lose my chance.

"C'mon, be lazy," I said to myself, trying to plant my thoughts into the arriving driver via some form of telepathy. “Make the other guy work the gate.”

I laid as flat as possible, down over the edge of the ditch, peering through the tall weeds and grass that bordered the narrow country road.

The driver swung down from the cab and began to open the outer gates. Once he pushed them back, he would move to the inner set. And here came my full tanker, freshly filled from the overhead pipe array. I had watched as mostly all diesel was loaded into the long smooth trailer. It was exactly what I needed. But this guy’s timing was going to blow it. If the gates were open, my truck would just roll out and leave. I had to stall them. I needed my tanker’s driver to be the one who closed the gates.

I used the only supplies I had. Loose gravel. I tossed little pieces of the ground-up rock into the air and it rained down upon the empty tank that sat outside the gates. Ting, ting, ting. The empty aluminum chamber echoed with a mysterious hollow sound. The man stopped and turned around. He bent down and looked under his truck. He turned back toward the gate, reaching for the lock. Ting, ting, ting. Another volley of gravel bounced off the target. It wasn’t much of a tactic, but it had his attention.

He let his key ring drop back against his hip and made a complete round, checking his truck for the source of the noise.

Any more sound from me would be muted by the sound of the approaching truck inside of the complex. My tanker was approaching the gates.

The guy outside hollered, “I’ll open ’em. You close ’em?”

“Sounds good,” came the response from my driver.

This was perfect. The gates were opened, and the first truck drove through, headed for the back of the terminal to stage his position under the fill racks.

My truck pulled through, leaving the cab at the edge of the road, turned just a bit to the right. The driver swung the door open and prepared to jump down to the ground. And just then, I sneezed. And not in the muffled way that your aunt uses a lace tissue in church to mask a slight nasal itch. I mean a full-blown dust, pollen, and cobwebs jammed up your nose sneeze. The driver looked in my direction and I could feel his eyes searching the edge of the roadway as I stared straight down into the dirt. But my sneeze was immediately followed by his air brakes reloading. He looked behind the cab of his truck, checking his connecting lines. His curiosity was settled by the hiss of the brake system. He jumped down, leaving the door open.

As he walked away from the cab, I was coming up from the ditch, behind him. He continued toward the gates and I crawled up into the cab. As he closed and locked the inner-most gate, I released the brakes, jammed the truck into gear, and pulled away.

At first, he tried to run after me. "Hey!" he called out. "Heyyyy!" As if I actually might stop. But that was highly unlikely. I watched him trailing his runaway truck in the rearview. I'm not sure how old he was, or what his athletic DNA held, but if he had run track back in his high school days, we might have been a close match. And, like me, the 100-yard dash would not have been his event. His arms swung around in circles, his steel-toe work boots losing traction as he accelerated. Finally, he tried to stop and turn, but the smooth soles went out from under him and he hit hard on his backside. His only recourse was to shake his fist at me. He got up and ran back toward the terminal gate.

I hadn't even thought about it, but I had his keys. He'd locked himself out. The first diabolical plan of my life had worked, and even better than I thought.

I waved as I passed Alex at the next corner.

“Hey, we got us a rollin’ pipeline!” I heard come across the walkie-talkie.

“Keep these on the rest of the way, just in case. We’ll get out of range, but you keep going. Take it slow, but don’t stop. Keep moving until you get there. I’ll be there eventually. Backroads. Slow.”

“I love you, Dad.”

“I love you, bud. But don’t use my name on here,” I shot back. Having just committed a felony, I was a bit paranoid.

““Dad” isn’t your name,” Alex responded, dryly.

“Yes. Sorry. I just...”

“Ha-ha. Love you, Dad.” Alex laughed as we headed north toward Iowa.

•

CHAPTER 21: HOME SWEET HOME

It was evening when I arrived at the old hometown. Alex and I had been separated for most of the trip, but reconnected on the walkie-talkies a few miles outside of town. It was comforting just to be close to Mom and Dad's house. It was the feeling of home that we all carry in our hearts.

The town looked empty. It was silent and eerie, and I'd be lying if I said I didn't feel incredibly uneasy as I drove up the side street, just east of downtown. Anyone who saw me would question what was going on. It was highly uncommon to have a fuel tanker roaming the streets of their small town. But I knew that I could make the turn at the top edge of town and come back down a mostly vacant street to the alley behind the house. The ones who saw me might wonder where I was going, but most wouldn't figure out where I'd gone.

I saw a couple of figures watching from pulled-back shades and curtains. When I was a kid, I knew everybody in town. From the young families with kids in my school to the retired farmers who had moved to town when they either sold to larger operations or turned the farm over to their adult children. It was a great mix of solid people, hardworking and dedicated to family and community. The place used to be as neat as a pin. Everybody knew everybody, and that was okay. But now I only knew a few of the residents, the holdovers from my parents' generation and some of the kids who'd stayed to run businesses and raise their children in a less hectic environment. It was probably a good choice. And it had its freedoms.

The people at the windows were unknown to me, and I couldn't even get a good read on their age. Usually it was the older folks that were the nosy neighbors, peeking and gossiping about the goings-on around town. These days were different though, and with no power for entertainment on the screens, they were likely to revert back to the old-time ways of hanging out on the porch and talking to the folks who lived next door. What a novel concept. Tomorrow, they'd be asking who saw the tanker truck, and where had it gone?

We came to a stop behind the folk's house, back in the alley behind the pine trees that served as a wind block from the north. They also served to block the view of the neighbor's yard to the back, who, before abandoning his place for a job in the city, packed the place with old machinery and building remnants. It was kind of a junk heap, but pretty decent camouflage for the tanker and my pickup.

Alex had come in from the other side, so we'd be separated in case either of us was stopped. We met, nose-to-nose, in the alley. I preferred that nobody know we were in town. There would be a lot of questions about what we'd seen, what we'd heard, speculation, conjecture, and too much curiosity about our plan forward. I preferred to simply pass through, pick up some supplies, add Mom and Dad to our group, and move along.

We opened the back door and peeked in. "Hello. Mom? Dad?"

"In here," I heard two voices say, almost in unison, as if they were expecting guests. That was odd.

We stepped into the kitchen. It was mostly dark outside, but there was enough ambient light to see some items on the kitchen counter. A glow of candles came from the dining room.

"What are you two doing here?" was the next response, and what I'd expected in the first place.

"Hey, hi!" said the other couple, sitting at the table amidst some candles, an old lantern, playing cards, paper, and pencils. Evidently it was game night.

"We're playing Pitch, do you want to join us?"

"No, thank you. I think we're probably just looking to lie down, take a break from driving, maybe go down to the basement and play pool." Wow, that was a weird string of options, but it was what I said.

And in an effort to fix my odd statement, I added another twist. "What I'd really like is a shower." I said.

"I don't think that's in the cards. Pardon the pun," joked Alex, with a smile.

Mom and I laughed. Dad looked at us with his standard "I really don't get your humor" look. The other folks just looked puzzled.

"So what are we doing, Dad?" came a great question from Alex, who was eager to make some sort of determination about what was next. And he was sensing my uneasiness with the neighbors. I'd known these people all my life but could not remember their names. My mind was elsewhere.

He tried to help me out some more. To break the silence, he said, "Did you want to check out that stuff in the basement? Remember?" Alex asked again, followed by a wide-eyed expression that let me know this was a directive and not really a question.

"Yes, yes, down in the basement." I finally managed. "So sorry. We'll be back up in a minute. Can I borrow that lantern?" Down the stairs we went.

I heard my Dad excuse himself from the group. He followed us downstairs.

Dad stood on the bottom step, holding the stairway post.

"What's going on?" he asked. "We've heard all of the power is out, coast-to-coast. But why are you here? How did you get here? And where's Rachel?" His voice cracked. "Where's Rachel?" he asked again, softly, with tears beginning to well up in his eyes.

"Dad, I think she's fine. I really don't know. She was traveling. I'm sure she's alright." I was trying to reassure myself and Alex as much as I was trying to inform him.

"We can't stay," were my next words. "And they can't tell anybody that we're here," I added, pointing to the ceiling above me where the neighbors sat with Mom at the dining room table.

"Alright. Understood. But can I ask why?" He stepped on down into the basement, closer to Alex and me.

I ran Dad through the brief about our travel plans, moving everything to Montana, which he had known about. But then, everything changed. I went through how we were split up by my client's schedule change, other commitments, and on and on.

He had heard bits and pieces of the Moberly plan a number of years ago, but said he didn't really recall the details. "I'm not sure I remember all of that," he said.

His response implied that he'd thought I was a bit over the top with my schemes, and while he entertained my talking points, he really hadn't paid much attention at the time. That was okay, the plan wasn't for him, it was for us. And, Alex had followed it brilliantly. I was incredibly proud of him. He's a good kid, and I always want the best for him.

"I'll be going back to Tennessee," said Alex, as a somewhat off-track comment to the conversation. I was a bit surprised.

"I need to go back, Dad. I needed to follow through, because I knew you'd be there for me. So I had to come. But, I've got to go back. I hope you and Mom understand that. I love you both, so much, but..."

He had obviously been thinking about this during his past few hours on the road. He said it was all he could think about. All the various scenarios, and none of them worked if he went with me. He had his commitments, his passions, and his dreams. And they weren't with me and his Mom anymore. Just like mine hadn't been in Iowa. I understood, and we both knew his Mom would understand too.

"I'm really sorry," he said, as a big tear rolled down his cheek. "I love you. I love Mom. So much. I just..."

"It's okay. It's okay. I get it, bud. I understand. I'm so proud of you. Thank you for coming to meet me. This is all going to be okay," I offered, my own tears running down my face again. "We'll get you set up and back to your truck tomorrow. I'll plan that out tonight. You need some sleep. We all need some sleep."

"Hey, Dad?" he responded. "Right after I beat you at ping-pong." He motioned to the ping-pong table over his shoulder.

Ping-pong had been a thing with us forever. Dad had taught me how to play on that same table in the basement. I had taught Alex on a miniature table at first, and eventually our own full-size table in the dining room. That's right, in the dining room. They don't have basements in Texas, and our kitchen area was big enough for a formal dining table, so we took out the chandelier and put the dining room to better use. Anyway, we had played almost every morning before he went to school, and we'd continued it as our personal bonding tradition every time we were together and had the opportunity.

I'll always remember those last games in the basement, by the lantern's light, the three of us. Even in stressful, scary times, you can find happiness if you look close enough. We were so blessed to be together. I think he even let me win a couple.

Eventually Dad went back upstairs, and Alex curled up on the basement couch. I heard Dad tell the neighbors that he didn't know exactly what was up, but he did ask them to please respect our desire for privacy for whatever reason. They agreed and promised to keep it quiet. They said they hoped everything was alright.

Dad said, "I'm sure it's perfectly fine. But you know Jake." The guy let out a laugh, and I heard the front door close.

I went upstairs to talk with Mom and Dad.

Their power had gone off three days ago, just like everyone else's. In fact, it hadn't really gone off, it just didn't come on that morning. They'd been having occasional brownouts, and their little town was just not high enough on the ratings scale to pull any preference when it came to distribution. They'd gotten used to it. That's why they had plenty of candles, lanterns, and oil. It was as if all this technology had returned them to the late 1800s. One modern touch was the small diesel generator Dad had installed behind the house.

I asked them about coming with me, but they were adamant. Dad had been in the Army. He'd been to war. He'd fought real live enemies, actually killed men, and returned to a quiet life of farming and running a small business. He wasn't afraid of a little darkness, and he wasn't about to leave his home. My Mom felt the same. This was her hometown, the house she and Dad had built before I was born. They weren't going anywhere. Plus, they had prepared for long winter blizzards, and they viewed this the same way.

They had also watched the unfolding events of the past year. The food shortages, the increasing failure rates on the system, and the change in the people around them. While there were a growing number that were on the edge, they felt that this area was a known quantity. The majority of their inner circle was solid, making it their best defense for the long term. They also were concerned that if they left, everything would be lost. The contents of the house, certainly, and perhaps everything else, would be taken as the unprepared masses from the city began to move outward. They had discussed it before, and they believed it would be okay.

"A number of us have talked about this, too, Jake," said my Dad. "I never thought I'd be fighting for my life again. But I certainly will. So will the other guys."

My doubts were greater than theirs, but I respected their position, and they respected mine. I helped Dad get some rolls of insulation down from the garage attic, and we wrapped them around the deep freezer with duct tape, giving it another 10 inches of insulation. We slid cardboard underneath it and filled the space between with spray foam, like you put around outside water pipes. If they didn't open it very often, the food in their lift-top freezer likely would last until they had consumed it. They had a full beef, most of the prior year's garden harvest, and about 20 loaves of Dad's homemade bread. Dad said they'd get by for a quite awhile.

But not more than a year I estimated in my head, maybe two at the max, if they started stretching right now.

When they'd sold the business, a grocery store, Dad had stocked up shelves in the basement with all sorts of inventory the new owner didn't want to take on. So they had cases of green beans, chili, cream style corn, window cleaner, paper towels, and more. One entire side of the basement looked more like a 7-11 than a residence. But he said, "It'll keep." And so it did. And hopefully not everyone in town knew what all was down there.

For protection, he had a sniper rifle that was in pristine condition – a memento from the war that had earned him more than one medal – a BB gun, two 12-gauge shotguns, and a couple of .38 revolvers, police issue, from the county sheriff's posse. Dad had served his community well, so I hoped they would now return the favor if he or Mom needed anything. It was hard to leave them there. I prefer not to think of them in any way except exactly like I last saw them. It simply worries me too much. One day I'll see them again. I just don't know when or where. •

CHAPTER 22: EVERYBODY UP

Dad woke everyone up at 5 o'clock. He was always an early riser, much to my detriment when I was a teenager. We filled every gas can and mason jar we could find with diesel and gasoline from the tanker, including the neighbor's – as reimbursement for their silence.

Dad had a 120-gallon farm tank for the back of his pickup that we moved over to my truck, inside the topper on the back. We put it clear up against the back of the cab, so the weight would be centered in the truck. It was going to be a lot of weight, but I'd beefed up the suspension when I bought the truck, in case I needed to pull Alex's band trailer for some reason. I always tried to be prepared. We filled it to the brim and topped off his generator tank as well. We also filled the tank behind the backyard neighbor's house, since he wasn't around anymore and it was a perfectly good tank. Nobody would ever dream that it was full, and it would give Mom and Dad the ability to run the deep freezer on occasion. When winter hit, it would give them a safety net for heat.

We also built a quick but deterring fence around the firewood pile, just to keep anyone from dropping by for easy pickings. Dad said he and Mom would move most of it into the garage and let the car sit out, as the wood now had more value. How times change.

Our last stop was the fire station, where we emptied the last of the diesel into the barrel of fuel they kept for the fire trucks. Dad had a key, as did a lot of the guys in town, as it was a volunteer fire department. It was the least we could do. But what if the town did have a fire? What if it were a big one? They could run the pumps for a while, but they couldn't refresh the water into the town's water tower. Not without the big water pumps down at the main well – they require a ton of electricity.

Dad told me that the city council moved to shut down water usage as soon as they heard the power outage was nationwide. They had turned off the main valves at the tower, and everyone had to go to the tower with personal containers. It was being guarded by a rotating shift of volunteers, including him. His first shift was the following day. He said they gave the old guys the daytime hours, because they thought they couldn't stay awake on the late shifts. I think all of those were wise decisions, but I still didn't know what would happen in the event of a big fire. All of the fuel would be consumed, all of the water would be gone, and it would be a huge problem. They would probably be better off just letting someone's home burn, as long as it didn't threaten the entire town. That's an incredibly cold way to think, but that's the reality now.

Their neighbors, the folks who were over playing cards, had an old windmill on their farm, now operated by their son's family. It wasn't the power-generation turbine-type of windmill. It was an old-fashioned water pumping windmill. And while the well had been converted to an electric pump, they had kept all of the apparatus in good condition and could convert it back pretty easily. If the gearworks had suffered the same issues as the big turbines, with the corrosive sulfur ash and dust, then they still had the hand pump to draw up water. So, with a few of these old hand pumps around, most of the townspeople would have some access to fresh water at least. I was glad about that. With that reminder, I added 50 gallons of fresh water to my truck's load as well.

Dad insisted that he go with Alex and I back to Alex's truck, but I wasn't about to risk something happening that left Mom at home alone over the longer term. That just wasn't going to happen. It was a bit of a standoff, but I won. I don't know that I'd ever gone fully against Dad's wishes before. Even in high school, when he set my curfew earlier than everyone else's, I toed the line.

When I was in my junior and senior years, we had sports curfews.

If you were an athlete, you had to be home by 1 a.m. on Friday and Saturday nights, and 11 p.m. every other night. If a coach or teacher caught you out past curfew, you missed the next game. So, everybody followed it pretty tight. But Dad's curfew for me was 12:30 a.m. on the weekends. That was a half-hour earlier than anybody else.

"What's up with that?" I had asked.

"Well," he said, matter of factly. "We live in a rural area. So, wherever you're at, you're going to be at least 20 minutes from home."

"Okay," I agreed.

"And whatever you're thinking about doing, it'll be midnight before you get up enough nerve to try it."

"Okay," I laughed.

"So, that only leaves you 10 minutes – and I don't think you can pull it off." He looked straight at me, with a somber look of wisdom, truth, and righteousness.

"I'd say you are probably correct," I admitted and I smiled. He slapped me on the shoulder, and we went back to whatever it was we were doing. He was an awesome Dad. The best.

But no matter how amazing he was, he was not going to make the trip back to Alex's truck with me. We did, however, borrow his truck for the trip, as it wasn't packed to the gills with diesel fuel, water, computers, and all the other crap I was hauling in mine. And I just realized, during our entire time at home, nobody asked how or where we got the fuel truck.

I wanted to return the fuel truck to the area where we'd "acquired" it for a number of reasons. First, it would keep suspicion focused in that area, and not up around hometown Iowa. And frankly, I wanted them to have their property back. I know we took the fuel, but I wanted to keep the incident to a minimum. Look, I'm not a professional thief, so just accept that I wanted to return the truck. They'll need the truck to haul fuel to others. I cost them a day's use of the truck and the fuel. I'll call it even.

So Alex and I started our journey late in the day, after everything was fueled and packed. We had over 100 gallons of diesel for him to take, along with water and canned food from the basement store. His plan was to not stop until he arrived back in Tennessee, except to fill with fuel in two very remote places. That would get him back home. Back to Holly and her family. They would be fine.

I pulled out from behind the fire station after filling the big red barrel. Dad waved and started walking up the street toward the house. If anyone had been watching, that would look somewhat normal. He'd met the regular fuel truck there many times before. And it could be logical that the fire department was getting fuel due to the circumstances. It could pass as legit. I figured we were in the clear.

At the same time, Alex was heading out of town on the other side, in Dad's truck. If anyone noticed Dad's truck over there, it was unlikely that they'd simultaneously see him walking up the street on the other side of town. I suppose if they did, it would simply make him eligible for sainthood. Anyway, that was the plan.

Alex and I met up about 10 miles outside of town, along the route we'd charted. It seemed that any traffic that was out and about was occurring in the early evening. I'm not sure why, but we decided it was best to be out on the road with others for this trip, helping deter curiosity about the tanker as well as bringing it back to its origin after dark. That was most important. And, we didn't want anyone to associate one vehicle with the other. So we traded leaders, with Alex passing and taking the front for a while. He'd get a few miles ahead, then slow down and let me catch and pass him. I think it was a good plan. •

CHAPTER 23: I MISS THAT KID

By 9 o'clock that night, the roads were vacant. Luckily, we were close to where we needed to be. Eventually, I took the lead, and honestly, I chickened out. We passed through a small town with a field full of old school buses and construction trucks on its outskirts. Some sort of "Used Trucks" lot, according to the sign. I swung the tanker down through the opening in the fence and lined it up with the rest of the vehicles. While the others were becoming overgrown with weeds, this one was still pretty shiny and it would be readily apparent to anyone passing by that it was out of place, new to its surroundings. But it may take a day or two for anyone to notice. That would be long enough.

I flagged down Alex with three clicks on the walkie-talkies and he picked me up down the road a ways. We had already wiped down everything we'd touched: the steering wheel, shifter, brake handle, valves, doors, etc. And I'd driven with gloves on, so unless they pulled a DNA sample from a strand of hair, I'm going to assume we got away with it.

Fifteen minutes later, we were back at the barn where we'd left Alex's truck. We drove by the first time at speed, to see if anyone was around or if anything had been disturbed. The old board we'd leaned against the swinging doors was still standing at a 30-degree angle, and the empty beer can I'd found and set on the other door's latch was still there. The entire area looked untouched.

Alex jumped out on our second pass and ran to the barn, throwing back the doors and pinning them open. I pulled down the road a little ways, to a wider driveway. We had decided that we didn't want to transfer everything back in the lot by the barn. If someone was to come by, we'd have no way out. If we were out on the open road, we could split up if we had to. Even if we weren't done loading his truck, we each had walkie-talkies and we'd selected a meeting point outside the next town. There were always plans within the plan.

But we didn't need our secondary plans that night. He pulled his truck up next to my Dad's, and we loaded the fuel cans, boxes, bags, and water. I gave him the tightest hug I had ever given him in his entire life and he hugged me back. We probably held onto each other for full minute without saying a word. No words were worthy.

There was nothing either of us could say. "I love you, bud."

"I love you too, Dad. Give Mom the same hug, okay?"

"You bet." I couldn't say anything more. My throat was too tight. He pulled away, and I waved as if I was going to see him again in just a few hours. But I knew that wasn't the truth.

I suppose that Alex could have driven that tanker back, close to where his truck was hidden, carrying everything he needed with him. But I, like my Dad, wanted to be with him. I needed to see him get into his own truck, know that he had fuel, food, and protection, and watch him set out on that road back to Tennessee. I needed to see that, to know that, to have that peace in my heart. Because honestly, I didn't know if I'd ever see him again. Just like my Mom and Dad, I know we'll all see each other again. I just don't know where or when. I pray that he's okay. I know he's okay. I know that God watched over him as he made his way back to his girl and his life. I know. I just know.

I jumped in Dad's truck and headed back to Iowa. I'd surveyed this road on Google Maps, traced it in the atlas, and now I was driving it for the third time in 48 hours. I missed my son already, and I missed my wife. •

CHAPTER 24: BACK HOME, AGAIN

It was around 3 a.m. when I pulled back into Mom and Dad's driveway. As Dad had stated, the car was outside and the movement of firewood into the garage had begun in earnest. I brought his truck in against the house as tight as I could to discourage anyone from taking fuel, the battery, I really didn't know what else. It just seemed like the best idea. But were there any good ideas?

If this lasted for months, which was highly likely – or a year, or more – what was parking the truck close to the house going to accomplish? What was any of this going to accomplish? Mom and Dad had an amazing food supply, but it wasn't going to hold out more than a year. I mean, nobody had that amount of food on hand. What were all of those people going to do? What was going to happen when the average house down the street was out of food in four days? What was going to happen when the people who thought they were seriously prepared were out of food in a month? There was going to be a lot of desperation.

•

CHAPTER 25: LEAVING IOWA

It was hard leaving Mom and Dad behind, but it was their lifelong home, the town they'd both grown up in, where they'd fallen in love, got married, built a business, and raised me. I don't know how you get much more *home* than that.

The house itself was even built by them just a couple of years before I came along. It's the only home I'd ever known, and it was where all of my childhood memories were made. I don't know what's become of them during this time, honestly. It's one of the things I don't like to think about because I'm not sure if they made it. And if they did, what they had to endure. But that was everyone's choice, and I love and respect them too much to try and override those decisions.

I waved as I pulled away, like I had done on Saturday nights as a teenager, heading off to cruise town or hang out with friends. And like I'd done on numerous Sunday nights, heading back to college, with my fresh laundry folded in my basket in the back seat. Dad had his arm around Mom, and he gave her a squeeze. She looked up at him. I knew she'd have tears in her eyes. I know I certainly did.

It was around 4 o'clock in the morning when I pulled out, still dark and with a couple of hours to go before any serious sunlight would be at my back. It was my goal to be crossing the Missouri River exactly at sunrise.

I love driving west in the morning. The spectacular lighting that God brings to the world, with the sun's warm soft glow that saturates the colors and brings an artist's touch to the details and textures. It's as beautiful as it gets.

And the blinding sun keeps you out of the gaze of folks traveling east or looking east, into the sun. You are on them and past them before they even know you are there. Ah, beauty and stealth, all in one package. Of course, that was before everything became hazy and gray. I hoped that the thin clear slit of atmosphere closest to the earth would give me about 20 minutes of sunlight, as it shot in directly from the east. Then the sun would be back above the curtain created by the smoke and ash.

While Interstate 80 was right there, begging me to jump on and fly, I simply couldn't trust it. There was still some traffic out there, but it was scarce. My parents had watched I-80 grow from an idea in the early 1960s to one of the nation's most important lifelines, buzzing with freight and travelers. It was one of a handful of major arteries linking the coasts and providing effective access across the flyover states. It had been in need of widening for years, as both lanes on each side remained consistently heavy both day and night. A third lane would have been a nice luxury for the long-haul truckers and travelers alike, but the past couple of days had seen traffic reduced to a dozen or so vehicles an hour, if that. And I couldn't really wrap my head around where those people were coming from or going to, and more importantly, how they had the fuel or power to be out there at all. I had decided long before this even began, back in the days of talking and planning, that backroads were the safest way to go.

My route to Montana was restricted by a couple of things, in fact, two specific things. Bridges. I would have to cross the Missouri River on the west side of Iowa. My choices were Highway 30 at Blair, Nebraska, or Highway 175 at Decatur. I'd go with Blair as my first choice. If that didn't pan out, then Decatur was upriver to the north, which would still take me in the direction I needed to go. And, if that was a no-go, then I'd keep moving north, up and over the top of the river's basin through the Dakotas. Plans A, B, and C, already determined.

But Plan A was Blair, a small city of just under 10,000 people. At the extreme north edge of the Omaha–Council Bluffs metro area, it was still pretty rural. It sat in a bit of a valley, nestled by the hills that bordered the Missouri River and the broader flat lands that surrounded it. It was where the Pacific Railroad had decided to take its route west in the earlier days of our country. So I let those frontiersmen and engineers help guide my course as well.

They would have been concerned about some of the same issues that I was worried about. Ease of progress, safe sight lines, and efficient transport. That was what it was all about. Safety and efficiency and making progress.

Ultimately, I needed to get to Highway 2 or Highway 20, my favorite choices to connect me with Colorado. But once there, I'd almost have to run Interstate 25, and honestly I was concerned about that. It seemed like forever away, at least at this point. One mile at a time.

When I pulled out of my hometown, it was as if the entire little village was asleep. The people, the dogs, the lights, everything. We get very conditioned to street lights, yard lights, and their glow upon the landscape. Driving down a city street at night, we move from pool to pool, the circles of light telling us of intersections and homes, and providing us with a sense that makes us feel safe and connected, even if the streets are vacant.

But when absolutely all of the lights are out, it's different. It makes us feel a bit uneasy. It's a bit too dark. A bit too quiet. And it makes us feel alone.

The horizon to the west was still blinking with some red aircraft warning lights on the top of the wind turbines, though. Mom hated those red lights. More than 200 of them in that county alone, all blinking in unison. While the turbines had stopped, many of the lights, still on battery backup, pulsed their unending waltz tempo. Blink, one, two, blink, one, two, blink, one, two. Every three seconds, they would string the horizon like Christmas lights. To some they were pretty, a modern touch of decor on the rural landscape. To others, like Mom, they were an eyesore, distracting and unnatural atop the cornfields she had been gazing across since her childhood.

I swung to the right at the fire station and headed west on "Old 6." Known decades ago as "White Pole Road," it had once been a lifeline between the coasts. That little two-lane highway had carried travelers and goods from around the world, feeding little towns like ours with gas station trade, shoppers, and restaurant-goers eager for a homestyle meal and homemade pies that stood 4 inches thick. The brick Main Street was still there, and was, in fact, seeing a bit of a resurgence as people from the urban areas began longing for some attachment to their roots and a place to escape the increasingly hectic lives that total modernization and technology had inflicted upon them. Whatever drove the change, it was good to see some revived storefronts along with some umbrellas and tables out on the sidewalks.

I saw a flashlight sweeping around out by the town's primary water well. While I hoped it was someone from the town's maintenance department, working to see what they could do to drive the pumps, I was pretty certain it was someone getting both curious and desperate about water supply. The dusty ash in the air traced their beam of light as they walked around the little concrete building that sat in the river bottom.

Most of the bigger pieces of ash had cleared down around ground level, settling into a fine gray dust that glazed everything like a dingy coat of flat primer paint. But up above what I guessed to be a thousand feet or so, it was still a solid opaque cloud. And it seemed to continue to grow more dense. In fact, this morning, there may not be a sunrise at all. I checked my bandana. Mom had tied it around my neck in case I needed a dust mask to breathe.

As I passed the little road that led down to the pump house, I saw that their tracks had come from the west. Whoever it was, they weren't even local. No other tracks yet disturbed the powder that had settled onto the roadway during the night. I was evidently the first to leave town.

I passed the infamous Eisenhart Schoolhouse Corner and smiled. It was one of my own inside jokes. Everyone knew the Eisenhart Schoolhouse Corner and it was a common landmark for local directions. The problem was, if you weren't from around here, there is no schoolhouse building at the corner. In fact, I think it was torn down in the 1940s, making that corner a cornfield for nearly 100 years. As irony would have it, the very next corner actually did have a schoolhouse built on it. That was where I went to high school. A modern brick facility with a big gym and beautiful natural amphitheater-style football field. It was a great piece of my own history. But although that incredible, physical, actual schoolhouse sat on 'that' corner, it was not on the "Schoolhouse Corner," as everyone called it. Maybe this is why people use Google Maps.

Anyway, no one was at either schoolhouse corner that morning, and there were no tracks to show anyone had been. The world had gone quiet. •

CHAPTER 26: AM I CRAZY?

I began to wonder about my sanity for the first time. Perhaps it was brought on by the comfort I found being in familiar surroundings, having spent a day at home with my parents and my son. But whatever the cause, my decisions and choices suddenly seemed abnormal.

The power had been off for a few days. But I had lived through power outages in the past. Dozens of winter ice storms, summer wind storms – both common in Iowa when I was growing up. The electricity had gone off for a few days at a stretch, and we all survived. No one back then had felt the need to steal a fuel tanker or stay within reach of a weapon. Was I going crazy? Was I implementing this plan simply because I had a plan to implement?

Maybe this was some distorted self-fulfilling prophecy that I was carrying out because I'd scripted it in my mind. Maybe the power failure was just a trigger to some personal instability. I mean, I remember going back into a store to pay for a pack of gum I was holding in my hand during checkout. When I got to my truck, I'd realized I hadn't paid for it. I felt guilty. I had gone back in, apologized, and paid for it. The clerk thought it was a bit unusual, but I felt better. Now just a few months later, I had almost nonchalantly committed a felony.

But I knew I was right. I just knew it. Somewhere down deep in my gut, where you feel those animal instincts, that quiet and mostly dormant inner voice that has learned from centuries of experience – carried across our genetics from our ancestors – was giving me a clear message. The geese knew they had to fly south in the winter, and I knew I had to get to Montana.

I was reassured when I drove by Crawford's place. They had the biggest farming operation in the area, with thousands and thousands of acres in play. There was a dim light glowing in their side yard area, toward their barn and machine sheds. With a long determined look, I could see reflections of the light on a number of pickups and SUVs. A row of vehicles sat in the drive. From that observation, I assumed all of the kids and their families were gathered at the homeplace, no doubt bringing their supplies with them. The main house would have deep freezers with homegrown beef and a massive pantry of food stocks. And, out around the shop they'd have generators, along with hundreds of gallons of diesel fuel, maybe more. They'd be alright for quite a while.

As I passed, I also noticed their front drive. It had been barricaded with steel posts, fence panels, and barbed wire. They had begun to put together a fortress between the outside world and themselves. Maybe I wasn't the only one acting a bit crazy. I was in good company.

I started running through the schedule in my mind. Getting to the river and getting across were the first hurdles of the day. It was about 100 miles to my target point, which meant it was five gallons of fuel away.

A successful crossing at Blair would be the start of my long run across mostly rural America. I glanced at my map, highlighted and taped to the dash. I was about to start stairstepping up, across, and down the backroads that would take me to the river, and I was having some second thoughts about the interstate. It was right there. Calling to me.

These days, Interstate 80 had almost no traffic. And there were no stop signs, no tight corners, and mostly no inhabitants along its roadside. The little towns had all been bypassed by the project back when it was built. It had rendered most of them obsolete as it passed nearby, yet avoided most of their populated areas. I would certainly make better time and use less fuel if I opted for that route.

My fingers drummed the top of my steering wheel. My inner voices were growing louder, arguing with each other. Just then, my decision was made for me.

An ambulance from the neighboring town came flying down a side road and pulled out onto Highway 6. It was about a half-mile ahead of me. Another car, obviously a volunteer first responder, with blue lights flashing, pulled onto the highway behind it. That was my ticket.

I had "borrowed" Dad's blue dash light from his truck. He had once been our local volunteer fire chief and served that role for many years. Although he had long since retired his position, he had kept the light as a memento, and it had sat on a shelf in the garage under a coating of dust. I'd taken it down and dusted it off a few times over the years, once sticking it to the roof of my car and plugging it into the cigarette lighter just for fun. It had come to life, whirled and flashed and threw a rotating blue beacon across the neighborhood. I had giggled with boyish glee. Guys like those kinds of things. Anyway, for this trip, I had taken it and stashed it on the floorboard, behind my seat with the food and snacks Mom had prepared for my journey.

The closest hospital would be about 30 miles west. I didn't know who the patient was, but I knew that an ambulance heading west, out here, was destined for either there or Omaha, and either was fine with me.

I rummaged around behind my seat until I felt the smooth dome and the curly cord attached to it. I popped it up on the dash and plugged it in. As a reminder, you should put a dark towel or a hat or a jacket – or something dark and flexible – on the backside of the light before you turn it on. The momentary blindness caused by the blue beacon was beyond startling, and I nearly lost control of the truck. Good Lord, I knew better than that.

I let them get a mile or so ahead of me, out of recognizable sight, but close enough that I could see the lights top an occasional hill. We hit interstate doing about 90 miles per hour, and they never slowed down. They ran me all the way to the Atlantic exit in about 10 minutes and when they pulled off, I just kept on going. We had passed a couple of state troopers parked alongside the road and they didn't give us a second look, even though I had a rack of fuel cans and an old bike strapped to the back of my truck. I guess it was dark, and we looked legitimate enough. Anyway, if my memory served me correctly, that was likely the entire law enforcement contingent between here and the turnoff to my river bridge. I felt a bit of stress drift away.

Dad's blue light was flashing strong, and the tires were humming the sweet song of speed and distance. I just knew this was right. My gut and my heart told me it was right. The focus had to be on getting to Rachel. Even if I was crazy and this was some sort of emotional or mental breakdown on my part, I just had to get to her. That was my job now.

It had always been my job to be a good husband, provider, protector. But those words are just words this day and age. She could provide for herself. As a smart, educated, capable woman, she didn't need me to provide for her. And as a far better marksman than me, a far better fisher and hunter, she really didn't need me to protect her either. I half laughed. Maybe I needed to get to her so that I could be provided for and protected. Whichever it was, that was my job, my hat to wear, and so I went to where I needed to go.

I followed Interstate 80 all the way to the western edge of Iowa, where it intersected I-29 running north. The exit for Blair was shared with the town of Missouri Valley, Iowa. It had once been a major truck stop location, where truckers would bed down for the night before heading into Omaha for deliveries. This intersection, like so many others, had suffered a lot of turmoil across the past few decades. First, the imposed fuel shortages had dried up some of the smaller operators. They simply couldn't compete for the fuel resources they needed to serve their customers. Then, a well-timed change in legislation brought a gush of resources onto the market and a few well-placed operations captured the majority of the market. It was almost as if the folks in Washington had some profit motive that aligned with the fuel prices and real estate. Hmmm...it was uncanny how things like that worked sometimes.

Anyway, the fuel flowed for a while, once the carbon tax rates were established. And my, how the revenue poured in – and the votes were purchased. At least, that's my take on it. Ultimately, once the carbon taxes got high enough, the trucking industry was forced to adopt the concessions offered by the lawmakers.

No diesel could be burned by commercial haulers within a 30-mile radius of most cities. They had to switch to full-electric to enter the urban zones. This kept the "pollution" out in the country, along with the windmills and the solar panels, so the city folks could breathe in the good clean air. And with those regulations, of course, came the banning of diesel distribution points inside those same circles. Again, closing down places like the ones located here.

The energy transition had been a costly one for so many facets of industry, and for so many entrepreneurs who had their investments and livelihoods shut down or trampled by the whims of others. It's depressing.

The point is, constant fluctuation in the rules, changes of the laws, combined with the push to diesel/electric and the bans on fuel usage in the cities, had turned this once buzzing intersection into a ghost town. The hot spots these days were at 200-mile increments from the major cities. That was about the distance most travelers could get from their battery sets. At first, we had seen the charging stations start popping up around 120 miles out, as the early adopters learned how to plug-hop from point to point. But now, batteries had improved and the new hubs were out around 200 miles.

I had tucked away the blue light about 20 miles back, not wanting to push my luck. Besides, if I'd been stopped by a sheriff or local police, I wouldn't have a good story to accompany my bit of theater. They'd likely know the first responders in that area, and I certainly wouldn't be one of them. So, Dad's little helper had done its job for now and needed to go back behind the seat. •

CHAPTER 27: THE BRIDGE

The exit ramp was coated with dust, and I couldn't see that anyone had beaten me to the top of the hill on this particular morning. I did see what looked like a Jeep parked in the drive of one of the closed truck stops. And I could see a cigarette ember burning in the driver's seat. It was an odd place for security and not a logical place for a traveler's nap. My heart rate increased a little, and I adjusted my grip on the steering wheel. I rolled my shoulders and checked my seat belt. It was as if I were preparing for a punch in the face. But nothing came of it.

The bridge was in sight and I turned off all of my lights. A dusty black truck...on a dusty dark road. But I wasn't going to get the blinding sunrise I'd hoped for. While my plan had included the sun's morning rays to break the horizon and diminish the view of anyone looking east, it was not to be. The dark cloud in the atmosphere had grown far and wide, likely beyond the east coast by now. There was a bit of a light essence behind me, but all it did was highlight the dust I was churning up. Not helpful. I slowed down a bit.

I crossed the river bridge with no problem. As I made the slight bend down into town, I heard a spark of static on my CB radio. After so much silence, I had forgotten it was even on.

"Ready..." I heard someone say slowly, in a hauntingly quiet tone.

The minor dust cloud in my trail had calmed down a bit, and I could see that back behind me, about 200 yards, I had a follower. It was a tight little profile and I guessed it to be the Jeep from the interchange.

No sooner had I looked back to the front than a cable shot up across the front of my truck. My normal self would have stopped, to avoid damage to my truck. Because a tight cable usually means a closed parking lot, a gate you're not suppose to use, or security to keep you out. Stopping would have been the proper response. But it happened so fast, my reactions were not from my normal self.

"Pull it!" squawked across the radio.

I was already on the gas and the cable hooked into my grill guard. The truck lurched and the nose dove down deep, but then it gave, springing up as a lamp post from the corner came crashing into the street behind me. A smaller pickup-like thing came sliding in from the other side of the street, from behind a stack of road signs and smashed into the long, tall lantern. Both were tied to opposite ends of the cable. I was full on the gas and swung a hard right. I needed to get to Highway 75 and head north out of town. The Jeep stopped and picked up a few guys at the intersection. The little truck had come undone, but I was still dragging a 50-foot light pole behind me like a noisy anchor.

The pole flung around dangerously, hitting parked vehicles, ripping through street signs, and leaving a debris field in my wake as I tore through the eastern side of Blair. Shit! What did they want. Fuel? Money? Food? My truck?

I'd reviewed my town map after the ambulance had turned off, to make sure I knew my route through town. I hoped that nothing else was waiting for me. I had to stay on course or risk driving down some dead end. Riverside towns and cities always have stray streets that end at the river. I had to stay sharp. I couldn't get trapped. Turning around with this contraption fastened to my truck would not be an option.

A big blue mailbox, half full of bills and coupons, and maybe a love letter or two – hey, gotta stay optimistic – sprayed into the street as the pole ripped it from its station. Some new landscaping and a freshly planted tree also became part of the carnage as I swung around the last corner before the highway. The Jeep was a couple hundred feet back, avoiding the sweeping silver pole.

Dad had insisted that I keep my guns up in the front with me. That had been a solemn statement that he had spoken softly yet firmly as I was preparing to leave that morning. In our family, we had "suggestions" when I was growing up. Those things that your parents said that were like, "You might want to take a jacket," and of course, you never did. You just shivered on the bleachers watching the baseball game and told yourself, "You know, maybe I should have brought a jacket." It's those suggestions that typically become the root of the self-taught lessons of youth. It's the seed that's planted that makes you think about something just enough to learn from the dumb thing that you did anyway.

Then there are "directives." I had these with Alex, too. He would always know when it was a directive and give some raised eyebrow response like, "So, I guess that's a directive?" Those were the things that the parents said as if they were slight suggestions but deep down, they were direct orders, to be obeyed regardless of how the child felt. It's those directives that kept us out of drunk friends' cars, kept us safe around power tools, and stopped us from eating the chocolate pie before Grandma served the Thanksgiving turkey. The directives were to be followed. Always.

That morning, Dad's directive to me had been to have my guns in the front with me. His exact words, spoken with the voice of a man who had been in the front lines of a war, in hand-to-hand combat with true enemies, were, "You'll keep the guns up front." It was a quiet statement, made as he handed me the cases. Mom didn't even hear him. But I heard him. And I took the cases and set them up for easy access.

As I hit the last intersection in the business district, the lamp post caught on another pole and my truck swung fiercely to a stop, 180-degrees around, we were now face to face. The Jeep slid to a stop about 50 yards short and the doors swung open.

I opened my door and racked the shotgun. They ducked down behind the doors. Without hesitation, I unloaded two shells in their direction. The headlights popped and the passenger side window shattered. They scrambled. The doors closed. In a haphazard retreat, the Jeep hit the curb and nearly tipped over. It rocked violently and sped away.

I took a quick look around and assessed my damage. The cable had hooked into one of my tow rings on the front guard. What a blessing. This big heavy steel Ranch Hand bumper had paid for itself once more. It had seemed silly to have this thing on the truck in Dallas, except in rush hour traffic, where it actually seemed pretty logical. But it was one of those things I had questioned. And it had just proved out. I untwisted the cable and detached myself from the lamp. I swung the truck around and headed out of town to the north.

My adrenaline was surging. I'd never shot at anyone before. It was not a good feeling. They wouldn't follow me though. They'd wait for easier prey. But I was afraid that even with all of my planning, it may not be enough to get me through this. I had to stay at 100 percent. I drew a couple of long deep breaths, then I put fresh shells in the chamber. •

CHAPTER 28: NEBRASKA

There was a constant snowfall of ash now. I didn't know if it was all from the original blast or if additional eruptions were pushing more debris into the air. Maybe it was starting to settle out of the atmosphere. I really didn't know. The radio chatter that I found seemed to confirm that it was Yellowstone, but there wasn't much detail or consistency.

When I was back at Mom and Dad's house, I did what research I could, using my encyclopedia set for the first time in a long time. It would add to the story to say the set of old books was dusty and smelled a bit musty when I pulled the first volume from the shelf, but that wouldn't be true. As the collection still resided in its original place, on the bottom level of the living room bookshelf, it had been dusted at least once a week, and likely each volume had been taken from the shelf, fanned, cleaned, and repositioned at least once a year by Mom. She ran a pretty tight ship.

I had never overused the encyclopedia. Except for occasional school projects and some curious referencing from time to time, they actually hadn't been opened very much. They were pristine.

I looked up information on volcanoes, then searched for natural disasters, finally coming across an inset article about Yellowstone and the caldera that made up the majority of the park's acreage. Evidently, it's a geologic feature that functions like a volcano, a giant vent for the earth's molten core, where magma and pressure rise up to very close proximity of the crust, releasing pressure and gasses through groundwater, creating steam that erupts as geysers. Old Faithful is simply the world's most well-known and most highly photographed pressure release valve.

In our early years of trekking to Montana, we'd drive around Yellowstone on I-90 for what seemed like hundreds of miles. You might see an occasional bear, but mostly the wildlife knew where they were safest, as if the borders were etched into their instinctual DNA. One year, Rachel said, "It's ridiculous that we have never stopped at Yellowstone. We've got to do that." So we did.

On our first trip there, she booked us a room at the historic Lake Yellowstone Hotel. It was a good thing she liked to plan – she had to make the reservation nearly a year in advance. Once there, we would officially become tourists, joining the thousands that occupy the majestic park each day. It was indeed beautiful. And it was unlike anything I'd ever seen. Beautiful mountains, gorgeous valleys, and peculiar crystal clear pools that look so inviting, yet are so corrosive and hot that they would prove a deadly bathing choice. A few tourists have in fact died there over the years by ignoring the signs that warn to stay on the path. Stepping through a thin crusty surface into a bottomless chamber of steam is not a good way to go. Some have been literally evaporated as family members stood nearby, unable to do anything that would stop nature's ravaging beauty. I finally understood why millions of people trek there on vacation.

So I couldn't believe it would simply blow up. But, that's what they said about Mount Saint Helens in Washington, back in the late 1900s. A whole mountain. One minute it's there, the next it's not.

While we've never been to the Mount Saint Helens area, we have toured through Canada a bit. Back in 1903, the mining town of Frank, Alberta was lost to the Frank Slide as Turtle Mountain fractured, burying the entire town beneath a mix of massive boulders and dust. Dozens of miners had been working the night shift, deep in the shafts that perforated the mountain's core. At around 4 o'clock in the morning, they felt a rumble, then a shudder, then they were surrounded by incredible noise and dust. They ran for their lives, toward the entrance to the shafts. They were hundreds of yards into the mountain, but their run was cut short when they found themselves in open air much sooner than expected. While they were "safe" inside the mountain, the entire face of the mountain had released, crushing the town below and spreading rock and gravel across the valley. Few in the mining town of Frank survived. Most mining disasters are, of course, the other way around. This was unique, like so many actions of nature. Mankind tries to understand it all, but at the end of the day, it's much larger than we are.

So, even in my short life upon this earth, I had seen firsthand how these things did happen. But Yellowstone. Wow. That's going to be historic.

The encyclopedia said that there had been three major eruptions of the Yellowstone Caldera over the ages. (Even a set of encyclopedias from my distant childhood has accurate content on stuff that happened 640,000 years ago.) The largest eruption was the Lava Creek eruption, which deposited a blanket of ash that stretched from the Canadian border to the southern tip of Texas, and from the California coast to Illinois. Obviously the region wasn't defined as states back then, as the dinosaurs had little use for legal jurisdictions and tax collection districts.
The Lava Creek eruption had scored a VEI 8 according to the article, making it one of the largest volcanic eruptions in the history of the world, as far as we have discovered.

Another eruption, named Huckleberry Ridge, occurred approximately 2 million years ago. *Huckleberry Ridge!* That's what the soldier had said back in Kansas – the kid filling the fuel wagon, he said the group had been talking about Huckleberry Ridge. This event must be the same scale as that one, or at least similar in magnitude.

According to my old encyclopedia, Huckleberry Ridge had been the second-largest eruption in the Yellowstone area. The event put down another layer of ash that geologists have uncovered across an area similar to Lava Creek, but not as far west according to the overlay maps. Maybe it was jet stream winds or other factors, but the fallout of ash and debris seems to always blossom to the southeast. While the entire great plains are covered in soot and powder, the nearby northwest region – what we'd call Oregon and Washington, and the northwest ends of Idaho and Montana – remain mostly unaffected in all of the prehistoric blasts.

At least according to the information I'd found, that was the scale of Huckleberry Ridge.

That was the information I was looking for. I needed to know if there were any prior eruptions and what the outcomes were. I'd seen similar information on the well-done educational signs that dotted the park during our visits, but I hadn't retained any of the detail. That's what I needed now, the specifics, so I could plan my route with some degree of certainty, some amount of historical perspective.

And so it was that I had chosen what I felt would be the most direct route, while maintaining a distance from evacuation centers and the population in general. I hoped to reach central Nebraska, then hook north, running the outer edge of the fallout line, working my way west across a stairstepped connection of state highways and county roads. It would be important that I run as efficiently as possible, as I only had so much fuel and I didn't know exactly how I'd obtain more.

If I were inside the evacuation circle, it would be easier to "obtain" resources by selectively looting fuel tanks and other goods left behind as towns rapidly emptied. With my hand pump, hose line, and filter, I should be able to find enough fuel to keep me moving. Of course, the way I was loaded, I should have enough anyway.

Don't get me wrong. I have strong ethics, and I'm an incredibly honest man, but we all have a gray line that we'll cross for the bigger picture. My bigger picture was getting to Rachel.

The guys back at the river bridge had proved I wasn't the only one whose morals were coming into question. I needed to be very aware of that when I was picking supplies, even if I thought a property was deserted. A wild-west-style ambush may be back in fashion these days.

I stopped and removed the license plates from my truck. They were a tracking device I could do without. I turned onto Highway 81 and headed north. •

CHAPTER 29: HEARTLAND

Moving up across Nebraska was a sad and constant reminder of what was happening to so many people. I had avoided the bigger towns, like West Point and Norfolk, bypassing them on country roads that reliably fall on a perfect grid in that part of the country. But the little towns that spotted the landscape, like Wisner and Hoskins, were a flurry of busywork and activity. People were standing next to loaded vehicles, talking with their neighbors but unsure of whether they would be bugging out or not. Norfolk was where I first encountered National Guard troops, guiding traffic to the east on Highway 275. It would take them down toward Omaha. I thought they should be taking those folks more north, up through Sioux City, with places like Minneapolis–St. Paul or Milwaukee as destinations. Omaha was already going to be overrun from the Denver and Cheyenne refugees.

That was one thing I had not counted on in any original plan or my most current route selection. I hadn't considered the mass movement of the population.

Highway 20 was a solid line of cars and trucks headed east. The westbound lanes had been blocked to access at any major interchange, and all lanes flowed east. It was the Midwest's version of the contraflow traffic rules they put in place down around the Gulf Coast preceding a hurricane. We've all seen those images on the news, when traffic 12-lanes wide is running north out of Houston or Miami. Just replace the BMWs and Range Rovers with Subarus and F-150 pickups. Well, in reality, it was a line of overloaded Prius, Leaf, and E-Phaze autobots, with an occasional farm truck. I don't know what the cargo capacity is for a Prius, but many that I saw were far beyond it. And the collateral damage was becoming apparent.

I had hoped to zip right across Highway 20, continuing a northward section of my yellow highlighted map line. Earlier, I had hoped I might be able to go west on 20, but that wasn't going to prove out. The intersection was blocked by the National Guard. The stream of Wyoming plates was endless. Dozens of cars littered the shoulders of the road with a host of issues ranging from depleted batteries to flat tires to complete structural failure. I don't know who thought that you could strap an entire bedroom suit onto the roof of a micro SizzerBot, but the shattered windows and collapsed door pillars showed it wasn't within the car's load spec. What were these people going to do?

The shouting public, not wanting to abandon their property, and the loudspeaker Guardsmen instructing them to get into the carrier trucks, with minimal belongings – it was worse than when the airlines restricted passengers to only one carry-on bag. The airline folks smiled and gave you a yellow tag for free stowage below on the plane. The National Guard takes it from you, throws it on a pile in the ditch, and pushes your ass up into the truck. There are no first class seats today. Tempers and frustration ran high on both sides. I swung around and headed back into the countryside.

It was also my first encounter with the walls of handmade signs and graffiti posts, saying things like, "Janet Moore.We'll be in Milwaukee," "MISSING: Mark & Tracy Johnson" with a phone number. But, the phones weren't working. There were no photos, because nobody could print them out. Most gave names and potential meet-up points. That was smart. One wall had what must have been more than a thousand signs. It was an early indication of the human toll.

Two miles from the main intersection, I was able to cross on a gravel road. The line of traffic was steady, but Dad's rotating blue light was again put to use as I faked a little "official business" and was allowed to cross. I added to my "shopping list," wanting to find an OFFICIAL license plate for the front of the truck. I'd stay on the lookout for that.

There were people walking at this point. We would be about 500 miles from Casper, Wyoming, and the electric cars were dying by the hundreds. Actually, I'm not sure how they even made it this far. I suppose the military had a portable charging deployment, maybe powered with diesel generators. I really don't know.

If I were in charge of that, I'd try to route everyone along a common pathway, and I'd stage charging stations – like water stations in a marathon or triathlon race – so people could pull over and charge. They'd need to be staggered across the distance or else the backlog would jam the road and nobody could pass. But how much of that type of equipment would the military have on hand? It would be an oddball need, and likely wouldn't land high on the list of any appropriations committee. So again, if it were me, I'd send those units deep into the zone, giving evacuees the greatest opportunity for distance before I just couldn't support them anymore. Then they'd be on their own. Stranded, but safe.

That's what I was seeing. Thousands and thousands of people now, safe but becoming stranded. And I was still in Nebraska. I assumed the bridge at Yankton would be a long delay, and that meant wasted fuel or battery, sitting in line, creeping forward three feet at a time. Had I been able to take Highway 20 west, my bridge-crossing issues would be behind me. I'd be south of the Missouri River Basin that travels the entirety of my route, from Iowa to Montana. I should have just gone north in Iowa, avoiding the whole river crossing issue altogether. But I had wanted to push west. I needed to stop second-guessing. Every plan has its problems.

According to my atlas, there was a little county road that crossed the river out by Springfield, Highway 37. It was a thin gray line on my map, but it looked like it crossed the river. Hopefully it would be a route missed by most. It certainly wouldn't be an official crossing point, as the military would need higher load capacity bridges for their equipment convoys. And, if anyone's autobot were using a built-in navigation system, these backroads were probably not even coded. I decided to give it a shot. •

CHAPTER 30: LEWIS & CLARK

If you've never been to the Gateway Arch in St. Louis, I'd highly recommend you add it to your list. I assume it still exists and will likely reopen one day, when our world returns to normal. As I've said before, I try not to think about the true reality of those things. It makes me emotional. But it's an architectural delight, with little egg-shaped pods that convey visitors to the observation windows at the top of the structure. It's a perfect rendition of mid-century modernism, designed in the mid-1940s and finally built in the mid-1960s. The futuristic pods, joined to industrial-era gear works and cable systems, are a physical and idyllic blend of the country's trajectory through iron-borne strength and star-bound vision. That said, they also had a great museum in the basement, deep beneath the arch itself. The movie theater showed an incredible documentary of the Lewis & Clark expedition.

There were hundreds of men, literally pulling huge barges of supplies up the Missouri River by horse and by hand. The journey would have been difficult enough going with the current. I can't even imagine the efforts required to move their necessities upriver against the flow. The men and horses walked on the rugged shoreline at times, but mostly in the shallow edgewater, around the downed trees, limbs, and snags that make up any riverbank.

Setting out from St. Louis, headed for the Pacific Ocean at the extreme northwest corner of the continental United States, they eventually passed through this very area. And while many of us forget their grand adventure, this area certainly had not forgotten. Lewis & Clark Park, Lewis & Clark Trail, Lewis & Clark this, and Lewis & Clark that. Lewis & Clark signage and namesakes littered the landscape as I ran west down a deserted backroad.

I stopped at a roadside display and read about a hunting party that had harvested some buffalo from this exact spot to feed the crew as they worked their way north and west. I can't imagine what that was like back then. I was thinking I had a rough go ahead of me, but it was nothing compared to their journey. I had maps, I had paved roads, I had walkie-talkies. They charted the river, they documented the plants and animals, and to survive, they hunted. I had a can of SpaghettiOs laying on the motor's exhaust manifold warming for lunch, I remembered. I had it easy.

While I had actually stopped for nature's call, I had regained some perspective on where I was in the world and in the timeline of our country. We all have it so easy, relatively, and we owe it all to the type of men that were willing to commit their lives to those efforts. We struggle with the stress of too many e-mails and the frustrations of rush-hour traffic. A great many of these people died, to help secure this nation – for us. So that their descendants could complain that the latte doesn't have enough foam. It's an eye-opener, or it should be.

Sitting just inside the chain that closed the park's entrance was a work shed, a maintenance shop for the park. I jumped the chain and looked through the garage door windows. There was a small utility truck – in my day, we called them "Gators." Kind of a working man's golf cart. Those were usually gas or diesel, not electric, so maybe there was fuel. I had a small flashlight on the lanyard around my neck. I held it to the window and lit up the inside of the small shop. A 60-gallon drum in the corner had a hand pump on it. That was promising. I tried to take a deep sniff of air. Could I smell gasoline or diesel fuel? The side of the barrel had a greasy film on it, thick with dirt and grime. It reminded me of the diesel barrels we'd had at our farm when I was a kid. Gasoline evaporates pretty quickly, so it doesn't stay wet on the surface. Diesel has more oil in it, I guess, and it stays damp and greasy for quite a while. Anyway, this looked like diesel.

I didn't want to put it directly into my tank, as it may have water in it, or it could be dirty, which could clog an injector or a filter. Hmmm. I took a good long look around. Another opportunity for the binoculars. Nothing. Everybody was on the highways.

The extra gas cans I had strapped to my back carrier were the most convenient. I drained four of them into my truck's fuel tank and carried the empties over the chain to the shed. The side door had seen a lot of weather and pushed open pretty easily, not even locked. My guess is, there's not a big problem with theft out here in the heartland, where Lewis & Clark once hunted buffalo and dined on wild maize and honest whole wheat loaves. I rocked the barrel, it was heavy and sloshed when I tipped it. I had no idea how old the fuel it might be, but the barrel was about three-quarters full, so I assumed it was used regularly. And it was diesel.

I checked the Gator for a license plate, remembering my shopping list and hoped I might come across a stray "official" plate for the front of my truck. No luck on the license plate, but I was happy to have renewed my fuel supply and filled my truck to boot. I grabbed a handful of honey-roasted peanuts as I slid back behind the wheel. It wasn't one of my trademark 10-minute stops, but it was a nice little break. I took a deep breath to regain my focus and turned the key. On to South Dakota. •

CHAPTER 31: LATEST NEWS

I was scanning my radio from time to time, hoping to find a bit of news. However most of it was pretty refined these days, providing embedded directives and pre-approved narratives meant to keep everyone supportive of the system and our "leaders." So I, like the others in the now-minority of America, had learned how to glean past the buzzwords and platitudes and hype and come away with some nuggets that we might be able to assemble into useful information. I also hoped that a disaster of this proportion may give way to some neutral truths and actual facts that everyone might be able to use.

A few minutes into my scan session and an AM station locked on. It was giving the Emergency Alert tone, and a recorded message was saying to stay tuned for important information. It was a station based in Sioux Falls, broadcasting a prerecorded message about road closures. I-90 had been officially converted to contraflow traffic only. Just eastbound traffic on I-90. All drivers should maintain a 40-mile-per-hour speed and pass through Sioux Falls. All entrance and exit ramps were closed. Drivers should pass directly through the metro area en route to Minneapolis.

How would that work? No stopping in the urban area where the most resources would be? Of course, there would be no electricity to pump the fuel or recharge the batteries. Stopping the traffic would simply strand the people in an already dense urban area. That would just add to the issues. So what do you do? Leave them stranded out in the country? I guess so. Wow. Alex was right. This was going to be bad. Really, really bad. I should have thrown out my computer equipment at the Lewis & Clark park in exchange for the fuel barrel and its remaining few gallons. Swapping $50,000 in Apple MacPro servers and high-res monitors for around eight gallons of potentially dirty diesel? It might have been a good trade.

Another message came on, asking drivers to be cautious of masses of pedestrians walking down I-90. The message went on to instruct those walking to stay as far to the left as possible. I wondered how those walking would hear the message.

I looked for a thin gray line on my map to get me across I-90. I had to avoid as many people as possible.

Highway 44 was another straight shot from the west, and a lot of evacuees had discovered it. While the National Guard was working hard to control the interstates, which were actually designed for the strategic purpose of moving troops and equipment around the country, the secondary routes had become loaded as well. I needed to keep moving north. Once I was in North Dakota, I'd consider tilting west.

The air here was saturated with sulfur, and I put my bandana to work, even inside the truck. Chatter on the CB had said that, while the control grid for the tens of thousands of wind turbines had crashed almost immediately, the sulfur dioxide, sulfuric acid, and sulfuric everything else that was settling on everything was locking up the gear works and power-generation components inside the rotor units and on the pivots. One trucker said he'd seen hundreds that had locked and more than a dozen that had burned or were burning, adding to the dark haze in the sky.

The Power Strip would be proven a complete disaster, but that realization would come too late. A lot of us argued against it from the moment it was proposed, but common sense just couldn't overcome the narrative and continual bombardment of messaging from the media. Working with an oil and gas major, we even had some within our own ranks that pushed for the highly promoted project.

The promoters promised an almost endless supply of clean, renewable energy, generated from millions of acres of solar panels and hundreds of thousands of wind turbines, all planted and arrayed across the "wasteland" of Nebraska, Kansas, North Dakota, and Oklahoma. The windmills extended into Iowa, with hundreds of them around my hometown, but the project's focus was out west. Relatively inexpensive land was either bought up or seized via eminent domain for the country's largest single infrastructure project since the interstate highway system was started under the direction of U.S. President Dwight D. Eisenhower in the mid-1950s. The projected cost of The Power Strip would make that little highway project look like a drop in a bucket.

The storyline was that it would be paid for by those who didn't use it, promoting its use by levying fees and taxes on those who were locked in the dark ages of fossil fuel. And yet, most of the fossil fuel giants had eagerly joined the narrative, seemingly bent on outlasting each other as the weaker players were crushed under the weight of regulations. They pitted themselves into a survival-of-the-fittest mode and went all in on an idealistic duel to see who'd be the last one standing. While they viewed it as a duel, I saw it as more of a circular firing squad. Nobody survives those, I had said. But nobody was listening to me. They were much more educated and certainly had more in-depth knowledge of their own industry. But in my opinion, it just defied logic.

Anyway, the narrative was spun, the public was hypnotized, and the funding was appropriated. Originally sold to the masses at around $2 trillion, the final bill was probably closer to $20 trillion. The land grabs by the politicians and their friends would have filled endless newscasts, had it been reported, and the backroom deals for how the power would be distributed must have been masterfully played by slick negotiators from the coasts. Because that's where it all went. By the time the checks were written and the deeds transferred, most of the land was held by East Coast real estate syndicates, and the actual electricity, the original purpose of the project – to "supply the entire country with a nearly endless source of clean, renewable energy," if you recall – was hijacked for political gain. Does your state need more power from The Strip? Well then, you had better vote correctly, because the gigawatts were controlled by the elites in Washington. It brought new meaning to the term "power broker." •

CHAPTER 32: DOMINOES

So, what set us up for this fall, this cascade of events that would put all of us in the dark?

The drag on the power grid had been growing for years, and ongoing legislation further reduced inputs to the system. On the West Coast, the California lawmakers had caught themselves in a pickle while not allowing any woodlands to be maintained and having overloaded electric highlines spark random fires in the tinder box they'd created. Rolling brownouts were commonplace and the faithful public had adapted to their rotating car-charging schedules. Ah, the Californians! They had long been on the cutting edge of this utopia.

The political push had been on for decades, from global warming to global cooling, to climate change, to climate chaos. I'm sure you've heard the terms and become familiar with the slogans. I had always enjoyed listening to the narrative as the titles evolved, the facts were reformed, and the agenda was kept on track. These folks were indeed masters of their craft. And along the way, there was always the recognizable slant to whatever it was, intended to manipulate the people toward the proper realization – in my opinion.

"My carbon footprint" became a social media catch phrase and status symbol. One of the world's ugliest logo concepts – remember, that's my biz – was the shoeprint decal with the rating stamp inside. If a restaurant had a shoe size greater than 3, their customers would shun the place, making it taboo to even consider dining there. If the vegan salad wasn't chilled via some geothermal net negative emissions array, well, you simply couldn't be seen dining there. It was nuts. If a business didn't display the "barefoot" insignia, it was off-limits.

As I've already said, coal usage was stopped first, as nearly limitless funding was put into expansive solar farms in Wyoming, Nebraska, and Kansas. These were tied to the massive cross-country power infrastructure that could feed the cities of either coast. Gigantic tracks of flat land, inexpensive for the installation of hundreds of thousands of solar panels, had been claimed by eminent domain cases. "The Power Strip," as it came to be called, was the pet project of every politician who claimed to hate big business. But clearly, they were funding what was becoming the country's biggest business for their friends and contributors. Offshore wind farms became popular along the West Coast as well, but the East Coast fought hard to keep them away – claiming they were just too unsightly – while at the same time protesting for more clean energy. Of course, they were more than happy to fill the flyover states with windmills and solar farms, far away from their pretty seashore views. As the push for transition accelerated, the country's electrical infrastructure teetered on failure, overloaded by a burgeoning generation of all-electric cars, buildings, and lifestyles.

Each night, as the nation slept, their 240 million Teslas, Volts, Zaps, and Shimmers were plugged into 240 million wall sockets, recharging for the night. The "heavies" – trucks used for freight – had shifted to either natural gas or diesel electric, like a locomotive. Restricted to their batteries in urban areas, they transitioned to diesel once they were out in the country, again saving the air in the cities, transferring the pollution to the countryside.

It had become a never-ending and expanding cycle for the system. Each day, the buildings were made the optimum temperature for the inhabitants, as the machines and servers and data mines hummed 24/7. And each night, the autobots returned to their docking stations and reloaded for the next day's commute.

"Teleworking" had failed, as the companies' best attempts to utilize geotrackers, observation cams, keypad sensors, and activity algorithms – to keep their employees actually working – had been consistently outpaced by those who developed high-tech countermeasures to help them avoid their tasks. They had track masks to keep cell phones pinging from the "home" location; delayed video feeds to "show" workers sitting at their monitors; modulating heat tips to fake touchscreen interactions; and dollar-an-hour bot servers to drive endless error loops and falsify login times. Which means that nobody had done anything for a few years, except go to yoga and sit around at Starbucks.

So, everyone had been called back at work where their employers could keep an eye on them.

By the time the sun came up each morning, all of the urban battery centers were drained and the switch was on to the wind turbines and the solar farms. There was no job quite as stressful as the systems engineers who monitored the bots that tweaked the inputs, especially on cloudy days with no wind. Conservation, LEDs, and other efficiencies had reduced the draw, but midsummer was tough. Some of the newer airlocked super-efficient buildings had even been retrofit with windows that opened – so a breeze could flow through during brownout. In fact, I'd seen a recent ad campaign on-screen. "Introducing...windows that open!" Wow, what will they think of next?

But all of the promises, even if well-intentioned, had fallen through. With no real energy mix to supply our energy needs, we were all dependent upon one source. One solution, developed by the politicians. It was destined to create a worst-case scenario, just as it had eventually done with healthcare.

So, by the time the sun was coming up that morning, the morning after Yellowstone, thick ash had already begun to fill the skies over the heartland. There would be no solar reload. And as the ash, loaded with the corrosive sulfuric acid that was so prevalent in Yellowstone, settled onto the rotors and pivots of the turbines, it began to cause immediate havoc on those components as well. It was a perfect storm, as tremors shot west to the California coast and disrupted The Power Strip and its battery centers. Major transmission lines went down, all the way to Texas. By the time the East Coast woke up to full batteries, there would be no switch of power. Outside, the day would grow brighter, but inside, the lights would grow dimmer.

Hospitals had emergency generators, and they were stocked with diesel. So were some of the older office buildings and a stray home or two – if the owner were a bit of a pessimist like me. But 200 gallons of fuel will yield only so much electricity. And if there's no electricity to pump more fuel, or no available fuel to pump...well, it's a small bandage on a major wound.

The refineries outside of Houston and Baton Rouge were about all that remained these days, except for maybe one out east and a couple of small units tucked away up in Billings, Montana, mostly for a military reserve. Everything else had been mothballed as carbon taxes soared and regulations made them infeasible to operate. And it didn't matter anyway, because all the cars were powered by the wall socket in the garage, right?

It amazes me that the majority of the people are not sure exactly how the power gets to that wall socket to get into the car. I would think common sense would tell them it doesn't just form in the sheetrock and escape through the thin slits in the plastic plate. Didn't any teacher in the course of their education explain that it's actually generated from the burning of natural gas, or diesel, or coal? Or, until today, solar panels and wind turbines? And, when the last two are the only options, the system may have some down time. *(At least my sarcasm has an unending supply.)*

Brownouts had become incredibly common, especially in the Midwest, but the backups would usually kick on and keep everything going. It was the constant cycle of drain and charge, drain and charge. Like pedaling your bike to the top of a hill and coasting down. Now, coasting down with a broken chain is no problem. Getting up the next hill however...that's a problem. So as the systems sequentially failed, so did the fabric of the daily routine. •

CHAPTER 33: CROSSING I-90, PART 1

I really wanted to stop and eat my SpaghettiOs, but thought better of it. I'd munched my way through two bags of honey-roasted peanuts and two Cokes. And I'd decided it was time to start rationing the Cokes, because the gravity of the situation was really settling into my mind. It was truly unbelievable. But if you're reading this, then you know. You've seen it, at least parts of it.

I-90 was about 3 miles ahead and I was worried what I'd find there. Based on my maps, this little road would either cross over or under the interstate, with no interchange. Hopefully it'd be a lonely stretch of road, passing over the highway. I didn't want to get trapped underneath anything, with people above me or above the truck. I didn't want anyone jumping on, trying to get the gas cans off the back. That was another realization. I stopped.

Nobody was around, so I stacked the fuel inside the cab with me. I had Dad's big farm tank under the cover of the "fishing hat" on the back and 10 five-gallon plastic fuel cans on the back carrier, wrapped with a tarp and topped by Alex's old bike, strung down with bungee cord. I stuffed everything from the cab into the back. My laptop, my Day-Timer, my backpack. All of it. Stuffed in under the topper.

I used the tarp to cover the seats and dash. The gas cans were hurriedly stacked and the tarp draped up and around them. For the first time in years, I wanted to avoid any advertisement. Alex's bike sat all by itself on the rear rack. It had great sentimental value to me now, plus I may have use for it before all of this was over.

There were two ways to approach this. I could go slow and attempt to sneak by, but that didn't seem plausible if people were walking. Or

I could go fast and scare them out of my way through the sheer size and momentum of my rig. However, something blocking the road was a possibility, and I couldn't risk an accident. If I wrecked, all would be lost. They'd pillage my fuel, take my truck, and I'd try to defend it, which could be bloody. It would be a catastrophe. I had to know whether the road went over or under. And I had to know if people were moving through or hanging out around the bridge. I wished I had Alex's drone.

I picked the binoculars off the dash. As soon as I saw Rachel, I would hold her and hug her and smell her beautiful red hair – and tell her, "Thank you for paying too much for those awesome binoculars at that auction."

I peered down the road and all around me. Nothing moving, no people. But I knew the interstate was just 2 or 3 miles ahead of me. It was pretty flat. The standard South Dakota terrain, cropland, pastures, and windmills.

Windmills. A windmill. That would give me an eye in the sky. •

CHAPTER 34: GOING UP

The idea was to climb up in the tower and use it as a vantage point to determine my exact location and whether the nearby bridge was constructed above or below the interstate. I'd never been inside one of these metal giants, but I was intrigued.

Don't get me wrong about any of this story, or the way I jump on my soapboxes. I think wind-generated power is great, and solar is awesome. In fact, we have solar panels on the cabin in Montana. It's logical. It's efficient. It makes sense. But a complete mix of energy sources, all of them, is the only way to feed humanity's drive for betterment. At least, our definition of betterment, and that's a whole 'nother debate. Bottom line, if we want to improve everyone's living conditions, on a worldwide scale, then it's going to require a lot of energy. Energy pumps and filters clean water, energy allows modern sanitation systems to operate, energy prepares fields and harvests food. Energy transports that food, powers hospitals, lights schools. Energy is the single fundamental component in every area of advanced civilization. So why restrict any of it? Again, it's all about logic. Or that's my opinion.

Anyway, I was kind of excited about climbing up inside the windmill. But I didn't want to become trapped up there. Add to shopping list: Parachute.

I remembered passing a work site back at the last corner. That would be where I'd stash the truck for my observation run. I checked it out with binoculars before getting too close. It looked abandoned. I pulled to the back of the work area and parked behind two shipping containers that set next to some crane arms and large steel tubes. It was a wind turbine maintenance yard, probably for one of the wind farms that fed The Power Strip.

I locked the truck and pulled my makeshift gas mask-bandana up across my face. The sulfur smell and dust were getting heavier, so I had thickened my bandana with a small Rain-X rag and some duct tape. I walked across the field to the closest wind turbine. These were the real deal out here. Over 300 feet tall, they were gigantic, but they were also graceful and elegant. While some would say that they plagued the landscape, they were almost hypnotic to watch as they gently rotated, in unison, as if dancing on the breeze. It was amazing how much electricity they could generate, with their complex gearing converting a seemingly slow spin into a high-velocity powerhouse.

But today, there was no spin, no generation of spark or power, even though there was a nice occasional breeze, certainly capable of turning the blades.

The hatch door was locked; no surprise. I'd carried my biggest bolt cutters with me, but it wasn't a padlock, either. Even with the binoculars, I couldn't tell exactly how the door was configured. So I'd brought along my biggest hammer and chisel as well. Yes, these are the things I carry in my toolbox, because everybody has a pair of pliers.

I wedged the chisel between the lock's edge and the metal door. It took a couple of heavy blows, but the lock wasn't built for bank-vault security. It was about as basic as my high school locker, although to be fair, my biology notebook was never stolen.

The door swung open with a shrill dry echo and I looked up the interior of the shaft. It was a long way to the top and the forced perspective of the narrowing tube magnified the distance. It looked like you could climb up to heaven from here; I hoped that wouldn't be my destination today.

The ladder was pitched at a slight angle, and there was a safety cable to snap onto a harness that I obviously didn't have, so it was just in my way. The ladder appeared to be built in 20-foot increments, more or less. Every section had a platform and crossover, so maybe, in case of a fall, you'd only travel down so far before hitting a platform. Or maybe it was structural, as the crosspieces were anchored into the sides of the vertical tube. Either way, it was exhausting and I had to stop and rest by the time I was on the fourth platform. I was afraid it might be dark by the time I reached the top, and that would do me no good whatsoever. I had to push through and make it to the top, quickly.

When I reached the generator pod at the top of the tower, I was blown away. The technology was apparent in the modular-built style, the mounts and maintenance points on the generator, and the controls. I wondered what the sound levels would be inside the unit when it was rotating at full speed, churning the gear works with intense momentum. It was impressive, but I wasn't there for a tour.

The top hatch didn't have a lock. Evidently they didn't expect visitors to drop in from the sky. The door was heavy and held a tight seal. The dust that had settled on it dropped into the pod and saturated the air with sulfur. I pushed myself out to my waist just to get a good breath. Then I peeked out into the hazy gray void that surrounded me.

Typically I'm not afraid of heights, but this was totally different. From the vantage point of the platform, you can't see the tower beneath you, so it appears that the top is just floating above the earth. It's very strange and very unsettling. I felt like I was getting sick, succumbing to a type of vertigo or dizziness. Like when you've enjoyed one too many spinning rides at Six Flags. You know the feeling. I needed to make my assessment and climb down.

But the blades were locked in a position that blocked my view. I'd need to leave the hatch and walk out onto the top of the housing. There was a thin rail, but it looked more decorative than functional. I thought about the cable that hung down inside. Maybe it was intended for going out on the roof as well. I looked back down into the shaft, and the darkness and perspective spun my stomach. As I reached for the cable, my body retaliated against me. The whole world became upended and I began vomiting down the shaft, down the ladders, and down the cable.

"Jake, pull it together. Do this." I was talking to myself, and I was not being kind. This is the kind of momentary weakness that causes errors, and this wasn't the place for a mistake. I needed to get it together, see what I needed to see, plan my action, and go. *"Come on! Do this."*

I clipped the cable to my belt. I decided to clip it to the side instead of the center back, maybe so I could keep my hand on it as well. I'm not really sure, it just felt more comfortable, and I didn't want to trip on it.

Gathering my wits, I stepped out onto the deck. Each small step kicked up more dust. It smelled horrible, and again I felt sick. It was like a thousand rotten eggs and every time I stepped it would puff up, releasing the stench. Just a few more stutter steps to the side, and I'd be able to see the bridge. The stutter-step move was from a high school basketball drill we used to do. Stutter steps to the side, so you don't cross your feet and get tripped up. You keep your butt low, your center of gravity down, and you hold a wide stable stance. That's how I moved across the top of the windmill. It creaked and moaned as a slight breeze pushed on the rotor. The entire structure wanted to turn, face into the breeze and spin easily. That's what it was designed to do. But it was frozen in space, the gentle wind stressing its long thin blades. It gave out a cry, like the recordings of whales, the pain descending through its long hollow tube. It was eerie.

I'd put on my jacket for the climb. I wanted the extra pockets for stuff and I wanted the binoculars, on the cord around my neck, to not swing and bang while I was climbing the ladder. It had been a good choice.

I unzipped the top of the jacket and pulled up the binoculars. I could see the bridge and it went over the highway. I was thrilled. There was a steady stream of movement going under the bridge, not moving very fast. It was a little too far recessed down from the edge for me to see, but it had to be vehicles, the tops of vehicles. There might be people walking, but if so they were too small for me to see with any detail from this distance. I counted the crossroads and decided I was around 2 miles from the bridge.

I strained to see if anyone was standing on the bridge. Even with these great lenses, it was just too far to see with any clarity. There was too much dust in the air, and I wasn't holding steady. The view shook from my nerves. I pulled the binoculars down and tried to gather myself. My vision was slow to adjust from the telephoto mode, and my head spun. A strong breeze caught the locked vertical blades and sent a shudder through the structure. The tower beneath me groaned and my right foot slipped in the dust. Wide-eyed, I looked for the railing, the edge, anything to give me some bearings. Was I sliding, was I falling, where was UP? I hit the rail hard on my right side, nearly flipping over the aluminum tube that ran just below my belt. My baseball cap floated out into the void and the world went into slow motion as I watched the black hat spin, catching the breeze for a moment and actually rising up, then twisting down into the gray.

My hands locked onto the rail as I dropped the cable in trade for something more solid. The slack cable slid back through the hatch opening, screeching and clanging on the ladder. I realized that I hadn't secured the cable's other end. If I'd fallen, it would have just hung me 100 feet above the ground. I got down on my hands and knees and unclipped the cable. I would be safer without it.

The cable raced back into the hole, a long metal snake dying a loud and violent death. It disappeared into a cloud of rotten egg powder, hissing and banging as it fell down through the tower. I crawled slowly back to the hatch. I'd seen all I was going to see.

Climbing down was harder than climbing up. I was unfamiliar with the distance between the rungs, unable to see my feet, and grabbing onto partially digested SpaghettiOs didn't help. It wasn't as strenuous, but it was far more stressful. Going up, I knew I'd be by myself at the top. Coming down, I worried that I may find that guests had arrived at the bottom. I'd brought my pistol, but this was no place for a firefight. Inside a solid metal tube with crossbars, angle iron, and edges, I'd probably shoot myself on a ricochet. I hoped I was still alone. •

CHAPTER 35: CROSSING I-90, PART 2

I found my cap just outside the door of the tower as I hurried back to the truck. I'd fanned through my footprints when I'd left, in case somebody stopped by. I wanted an indicator if there had been visitors. I didn't see any fresh tracks near the truck, so I was good.

My decision about driving fast or slow as I crossed the bridge was still under consideration. Moving fast, I would kick up a lot of dust and the people on the road would see and/or hear me coming. I couldn't decide if that were good or bad. It would provide an intimidation factor, but it would also draw unwanted attention. Moving slow would be better from a distance, as fewer travelers would be aware of my presence, but the slow speed would put me at risk as I got closer. I realized I was answering my own arguments, so it was decided.

The ash was beginning to accumulate pretty significantly on the ground. A stinky egg-smelling winter had arrived. Everything looked like old photographs. Similar to watching TV from the 1960s, all that existed were shapes, shadows, and tones, but no color.

It was getting late in the day, and I wanted to cross before anyone decided to use the bridge as a campsite for the night.

I had already covered my reflectors, turn signals, tail lights, and anything shiny on my truck with black gaff tape. Only thin slits remained in the tape across my headlights, which were always kept off. If I moved slowly enough, I just might blend into the landscape. And so I set out.

Less than one mile per hour was what my speedometer told me as I neared the crossover. I would crawl until I reached a possible sighting distance, which I had determined to be about 100 yards. At that distance, someone might notice me and climb up onto the road. So that would be my launch point. I'd go full on the gas and stop for nothing until I was far past the bridge, out of range of any possible runners or for that matter, gunfire.

Okay, here we go. I took one last look through the binoculars. Still nobody on the bridge as far as I could tell. Traffic was moving beneath on the highway. I put the pedal to the floor and the motor roared. It was the sound of my fuel economy dropping to zero, but I only had to drive that way for about 20 seconds, then I'd be past it. I laid on the horn for added effect. Gravel was flying past the sides of the truck and knocking on the floorboards. It was like sitting in a metal shed during a hailstorm.

Having spent so much of this journey in silence, I was now wrapped in noise and motion. The truck was fishtailing on the gravel, as if becoming light with the speed. I worked the steering wheel, constantly correcting the side-to-side drifting as the loose gravel and ruts fought for control. My eyes wide open, not taking a moment to blink, all of my senses piqued as the passing world fell into slow motion.

I saw the traffic below, moving east on both sides of the interstate. The movement was slow, a plodding traffic jam of trucks loaded with people and bags. An assortment of furniture, bicycles, and bedding hung from everything. I saw at least four cattle trailers, full of standing humans, being pulled by pickups equally loaded with bags and boxes. I saw autobots stalled in the median and in the ditches, one laced with bungee cord. The occupants were unstrapping a couple of bikes from the hood, making their own energy transition to pedal power. Dozens, likely hundreds of people walking, pulling carts and luggage, and pushing wheelbarrows.

Most every face was wrapped in cloth or old T-shirts to avoid breathing the sharp powder that hung in the air. Those walking would wave their arms at the vehicles, hoping to slow them and reduce the dust they were kicking up. Everything was in shades of drab gray. No matter how bright the colors may have been in the fabrics, everyone was draped in gray, on a gray road, in the gray air, under a gray sky. I saw families walking together in clustered groups. I saw a father carrying a small child on his shoulders the way I used to carry Alex. The kid was nestled on the back of the guy's neck, his head on top of his father's.

I wondered where they had begun their journey. Had they evacuated from Gillette, setting out in their new Zap MiniVan XL, with leather seats, entertainment displays, and seven active WiFi hot spots? They would have brought coolers with everything from the refrigerator, hard drives with family photos, extra clothes, and a few toys for the kids.

Had they been among the first to get out, or did they hesitate, not trusting what they'd seen on the news? Did they have a full charge on their vehicle's battery set, or had they suffered from rolling distribution brownouts? Maybe they were on an even-day schedule with their minivan, leaving them with whatever juice remained from the prior day's trips to school and errands. I imagined that they made it through Rapid City, where ash would now coat the faces of Mt. Rushmore just as it coated their own. Their van would have cashed in somewhere in the hills around Wall, and they'd have spent some time trying to decide what to take with them. Perhaps they feasted on what was in the coolers, giving themselves a boost of calories to fuel their bodies in the days ahead. Had they thought to bring backpacks and tactical pants and vests with lots of pockets to help carry necessities? Did they bring their most comfortable walking shoes or did the kids just grab flip-flops? What about extra socks? Scarves?

The child on the father's shoulders was wearing patterned pajamas, probably what he had on when they put him in the car. They were unprepared. And they would be walking like this for days. In the speckled dense air, the only thing that was crisp and clear was the look on the father's face, as he looked up at me, up on the bridge. Walking in the median, he made a momentary stop as I flew over them. I'll never forget it. A single second of time, etched into my memory for eternity. I can still see every detail.

I don't know how fast I was going when I crossed the bridge, but I felt the whole vehicle might go airborne as I hit the peak of the crossing. It was formed with a gentle arch, just slightly higher in the center. The road surface changed to concrete and the roar of the gravel fell away. There was a moment of near silence as I crossed over them, like a small black rocket in a blaze of colorless flame. My dust trail alone would deter anyone from following me, and a shooter, well, they wouldn't be able to see anything for a couple of minutes after I'd passed. My heart raced as I landed on the other side, and the gravel once again bombarded the undersides of the truck. I let off the gas, and the truck settled down into itself. Time began to flow at its standard pace, and I felt like I was in control again.

In about a half-hour, I'd try to make a cut west on Highway 34, restarting my zigzag pattern toward North Dakota. Highway 83 would be my goal in the morning. It would trace the Missouri River to the north and west, and once again I'd be following Lewis & Clark. I just needed to get a bit farther away from I-90 and its flowing humanity before stopping for the night. •

CHAPTER 36: WHERE THE BUFFALO ROAM

I made a left on Highway 34 and proceeded west. I hadn't seen anyone in a while, and the road remained empty as I reached my cruising speed. It was definitely dusk now, with the sky's light fading quickly.

As soon as I reached speed, I felt a shudder in the truck. Great, a flat tire. That's what I needed, with my jack buried under everything else in the back, plus, no way to fix it. I had a good spare, but I wanted to keep it as a spare. And, given the situation, there would be no way to repair it. How would a shop even pull it off the rim to make the repair? Regardless, everything was closed. But even if I broke in, what would I use? The air-driven tire machine? No, no compressor power. How to heat the patch? The electric heat iron? Even if the tire could be fixed, how would I refill it? The same compressor that wouldn't power the tire machine wasn't going to put any air in the tire.

I added to my shopping list: *extra tires from a similar truck*. I needed to be carrying multiple spares.

Even as I slowed to a near stop, the motion continued. No, this wasn't a tire, it was more of a vibration. Maybe a bigger mechanical issue. A U-joint, a tie rod? Something pulled apart from dragging that street lamp across half of Nebraska? That cable might have torn something loose. *Damn it*. I stopped the truck.

The shaking continued even though the truck was stopped. Was it an aftershock? I know earthquakes have aftershocks. I didn't know volcanic eruptions did. Maybe another eruption? Maybe I was heading west too soon? I looked to the horizon ahead, maybe a quarter-mile to where the road dropped over the ridge. A line of haze seemed to grow, moving in my direction.

Suddenly the air began to fill with dust. The shaking grew more intense, and then I saw them. Hundreds of them, headed straight for me, rushing past me. Covered in white ash and powder, they moved in a cloud. Massive buffalo, a herd obviously spooked from the world changing around them and the sky falling and the rotten smell and the endless dust. They parted around me, breaking like the water in front of a ship. The group became more dense and a big male, I'm guessing, clipped the corner of the grill guard, rocking the truck, pushing me into an angle on the road. Another caught the left rear corner, bringing me back into alignment. The passenger side mirror snapped from its mount, replaced by a tuft of thick black hair. I hit the button that rolled in the remaining mirror.

The thunder from their hooves was incredible, bouncing the truck as they scraped by on both sides. And then, in just a few moments, it was over.

I sat in a cloud of ashen dust. Like a dense fog, it surrounded the truck. I couldn't see two inches beyond the surface of the windows. I turned off the truck, not wanting to suck the powder into the air filter on the motor. Another item for the shopping list: *extra air filters*.

I hadn't thought of the wildlife until that moment, really. I had been so focused on me, us, family – *people*. I hadn't given much consideration to the animals.

The last time we were in Yellowstone, we saw black bears, grizzly bears, eagles, deer, and most impressively, elk. On our second day, we had driven a section of the main loop, looking for interesting hiking trails and side roads. We had taken a beautiful hike in the morning, stopping to sit atop some rocks and dine on some incredible sandwiches Rachel had made. Give her some whole-grain bread, a fresh tomato, half an avocado, and some leftover bacon, and she'd spin up a five-star lunch. Some marmots came out to beg for scraps. Evidently they hadn't read the signs that told us not to feed them.

I wondered where the marmots had gone. Those two in particular. I wished that I'd given them some bacon, even though it may have increased their cholesterol.

But the elk had been the stars of the show. Coming in from our second hike of the day, we'd made a wrong turn. The map wasn't drawn quite right, and we'd taken a winding road that led us far from the park's hotel. By the time we realized that we were lost, it was dark.

We had joked about some of the signs we saw posted throughout the park – "Caution: Elk Herds Ahead" and "Slow: Bears Crossing". Having not seen many animals at all that day, we had laughed about the signs, thinking they were more of a marketing ploy than a reality. It was a great reinforcement of the park's marketing, as the wildlife must surely be thick if they have to put out warning signs along the road. We made up new signs they could post, maybe down by the lake that would read, "Caution: Large Fish May Impact Hook," or smaller signs on the cabin steps like, "Danger: Chipmunks Below."

The day had been a long one, and we'd taken in a lot of sights. The road was empty, as all the other tourists – those who'd read their maps correctly – were either enjoying a late dinner or were already sacked out in their cabins. We were the only car on the road.

It was just us. And an entire herd of elk. There was a bit of steam in the air, rising off the road from the day's heat, and they appeared before us like a dream. We were crossing a large meadow and so were they. I'd only been driving about 10 miles per hour, so I quickly slowed to a stop. The biggest one turned its head and looked directly at us. He moved to the shoulder of the narrow road and returned to grazing. I turned off the headlights, and our eyes adjusted to the moonlight, which was pretty full that night. They were all around us. We rolled down the windows and just sat there. We were the human display in their zoo. Sitting inside our glass cage, they moseyed by, looking in with curiosity and returning to their grazing. I knew they were large animals, but with us sitting and them standing, the comparison was profound.

I don't know exactly how long we sat there, but eventually the last ones moved by, and the road ahead was clear.

The next morning, we returned to the same spot, to see if *our* herd was still around. We saw only two, but they passed by us and waded down into the lake, fording the glassy water to the other side. Their heads and majestic antlers were all that broke the surface, trailing soft wakes of water behind them. At the other side, they walked up into the grass and disappeared into the trees. One of the most beautiful things I've ever witnessed.

I said a prayer for them. I hoped their instincts got them away from the danger. And I hoped that the buffalo that had just passed me would find some clean pasture, some tall lush grass, not yet coated with gray.
•

CHAPTER 37: SLEEP?

As the dust sifted to the ground and my viewing distance increased, I moved the truck to a smooth area just off the road. I seemed to be at the edge of a fallout zone. I didn't really know how those things worked, maybe the wind, maybe the atmosphere, or maybe just the weight of the dust and its ability to travel. Whatever the reason, driving west on Highway 34 had been like heading into a blizzard. Ash had drifted into the fence rows, and it was accumulating heavily on the road. It had increased from less than a half-inch to more than 4 inches in just a few miles. I decided to go back to Highway 281. That had been clearer air and a cleaner road. I couldn't risk getting stuck or losing sight of the road. And I needed to keep my engine running and myself breathing. So my earlier plan would change.

The next decision would be whether or not to stop for the night. In the haze of daylight, I could move stealthily, and I could see my surroundings. At night, I'd need to use my headlights, and that could give me away. I wanted to keep moving, but as I'd come to learn from an old client, "Safety first." All of my machinery could use a rest, and I would be better off letting my adrenaline level taper down.

I should spend the remaining daylight looking at my maps and preparing for the next day. But I had to use all of the remaining light to gain distance. That was the best use of that resource. Everything had to be considered in that way. I needed to maximize everything that was available to me.

I drove until it was just too dark to see. Time to call it a night.

Tomorrow would bring another interstate crossing. I-94 ran across the lower third of North Dakota, connecting Bismarck to Fargo. It would also be an evacuation route, bringing people from north of Yellowstone, the Billings area, and really all of eastern Montana, toward the center of the country. The more I thought about it, the more I questioned my choice of sleep.

The cab of my truck was still stuffed with big plastic gas cans full of diesel fuel. Honestly, its somewhat sweet aroma was better than the sulfur that filled the outer world, but I didn't want to become asphyxiated on fumes. So I redecorated my mobile home once again.

I topped off the truck's main fuel tank using four of the portable gas cans. It was best to empty those so I could grab more fuel if the opportunity presented itself. I also decided it was time to fashion some holsters for the shotgun and pistol in case I needed to use them while driving. I needed to be able to work the weapons inside the vehicle if necessary – to turn, aim, fire if it came to that, and reload. I needed more space.

My favorite workstation had been carefully disassembled and stacked in the back, beneath my other necessities. The sleek black metal and glass table was a high-tech desk that raised and lowered so that I could sit or stand as I worked. The glass surface was great, because I could stick Post-it notes to the underneath side and still mouse across the top. I'd seen it in a designer's magazine article, a biography of one of my favorite peers. Their offices were everything I'd always dreamed that mine might be – brick, iron, wood, glass. Classic and classy. And I'd seen that work table there. It was an awesome work platform.

And it would now be stacked along a fence row, to one day be found by a rancher who would wonder how in the hell it got there. Along with it, they'd find the complete Pantone collection of color swatches, so that perfect shade of teal would always match, in print and on the screen. I reasoned that it could all be replaced and certainly wouldn't be of any use to me in the coming days. In total, it was about 4 cubic feet that I could put to better use.

The gas cans went into the back, behind the big metal farm tank we'd swapped from Dad's truck. I took inventory and wrote some notes on my map.

I had used about 20 gallons of fuel to get to northern Nebraska. It had taken me another 20 gallons to get to North Dakota. My trip had started with almost 200 gallons of diesel available – 25 in the truck's normal tank, 120 gallons in Dad's farm tank, and 50 gallons in portable plastic gas cans. If I could average 20 miles per gallon, it would give me 4,000 miles of range. It should be enough to get me to the cabin in Montana, even considering my horribly inefficient route. I'd picked up another 20 gallons from the park maintenance shed in Nebraska, but I'd save that for last, as I couldn't trust its age or quality.

On top of my lifeblood, I draped the tarp, borrowed from the barn in Missouri, to hide the farm tank from immediate view. My truck tank was full, and I shouldn't need to access any of the extra fuel for awhile. I decided to take on the look of a more-local evacuee and put my oldest computer crate on the back carrier. I determined my clothes were somewhat expendable, so I stuffed half of them into the crate. Peeking from the corner of the wrapped crate was my smallest computer monitor, for visual effect. It looked haphazard and randomly assembled. Alex's bike was strapped to the top of it, with two of the empty gas cans hanging on the other end. My hope was that looters might see the monitor – valuable in any normal situation – or the gas cans, and go for those items first, giving me time to pull away if I got in a pinch. If they got those items, no big loss. This interstate crossing would be worked in a smarter manner.

It was pitch dark when I completed my remodeling project, but I was happy with the results. To celebrate, I opened a can of tomato soup that had been warming in the engine compartment, wedged between the radiator and a support bracket. I washed it down with some Iowa tap water. *Delicious*. But I wanted to get more miles beneath me. My body was still wide awake. I was restless and anxious to stay on the move. I set out into the void.

Of course, driving in the dark has its issues. With my side window down, I hung my body out like a dog, exhilarated by the joy of riding in a car, my ears and tongue blowing in the breeze. That would be Gus. A long trail of slobber streaking back across the windows and side, wearing the size of smile that only a dog can display. But I wasn't traveling fast enough to blow back my ears. In fact, it was so dark, I was rolling along at a speed just fast enough to hear my tires on the gravel. The quieter the tires, the more likely I was in the main grooves, rolled smooth by the farm equipment that mostly ran these roads. When the gravel got rough and loud, I was running too close to the edge. I was driving by sound. I didn't have any other navigation device that would give me the level of detail I needed. If only I had night vision goggles.

Wait! The truck had a kind of "night vision" on its backup camera. I could drive in reverse using the truck's camera for guidance.

I got out and surveyed the road. It would be wide enough to make a multipoint turnaround; I'd just need to be patient about it. Okay, then what? Is left right? Is right left? The image on the display was backwards, so it would match what a rearview mirror would typically show. One of the leftovers from the original age of motor cars.

After a couple of minutes driving at nearly zero miles per hour, I gained the courage to drive a bit faster, as long as the road appeared straight – and in this part of the country, it almost always was. As long as nothing else caught my attention. I had to keep all of my focus on the little dashboard screen. Looking up would reset my sense of left and right, and I'd need to hit the brakes and reset my senses again. I nearly clipped a mailbox with my single remaining outside mirror. It startled me as it crept past the window in my peripheral vision. I jumped and hit the brakes, sliding the truck onto the grassy shoulder of the road. Too fast, I told myself.

Eventually I was close enough to I-94 to pick up some CB chatter. The radio stations were still all static, so the truckers' news report was all I had to go on.

I backed into a field and shut off the motor. I listened to the CB for a bit and marked some notes on my map. Everything was quiet outside. I had a plan for the morning, so it was time for a nap. •

CHAPTER 38: JAMESTOWN

Sunrise was just a dull glow in the air as morning broke outside of Jamestown, North Dakota. I wanted to get an early start while people were still tired from either sleep or a lack thereof. The truckers' chatter during the night had told me that Jamestown's exits, which appeared on my map to be three small tightly clustered interchanges, were blocked by the National Guard. All lanes of I-94 were running east.

My plan was to join up with the eastbound traffic just west of Jamestown. I'd ride along with the flow, learning what I could from passing through town and hoping to get lost in the confusion of traffic. I'd make the break north when the chance came along.

The signs for Frontier Village took me back to younger days, when we'd traveled the country for fun instead of survival. I wondered if there would be anything useful at the museum, but my daydreaming was stopped by a man pounding on my fender. "Hey, dumbass, give us the shoulder!" he yelled and motioned for me to move farther left on the road. I hadn't even seen him. Stopped in the traffic, he was actually making better time walking with his backpack and gunnysack. Another body, also draped in what appeared to be bedsheets or blankets, walked beside him, pulling an old Lil' Tykes wagon that was overloaded with garage crates and a large stuffed panda bear – the kind you win at the state fair by putting the ball through the impossibly-sized hole or lifting a bottle with a washer and string. It seemed like an odd choice to bring along on such an expedition, but it was obviously an important possession.

I checked the placement of my pistol and shotgun. I reached for both without looking. The grabs were sloppy. I ran through a couple dozen reaches, making sure I hit the grip every time. That was better. Practice makes perfect.

People were milling around the interchanges as the line of cars and trucks hit town. Nobody was interested in the computer monitor or gas can bait I had dangling from the back rack. If they were walking, they couldn't carry anything else. If they were in vehicles, they wouldn't risk stopping. So Jamestown was pretty civilized compared to what I'd seen yesterday. The walls and posts were plastered with "missing" signs and "find us" signs, like I'd seen farther back.

The Army trucks that blocked the exits and entrances were serious rigs. They were the big, 6- and 8-wheeled, all-terrain haulers that are usually reserved for practice drills or flashbacks to the never-ending Middle Eastern conflicts. It was a unique picture. I wasn't accustomed to seeing tracked infantry carriers ringed by soldiers in full-fledged military attire, sporting full-out automatic weapons, standing in the parking lot of Dairy Queen. Times have changed.

At the second interchange, a group of MPs were sorting vehicles. I covered my holsters with a towel and wiped some spit up across my face to smear the grime. It might sound a little gross, but I did not want to appear inviting.

"Destination?" asked the young man, probably about 22 or 23, based on some remaining pimples mixed with a scruffy crop of day-old whiskers. He looked exhausted.

"Grand Forks...well, Canada." I quickly edited my reply, hoping to be shifted to a northbound route. He looked a bit perplexed and squinted at me. "Canada. Home," I said, exaggerating my own exhaustion. I sounded like a caveman, speaking in one-word grunts.

He motioned to the young gal who was questioning the driver ahead of me. "Canada," he hollered. She waved in acknowledgment, and he motioned for me to move forward.

"Canada, eh?" she said, offering some humor.

I smiled. "Thanks for the laugh," I said.

"Sorry about your truck," she replied.

"What?" I was going to ask what had happened to it. I was sure the buffalo did a number on the sides, and I remembered two or three had actually hit the truck, but those were on the passenger side. Before I could finish my question, she pulled a spray can out of her holster set, made a quick check of the label, and painted a big red "C" on the front left corner of my hood.

"Keep moving north," she said. I thanked her and moved to the farthest left lane. I pointed to my "C" and a row of armed MPs waved me through. And that was my last visit to Jamestown. •

CHAPTER 39: MINOT. WHY NOT?

My intended route was to zigzag northwest, picking up Highway 2 west of Minot, North Dakota. The citizens band radio chatter had said they were running Highway 2 as a westbound supply route, running emergency equipment, search and rescue, and other gear in from places like Minneapolis–St. Paul. The top half of North Dakota is sparse, and since they shut down the oil fields out around Williston, there were no jobs and really no purpose for living there. It's beautifully rugged country, but you have to really want to live there. Who knows, when all of this is resolved, it may be a boomtown once more.

I'd guess the Bakken Field will once again become an energy source, with a likely resurgence of fracking and drilling to help recover the country. We still have the infrastructure, and we still have enough of the "old" systems in place. It will just take a shift in thinking and politics – typically mutually exclusive – to make it happen. Or maybe the "carbon footprint" left by this event will be the final straw that literally cooks all of us.

At this point, I'm just a storyteller, standing in his garden in Montana, so those details are beyond my pay grade for now, and I probably won't live long enough to see exactly how this all plays out. But returning to the story...

I was on my way to Minot. "Minot. Why not?" I said out loud to myself. It wasn't that funny, but I smiled anyway. Wow, two smiles in one day. Maybe things were looking up.

I started thinking about Rachel. And Alex. And Mom and Dad. I had to let that go for now. It wouldn't help. But I missed Rachel. We were almost always together. We were a good team.

Meeting her for the first time had been such a fluke, a blind date set up by a mutual friend in the ad biz who was always getting into everyone's relationships. It was a hobby for her to matchmake her circle of friends, so we were never really sure if she truly felt we'd be good together or if she was just looking for a new project. Whatever it was, it ended up being a great fit.

Rachel lived life closer to the caution tape than I did, traveling the world, modeling, and drinking in the rich experiences that every culture had to offer. She had stories of Asia and the islands, limousines and private jets, magazine covers and fashion icons. My stories and experiences were mostly set within the United States, and my transport novelties had always been hot rods and classic cars. But she loved my stories as much as I loved hers. I guess we just have a deep mutual appreciation for one another.

Our last trip together had been to Big Bend National Park, in far west Texas. I was familiar with it because Neil Peart (the drummer and key writer for the band Rush) had included it in a book he'd written entitled *Traveling Music*. I'm not much of a reader, but I'm a solid Rush fan. According to his book, he would escape to a cabin in Big Bend and write. He said being out in nature, in the open spaces, would open his mind to ideas. Rachel had given me the book with a note that said, "I know you don't read, but this is a book about road trips and music – written by your favorite drummer. Can't be all bad." And she was right. It was a great read. And we'd talked about making an escape to Big Bend ever since. It just never fell into place.

But the year before everything went crazy, we had finally taken the trip. Rachel planned it out, which meant it would be an incredibly nice journey. We had started with a road trip to Marfa, an artsy enclave with a diametric lifetime-cattle-rancher-meets-escaped-urban-hippy vibe that even includes a government-funded viewing platform built on the outskirts of town for watching the famed "Marfa Lights" – a possibly paranormal or UFO-based phenomenon that helped put the place on the map. The town has some great art galleries and is a magnet for talent, if not actual alien space men. Two nights in Marfa got us about as far removed from the Dallas hustle as any place we could have gone.

Next up, the beautifully historic Gage Hotel in Marathon. Refined and classic, we found the place impeccably restored to its cattle baron and oil tycoon glory. If you're looking for five-star lodging in a town with a population of less than 60, this is your place.

It was a great escape. We always had so many things going on in our businesses and work lives, it was difficult to just unwind and find intimate time together. So our most romantic moments were usually when we were out of town.

The hotels had been great. One, a modern contemporary style, was sleek and minimalistic with a beautiful pool area; the other, a rustic step into the wild west – had the wild west offered 300-thread count linens and a deep-tissue couple's massage. Modern times have indeed brought some improvements.

But what I was thinking about, where my mind wandered to, was our drive through Big Bend. It was every western painting you've ever seen come to life. Sweeping color-banded plateaus rising from sagebrush-covered desert, standing in a pool of hot sunlight while watching a rainstorm cross the other side of the valley. It was mystical and rough, with bright supple flowers sprouting from harsh thorned bushes. I now understood the attraction felt by the artists. It was inspiring.

And so, too, was Rachel. She always inspired me in so many ways. Uninhibited and bold, she never feared finding the edge. One moment I was looking out to my left, enjoying the view scrolling past the window, the next I was looking back at her as she unhooked her bra and slipped it out through the sleeve of her fitted T-shirt. Her movements were paced and sensual. She kept her sculpted face focused on her shirt but shifted her eyes towards me and smiled. Her thin shirt traced every detail of her body. She was obviously playing with me, and I was loving it. I started to slow down, looking for a spot to pull over.

"You just drive," she said, as she began to undo my belt. She is so amazing to me, and so amazing in how she treats me. She ran her hand down against my thighs and released me from the confines of my hiking shorts. She knew exactly what she was doing. "Just drive," she reminded me as the tires again ran across the rutted edge of the road. It was getting hard to focus.

She slipped off her silky shorts and tossed them up on the dash. She leaned over and put her head in my lap. Simply driving was becoming a real chore at this point. She laughed at me as the tires once again rumbled on the edge line. "You can find a place to stop now," she said in a light, coy voice, kissing my neck. I pulled into the next scenic overlook and slid to a stop.

In a moment, she was over the console and straddling me. I ran my seat back as far as it would go and reclined it nearly flat. I pulled her down on top of me and melted my mouth into hers, gently biting her lip and nibbling on her neck. She moved and took me into her warm soft center. She giggled for a moment and then whimpered as I began moving her on top of me. Her body had always been perfection – toned and curvaceous, with poster-girl breasts and luscious red hair framing her face. That's where she really shines, with soft blue eyes, a quick, easy smile, and elegant demeanor – I am truly a lucky man.

We moved slowly at first, kissing, renewing ourselves to one another, then moving with raw passion as she began to tremble around me. She pushed me deep into her, and I felt a sense of release I hadn't felt in months. She continued to grind her hips onto me, tilting her head back and lifting her incredible body over me. She panted a few times and dropped her body onto mine, where we lay, sweating and out of breath. I wrapped my arms around her and held her tightly. She nuzzled into me and we just lay there, absorbed into one another. It was beautiful.

After a few minutes we looked around to see if anyone else had stopped. We were still alone, so we lay back together for a while longer, 100 miles from anywhere – a million miles from where we'd been.

Eventually we took the time to actually look at the scenic view where we had stopped. It was okay, but it didn't surpass what I'd just experienced. God has created incredible things, incredible settings, and one incredible girl. I'm a big fan of His work.

I couldn't wait to see Rachel again, to have her fall onto me, to feel her body, taste her skin, and feel her close to me. I missed her deeply, and so my endeavor must not fail. •

• •

NEXT: "RACHEL'S STORY" CHAPTERS 1 – 11

Jake's story will follow, picking up at Chapter 40.

...far beyond the bridge at
Moberly, Jake pushes on to meet
Rachel in Montana ...
ORIGINAL
Coca
SPAGHE

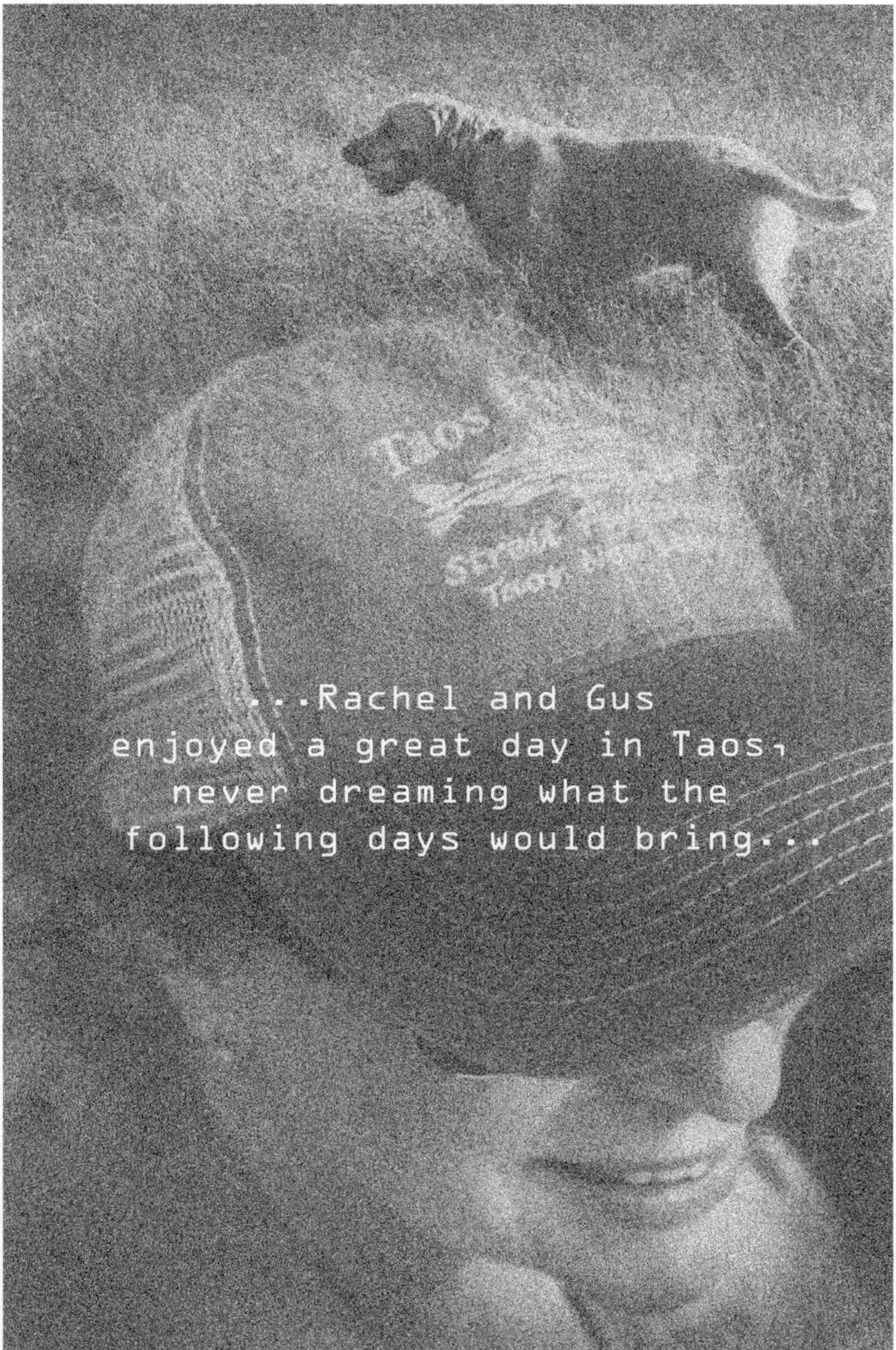

...Rachel and Gus
enjoyed a great day in Taos,
never dreaming what the
following days would bring...

• •

RACHEL'S STORY

RACHEL'S STORY
CHAPTER 1: LOVE OF MY LIFE

Rachel was the love of my life. Strong, confident, intelligent, and beautiful. She came from good stock, growing up in the same kind of rural church-going environment that framed my childhood. The pictures from her teenage years show her to be cute as a button, tall and lean, with tumbling locks of strawberry blonde hair. She says she wasn't popular with the boys. I don't believe that. I think they were scared to death. I would have been as well. In fact, if it hadn't been for a blind date scenario, I never would have approached her.

She asked me that question on our wedding day.

She said, "Would you have asked me to a dance? Or if you'd seen me sitting by myself at a bar, would you have come over to talk with me?"

"Hell, no," was my honest response. I laughed. "Are you kidding me? No. I haven't got enough game or swagger or whatever that requires. No. I'm sorry, I just wouldn't have."

"But, it's just me."

Yes, but she has never seen herself through a man's eyes.

Before being formally introduced, I'd actually seen her many times. She was a model, booking through a Dallas agency that provided talent for photo shoots, TV ads, movies, and the like. Her niche had been high-end fashion and runway modeling. Elegance, glamour, and always a bit too much attitude in that world for this farm boy. So the models

I'd hired for swimwear and lifestyle clients had always been the cute, cheerleader-who-lives-next-door type. I felt it was appropriate for the ads and branding we were generating. The runway models were just too sophisticated for me and typically not aligned with my clientele.

Yet as it turns out, my elegantly glamorous cosmopolitan lady can out-hunt and out-fish the purest redneck on the plains. It's a mix that some of her earlier boyfriends just couldn't grasp, or maybe needed to compete with. For me, it's just a joy to watch her in her element.

As our dating became more and more serious, she told me directly, "Do not ask me to marry you." She said the decision was too big and important to be pinned into some theatrical moment, prearranged with a dinner, flowers – for some, the jumbotron at a Cowboys' game – and she wasn't going to answer a question that important in a moment of packaged tactical strategy. And I was fine with that. Frankly, it took the pressure off of me.

So one day, after being together for around two years, while we were walking along a beautiful mountain trail, listening to the birds and the nearby rushing river, she just stopped and looked at me. "Jake, I can't imagine living in this world without you by my side. Will you marry me?"

It was magical. The moment I'd dreamed about since I was a boy. Well, it was magical, and incredibly special, but boys don't dream about stuff like that. You know, we just don't. But that doesn't diminish the event in any way. It was an awesome moment, even though she didn't get down on her knee – and I still kid her about that. Anyway, I grabbed her and held her.

"Yes. I would be honored. I thought you'd never ask!" And that was true.

I had decided that she probably wasn't ever going to ask, and that was going to be okay. But I'm so glad she did, and I am honored to be hers.

•

RACHEL'S STORY
CHAPTER 2: THE MOVE

We had long talked about moving to Montana. It was one of those bucket list conversations, when you bring up things you'd like to do, some of which simply won't happen without a lottery win – and since we never bought tickets, even more unlikely. But you still talk about them. You talk about the things that are out there, just within reach if you twist just right, make the right moves, and aren't afraid to fall from the ladder. Those are always the best apples, it seems. We had certain apples that we reached for.

The change in my work situation shook our ladder, but we were close, so we decided to reach for that one big apple, risking the fall. We would will it into our grasp, and we'd catch each other if it all toppled down.

The big yellow Penske truck was packed tight, but not overly so. We'd sold the majority of our furniture and material possessions, and what we really loved or needed we'd wrapped in bubbles and blankets and strategically arranged in the truck. We could have stuffed a smaller truck, but it would have made the process more difficult, and a smaller truck may have struggled to tow our vintage Chevy K5 Blazer on the trailer behind. One of the things I just couldn't part with, it would now have a more logical home in the mountains, and maybe actually see some off-road mileage on the tires. Since its restoration, all its big knobby tires had ever felt was smooth concrete and asphalt. I knew it'd enjoy its new home.

Rachel had made a nest for Gus, up on the passenger seat. I'd thought it best to have him ride in his soft-side crate, but she wasn't going to make him endure confinement for the four-day ride. So she wrapped the seat with towels, and we strung some bungee cords to persuade him to stay on his side of the cab. They'd have a good time. She'd probably pick all of the music.

When our departure schedule had been derailed by my client, she decided to go it alone. The truck was already halfway packed, and it didn't make sense to delay the start of the trip. Besides, I could almost catch up if it were only a couple of days. It was so great to have a wife who was an international fashion model as well as a damn solid gear-jammin' truck driver. She'd spend the first night of her journey with some friends in Taos. •

RACHEL'S STORY
CHAPTER 3: CHECKING IN

"Hi, Beautiful," she said with a bright smile in her voice. With her killer looks and Sophia Loren style, I always loved it when she called ME "Beautiful."

"Hi, babe. Did you make it to Taos?"

"Yep. The truck's full of fuel, and Rick helped me check all of the straps and tie-downs, so it's ready for tomorrow's trek. Debbie's opening some wine. We're going to sit on their patio and gaze at the stars."

I had nearly forgotten about that. The stars are incredible out there. With a bit higher altitude, cleaner air, and no city lights, the galaxies and constellations were right there. You could almost reach out and touch them. I was looking forward to that as well. Crisp fresh air and diamond-filled skies.

I suppose the skies were like that everywhere, long ago. On my first trip into the mountains, I'd been overwhelmed by the stars. Looking up at the patterns, I'd wondered how the old mariners did it. I understood the premise of the sextant, looking through some rustic telescope to triangulate the distances between the stars, considering the rotation of the constellations to determine your earthbound location. But we hadn't covered any of that in my astronomy class. We were too busy looking at the amazing digital images that the Hubble telescope provided. Those images were incredible, almost surreal, and they gave us a sense of scale that was beyond our grasp. Light years, millions of light years, that's the measuring stick of the heavens. Vast. Expanding. And mostly vacant.

I assumed the Hubble, like some other great pinnacles of achievement, was still floating around out there, hibernating until some future awakening that might pull it back into service. It's a worthy dream, and mankind is good at dreaming.

“Wish I was there.” I said.

Rachel replied, “Me, too.” We shared a few moments of silence, just being connected. And I knew she was safe. It had been a lot of miles and the first of many long days for her and Gus.

Tomorrow, she’d make her way up to Salt Lake City, another of her favorite places. And that would be her second stop on the journey.

“How’s Fuzzy holding up?” I inquired.

“He’s doing great. We took a little walk in the middle of the day, and he chased a bird through some stickers and mud, across from where I stopped for fuel. So, he got a bath from the convenience store water hose. You know, the usual. Then he slept like a dog. He was fine. We had a good day.”

I told her I loved her and asked her to scratch Gus’s ears for me. That was our thing, a bonding between Gus and me.

“Tell Rick and Debbie ‘hi’. I love you.”

“Love you.” •

RACHEL'S STORY
CHAPTER 4: SALT LAKE CITY

Departing Taos with no issues, Rachel made good time and found a nice spot to stop for the night. A healthy dinner across from the hotel had also provided a few leftovers to enhance Gus's dinner bowl. They were both tired from the travel.

She had just gotten back to sleep. Gus had decided that a late-night outing was needed, trying to stretch his four legs and gather a little freedom after being penned up in the truck for 12 hours. He was a good traveler, for a dog, but this was beyond his typical joy ride distance to the local park. While he had been to more of the United States than most people, he was used to traveling in the back of a much more refined vehicle, cozy and nested in his soft-sided traveling crate. And Rachel had wanted to avoid any midnight barking at the hotel, so she was happy to get him out and about.

It could have been a room service cart careening out of control down the hallway, delivering a 2:00 a.m. snack to some newlyweds, but recent events had somewhat lowered Rachel's requirements of star ratings on her lodging. Plus, she had Gus and was driving a large rental truck, towing another vehicle. The Ritz Carlton would not have been her choice on that evening, even if there had been one available. But the rumble and noise brought her to attention, and Gus held an inquisitive look that she'd not seen before.

"It's okay, buddy," she said, speaking more to comfort herself than the dog. She'd been in an earthquake in California once, where the ceiling tiles in the building had raised up and fallen back into place as the ripple passed through the structure. It was like seeing dominoes fall from beneath a glass table, eerie yet somehow logical and not all that scary.

That was the sensation she felt, like some deep rolling thunder passing below the hotel. There were a few moments of silence, and then the alarms went off. Shrieking and wailing, the hallway alarms ignited throughout the hotel. The backup lights kicked on as the rest of the power failed. She'd practiced for this, but she still rolled her eyes, knowing Jake would be proud that his half-crazy drills and methodologies were actually proving useful. Her bag was already packed for exit, so a quick grab of battery packs, multiplugs and her Critical Box, followed by a fast look out the edge of the window – always need to be aware of your environment – and she was out the door. Even Gus knew the drill.

Rachel thought about their discussions. Jake had not been shy about his desire for the entire family to be prepared and confident in an emergency situation. He had said, "Life or death shouldn't be a 50/50 shot." He wanted his team to be comfortable in situations where most people are not. Being ready makes all the difference. That's the difference in taking advantage of a saving opportunity versus falling victim to the circumstances that surround you. You aren't looking to take advantage of anyone, but if there's only two water bottles left at the hospitality table in the lobby, you want them both to end up in your wife's backpack as she flies out the door. He would be proud. He always had little analogies that cut through the BS and made the point in a profound yet simple way, and the lessons were easy to remember.

Her friend Debbie, who she'd just seen in Taos, still used "keys in hand" every time she shut her car trunk. We had shared that concept one night at dinner. Talking to yourself, making a physical contact with something, it commits it to memory, so you aren't left saying, "Where are those keys? Crap, did I just lock them in the trunk?" Debbie remembers that trick, and she has not lost her keys in more than 30 years.

Rachel needed to make a quick assessment about any damage and whether or not she could maneuver her multitruck rig out of the parking lot. A bunch of panicked drivers, clogging up the exit or backing into one another, could really slow her down if she needed to make a hurried departure.

She made it to the parking lot ahead of even the desk attendant. All of the surrounding buildings had switched over to backup power, although that wasn't as uncommon as it used to be. Out here, where most of the generated power was priority-designated to The Power Strip – meaning the generation corridor that fed electricity to the coasts – it was pretty common for their demands to outbid the local needs. Nobody seemed too excited about the lack of power or the tremor. A few people were walking around the entryway, shrugging and making small talk, and eventually drifting back to their rooms. She made sure the truck still had clear access to the street and headed back to bed herself. Sleep doesn't require much light, so she was quickly curled up with Gus, and both were sound asleep.

Her morning alarm chirped gleefully. Rachel was an early riser, always up and around before the sun even thought about cresting the horizon. Gus gave her a wet nose kiss accompanied by his standard morning whimper. Time for another walk. He was an awesome dog, a beautiful yellow Lab, quiet-tempered and an excellent person all around. His only drawbacks were his talent for shedding, which we believed to be unmatched by any other critter known to mankind, and his on-off switch in regard to activity and sleep. "Thirty hours a day," is what we'd always said about his sleep habits, interrupted by four 2-mile walks, each requiring a dozen or so retrievals of his oversized squeaky tennis ball and, if the opportunity presented itself in any way, a swim. It didn't matter if it were the backyard pool, a neighborhood fountain, or a murky drainage ditch, Gus was always ready for a quick dip. Rachel had packed towels in the cab of the truck, just in case. •

RACHEL'S STORY
CHAPTER 5: GOTTA GO!

The rumble came again. This time it was severe and steady, lasting what seemed like minutes. She grabbed her bags and Gus and ran for the truck.

Against the first glimmer of sunrise, Rachel could see that the entire sky to the east was black. The shaking had stopped, but there was a deep tone in the air that was completely new to her senses. They say tornadoes sound like approaching trains, hailstones on the roof have unique impact signatures, and you can gauge the distance of lightning by the time delay in the thunder. These are the sounds of nature that we've all grown up with or that we've been told about at some point. But this sensation was unique. The deep moan evoked a residual endless echo that didn't seem to be emanating from any real point of origin. It was as if the atmosphere itself was saturated with long, low sonic waves, or that it was coming through Earth itself. Rachel flipped on the radio in the truck to see what was happening. It was pure static.

She stuffed her night bag in the space between the seats and coaxed Gus up into his perch on the passenger side. He was whimpering, disturbed by the low-frequency tone in the air.

As you would expect, she was the first out of the parking lot behind the hotel. She'd calculated the length of her rig when she parked, allowing enough space to bend the truck and trailer around the light poles – scarred from others who hadn't calculated quite so well – and join the access road to Interstate 15.

"What the hell?" Rachel exclaimed, slamming on the brakes, as a family towing a boat cut across the edge of the hotel lawn and lodged themselves in the road.

The guy had tried to short-cut the turn, and while his micro RV had survived the curb's 12-inch fall, his boat's motor, locked in the down position, was now jammed into the yard, anchoring him and his entire contraption to the concrete edge. His menagerie blocked the entire roadway.

"Are you f-ing kidding me?" Rachel could not only hunt, fish, and drive on par with any workin' man, she could conjure the same vocabulary when the situation arose. She did not suffer fools well, and this guy had clearly earned that title.

She explained the situation to Gus pretty efficiently. "Stay!" she commanded, as she spun down out of the truck and slammed the door. This is what scared her the most about any kind of weather event, like icy roads, snow storms, or hurricanes. It wasn't the actual event. It was the erratic reactions of people, the morons who screwed it up for everyone else, because they'd never considered even the basic preparation of parking their damn boat properly or knowing how to exit a damn parking lot. It seemed pretty simple. She was not happy.

"Nice driving, A.J." she complimented under her breath as the man shifted back and forth into reverse and continued to spin his tires on the blacktop.

"Hey!" she hollered, motioning him to roll down his window. "You'll have to unhook it. You're dug into the propshaft on the back end."

She didn't know what he'd do once he had that accomplished, but at least it would separate his rig and she could slip past. That was her main agenda and honestly, she didn't care how he resolved it. She just wanted to get on the road and away from the idiots. •

RACHEL'S STORY
CHAPTER 6: IT'S YELLOWSTONE

Waiting for the man to crank up the hitch on his boat trailer, Rachel returned to the truck. Others were now stacked up behind her rig, waiting for the same solution to unfold.

"Sorry," repeated the guy's wife to everyone. "Sorry."

It was like a needle stuck in the groove of a record. The constant statement offered by the guy's wife as she stood next to the RV, waving like an ambassador to the frustrated travelers who thought honking their horns would speed the process.

A young driver tried to run his autobot on the manual setting, choosing the sidewalk between the pool and the corner of the hotel. It was clearly not a good choice as he and the vehicle fought for control and he ended up pinched between a small evergreen tree and the pool's perimeter fencing.

"They are out in force today," Rachel thought.

Most of the travelers had the usual array of self-driving cars, and they left them on autopilot. So the vehicles had staged themselves in a perfect utopian order, 10 feet apart, in precise alignment, awaiting their turn on the invisible thread that would guide them to the highway.

Rachel was passing by one of the smaller bots. The couple had lowered their windows to partake in the conversation.

"This is why we shouldn't drive ourselves," offered the middle-aged man as he pushed up his glasses and returned to his book. He and his apparent wife sat facing each other in a new E-Phaze-200, which didn't even give him the option of a steering wheel. Any manual driving utilized a joystick that looked more like a video game controller than an automotive system. His wife agreed, stating it was "nonconformists" like that, who remained in the "dark ages," who kept us all from advancing on our predefined paths. "It's an analogy of our times, really," she posed. "He needs to get with the system."

Just then, the young desk clerk came running out into the parking lot.

"It's Yellowstone!" he yelled. He was both excited and shaken.

"It's Yellowstone!" he exclaimed once again, and he ran back into the hotel.

Rachel gave Gus another "Stay!" command and grabbed the keys out of the Penske truck, along with her backpack. She jogged quickly past the candy-colored autobots that now snaked around the majority of the parking lot.

"There's a couple of stations showing it now," one of the drivers offered, staring at the screen that filled his dashboard.

Rachel stopped for a second to see the channel. It was a news streaming app, possibly unique to the car brand. She continued into the hotel to get a broader assessment.

"It's Yellowstone!" the kid yelled again, somehow unaware that everyone within earshot had already gotten that part of the story.

"What else are they saying?" Rachel asked. "And, how far from Yellowstone are we, exactly?"

"I think, like, maybe 100 miles," he said. "I'll look it up."
He pulled his device out of his pocket.

"Maybe it's a thousand." He paused for a moment of thought then continued, "I've never looked it up before."

"Didn't you grow up around here?" Rachel inquired.

"No. I'm from Ogden," was his response.

Ogden was about an hour's drive north, which she thought would have qualified as "around here." Wow. He must be related to the kid whose car was currently lodged in the tree just outside the door.

Rachel decided this rabbit was not worth chasing.

An older lady was sitting close to the large flat screen that adorned the wall above the lobby's well-intentioned fireplace. While not an actual fireplace, it had a digital display of a burning log video loop and a fan that blew warm air from the vents beneath it. It had a certain commercial charm.

"Ma'am, have you heard the full story? Are we at risk here?" Rachel tried to be calm and friendly, yet somewhat direct in her questioning.

"Oh dear, it's just awful. Dreadful. It's just terrible." The lady had a long list of adjectives but not much information to offer.

The screen returned from its commercial segment to show three newscasters sitting behind a glass desk, surrounded by large screens, most of them showing the same telephoto shot of a wall of black smoke, backlit by the sunrise, as morning broke.

"We're still trying to get online with Idaho Falls, about 100 miles from the epicenter of the blast, but we seem to be having some technical issues, Lori," said the announcer, handing the story off to a field reporter, evidently at the same location as the camera.

"This is Lori Owens. I'm standing next to Interstate 15, just north of Pocatello, Idaho. We are approximately 160 miles from the center of Yellowstone National Park – or what used to be Yellowstone National Park. It's unclear exactly..."

"Holy shit," Rachel gasped. That camera shot was from 160 miles away! The horizon line at that distance is so far removed, nobody should be able to see anything from the ground. That meant the wall of smoke filled the entire atmosphere.

The older lady glared at her, obviously not happy with her language.

"Sorry," Rachel offered. "It's awful. It's terrible."

"That's what I said!" the lady huffed and turned back to the screen.

The reporter continued. "Residents in Casper and Cheyenne are being evacuated to the east as strong sulfuric gas and ash have already started impacting those cities. First responders in smaller communities have been asked to make neighborhood rounds to promote evacuation, but many have not been reached. The Power Strip was heavily impacted as tremors brought down power lines as far south as Santa Fe. The mayor of Denver has stated they may be asking residents to prepare to evacuate as well, but for now they have issued a shelter-in-place order, requiring everyone to either stay at home or return to their homes until further instructed. Greg?"

"Thanks, Lori. We've got road closures to announce, as I-15 north of you has been closed due to damage and concern about bridge collapse. Hold on. We've got a report that two small refineries in Billings, Montana are on fire. We're having difficulties getting images. It seems a lot of infrastructure damage has resulted from the blast that peaked area sensors at around 8.0 on the Richter Scale. The resulting quake shattered pipelines and sparked fires across the foothills region."

"And that's why we've moved to an electric-based system, Greg," added the blonde lady at the end of the glass desk. "Can you imagine the carbon being released by those refineries? It's deplorable."

"That's not all that's deplorable," Rachel said out loud as she ran back to Gus and the truck. Her timing was nearly perfect as the man had finally managed to unfasten his little RV from his sunken boat trailer.

"Never had a boat before," he offered, as if the boat had willingly sabotaged his incredible driving skills.

Rachel was halfway through another silent "idiot" statement, but she noted the Wyoming plates. Her attitude softened as she thought about their plight.

"I'm so sorry," she said.

He looked at her unknowing. They were probably lucky to have been away on vacation, but they could be in serious trouble now. She saw a couple of small suitcases through the back window of their little camping truck. The kids wore flip-flops and pajamas. They probably don't even have an extra set of batteries for their flashlight, Rachel thought. Actually, they probably didn't even have that.

She jumped up into the truck and pulled around the van.

"Oh, my God. Jake!" She stopped at the intersection. Where was he? •

RACHEL'S STORY
CHAPTER 7: WHERE'S JAKE?

She reached to dig her cellphone out of the backpack that was stuck between the seats, caught on one of the bungee cords that was supposed to keep Gus on his side of the truck.

Gus gave a loud whimper. His protector's heart told him something was wrong. He pawed at the bungee web and twisted through to be in Rachel's lap.

"Gus, back," Rachel implored, as Gus continued to climb through the dividing lines, struggling to get to her side. "*Agh*. Fine, come here."

Gus reached her lap, all 100 pounds of him. His tail wagged, and he licked her cheek.

"Good dog," she said.

Now to get to the phone. It was all so much easier with a full-grown yellow Lab sitting on your lap, pinned between you and the steering wheel of a rental truck.

"Good dog," she sighed.

She called Jake a number of times. Driving and hitting *redial* for the next hour or so. "All circuits are busy," was all she could get. She tried Alex in Nashville. Same thing.

As the news on the screens had said, I-15 north was closed. Following the guidance of the big orange arrow signs, she joined Interstate 84, moving northwest. She had two destinations in mind. First was the lake. That was where they had been headed. It was always the goal, and it had been the destination they'd decided on in case of some major event. Even though she had fought hard for her preferred location in west Texas, Jake had always said he'd rather freeze to death than die of thirst.

"Balmorhea," she'd always countered. The oasis in the desert. Fresh water, no freezing cold. That had always been her pitch, but they had the cabin up north, so that was the agreed-upon destination.

She knew that Jake had no idea how much wood was required for a full winter's heat, but she had caved. Besides, what were the odds that they'd ever use these plans?

Her next choice, if this event had destroyed the lake house, or the lake, was Newport, Oregon. She'd seen some houses there, for sale online, and she loved the views along the coast. She'd never been there, but it was someplace she could certainly see herself being. She and Gus, running down the beach. But she wanted Jake to be part of that story too, along with Alex and his girlfriend. She could picture all of them together, eating dinner on the deck, listening to the surf. But she had to let Jake know her plan.

And just like that, her phone rang. She answered immediately.

"Hey, I love you!" she exclaimed, in case the call was dropped.

She began spilling her story to Jake, telling him where she was, what roads, what direction. Her plan to get to the lake by going up and over the top. From what she'd seen, most all of the destruction and fallout would be to the southeast. She planned to come in from the northwest. But how would Jake get there? It wasn't going to be just a question of geography. It was going to be questions about fuel, food, and, most importantly, the strain on society.

"Have you talked with Alex?"

Neither one of them had been able to get through, but he was a long way from the Rockies, thousands of miles from the eruption. His issue wouldn't be the physical fallout, such as the ash and sulphur, but the other fallout – the near-certain nationwide power failures and the impacts to the food distribution systems, the financial systems, and, just like his mom and dad's issues, how the population would deal with this as a whole and as individuals.

Rachel and Jake covered a lot in their brief call, and Rachel was able to tell Jake about her "Plan B," which meant going to the Newport area if the lake wasn't going to work. Then the call had dropped, and the lines were dead. She'd need to develop a solid plan, from scratch, on the fly, and execute her plan with perfection.

She looked at Gus, who had returned to his seat and was now looking intently through the windshield. "We're gonna do this, Gus." •

RACHEL'S STORY
CHAPTER 8: A LITTLE FAMILY BUSINESS

So that was it. Her decision was made, and she needed to get to work. The first thing she needed to secure was fuel. Like everything else that size, her rental truck was a hybrid. Some were propane or natural gas, but she had wanted diesel, which Penske offered. However, she had no ability to just plug it in and charge the battery set. All of her power was generated from the truck's motor, so diesel was her required energy source. And she was glad that it was. If she remembered right, the tank held 40 gallons, and, because she'd heard one too many of Jake's lectures about keeping the top half full, she'd filled last night before checking into the hotel.

She looked at her map. She'd stop and get fuel – if there were any fuel to get or any way to get it – at Hazelton or thereabouts. That would be a couple hundred miles out and the map showed two exits. She weighed her options for fuel.

The larger cities, like Twin Falls and Boise, might be drained by the time she got there, depending on how people reacted. The smaller towns may be better odds, but they'd have smaller operations to begin with, so they wouldn't have as much storage tank capacity.

"Think!" she yelled at herself. Gus looked startled and crawled down onto the floor, curling his tail between his legs.

"I'm sorry, buddy," she said to him in a soothing voice. "It's okay. You're okay."

He looked up with his eyes only, his nose planted firmly between his front paws. He could sense the intensity, so he was taking cover.

"Bigger town, smaller station," Rachel said out loud to herself. "On the opposite side of the traffic flow... the inconvenient side. The side that other people wouldn't use." As she talked it out, she knew what she was looking for.

Almost to Hazelton, Rachel began to watch the billboards for fuel. Big bright shiny panels promoted the bigger truck stops, with red and green digital price displays that had gone dark from a lack of electricity. Then, a bit back in the trees, she saw an older, painted billboard, advertising friendly service and clean restrooms. It had an arrow with "1/2 mile" painted in it, along with the tag line, "We Treat You Like Family." It appeared to have been repainted somewhat recently. That was the place.

As she continued to roll west on I-84, she was noticing the drop in traffic. No big evacuation to the west. It was as if they were on the safe side of a fire line. Maybe it wasn't as bad as she'd thought, maybe she and Jake were getting too worked up about this. Then she saw a line of vehicles coming fast on the eastbound side. It was a solid line of National Guard rigs, tankers, heavy equipment, and fire and rescue trucks. One of the bigger trailers had type that she could read. "Portland Fire & Rescue" My God, that was almost 600 miles. That means they were on the road immediately. She hadn't overreacted. This was bad, and it was going to get worse.

And the line of vehicles continued as she made her exit. "Tommy's Bait & Gas" was, as the sign said, about a half-mile from the exit ramp. The big truck stops had built at the next interchange, opting for the hilltop view and easier on/off access. Tommy, or more likely Tommy's dad or grandfather, had built their bait shop back before the interstate came through. Their place was situated for the folks who were headed out to do some fishing. They were the last stop on that road before reaching the little lake that sat just outside of town – and nobody was going to the lake today.

As Rachel pulled in, a young woman was unloading coolers packed with ice from the back of a small delivery truck. It had the same "Tommy's" logo painted on the door.

"Excuse me, do y'all have fuel?" Rachel asked.

"Sorry, we're not really open," said the lady, struggling with the large and obviously heavy box.

“Here, let me help with that,” said Rachel, grabbing one of the handles and walking up the steps into the store.

“Thanks,” the lady said. “But, we’re not actually open. We’re just trying to save everything.”

“Save everything?” Rachel was sure she knew what the young woman meant, but she wanted to drive some more conversation and get some more information. And she desperately wanted to fill with fuel.

“Yeah, the power’s off again, so the coolers shut off. We’ll lose the ice cream, the milk, all that stuff.”

A young man, maybe 35, with an outdoors look and red plaid shirt, came in through the side door. He looked like he’d stepped right off of a Bounty Paper Towels package. That must be Tommy.

“Tommy?” Rachel asked, taking a shot with her female intuition.

“Ha-ha,” the guy laughed. “Tommy was my grandpa. But, yeah, I guess now I’m Tommy.” And he followed up with, “I guess you’ve met my wife, Laurie. I’m sorry, we’re closed, because of...well, you know.”

“Yeah, your wife said y’all were closed. I need to find some diesel somewhere, before it’s all gone. And your sign promised clean restrooms.” Rachel hoped some humor might win some points.

The young lumberjack told her that they did have diesel, in fact a few hundred gallons of it, but no way to pump it – because the electricity was off.

But Rachel was pretty sure she had a hand pump, because it would be part of the Emergency Box that Jake had assembled for her. Of course.

She asked if she could buy some fuel if she could pump it. The couple agreed, because they were more focused on their cooler situation, and they didn’t see how some lady and her dog were really going to accomplish that.

Rachel opened the lock on the back of the truck and rolled up the door. Everything was holding together pretty well. One of the crossbars had come loose, letting some stacked containers tip away from the wall. She pushed it back into place and cranked it tight. The Emergency Box was there at the back. It was a good sized plastic tub, sealed with red duct tape. "EMERGENCY" was written with a Sharpie in Jake's trademark handwriting.

Rachel undid the tape and unlatched the tub. It was like finding a pirate's treasure without the jewels. There was a small set of tools, a short loop of cable and carabiner clips, duct tape, a multitool, a 6-inch hunting knife, a 25-foot extension cord, a 10-foot garden hose, D-size batteries, and a camping lantern, along with a pair of tactical pants, her hunting vest, and hiking boots. At the bottom was a tarp and an inflatable pillow. And under the neatly folded tarp, was a case with a 9mm pistol and about 200 rounds of ammo, all in clips. Jake wanted his girl to be prepared. But most importantly, about halfway through the box, Rachel had found what she needed. A small hand pump with a coil of plastic hose. If it would reach the liquid in their tanks, she could get her fuel.

"I don't believe what I'm seeing," said Lumberjack Guy as he walked toward Rachel.

She had parked her rig as close as she could to the store's underground tanks. Opening the fill hatch, she'd unfastened the cap and looked inside. The plastic tube was too curled from its package to make it down into the fuel. But she'd seen places like this check their fuel levels when she was a kid, with a long yardstick pole marked with lines and numbers. She'd seen her grandfather check tanks at area ranches, with a roll-up ruler and a weight. It was like a giant dipstick. They'd open the lid and run it down into the fuel tank. They'd pull it up and see where the stick was wet. That's how they knew how much fuel was left.

The store's dipstick hadn't been used in a long time, probably replaced with a digital sensor. But she'd found it hooked under the awning, where Tommy's grandfather had likely last put it. With that long smooth pole and some duct tape, she had fashioned the perfect siphon tube. Spinning the crank on the little pump, she was halfway through filling her tank.

"How are you doing that?" asked young Tommy. "Did you have all of that with you?"

"Well, I had some of it. And you had some of it. You said, if I could..."

"Oh yeah, I know what I said. Can you fill our trucks, too? Maybe some gas cans?"

Before she was done cranking her little fuel pump, Rachel had filled her truck, Tommy's delivery truck, and his wife's pickup. Plus, she filled eight 5-gallon gas cans originally designed for outboard motor boats. They were willing to sell her half of them because they were so impressed with her skills.

And just like those guys back in high school, they were a probably a little scared. She'd put the 9mm in its holster and now had it clipped to her belt.

Tommy's wife asked if she could give her a hug before she left.

"Thank you so much," she said. "If it hadn't been for you, we'd run outta gas, but you showed us how to do that. And you helped with the ice and everything. We just hope you get where you're going." She smiled and looked at Tommy.

"Yeah, it's been real interesting." said Tommy. "Hey, can you say 'Y'all' again for us?"

"Sure. I hope Y'ALL have a great day. And thank y'all so much. I really mean it," Rachel drawled out with as much southern accent as she could muster.

"You guys take care of one another, okay?" she added in her natural voice as she looked at them for a moment.

They weren't much older than Alex. A young couple, working hard, working together, to continue the family business. It was pretty perfect. If only the world would get out of their way and let them do it.

Tommy gave a piece of beef jerky to Gus, who eagerly jumped up into the passenger seat of the truck. The restroom was indeed clean, and the service was incredibly friendly. Just like the sign said. •

RACHEL'S STORY
CHAPTER 9: NONSTOP

Now Rachel had 60 gallons of fuel, between the truck's main tank and the extra gas cans she's picked up at Tommy's. Loaded the way she was, towing the Blazer, she was only getting around 11 miles per gallon.

Making some calculations, she sighed. If she really watched her pace, she'd make Coeur D'Alene, but she couldn't make the lake. She'd need more fuel at some point. But she planned to drive all the way, nonstop.

She tore the pages out of the atlas and fastened them to the dash with duct tape. She marked the distance, estimated the times, and made notes on the map with the Sharpie from her backpack. Rachel knew her route. She had her plan.

She was pretty sure that the lake house would be okay. There wouldn't be any power, but there were a lot of other resources. In fact, an abundance of some things. It would all be okay.

There was a void of information, though, with no news about anything. What was the time projection for getting it all back online? How much of the country was affected by the eruption, by the fallout, by The Power Strip going down? She was doing her best, balancing the news reports she'd seen with what she was now hearing. The rental truck didn't have a high-end sound system to start with, and the radio was basic. Just AM and FM, and the stations out in these parts were mostly local affiliates or owned by individuals. Either way, they didn't have the resources for long-term generators, so by mid-afternoon, the stations had mostly turned to static.

Between Twin Falls and Boise, there was no traffic. Stay-at-home orders had been issued to the masses. Evidently, folks were listening.

The air had been getting heavier and heavier. She had thought it might clear out as she moved further west. In the morning, there was a smell of rotten eggs or broken sewer pipes in the air. Now, it filled each breath with a stale taste, and the thin haze of dust gave everything an odd glow. As it settled, surfaces became dull and colorless.

The sun was still shining brightly though, as it arched into the western sky, just slightly ahead of the growing atmospheric cloud. If it hadn't been for the circumstances, it may have been a wonderful spring day.

I-84 is a beautiful drive, as it winds along the valley, then follows the high plains into Boise. That's where Rachel planned to turn north, following Highway 55, then Highway 95, toward Lewiston. She looked closely at her maps, marking some distances and thinking about what lie ahead. Wait. What's that road? There was a road that wasn't shown on the regional map, only on the Idaho map. Highway 12, running northeast. If they'd let her, she could cut across to Missoula – yes, cut across on Highway 12 to Missoula. That's what she needed to do!

She calculated the distance. That would be under 500 miles, in fact, right at 460. She'd have enough fuel to make that distance without stopping. It was a mountain road, with steep inclines and sharp turns, but she could do it.

That was her plan now. She'd be in Boise by 3 o'clock, maybe a bit later. The drive to Grangeville would be another four or five hours. That's where she'd find Highway 12.

"Nine o'clock," she said out loud. "Gus, we're gonna go 'til 9 o'clock, then we'll catch some sleep. You'll be jumping off the dock by lunchtime tomorrow!"

Gus was thrilled. He wagged his tail and stood up in the truck. He knew the words "jump off the dock," and it was one of his favorite things. Rachel was talking with Gus, trying to keep him on his side of the truck, when she saw the roadblock ahead. State troopers lined the road, bringing everyone to a stop. •

RACHEL'S STORY
CHAPTER 10: LONE STAR

After sitting and idling for just a couple of minutes, Rachel realized she was wasting precious fuel. "We can't just sit here," she said to herself, and to Gus, as she shut down the engine.

Gus had heard a lot of one-sided conversations from both Rachel and Jake. He could tell from the tone whether to be happy, supportive, or run for cover. When food was discussed, he was thrilled. When talk turned to finances, he seemed a bit puzzled, and when the words "walk" or "ball" or "lake" or "go" fell into the conversation, he went bonkers. When he was home with Jake, and Jake had computer issues, Gus knew it was best to curl up under the table in the kitchen.

After 20 minutes of starting and stopping, Rachel reached her place at the front of the line.

"Hello, officer, what can I...?" she started to say.

"Destination?" He'd probably talked to a few hundred people today, so the chit-chat was over. "Destination, ma'am?"

"Um, well, Kalispell ultimately, but I thought I'd..."

"Where are you traveling from, ma'am?" His partner was making a circle of the truck, looking underneath and around the trailer with the Blazer on it.

"Texas plates!" shouted the partner, from back behind the trailer.

"Are you from Texas, ma'am?" the officer asked politely.

"Well, yes. Yes, I am. I'm on my way to..." Rachel again was cut off.

"Then Texas is where you shall go." He pulled a bright orange piece of paper from his clipboard and wrote "TX" on it with a fat-tip Sharpie.

"Place this on your dash. Turn around here and return to Texas."

"Are you kidding me? How am I going to do that?" Rachel couldn't believe that was what he really meant. How could that even be a consideration. "Are you crazy?"

"Ma'am, are you questioning me?" his voice lost its politeness.

"Yes. Yes, I am. Tell me, where will I find fuel? How will they pump it? Where will I stop? What will I eat? Can you answer any of those, sir?"

The partner came up to the side of the truck to join the conversation. "Orders, ma'am. Everyone is to return home. You'll be safer at home."

"What sort of scripted bullshit is this?" Rachel asked, also losing her politeness. "You're going to send me...a lady...by herself, back through 2,000 miles of dust and chaos without any fuel or food...or a plan for her safety? Your mama needs to smack your face."

Rachel stood out on the step of the truck.

"Yep, she's from Texas," the second trooper snickered.

"Turn it around!" The first officer stated, firmly, motioning her with a pointed finger.

"Roberts. Badge 337. Idaho. Hey, Roberts, you ain't seen the last of me." Rachel slammed the truck door and pulled forward, accidently catching the front fender of his cruiser with the big front bumper of her rental truck. Her bright orange paper reflected off the front glass.

As the wall of troopers turned her around through the median, Rachel saw others being issued orange papers as well. They appeared to be nodding and agreeing, thanking everyone for their help.

"Sheep," she said under her breath. "Frickin' sheep."

Just out of sight from the roadblock, Rachel pulled from the road, onto a wide spot on the shoulder. This would not stand. She ripped up the orange tag from the windshield and threw it behind Gus's seat. Gus ducked and gave her a look. She'd go back an exit and take a backroad. But first, she'd improve her odds. Digging through her backpack she found the multitool from the Emergency Box.

"Sorry, ole girl, it's time to hide your identity," she said to the Blazer as she undid the license plates and stuck them under the floor mats. She also took another moment to crawl up inside the back of the truck. Rolling up the big back door, she looked around at the containers and tubs. Jake always labeled everything, so if it was there, and it wasn't too deep, she could find it.

"Cookware? No. Christmas? No. Okay. Three more stacks, then I'm giving up," she said to herself. She knew she needed to get back on the road, especially with this delay. "Damn it."

"Family? Maybe." Of course it'd be on the bottom of the stack. Rachel unfastened the cross bar and slid another stack toward the center of the truck. She opened the box labeled "Family" and there it was. Exactly what she was looking for. It might come in handy. She rolled the big door shut and jumped down from the loading deck. Back behind the wheel, Rachel peered down the road ahead. There was a big green sign. Next exit, one mile. That would work.

Rachel sat there for another minute, reviewing her maps, worried about her backroad plan. There weren't a lot of good options. All steep and winding. But that wasn't her biggest problem. Flashing blue lights pulled up behind her. State troopers again.

Her mind was spinning. What's the story? *What's her story?*

"Ma'am, are you okay?" the young female officer asked. "Is there a problem?"

Rachel raced through the likely questions, the possible answers.

"I'm looking for my purse," she finally said. "I stopped a ways back, trying to get gas, and I must have left my purse."

"Do you have any ID?" asked the officer, followed with, "Ah, yes, in your purse, right?"

"Yes, that's where it'd be. I'm trying to meet my husband in Wyoming. We're..."

"I'm sorry, ma'am. Nobody is going to Wyoming."

"Why not? What's with all of the police cars I saw back there, is something wrong?" Rachel's acting skills were as solid as her hunting.

"I see your truck plates say Massachusetts, I assume that's just because it's a rental," the officer inquired. "So where are you coming from?"

"Well, home actually. Kalispell. But the roads have been blocked, I've gotten lost, I'm not really sure..." Rachel let her sentence break and hang, waiting for the officer to fill the void.

"Ma'am, you'll need to head back to Montana. Everyone has been ordered to return to their homes. Here...I'll give you a pass-sheet so you won't have to bother with the roadblocks." The young lady pulled out a thick black marker. She placed the bright blue "westbound" sheet of paper on Rachel's dash. It would be her passport. "MT" was written in big black letters. Montana.

The officer reached down toward Gus, who was out and about, checking on the situation.

"Oh, can I pet him?" she asked. "I love dogs...especially Labs."

"By all means, and he'll be happy to give you some souvenir hair!" Rachel noticed the stripes on the woman's sleeves. "Miss, are you a sergeant?"

“Actually, I’m a captain. This is my sector. I’m in charge of the whole area. Why?”

“Can you sign my paper, so I can show people who gave it to me? You know, just in case.” Rachel was setting the stage for her next performance.

“Sure.” The young woman wrote a note on the Blue sign, giving Rachel permission to drive on any road she deemed necessary to reach her destination.

“Don’t let anybody stop you. Tell them you’re traveling under my authority,” added the young woman.

“Oh, don’t worry, I will. Thank you so much,” Rachel smiled.

And with that, Rachel turned around and headed back to the line on the other side of the highway. She couldn’t wait to put another dent in Roberts’ fender. •

RACHEL'S STORY
CHAPTER 11: I CAN DRIVE 55

Reconnecting with Officer Roberts was a pure joy for Rachel. The big yellow Penske truck caught his attention while she was still far down the line. He left his post and walked back toward her.

"Ma'am, you can't just..." he began to rerun his script on her.

Rachel held up the bright blue tag and pointed to the signature at the bottom.

"You might want to check with your superiors," she said with a flat expression. "Perhaps give your captain a call?"

"Hey!" he hollered back towards the line of officers checking drivers. "Let this one through. She's good." He tipped his hat, but it wasn't chivalry, it was to say, "Well played."

Rachel pulled out of the line and passed them all along the shoulder. She gave a short honk and waved to his partner, still standing at the front of the line.

"What the...?" The guy looked back toward Roberts and raised his arms.

Rachel had a gift for persuasion. I always said she could sell ice cubes in winter, and I believe she could, whether someone wanted them or not.

Another roadblock was set up on the north side of Boise, but her Blue passport tag got her through with only one question: "Ma'am, do you have at least 250 miles of range in this vehicle? Fuel or power?"

"Yes, I do. I'm all set," her politeness had returned, and these guys seemed to be helpful and courteous.

"At Grangeville, you'll find a temporary charge station, but that probably won't work for this vehicle. I don't know about fuel supplies. That may be scarce. Do you understand what I've told you?"

"Yes sir, I do. Thank you."

"Be safe, ma'am. 55 can be a hazardous road sometimes." The officer seemed sincere and he gave her rig a long look as she rolled past. He appeared to wonder how she was going to get where she was going with a truck that size, pulling a trailer.

Highway 55 is designated as a scenic route and for good reason. The highway follows the river valley through a stunning mountain range, loaded with numerous species of trees and wildlife. It would have been more fun to drive with her old Porsche, but that was in a different time. The Porsche had been sold for the move. While the Montana roads would have been a delight in the little convertible, it was sold to clear the way for the next chapter of life. Maybe another Porsche was in her future. She'd wait and see.

Running alongside the river, her big rental truck wasn't the only moving van on the road that day. At least three big trailer units passed her in the hills, one with "Spokane or Bust!" written in the dust on the back.

She started noticing the license plates, especially on the trucks and vehicles loaded with bags and bikes. Most were from Wyoming, so she assumed they had evacuated from the western edge of the state, probably heading up-range of the fallout. She wondered how someone would start over following that kind of event. Do you file an insurance claim? What if your house is still standing, but the city is just simply closed? And without power, how do you file anything, find any records, trace any ownership, prove any place of residence? This was going to be a big mess. She was glad to have her Critical Box and records with her. She felt lucky.

She wondered where Jake was on his route. It seemed like forever since they had talked. At least she knew his route, and he knew...*damn*. He didn't know her route. If she cut across on Highway 12, it wouldn't be what she'd said. It wasn't what she'd told him she was going to do. But that's what she had to do. It was the most efficient way. It would get her there, and that's what was important.

Gus was sound asleep on the floor, curled tightly with his head resting on the transmission hump, by her right foot and the accelerator. It had been a long day for him, with much less sleep than normal. Rachel smiled. Maybe he wouldn't want to go for a walk at midnight. That would be positive.

What the officer had said about fuel was important. But if she'd figured it right, she wouldn't need any more fuel to make the lake. •

• • • • • • • • END OF "RACHEL'S STORY"... FOR NOW • • • • • • • •

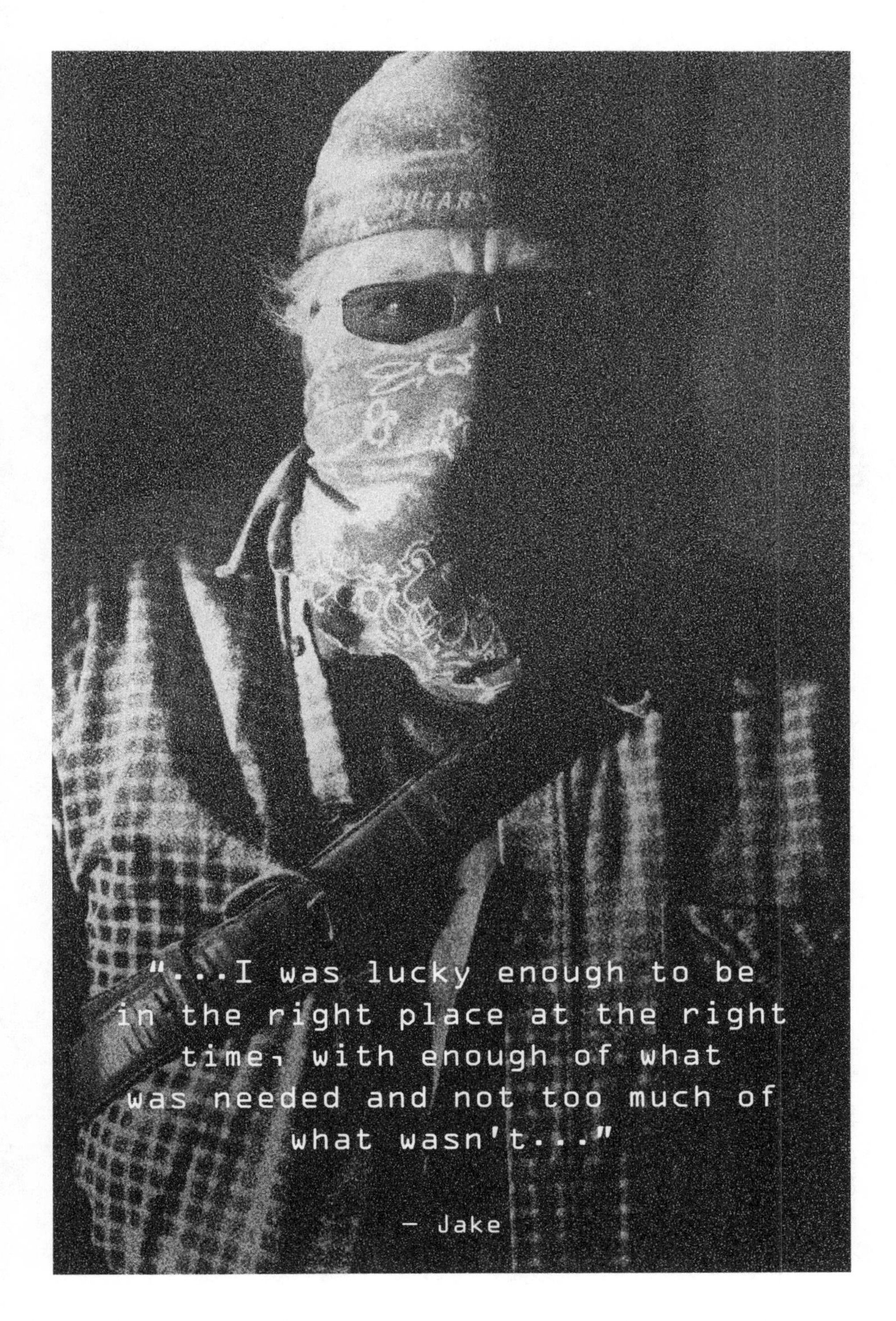
"...I was lucky enough to be
in the right place at the right
time, with enough of what
was needed and not too much of
what wasn't..."
— Jake

"...and we shall harvest the sun
just as we harvest the crops.
Across the vast wastelands of the
central plains. And there will
be abundance for all. This is the
promise. This is the future..."
— Presidential Speech: The Power Strip

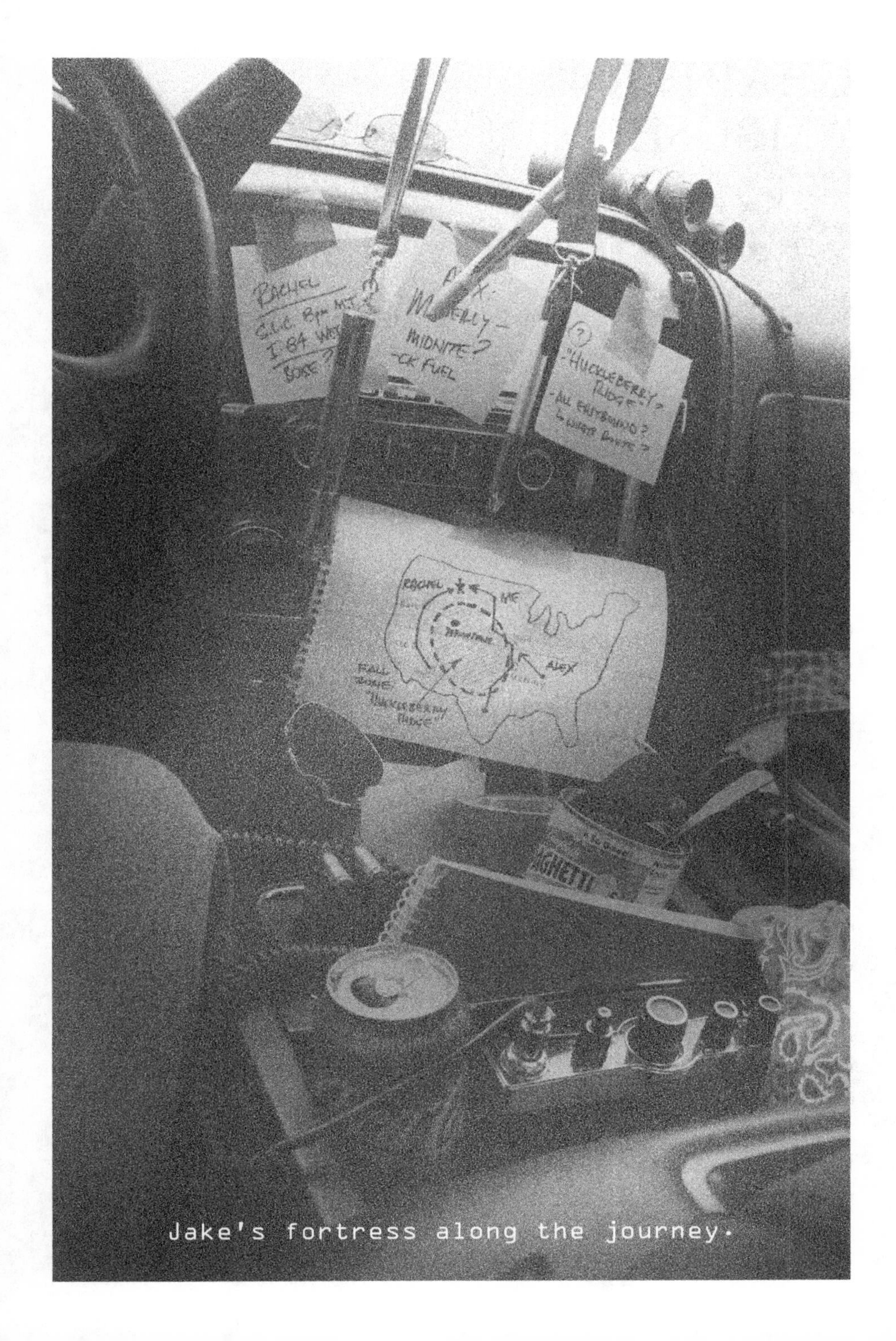

Jake's fortress along the journey.

CHAPTER 40: AMBUSH

Northbound from Jamestown, I decided it was time to move back onto the backroads. I'd been able to make good time on the main routes, but the heavy fall of ash was pushing the holdouts into evacuation mode, and the well-marked routes were being traveled by people who simply weren't prepared. Their only choices were roads with good signage, because most of them had no idea where they were without their onboard nav systems leading the way. I wanted to avoid all of those folks and their dead autobots.

In fact, by the time I'd reached South Dakota, most of the autobots had died off, littering the roadsides. I'd pushed a couple off the road in Nebraska, and South Dakota had raised the tally to around a dozen. I should have been marking the bodies on my fender, placing little lightning bolt icons to record my kills.

That heavy grill guard had come in handy a number of times. Saving me from the ambush in Blair and now, daily, to push the drained-battery vehicles out of the way.

The autobots were an interesting species of technology. When they were running out of power, most automatically cruised to the side of the road, as programmed, to die. Kind of like old dogs you read about in the storybooks of youth. They know their end is near, and so they wander off to be alone and not bring the danger of vultures and night creatures to their pack once they've passed. It's amazingly elegant in its rawness. It's a final act of taking care, doing their job. So, the autobots, knowing from their GPS locale that their end is near – and no charging port is within range – wander off the road, into a parking lot, or under a lamppost, to die. And there's such rich irony in the lamppost scenario. They were so close.

But without GPS systems, the autobots were lost, and most of their drivers were as well. Even those who knew how to drive, or once did. Whoever would have thought that in America, land of the classic tail fin, cruising the loop, parking with your best girl, and the entire car culture, the generations would devolve into this.

But there I was, pushing a couple of the newest heaps off of the road. Their thin alloy and plastic bodies gave easily to the force of my solid truck, and their thin little tires didn't put up a fight at all. There was no resistance of friction in their overly-hardened treads as I slid them to the side.

I knew why they were out there, mostly. The cars were likely on the road because the passengers had attempted to drive them. Overriding the system, most had no idea how to operate it – steer it, stop it, accelerate it. Each one I'd seen had been wrecked to some degree, run into a tree, a signpost, a bridge rail, something.

The complete lack of automotive knowledge started when the automakers began covering up the motors on the last series of fuel cars, allowing only the manufacturer's service techs to access the working components. On some, the oil didn't even need to be checked. All people knew was...fill it with gas and *GO*.

The autobots made it worse. Now, you just get in and go. You didn't even need any training or skill. No Driver's Education, no basic understanding of how the vehicle worked. All you had was a quick video tutorial of how the electronic entertainment gadgets operated. There were a lot of those.

I can't imagine not knowing how to drive, and drive well, on a performance level. But I was a dinosaur in that regard.

Today's barricade appeared to be made of an old wrecked Tesla missing its battery pack, a Zapper mini-truck, and a broken-down, gas-powered Saturn. I hadn't seen one of those in forever. The whole assortment was a bit odd, and I wondered how long the Tesla had been sitting there.

Long enough for someone to rip out the battery pack? That seemed unlikely.

I was deep into the country, running a road that paralleled the main highway. Maybe 2 miles off. I'd just passed an abandoned trailer house that looked like it might have made a decent meth lab once upon a time.

As I began to push the second vehicle away, I took a closer look at the Tesla. It looked like the battery pack had been ripped out long ago. Two of the side doors were off and the interior of the car was full of dirt and weeds. It hadn't just stalled out. Had it been dumped here? Or had it been placed here? I backed around, changing my view toward the old trailer.

A voice rang out. It came from the porch. "SHOOT HIM! GET THE TRUCK!" Shrill and pitched like a dog whistle, she was pretty direct with her instructions.

Who was she talking to? I looked around in all directions. A man had approached me from behind, carrying an old bolt-action rifle. He swept around to my side, about 30 yards out. I was stuck between him and the pile of cars.

"Damn, I can't just shoot him," he yelled back at her, his gaze still fixed on me.

"Hey, whoa...", I said. "You aren't gonna shoot anybody."

"Get him, baby. Get him!"

Wow, this woman was serious. We were only a few days into this, and this is what people were becoming? I had thought the incident at Blair was over the top. But these folks had really lost it.

"Look, man, just get out of the truck. You heard her." The man was shaking. He was probably about 40 but looked to be pretty well worn.

She was too far away for me to tell much about her, but both looked skinny and ragged.

"C'mon, you worthless piece of shit! Shoot him! Dumbass. Do it!" she barked.

"Hey, look man, I don't mean to cause any trouble." I was stalling for time and sliding my Glock out of the holster on the console. "I'm just a little lost."

"DO IT! Damn it. Loser!" she cried.

I decided I had been wrong. It probably was still a meth lab.

He continued to swing around toward the front of the truck, actually losing his advantage over me as he came out of my blind spot and fully into view. My Glock was resting in the corner of the lowered window, under my left arm. I could aim it by the laser. I placed the red dot on the center of his chest.

"I'm not giving up my truck, and I'd suggest you just move back." I kept my voice as calm and steady as possible.

He laughed, holding the gun at his hip, angled into the air.

"What's he sayin', baby?" the woman inquired.

"He's tellin' me to move back. You know, I'm tired of everybody tellin' me what to do!" He was really unstable, maybe drunk or high or both.

He wiped his left arm across his face and chambered a round in his gun, but he continued to hold it in a low awkward position. I guessed he was mimicking some movie he'd seen. If he shot at me, he was going to shoot from the hip and probably miss me. But he might get lucky. He continued to swing around. He was now directly out from my side window and a bit closer. Maybe he expected me to get out of the truck?

I scanned my laser dot across his body. Could I actually shoot someone? There's no way I could kill a person. Could I?

Maybe his knee – but he'd need to walk. Maybe his shoulder – but he'd need that for working, for growing food, which is likely something he hadn't considered yet. *Damn.* Either of those would still leave me at risk. Indecision is not your friend in this type of situation. And it was probably going to get me killed or horribly wounded.

The crazy lady on the porch continued to scream at him. Degrading him, cursing him. Demanding my death. And while I was beginning to actually fear for my life, I couldn't help but feel sorry for him. Was this his daily existence? Did she scream at him like this about everything? The unpainted house, the unkept yard, and what I observed to be a serious lack of finances. Had they simply smoked it all away? It looked like a pretty rough way to live.

In her tantrum, she let out another shrill, "SHOOT HIM!"

Spurred by her growing rage, he lurched toward the truck, taking a long fast stride, raising his gun until I saw the open end of the barrel.

Almost instinctively, I pulled the Glock from beneath my arm and squeezed the trigger.

As he moved, he was spinning, throwing his aim back toward the porch. The two shots came almost simultaneously. He continued his rotation and his face came back around to mine. He fixed his gaze on me as his body hit the side of the truck, the tip of his rifle scraping a long deep line in the door as he fell.

I looked toward the porch. Atop the rotted wood stairs I saw the bottom of her feet. A strip of her shirt hung from a snagged nail.

Once the echo of the shots had cleared from the pasture land around us, there was silence. No barking dog, no breeze, no bird in a tree. Just a deafening quiet that I'll never be able to erase from my mind.

I was numb. What if he hadn't shot her? What if he had dropped his gun just as I fired? I considered that as well. What if all of that had gone differently? Could I have left her as a witness? Could I have shot both of them? I just couldn't do it. All I could do was what I needed to do. All I could do was what I did – save myself and get away.

Getting out to move him would have been an opportunity for evidence to be left behind. My tracks would be covered in a deep layer of dust before anyone else drove this road. Even if someone had seen me, my truck had no license plates, no real means of identification, and there would be no manhunts. These individuals had chosen the course for all of us. I just happened to be the one that survived.

Maybe this is what war feels like to those in the field of battle. I won't pretend to have the heroic traits of a soldier, but even to be a hero, you've got to operate at a core that is pure and fundamental. Save your men, save your country, save yourself. Taking someone's life can't be fully gamed out in a simulation or model. The actions can, the logistics and the statistics can, but not the emotional impact. The games end, the simulation is studied, but the memories remain when it's the real thing. This was an all-too-clear understanding of some of the moments that Dad carried in his memory, from his frontline days in the war.

Through all of my childhood, my father was a loving, compassionate man, giving to his family and community. He was quick with a laugh, willing to provide some witty inspiration to any soul in need. He was a bright spot in many lives. And now I know how well he hid the dark pieces that most certainly lingered in his memory.

That small moment in time was so complex, and yet so simple. My worthy, loving wife was depending on me, and I was not going to fail her. Rachel was everything to me.

And that woman back at the trailer, she just wanted to take yet another thing from someone. My truck wasn't going to save her. Nothing was. Her countless wrong decisions had doomed her for a long time, I'm guessing. A fully stocked Chevy Silverado wasn't going to be her saving grace, and my death wasn't going to give her a second chance at anything but more failure. That was it. Cut and dried. And he was the willing henchman, doing her bidding as she mandated orders from her rotting throne of power on the porch.

When you listen to a news story, there is always time to contemplate "what if?" What if there were unforeseen circumstances that drove the situation? Was she always like that? Was she drunk, high, a lunatic? Maybe he was also. What would be 20 different ways to handle the situation, and how would each one play out in a 30-minute discussion of nuance and feelings and logic? What was their story, their history? And what were their childhood dreams? All of that is considered when the talking heads give their analysis. But, one single moment of reality was all I had.

I was in grave danger, threatened and at risk of having my life tragically altered. I did not threaten them. I did not approach them in any way, let alone in a manner that meant harm. Yet their only interest in me was to do harm. To kill me and take my property. That was the pure intent. That's why they had set a trap and waited to snare their victim. Those two individuals had threatened me. I defended myself.

They say the truth will set you free, and I fully understand that now. I found peace with it, and it only took me about 20 minutes to do so. Their lives had ended long before I drove up that road. I had other things to focus on. I was going to Montana, and nothing was going to stop me. •

CHAPTER 41: MINOT ON THE HORIZON

Highway 52 ran at a perfect angle for my route. If every road in the land had run at this northwestern slant, my trip would have been much easier. The evenly spaced little towns were reminders of the railroad days, originally placed as water stops for the steam locomotives that first brought commercial transportation to this part of the world. And I didn't worry about herds of buffalo much, as the maps all showed a long, wide reservoir, created by damming the Missouri River in the center of the state. The massive body of water snaked clear back to Montana, a barrier to the escaping wildlife. Hopefully the grasslands on its western side would provide them with a new home while theirs recovered.

The drive across North Dakota was pretty lackluster. I'd been on this same road before, years ago when Alex was working a tour. The summer circuit had taken him in a circle of the entire Midwest, hitting any town that had a decent-size venue. We'd been making a road trip to Montana and thought, "What the heck, it's only 600 miles out of the way. We'll surprise him at Minot. Why not?"

The landscape was, as I remembered, smooth and level, without much visual interest. But wide-open space certainly has its own allure. The vast horizons have a draw. It's like crossing a canvas that's yet to be painted. It allows your mind to open up to possibilities. It had a calming influence, and I'll admit I liked it.

The maps showed a pockmarked surface teaming with small ponds and lakes and sloughs. Remnants of the last glacial age.

Ancient glaciers had smoothed the land into flat plains, pushing the higher levels further south and cutting through to the rocky strata that now revealed itself through the top soil in many places. As the ice withdrew, over millions of years, the remaining "puddles" of melted water created the lakes that cover Minnesota. The Red Lakes area in far north Minnesota is an incredible example of that geologic history, remaining as the largest puddles from that age. And the North Dakota region has much of the same water-filled divots; it just lacks the soils necessary to grow the tall pines seen further east. It's an amazing study, how our great land came to be. The richness of the soil across the agricultural belt, the grandeur of the Rockies as they stretch from border to border, all formed through the incredible power of nature. And we saw it unleashed once again in this massive event. As I grow older, I am more and more in awe of the world in which we live.

Over the past few days, I had witnessed more of this country than most ever will. Maybe I should have felt more honored. Maybe I should have been more proud. But mostly, I was just focused on covering the distance.

As I got closer to Minot, I heard more and more chatter about military convoys heading west into Montana and down into the evacuation zones. I was hoping to tag along with one of these groups, but I didn't know how I was going to accomplish that. Most likely, I'd be rejected and turned away, per some safe-at-home orders that would point me back to Texas or Iowa. I was still working that part of my plan.

I picked up Highway 2 at Berthold, about 20 miles west of Minot. I saw signs for the Minot Airforce Base, which put a few things in perspective. If Minot was far enough outside the dense ash plumes, they could get cargo planes in and out, helping to supply the ground effort and quicken the logistics. They'd also have control centers, hangers, barracks, and support systems, like kitchens, food storage, and more, already in place. It was a very logical place to mount this type of operation.

All I wanted was to drive along with the flow of westward vehicles originating from Minot. I didn't need any of their supplies or resources, just access to the route. Surely there would be gaps. I'd just run in a gap.

•

CHAPTER 42: IN THE ARMY NOW

I decided that, even as a rescue operation, the military would have surveillance as part of their standard security protocol. So sneaking up on them wasn't going to go over well. My first idea had been to just jump on Highway 2 and head west, with the whole "forgiveness versus permission" concept. Maybe it would have worked, but I thought better of it. I pointed the truck east and looked for the first roadblock. A small group of old Hummers sat at the first exit I encountered.

"Whoa," waved the first soldier as I slowed to a stop behind their barricade. "Where did YOU come from?"

There were two other guys at the front of one of the Hummers. A thick paperboard box sat on the hood. They appeared to be eating sandwiches. Maybe it was lunchtime. By this point in the journey, I had lost nearly all track of time. But it reminded me, I needed to put another can of SpaghettiOs on the motor to cook.

"Hi. I'm actually headed west, but I wanted to get permission to use your highway," I offered, as honestly and concisely as I could word it.

"Canada, eh?" he motioned to my big red "C" on the front fender.

"Well, sort of, via Montana if possible." I didn't want to go any farther north than I had to. Highway 2 was pretty much the top of the world as far as American highways were concerned. Beyond that, I would be up in Canada. That would mean more distance to cover, using more fuel, and adding unknown issues. They could restrict what I was carrying, who knows. I really wanted to stay in the States.

"Well, first thing, we're gonna have to take you in to see the sergeant."

"He just came back from the west, clearing the road. He's gonna be surprised to hear that's where you came from."

That probably wasn't good. I was rethinking my idea; I probably should have just gone ahead and begged forgiveness.

The soldier pointed me toward the eastbound on-ramp and shouted, "Stay right behind me." I thought that was pretty trusting. In the dust cloud, I could have turned off almost anywhere and lost him, but this wasn't a county sheriff, without backup outside of my home town. This was the U.S. Army, and I didn't really want to piss them off.

It took about 10 minutes to reach the gate at the edge of the airfield. It opened as we approached, and a guard waved us through. We rolled up next to a long brick building and came to a stop. Two big generator trailers sat humming down at the corner of the building, with thick black cables running into the building through an old ventilation fan.

The soldier signaled me to pull into the Visitors parking space. "He'll get a kick out of that," he said as we got out and walked to the double-door entrance.

There weren't any guards at the door, and we stepped right in. The space looked to be an old gymnasium, circa 1950s, with dark wood strip floors and basketball hoops cranked up out of the way. The lines on the floor had seen a lot of use, but you could still tell where the center court circle was, and the free-throw lines. It was a flashback to my earliest basketball days. "Cool," I said, unable to stop myself from responding at the sight.

"Sergeant. A visitor," said the soldier, with the crispness I'd expected.

"So exactly where did you come from?" asked the sergeant. He was probably my age, but he was remarkably fit and lean. He was perfectly cast in his part, and he left no doubt who was playing the alpha role in the room. He was looking through some notes, and his eyes had yet to look my direction. "They say you're marked for Canada."

“Yes sir. The crimson ‘C’. That was a bit of a misunderstanding. I’m coming from Iowa. I need to get to Kalispell, Montana. To meet my wife.”

“Ha! ‘Crimson C’. That’s funny,” he chuckled. I wasn’t sure if he’d even heard the rest of my statement. He finally looked at me. “So, you’re coming from Texas?”

Texas? I hadn’t said anything about Texas. I’d taken the license plates off the truck. They were stashed in the back. One thing for sure, I was glad that I hadn’t put on any fake Official tags. I’d have a hard time explaining that.

But how could he know I was coming from Texas. I hadn’t even said “Y’all” or anything. My pause was noticed. He continued to fill the silence.

“Toll tag, up behind your mirror. Shows an outline of Texas. Hard to miss. Easy to recognize. The boys said you’d ditched your plates.”

“Wow. Yes, I used to live in Texas, but we’re in the middle of moving to Montana. My wife...” I was cut off mid-sentence.

“Your wife is already there, so you’re driving through the largest volcanic eruption the world has seen in a millennium, just to be with her? Is that your story? You’re either the most romantic husband in history, or you’ve got other motives. That’s where I’m placing my bet right now.” He nodded at the soldier who’d delivered me, and the young man turned and left the building.

We were in a nest of folding tables, communication cables, and screens. All around the gym, small groups of people, dressed in light camo, were making lists on marker boards and chatting in their circles. A large canvas tarp was strapped tightly in front of what might have been a small stage curtain. Multiple projectors were shooting images of maps, weather radar, and satellite images onto the big fabric screen. Obviously this was a logistics hub.

"Nice setup," I offered, looking around in detail for the first time. Looking more closely at the large screen, I saw it was tied to a small truss at the top, with grommets and short ties. Another strip of truss was tagged to the bottom, used as a weight to keep the screen smooth and taught. "Great rigging."

"So let me tell you what I know, then you can fill in the spaces," the sergeant said, marking a clipboard and handing it back to a woman sitting behind a row of monitors.

"You're on the wrong side of the country, no license plates, your truck is beat to hell, and you've got a worthless computer screen and two empty gas jugs hanging off the back...like some low-rent looter's bait. Inside, you've got a pistol slotted in your dash and a stub shotgun holstered in your console. And I'm guessing you've got enough ammo to reload them more than once. You're wired with an old CB radio and you're carrying what appears to be enough fuel to get you to Alaska. It looks like you're on the run, possibly using this event as cover. How am I doing?"

"Well sir, you were good until right at the end." His guys had obviously looked me over much more closely than I thought, and he'd been given the details before I'd ever arrived at his Visitor parking spot.

"I am certainly on the wrong side of the country. I should have passed through Colorado three days ago, on the way to our cabin in Montana. I was at my folks, in Iowa. My wife, the last I talked to her, was outside Salt Lake City. She said she'd see me at the lake. Then the call dropped." I could feel my face tense, my chin was quivering. I tried to keep it together, to maintain my own version of military coolness, but I couldn't do it. I was exhausted. I had been so tightly wound for so many hours. This emotional breakdown had been building for a while.

"I grew up outside Cedar Falls. Where in Iowa are you from?" his voice had softened a bit. Another Iowa boy.

"I'm from Casey," I said. "It's pretty small, but everybody always remembers the..."

“Happy Face water tower in Adair?” he finished my sentence.

“Yeah, right there on I-80.”

“I’ve been to both. You guys made your fair share of state tournaments if I recall. Did you play ball?”

“I tried to,” I replied.

“Haha. Let’s see what we can do. Take a seat. Over there.”

He motioned to a small section of bleachers that had been pulled out, mostly as a bench for coolers and boxes of snacks. Further down, another section had been pulled out and an assortment of backpacks were scattered on the rows. A couple of soldiers were taking naps, or just taking a break, laying on the stepped wooden seats. I heard a large jet land on the runway. I’d forgotten it was just outside the building.

“That’s the next one,” hollered a man from one of the work groups.

The two soldiers that had been laying on the bleachers were up lacing their boots before I could even react. They walked quickly through the assemblies of workers and gathered printouts and clipboards. All of the visuals on the big screen changed and four large maps went up in their place. Routes were marked in varying colors, some of the lines extended as far as Casper.

Casper would have been about 250 miles from the center of Yellowstone. An egg-shaped mass was overlaid onto the map. The top of it centered on Yellowstone and expanded out to the southeast. It was a dark gray, almost black, but I could see some detail of the map through the overlay. Another larger egg shape expanded a bit from the top of the shape, but mostly in the direction of Casper. It was red, and I assumed that wasn’t good.

The sergeant returned, alongside an older man with bars and stripes and a lot of other decor on his uniform. “Shit,” I said to myself. •

CHAPTER 43: NO NEGOTIATION

"The sergeant tells me you've come all the way from Texas to see us," the man said, extending a hand. "I'm from Tyler. Maybe we've met?"

He continued, which was fine, because I didn't really have much to say. I was thrilled with his demeanor however, as the situation could have easily swung the other way.

"Sarg tells me you can drive, based on your rig and the fact that...well... you're here." He nodded in agreement to himself. "So I've got a deal that you can't pass up. And I do mean that. You can't pass on this." And he nodded again.

"Alright, I can certainly..." I started to agree with him, but it was unnecessary as he simply took a breath and continued his banter.

"We've got routes working to Billings. That was our first impact point and we're expanding that out. So we need to put our folks and gear on the road to Casper. That's the edge of the lifeline. By the way, there will be no photos, not in here, not outside, not along the route. Do you understand that?" He stopped, this time waiting for a solid answer.

"Yes. Sure. Whatever I need to do. Of course." I hadn't taken any photos of anything to this point and hadn't even thought about it. It seemed like a pretty easy request.

"We need to put everything we've got on the road to Casper," he repeated, which made me wonder how much rest he'd had in the past few days. Assuming they'd all been deployed elsewhere, they're all probably into multiple days without sleep. "But we've got a generator station that needs to stage at Wolf Point. You familiar with Wolf Point?"

"No. No sir, I'm not."

"Wolf Point is on Highway 2. Corporal, bring it up on screen four, Wolf Point," he raised his voice for the room to hear. The lower corner of the big screen flashed, an outline of Colorado disappeared, and a new image came up showing an inset map from northern Montana. He continued, "Wolf Point. 223 miles from here, Minot. And 243 miles from Lewiston, Montana, which is here." He broke the projector beam with his finger to mark a point on the map.

"Do you know why?" He paused again, raising his eyebrows and looking directly at me. He shifted his stance. This time, he was expecting a reply.

I started processing it out loud. "Approximately 250 miles to either place, just a little less actually. But it's in the middle." I looked at the markings on the map. Evidently this was a test for something, and I needed to pass.

My contemplation continued, "Electric vehicle range is around 250 miles these days, so maybe you're staging an evacuation route. Maybe a secondary supply route for civilian trucks?" I paused. "But they'd need diesel," I mumbled to myself. "So maybe it's both? That makes sense. It's outside all of the rings your map showed. The red, orange, and yellow. It's in the blue zone. It would be the start of a route over the top. It could be a reconnection route for the coasts, maybe. That's just a guess."

"Good guess." The sergeant seemed happy with my response. He turned to his superior. "Thoughts?"

"Have you ever been to Australia?" the man asked. •

CHAPTER 44: AUSSIE OUTBACK

Both men walked past me to the side entrance. I followed because it seemed like the right thing to do. Outside on the tarmac, a C-130 transport was dropping its rear ramp. Trucks and trailers were staged behind it with more rolling up.

"Everything below us...meaning south...is being evacuated east. We're flanking it and bringing in support from the top. The target is Casper. That's the western edge."

"Do you mean 'eastern' edge? The gray circle?" I pondered.

They looked at each other for a moment.

"There's nothing in the gray circle," the sergeant responded. There was a single moment of silence that coursed through the air. It was a statement that stunned my senses. Even with their military training and professional aire, I could tell they were impacted as well.

"All rescue and recovery will be from that edge outward." His look was flat, the trained factual expression of truth. Solemn, but I could see a glisten in the corner of his eye. He was human.

"We need to drop a generator and fueling station at Wolf Point, but that means two troops and a chase vehicle. That would be required for the return. We can't just leave somebody out there. But it's a waste of manpower." The man in charge looked back at his sergeant.

"So, we'll set you up with the gear, load your truck, you make the drop, unload, and keep going west. It gets you down the road. And it saves our folks for the bigger picture." There was a slight pause. "Or you go to Canada."

That worked for me. Plus it would save me 200 miles worth of fuel. This was a no-brainer. "Yes sir. That works for me."

A young female soldier appeared at my side. "Keys?" She was right to the point.

I dug in my pocket and fished out my truck keys. "The remote is..."

"She's got it," said the sergeant. "She can tear down the motor and advance the cam if you need her to. Grab a bite. Tell the guy in the yellow hat to set up a cooler for you. Wash up and get some sleep. Back here at O-six-hundred."

"Yes sir." My voice had automatically assumed the staccato tone they all used. It wasn't with sarcasm, and it wasn't really intentional. It just seemed like the proper response.

Six o'clock in the morning seemed like an eternity. I hadn't had that much sleep in days, and I hadn't had the sense of security I felt around these people. They had a plan, a plan more thought out and detailed than mine, and it gave me reassurance about my thoughts, my plans, my intentions. I slept well.

Fifteen minutes early, I was back in place. The night before, I'd washed my face, turning the paper towels black with residue. I camped out on the bleachers for a while before checking in, watching the screens and radars and maps flash by as the teams worked through the night. Yellow Hat had given me a wrapped sandwich to snack on, ham and cheese, with an apple. The cooler was a thick paperboard box with a formed lid and indentions for handles. It held a few bottles of water, an apple, and four cans with pop-top lids.

"MREs" he said.

"Like SpaghettiOs?" I asked.

"Kind of. Maybe." He seemed amused by my question. "The cooler. Use it for as long as you can. It's strong enough to sit on. It's lined with foil and you can make a solar oven. Then you can burn it. Good fire starter."

"Nice." That made more sense than a plastic or Styrofoam container. I could see using it in a number of ways. I remembered the kid from the craft store and the whole "paper or plastic" incident. Justice.

"Is there suppose to be ice? In the 'cooler'?" I asked.

"Well, that's the irony. No. No ice."

The young woman reappeared with a different set of keys, really more of a T-shaped remote. She handed it to me and motioned toward the door. I grabbed my cooler and followed.

"Have you ever been to Australia?" she asked as we reached the door.

"No. The other guy asked me that." And it suddenly became apparent what they were talking about. There was my truck, on the fourth trailer in the chain.

At the front was a military issue semi-tractor with offroad tires 4-feet tall. It was a six-wheeler, coated with standard flat Army green. A Pantone 7498 color match. The military had always been pretty specific on its colors and patterns.

Directly behind was a tanker trailer, containing maybe 1,000 gallons of diesel, or it could have been more. Trailing that, a Caterpillar twin gen-set system with a small control room and towering stacks. The third trailer was a flatbed, strapped with crates and cables and smaller generators. Among the green and brown containers I saw two bright red charging stations with chrome logos: "Tesla." A fourth trailer carried my truck.

"Your truck's on the back. When you get to Wolf Point...here, check this map. This is the drop point. Do you see this? Check the sat image. Do you see? Exactly here?"

"Yes, yes. I see it." I was overwhelmed at the detail, the planning, the rig, it was just...overwhelming.

"You won't be able to turn around. Obviously. So you'll need to be exact on this route. Can you follow a map?" she asked.

I laughed. "Sorry, didn't mean to laugh at that. I've been following maps for a long time now. Yes."

Just leave the entire rig at the staging point. It's 36 feet off the road, on the left side. You'll leave the road driving west on the eastbound side. Do you understand that?"

"Yes, yes, it's on the left side."

"On the sat image. Do you see exactly where that road is?"

"Yes, yes, I see it." Geez, this lady was going to make a great parent some day.

She walked me to the back of the last trailer. "The ramps pull out from the floor. This is NOT a U-Haul, but it has some similar features. Just a lot bigger. The tire straps are the same. Have you used anything like that before?"

"Yes, yes. I used to be a classic car guy, so trailering cars, I've done a lot of that."

"Oh, cool. My grandpa had a '69 Chevelle! We rebuilt the motor together. A 396 big block with a double-pumper Holley. With a 4-speed. It'd haul ass, you know?" Suddenly the girl had something to say. We just needed to find her topic.

"Exactly. Yes! I love the Chevelles from that period. Awesome that you worked on it with him. Does he still have it?" It was nice to have a normal conversation with someone on a topic of mutual interest.

"He passed away. Just after the holidays. My dad has it now." I could see her tough shell had some soft spots as well.

"I'm so sorry. But I'm really happy for the memories you built with him. Always keep those close in your heart." I was thinking of Alex and the projects we'd done together. He grew up too far away from any grandparents to really experience much with them. That was too bad. But I was happy for this young lady – and she'd turned those experiences into a career path, so good for her.

"What's my speed in this? Braking distance? I've driven a lot of things, big farm equipment. You know, combines, wide disks, applicators. But..." Again I was feeling overwhelmed. We'd been walking beside it for awhile and it just never stopped. It was about a city-block long. "I'm gonna need some instructions."

We walked around to the cab door, and she stepped up on the ladder. "Take your seat," she said as she stepped back onto the side tank, giving me plenty of room to pass.

"Air brakes, power steering, and automatic transmission, so no shifting required. Not much different from your truck, really. We'll take you back to the highway and point you west. Then you just keep it between the lines until you get to Wolf Point. At Wolf Point you...." she paused and looked at me, waiting for the rest of the sentence.

"Move over into the eastbound lane, and pull off into the spot shown on the picture. It's about 36 feet off the road. On the left. I leave the whole rig there and unload my truck. National Guard will set it up after it arrives." I was pretty proud and she gave me a smile of approval. "The key. Where do I leave the key?"

"That's a great question. We never leave these sitting around. Where would you put it if you were doing this?" she asked. It was a good question. I felt like I was adding something to the process.

"Well," I thought for a minute. "People may try to steal the fuel, the batteries, stuff off the motor, the interior, the radios...."

"Oh, the radios." She looked back to a group loading other vehicles. "Marcus, you need to get the radios out of here!" She turned back to me, "Sorry, no radios for you. Could be classified."

"Man, I hadn't even thought about..." I started to say.

"There's a lot that hasn't been thought about. We like to think that we've covered everything, but every situation has snags. You know?"

I knew. In the past week, I'd stolen a tanker, trashed a town in Nebraska, and shot a man. "Yeah. Snags. I know."

The mechanic ran over and spun some knobs on the mounts, unclipped some wires, and within a minute, no radios.

"When he pulled the radios, you see that air duct, that flex tube under the dash?" I pointed to the black flexible tubing behind where the radios used to sit. "I'll push the key through the vent and just leave it unlocked. Might as well save the glass, so nobody breaks it out trying to get in. Your guys can just pull the vent tube and grab the key. It'll slide back on."

"Good answer," she gleamed. "I'll put that in the brief." •

CHAPTER 45: ON THE ROAD AGAIN

After a few more minutes of instruction we were headed back to the highway. I rode with another soldier who was bright and friendly, and who had a lot of experience driving these super-long rigs.

"They call these road trains in Australia," he said, talking above the whine of the turbo diesel motor. "You're gonna be right at 170 feet. We usually run three trailers, but your truck added a fourth. You'll be alright. Steady is the key. Easy. Steady. Nobody's in a hurry here."

I don't think we reached more than a few miles per hour on the road between the base and highway. Each corner had been well thought out and I could see how the roads had been built with these in mind.

"This is all built for this, isn't it?" I asked, referring to the sweep of the entrance ramp and degree of the turns.

"Yep, years ago. Way back," he said. He pointed to the bottom of the bridge, toward the top of the pillars. "Do you see those blocks? They look like steel cinder blocks, between the pillars and the crossbeams?"

"Yes." It looked like a little stack of spacers or shock-absorbing blocks. I remembered these from when I was a kid. They had a big construction project all along Interstate 80, outside of my home town. They jacked up all of the bridges that crossed over the interstate and added those blocks. I'd forgotten all about that. "So they could run taller trucks," I was proud of my answer.

"No, so that the new Intercontinental Ballistic Missiles could be transported without hitting the bridges," he said. "The interstate system was built primarily for military purposes. Transportation for commerce was just a broader long-term benefit."

I'd known that too, I remembered. Some article somewhere. That was started back during Eisenhower, yes I knew that, but what's with the little blocks?

He continued, "When they built the newer ICBMs, they had to be able to transport them around the country, to the silos, the launch sites, wherever they might be needed. And the bridges were too low. So they had to raise them. All of them. Gotta work the plan, you know."

An old Hummer pulled up next to us as we stopped on the highway. "This is where I get out," he said. "At 40 miles per hour, it'll take you about a half-mile to stop. And you'll want to stop easy. When you hit the brakes, the trailers will brake in sequence from back to front. It'll keep you straight."

"And, if they don't? If they don't brake in sequence? What happens then?" I asked.

He smiled. "Slow. Easy. Steady. Good luck."

I suppose I could have stolen the whole thing and taken it all the way to Kalispell, but they'd photocopied my driver's license, photographed me from three angles, retina-scanned, and finger-printed me.

When they finished the retina scan, I had asked, "Will you be drawing any blood?" I'd thought it was sort of funny, and not a bad question.

The guy had looked at me, somewhat puzzled by the question. "No. Why would we do that?"

The two soldiers stood beside their Humvee and watched me depart. I released the brake lever and slowly pushed the accelerator. The turbo whined and the cab twisted to the right, raising on the front suspension. I could feel each of the connections engage, from the truck to the first trailer, then the second, then the third, then the last one, where my truck dangled from the end of this spectacle. More than half the length of a football field. It was hard to grasp.

Traveling right at 40 miles per hour, I figured it would take me about six hours to get to Wolf Point. Barring any issues. •

CHAPTER 46: HIGH ROLLER

There's a line that appears in bodies of water, where the saltwater from the ocean mixes with the river water, creating a brackish mix of the two. Outside of Glacier National Park, there's a point where two rivers converge, one carrying beautiful blue tones, the other more pink, both toned from the granite particles carried from their cutting paths higher up in the mountains. It's yet another glorious view of our incredible world, God's masterpiece of creation.

While water seems so soft, it has incredible power and strength, cutting grooves, valleys, and canyons from solid rock. It just takes time and motion and more time. The clock of the earth is not interested in man's timeframe or sense of urgency. We will be here for a split-second, then we'll be gone. Nature will continue on until the sun eventually overtakes our blue planet. Eons from now, it may all start again, another breath of creation, another start, perhaps in another place.

Driving west from Minot was a peaceful return to my start in Texas. The morning I had begun my journey, thinking about the positive future that lie ahead, the miles had rolled beneath me in silence. My mind was full of thoughts and dreams of the life Rachel and I were continuing, in another chapter. Then nature had given us a surprise, upending our plans and putting us in a very serious race for our lives. I knew she was suffering turmoil on her side of the Rockies, probably scavenging fuel and wondering where I was. On this side, I was clearly beyond any of my expectations and plans, sitting high in the cab of an Army road train, heading for Wolf Point.

But eventually, as the streams mix and the sediment falls from the slowing water, it all becomes crystal clear and pure. I hoped our lives would follow the waters' lead.

And in the sky, I had the defined line of saturated gray ash and clear blue skies. North of me, probably miles across the Canadian border, the edge of the ash stopped, and a bright strip of blue extended down to the horizon. North of there, the skies would be as crisp as any other spring morning. I wondered how the systems failure here might affect the people there. Maybe significantly or maybe not much at all. It was hard to believe that in some places, life was moving along with normalcy.

Ahead of me, to the left, was darkness. I was still about 500 miles from the center of Yellowstone, but as the gray circle on the map showed, the devastation was broad. The maps I'd seen on the screen as I sat on the bleachers the night before showed more than 200 miles to the southeast were assumed to be completely decimated. I also knew that the refinery fires in Billings were adding to the darkness in the sky. They were only 300 miles out.

I'd driven through Billings many times and had spent the night there more than once. It likely wouldn't make many Top 10 lists for cities in America. It wasn't a mecca for finance or insurance, certainly not a center of high tech, and probably pretty mainstream when it came to education. The refinery jobs would have been good paying, but the ladders would have only gone so high, and any media coverage from the coasts would have given it negative marks simply for its role in the fossil fuel industry. However, its proximity to Yellowstone and the surrounding areas made for a unique and special setting. Any family who favored the outdoor lifestyle would enjoy every facet imaginable. The summers would offer hiking, biking, hunting, fishing, and more, while the winter would offer its array of activities, from snowmobiling to skiing. It was probably a pretty cool place to live.

Based on the overlay rings, Billings was just outside the gray, centered in the red zone that would be a dice roll for most of the inhabitants. Those making it out would be chasing I-94, becoming part of the stream of humanity I'd crossed the day before. Some may be continuing more north, toward Williston, my first checkpoint on today's drive.

Three hours out from Minot, I arrived in Williston, following my

40-mile-per-hour cruising speed limitation. And looking back in the mirror at the endless line of trailers that followed me, it was fast enough.

Williston sat almost on the border between North Dakota and Montana, and I was looking forward to putting my feet on the ground in Montana. The checkpoint on my highly detailed map showed I'd be stopping outside of town, close to the airport.

As I approached the small city, coming in from the northern side, I spotted an unending line of medevac choppers in the air, lowering into what appeared to be the city's airport. There was a sea of tents and trailers assembled and each of the landings was causing a flurry of activity. My guess was a mobile medical unit, kind of a M.A.S.H. operation. It could be served by the base at Minot and cover the area spanning from north Yellowstone, across Billings and down to Casper. A line of helicopters filled the airfield's taxiways, ranging from the big twin-rotor jobs, the old Hueys and Jet Ranger medevac units to the new quad-rotor First Impact search-and-rescue copters.

I tried to count the number of helicopters coming in on approach, but there were just too many. It was distracting to watch, and I had to get my mind back on my driving.

One of the quad-rotors buzzed out across my rig as I came down into the edge of town. It was sleek and futuristic, looking like an oversized drone that a kid would fly via remote control. I'd watched a documentary on those and it was fascinating. One of the units they showed had jet-fighter-style pods hanging under it for controls and equipment. The pilot could hover the craft and lower two pods down on a cable. In the forest fire simulation, he was safe in his pod until he reached the ground. The craft stayed in place on autopilot until the pilot popped open his encasement and freed a trapped fire fighter, placing him in the pod alongside his. They had showed the same process for a water rescue, with the small craft launching from a Coast Guard ship.

Following the quad, a twin-rotor was taking off and heading south as I pulled into the checkpoint.

"Not in convoy?" the man asked, stepping up onto the platform outside the door. He was wearing the same light camo gear I'd seen back in Minot, but he had an added face mask to help reduce breathing in the fine silt of ash that hung in the air. It muffled his voice a bit. The checkpoint consisted of barricaded lanes of the highway, funneling me down to a single lane that passed between a row of tents, protected by concrete barriers. A simple red and white striped board was all that actually blocked the road.

"I'm headed to Wolf Point. They told me to give you this." I handed the soldier the envelope and tags I'd been given by the sergeant. He pulled two sheets of paper from the envelope. The first page basically said that I was on a contract mission to deliver the contents of the rig to Wolf Point. The second page said that I should not be delayed or questioned about my mission. It was stamped "Critical" and initialed by a number of people. A three-star shape had been stamped into the top right corner of the letter with an embossing tool.

"So, you're our special package. They didn't think you'd be on schedule, but look at you. Three hours on the dot." He took the papers and motioned for me to sit tight for a minute. He stepped over the concrete wall into one of the canvas shelters. The soldier at the barricade gave me a nod of greeting. He was dressed to match the first guy, and with the face masks on, they were nearly identical twins. I waved from high atop my perch. It was actually kind of fun when I look back at it.

In an instant, the guy was back beside my window. "Alright, you're good," he said, waving for the second man to lift the barricade. The truck began to shudder and he lost his footings on the steps, slipping down to the ground.

"I'm sorry," I called out, thinking I'd slipped off the brakes or done something to lurch the truck forward. But I hadn't done anything.

I looked around at the controls, taking my hands off of the steering wheel and searching the dash and levers for an answer. It felt like another buffalo herd was approaching.

Outside, I saw the man holding onto the barricade as the end of it swung up into the air, acting on its own. I saw the canvas on the tents waving in a rhythm that looked like water. It was an earthquake or aftershock of some type. I pulled the brake lever tight, hoping to keep the train aligned in the queue.

The vibrations lasted just a few seconds, then passed. I looked down at the soldier who'd managed to slide safely to the ground between the truck and the wall.

"Had one of those yesterday," he remarked. "Hope they're about done." He waved again at the barricade guy, and the board went up.

"Thank you!" I called out to both of them. I received two hands up as I pulled through the little canyon of concrete.

I looked over at my own map, what I'd been working from before I became all official and everything. I saw the green dotted line running beside Highway 2 – another scenic route. An hour past Williston, the highway began to parallel the Missouri River once again. It was a scenic drive.

In some places I could see the river and the opposite bank. I noticed a lot of wildlife, deer and antelope, drinking at the edge, likely pushed north seeking food and water and safety. The river had become a natural barrier for them. At a low point in the road, I saw movement along the left edge. I started applying the brakes. They had told me it would take a half mile to stop, and it took every bit of it.

A group of elk, maybe a dozen or so, were crossing the road. They'd made it across the river and were heading farther north. The last one stopped to look at me. He was tall and majestic, the top of his head even with the top of my hood. Was he scared? Did he feel anxious? Or was this just another day of survival in nature?

Some people spend their entire lives thinking they are victims. But I think the truth is that we all have it easy. We can change our circumstances, move to other places, educate ourselves, and choose different jobs. The elk didn't have any choice that day, but he was holding his head high, taking a bold course of action. I remembered the beautiful elk we'd seen in Yellowstone. I tipped my hand to him as he passed, "Good lucky, buddy," I called out.

I'd be at Wolf Point within the hour. I was going to crawl through there at about 2 miles per hour, so I wouldn't miss my turnoff. What an embarrassment that could be. As the young lady had said, "You can't turn it around." •

CHAPTER 47: WOLF POINT

At the intersection of Highway 13, I stopped to make a final review of my maps and photos. Wolf Point was just 7 miles up the road and I needed to be spot on. My instructions were to pass most of the way through town. On the western edge, I'd see the Agland Cooperative, a grain elevator, on the left side of the road. I was to cross through its gravel lot and continue out the west side of the property into the grass median area that would place my train between the roadway and the actual railroad tracks that served the elevator. The local high school was adjacent to the location, which could be used for other purposes if the military needed.

I'd have one shot at getting this, as the satellite images showed I had no exit from the location. I was driving into a dead end. A perfect location for their needs but it was making me nervous. Maybe 2 miles per hour was going to be too fast.

The photos of the route they'd reviewed with me were extremely accurate, and I felt as if I was familiar with the town as I slowly moved down its main street. The church, the park, a car dealership, McDonald's – just two more blocks to go. I could see the grain bins, the tallest structures in town. There might have been a few people out and about, but I only recall one pickup truck. I was pretty focused on my destination.

Ahead was a nice red Ram pickup with a water barrel in the back. He slowed and pulled off to the side as I swung over into his lane. They had told me to cross over into the eastbound lane, so I was just following orders. He didn't shake his fist or give me the finger or anything. He just looked kind of amazed as my monster of a machine cruised by.

I found my target sign – "Agland Cooperative." Just a few hundred feet more, and I was there. I snaked between the building and two grain wagons, parked next to the highway. There was no turning back. Even at this snail's pace, it seemed my mind was on hyper-drive. There was the end of the lot. It turned to grass, lined with some small pine trees, the railroad on my left, and the high school. Yes, this was it.

I stopped when I thought that I was 36 feet from both the edge of the road and the edge of the railroad tracks. The positioning of this portable recharge/refuel station was brilliant. The distances from Point A to Point B, the placement between a highway and a railroad. Obviously the intention was to bring in replacement fuel via rail. Ingenious, actually. I was impressed. I'm usually pretty quick to complain about government expenditures, but the team on this project was earning their pay. I set the brake and jumped down off of the platform.

Taking a quick surveillance lap, it was like walking around a ballfield. I checked the trailers, tires, connections, and tie-downs. It all looked good. I just needed to unload my truck, grab my cooler and stuff from the cab, and push the key down into the vent. The National Guard would be along to put it into operation. I was pretty proud, and for the first time in this journey, I felt like I'd actually done something good for someone else. I smiled and patted one of the tires.

The red pickup found me and pulled off on the shoulder of the highway.

"What the hell is that?" asked the man, weaving his way through the pine trees, brushing the last branch from his face.

"Recharging station," I offered. I hadn't been briefed on what to say or not say and I guess I thought the place would be deserted. "The National Guard will set it up."

"How do you turn that rig around?" It seemed to be the most obvious question from anyone seeing one of these things.

"I have no idea," I said. "Can you give me a hand with these ramps?"

The ramps on my truck's trailer were slotted in under the main floor, latched in place like long thin drawers that would pull out and drop down on the end. I could drop them myself, but I wanted to put them back in their slots after unloading my truck. It just seemed safer and more complete.

I was unlatching the tire straps as he came around to my side. He looked up at my truck, noticing the wheels and tires and other accessories. It was apparent that it wasn't military grade.

"Are you civilian?" he asked. "The rig looks mostly military."

"Yeah. That's a good question," I answered, giving him no real response. "Can you grab this under here?" I passed the tail of the last strap to him and jumped up on the trailer.

I got in my truck, which now seemed very small and confining, and turned the key. It was also very quiet compared to the tractor I'd been driving. Two days before, this was a part of me, an extension of my limbs and body. But on this day, it seemed foreign, the controls all very small and tightly placed.

Backing down the ramps, it felt a bit more like home. I had my backup camera, the remaining side mirror, and the length of the hood seemed more reasonable. I turned around and pointed it toward the highway. That felt good. I realized that I hadn't really 'turned' the steering wheel on the big rig, I'd just sort of guided it along a straight path. This was better. I was back in my element.

I took a deep breath and hopped out, knowing I'd be getting more questions. I remembered dealing with that at car shows, when I'd taken one of my old classics out to a local show-n-shine or even the national auto shows. The most common question, "So, what's it worth?" or "What'd it cost?" What was a good answer for that? The real numbers were unreal to most folks, and the idea was always to promote the best interest of the hobby. So, you'd say stuff like, "It's worth a lot to me. It took a lot of time to restore," or "It's hard to say. I worked on it for a number of years."

And the guys who said, "Had one just like it." I can't count the number of times some guy came up to me and my handcrafted Camaro and said just that. It had a fully integrated racing suspension, high-output engine, tons of body and interior modifications, and custom paint. It made it into a couple of magazines, so trust me, it was truly unique. But this guy "had one just like it." Those were the good ole days.

So I laughed out loud when the pickup man asked, "So, what's this thing worth?"

I decided, since I really had no idea, to give the answer I'd always wanted to give, at all of those car shows. "Right at 7 million," I said, very matter-of-fact. "And once I set the security sensors, I wouldn't go near it. They monitor it from space, with those satellite cameras. It's crazy." This was fun. He was silent.

"In fact, they can probably hear us talking right now. They'll run a background check, you know, with voice recognition. Hey! Where are you going?" I guess he was done asking questions.

I slid the last ramp up by myself and grabbed my backpack and cooler from the cab of the big truck. I took one last look back across the string of trailers. *Damn, no photos.* That's okay, I'd remember it. I slid the key down into the air vent and shut the door. •

CHAPTER 48: SHAKE, RATTLE, AND ROLL

I grabbed a bottle of water from my paper cooler and put it in the cupholder. I was happy to see my pistol and shotgun were still nestled in their makeshift holsters, and everything looked to be in good shape. I checked my gauges. "Seriously?!" I was in disbelief. But what did I expect? It wasn't like they were a high-end service shop or car dealership. For some reason, I expected to see that my fuel tank had been filled. I'm not sure why I would have assumed that. Years of having my truck serviced by the best in the business, it had always been returned to me clean, serviced, and full of fuel. I guess the Army doesn't care if they have return customers.

Following the curiosity of the guy in the red pickup, I decided to get a few more miles out of town before refilling my tanks. I'd use up the individual cans and save the big farm tank for later. As a last resort, my emergency fuel would be the few questionable cans of diesel fuel I'd picked up back at the park in Nebraska.

As I've said before, the route was scenic. Even with the gray sky to the left and a lot of ash and dust hanging in the air, it was pretty. Gray powder had settled on everything, but it seemed more like snow. On the evergreens and pines, you could see bits of green needles peeking through, and the terrain was spectacular.

I pulled off the road on the river side and started my routine. I'd do fuel first, in case I had to bug out. That was a necessity. I'd check the tires, the underside of the truck. I didn't want to be dragging anything or have any leaks. Then a bathroom break. No facilities, but who was going to see me? Then I'd throw a couple of the MREs on the motor to heat. I thought about doing a taste test, putting the military MREs up against my SpaghettiOs for comparison, but it would be a waste of food. I'd try theirs and see what I thought. I'd had enough SpaghettiOs for a while.

It was peaceful, and I even heard a few birds chirp. Maybe I was getting far enough over the top to find some nature undisturbed by the eruption.

The truck looked good, the tires were holding up well, and the dents and scrapes accumulated along the way added character. I thought it would be getting easier from here.

Placing the MREs on the motor, the hood slammed down onto my head and I reeled back, cussing at the truck. Then I realized that the ground was shaking again. Another tremor or earthquake. I stood back from the truck. Not much to fear in the open spaces. The hood slammed shut. I rubbed the bump on my head, finding a bit of blood on my sleeve. It wasn't much of a gash, but it hurt.

More severe than the shaking I'd felt up in the cab of the big rig, this also seemed to continue for a much longer time. I staggered back to the side of the truck, and the world was still shaking. I noticed the piles of ash at the base of the trees. They were getting deep. Maybe this was why the limbs and needles had been so clean. Maybe they'd been shaken regularly, keeping them dust free since the eruption. The ash was also deep along the wooden fence line, drifted along the posts. I suddenly felt uneasy. This was not a good place to be, and I didn't know why. It was that age-old internal voice again.

The shaking continued to roll the ground beneath me, and I heard a thunder-like sound coming from the valley ahead. The gray clouds that had hung still in the sky appeared to be moving up and toward me. They were closer than I ever imagined. I saw a couple of trees fall, then a few more. A wall of gray water rushed down the river valley toward my resting place.

I jumped into the truck, slamming it into gear before even closing the door. I put the pedal to the floor and spun the steering wheel to the right. The truck spun around, nearly too far before I corrected the drift and fishtailed onto the highway, tires screeching, black smoke pouring from the exhaust. Red lights were flashing on the dash as everything was overloaded, too many RPMs, too much drain from the battery set, a loss of traction control, and for emphasis, the "Fasten Seat Belt" warning.

The two stray gas cans tied to the back rack came loose and tumbled down the highway. Within a moment I saw two flashes of red in my mirror as the cans were kicked up and disappeared into the wave of foam and debris that was coming up behind me. "Come on," I coaxed the truck. "Come on." My heads-up display on the windshield flashed when I hit 80 miles per hour, pulsing a speed warning. But I was hoping for 100. The truck shifted gears. I shot ahead, gaining some distance on the approaching mass.

"What the hell is this?" I called out loud. Another eruption? The river backing up? I was watching the mirror, checking on the churning monster chasing me up the road. I was looking back more than ahead.

His horn caught my attention, and I looked up just in time to regain my lane. The red Ram pickup passed by and the world again fell into slow motion. I heard the horn and looked up, twisting the wheel and swerving to the right, back onto my side of the road. He nodded and gave me the county line wave, two fingers lifted from the steering wheel. He looked at me with a smile as he passed. I noticed his water barrel was full, returning home I supposed. My expression would have been one of horror, and I saw his look change to one of question as I waved frantically at him to stop. But there was no time. He went past and I saw all of his taillights come on as the back of his truck rose from a hard punch on the brakes. His full fresh water barrel hit the back of the cab and exploded into a ball of clear liquid as the moving embankment of mud and gray foam smashed into the front of his truck.

I let off the gas, prepared to hit the brakes, but what could I do? Like the two red gas cans, his truck flipped up into the mass and disappeared, the remnants of the water barrel bouncing along the top of the wave for a brief moment, then sucked down into the mass. I was back on the gas. "100" flashed on my windshield as the speed warning buzzed. In a few moments, the destruction behind me fell from sight.

Wolf Point was a blur as I flew through the small town, laying on my horn to alert whoever might still be around the little community. I didn't know if the wall of sludge was still chasing me, or where it came from, but I knew I wanted to get north, to higher ground. Away from the rushing tide of water. Rapidly searching my maps on the dash, I found Highway 13 north. I slowed enough to drift the corner and point my truck back true with the road. Heading north, I glanced at the maps again, and I saw it.

Fort Peck Lake, the Fort Peck Dam. I had been right below it when the quake hit. The dam must have collapsed. Too much stress from the continual shaking. I hoped the stuff I'd left at Wolf Point would be okay, but I couldn't stop thinking about the guy in the red truck. There's no way he made it.

How many others hadn't made it? How many hundreds, thousands? What was the number? The Army guys hadn't said, but their expressions and the big grey circle were telling. I'd seen bits and pieces, but now the full picture was beginning to weigh on me. And there was no way west from here now, except in Canada.

I drove full-out toward the border. The animals at the river, the elk crossing the road, the guy in the red truck, all dead most likely. Everyone in Yellowstone, the surrounding towns, Billings, Casper. Catastrophic wasn't a big enough word. There were no words. And the fallout from all of it. No power, no food, no fuel. An entire nation in blackout.

For a minute I added my parents and Alex to the toll. All would die from the upheaval caused by all of this. And I'd killed a man as well. Death, destruction. It was too much. I broke down and sobbed. It felt like I might have a heart attack. I slammed my hands against the steering wheel. It was just too much. "Rachel!" I called out. "Rachel!" •

• •

NEXT: "RACHEL'S STORY" CHAPTERS 12 – 20

Jake's story will continue with Chapter 49

...they were almost hypnotic
to watch...as if dancing on the
breeze...But today, there was
no spin, no generation of
spark or power...

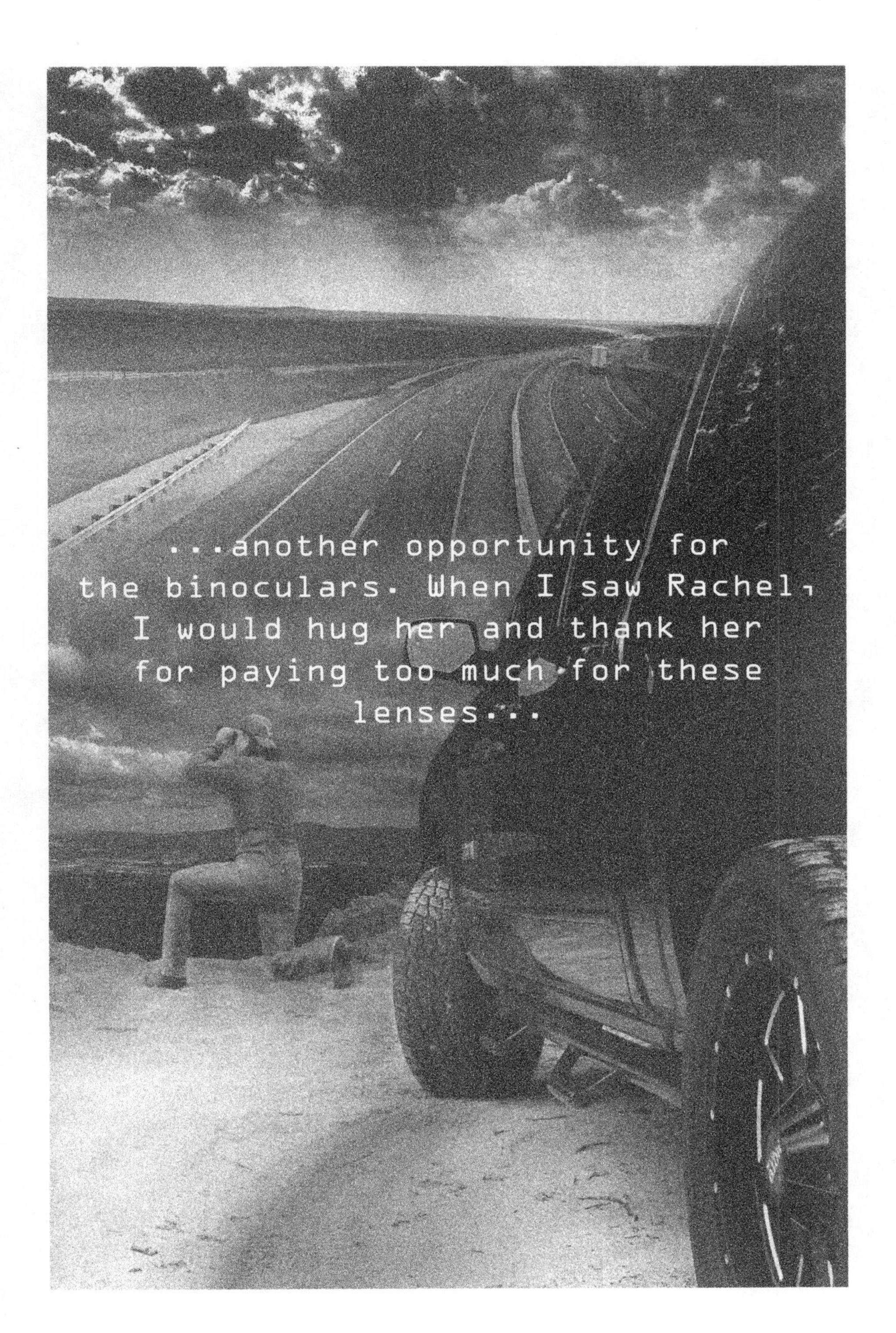
...another opportunity for
the binoculars. When I saw Rachel,
I would hug her and thank her
for paying too much for these
lenses...

RACHEL'S STORY

CHAPTER 12: HELL'S CANYON

New Meadows was her connection point for Highway 95, which would take her up to Grangeville where she'd cut across to Highway 12. But Grangeville would be the end of her saga on this night, and she'd tackle the final leg of the trip the next day. If she could only get through the main intersection at this place.

People were standing in the street, pointing and directing one another in an unorganized attempt to get their autobots into the charging queue. She'd seen other lines at a couple of charging stations. Both had handpainted signs sitting next to the road that said "No Power" or "No Juice." Her favorite was a sign at the place on this corner. It was one of the liquor store/charging port combo sites, with a plastic panel that read "No Power? Get Buzzed Anyway. BOOZE SALE!" Spray-painted on the pavement were the words "Cash Only." The store's lot was lined with dead autobots and EVs. Folks were standing around their cars drinking from paper bag-sleeved bottles. Economics 101 – no matter the situation – liquor sells.

Making the tight corner with her rental truck and trailer in tow, Rachel had slowed to a stop. A pair of autobots had evidently died midstream, clogging the path for everyone. A man halfway through his bottle stepped up on the rail of the truck and grabbed the mirror. "Can I help you, miss?" he slurred, swinging back and pulling the mirror completely out of alignment. His breath reeked, and his gaze was rolling.

"No. Off!" Rachel motioned, rolling up her window for some added protection. She'd hoped to hear some news, maybe from the people standing around the intersection, or some information about her route ahead. This guy was not what she'd anticipated. "Get off the truck," she said with a little more authority.

Gus's door flew open and a younger man appeared in the opening. "Let him help you, lady," the kid said, staring at her. He was holding the door and the handrail, beginning to climb into the truck. She looked back at the drunk, who was no longer weaving, but standing quite firmly on the top step of the fuel tank.

"Slide over," he said, very crisply. The alcohol haze had disappeared and she realized it had been an act. She looked around at the people on the street. Everyone was either sloshed or angry, pointing and shouting directions at each other amidst the stalled cars and the commotion.

"Okay," she said, lifting her hands from the wheel.

The kid to her right was in far enough to find Gus, lying on the floor. An errant step had put his work boot on Gus's tail and Gus spun up into the seat with a growl more vicious than Rachel had ever heard come from his gentle soul. His lips pulled up into a snarl, and he snapped at the kid's face.

As the kid fell back into the opening, Rachel popped her foot off the brake and hit the gas. The truck lurched and the kid tumbled to the pavement, the door slamming shut behind him. She jammed the truck back into Park and it lurched once more. In the same motion, she kicked her door open and the drunk fell to the street. Rachel stood out on the side tank, her 9mm training a red dot on his chest.

He slid on his back to the curb, his hands lifted, his eyes wide with astonishment. Some of the people standing on the corner began to take notice.

"Hey, we were just tryin' to help, lady."

Rachel held him in her aim until he was against the building. He looked around for his friend and the two slithered into the store.

"Can you move your car?" she asked of the couple standing next to the small yellow ZapLite coupe blocking the road. It was dead in the middle of her lane, blocking her turn of the corner.

“Not ours,” the guy said, stepping a bit away from it as he and his girlfriend stared at the lady with the gun, standing on the truck. “It’s not ours,” he repeated.

“Anybody?” Rachel asked. “Anybody own this?” she called out. She pointed her SigSaur at the little plastic lemon-shaped car. Nobody responded.

She checked on the guys who had disappeared into the store. It was dark inside, but she assumed they’d seen enough. She slid back into the seat and looked at Gus. He’d returned to his normal self, sitting on the seat, panting a bit, smiling at her.

“Ready, bud?” she asked him. She threw the truck back into gear. She pulled ahead, taking the yellow bubble with her. She couldn’t see it over the hood, but she felt the impact and she could hear it scraping along the street as she rounded the corner. A block down, she pushed it off on the shoulder and continued on her way.

As she headed north, the signs were not encouraging. “Hell’s Canyon.” “Seven Devils Campground.” Good Lord. She smiled when she finally saw a sign for “Heaven’s Gate” peak. The sign said it was at 8,429 feet elevation. She’d always pictured the entrance a bit higher. •

RACHEL'S STORY
CHAPTER 13: GRANGEVILLE

Rachel pulled into Grangeville. There were a number of signs for campgrounds and RV parking, but she had already made her choice in regard to lodging. She pulled the truck up next to the curb, taking more than her share of parking spaces. Maybe somebody would call the cops. They wouldn't have far to go, as her big yellow truck and trailer were now sitting directly in front of the Grangeville police station. It had to be the safest spot in town.

Jake would have been proud of this improvisation, she thought. They'd never discussed any details about where to stay or not to stay, except to typically avoid groups of people. Not knowing the area, and having a clear vision from the attempted carjacking incident just a few hours before, Rachel was willing to place her bets on hanging out close to the good guys.

She took down the bungee cords separating her from Gus's side of the truck. Stacking her backpack and cooler, she made a connecting section for her mattress. It had been a long time since she'd slept in a car. She and Jake had played around in various vehicles a few times on road trips, but that wouldn't really be classified as 'sleep.' One of his old classic cars had a bench seat, not nearly as modern as the sleek consoles and shifter panels found in newer rides, but certainly a lot more romantic.

As she lay there on her vinyl-clad bedding, she draped one of Jake's jackets across her for a blanket. Gus had pressured her into a brief walk around the parking lot, to stretch his legs and take care of business. She fed him on the ground next to the truck, and stroked his back. He'd done a great job, fighting off the guys at the intersection. If they'd been at home, he'd have gotten steak. This night, it was just the basic kibble and some of her bottled water.

Now that Gus was asleep, curled back into his ball on the floor, Rachel lay on her back and looked up toward the stars. Her view was partially blocked by a lamppost that, on any other night, would have been lighting the inside of her truck, making it difficult to sleep. But all of the street lights were dark. Only the small security lights in the hallways provided any light inside the police station. A couple officers were standing in the parking lot, charging their patrol units on the diesel generator. She'd try to talk with some of them in the morning and get an update on what was happening.

Her mind drifted back to her and Jake and the wide bench seats. She wondered why it was so much fun to make out in a car. Was it the risk, the naughty aspects of teenage curiosity relived or just the change in scenery? It certainly wasn't the comfort. Their king-size bed would be the best place for romantic activity, but that was just too boring and common. She let her mind wander over some of their more interesting locations, obviously the cars, his truck. She recalled one time, recently in Big Bend National Park. They'd stopped at a scenic overlook and had an incredible lovemaking session in the middle of the day. When they'd left the site, Jake was driving down the park road, empty of tourists, with views of a hundred miles in every direction. They'd come up over a small rise in the road, talking about the beauty and harshness of the desert. As they peaked the small hill, Jake had suddenly clenched his grip on the wheel, his body becoming more straight in the seat.

A small digital sign, sitting on a cart next to the road was flashing at them. It had said "Speed Limit: 35. ...Your Speed: 83." Jake had let off the accelerator and they both laughed. Wow. He had been distracted! They tried driving 35 for a while, but it was ridiculously slow, alone, on a laser-straight road, in the middle of nowhere. They settled on 70, just twice the limit.

Jake was far more tame than her, but he had brought her a lot of fun and excitement over their many years. He was loving and passionate, and he openly showed affection toward her. They'd attempted sex in a hotel elevator once, but there simply weren't enough floors in the building.

She knew her favorite memory, and her mind brought it back to her in fantastic detail. A hike in the mountains had provided a large smooth rock that jutted out over a rushing river. They had been out early in the season, before the tourists began flocking to the park, and they'd ridden their bikes up the closed road. Most of the place was still closed due to snow, so the roads were guaranteed to be one-way. Finding the head to one of their favorite trails, Jake had suggested they take a little walk, getting off the road. Rachel had easily agreed, and they dropped the bikes and started up the path.

But Jake had something planned that she didn't know about. His backpack was usually filled with granola bars, bottled water, bandages and splints, some type of communication device, and a set of maps, along with GPS trackers and the rest of his first aid kit. But that day, it was filled with something else.

About 100 yards up the trail was their lookout rock. A large smooth boulder that sprung out above a slot of rushing water, pushed down the gorge from the melting snow above. In late summer, the rock was 50 feet above the stream, deep down in the solid rock groove. But in early spring, the flow of water rushed from the peaks above, bringing the surface of the water up within reach from the rock. Mist from the churning water created a light fog up through the channel, the sun's rays generating a full rainbow of color along the water's path through the trees. At the rock, Jake opened his backpack and pulled out a thick plaid blanket, a small basket of cheese, crackers, and dried meat sticks, along with two thin glasses and a small bottle of champagne.

"Wow." Rachel remembered saying. "What's the occasion?"

"It's Thursday," Jake had said. "The first day I ever knew you existed was a Thursday."

They sat on the rock and dined on their crackers and cheese. She had prepared many picnics such as this for them over the years, for road trips, concerts, or just afternoons by the pool. It wasn't unusual for Jake to do nice things for her, for them, but he hadn't put together a picnic in quite a while, let alone one of this scale and quality.

She remembered toasting life and the wonders around them. The midday sun warmed the rock, and it was a comfortable place to be, undressed, and work on their preseason tans. Rachel lay on her stomach, and Jake massaged her back, tracing her muscles from her neck to her ankles. He took his time and rubbed her calves, the small of her back, and sides of her chest. She rolled over and looked up at him, the sun hidden behind the shape of his shoulders as he leaned over her. She had kissed him and pulled him down on top of her. He raised his hips and she spread her legs beneath him. No words were said, as each of them knew exactly what the other was feeling. They moved slowly together on the flannel blanket, the only cushion between them and the rock.

The moment had been divine. As the water crashed beneath them, coursing through the channels of the ravine, Jake moved on top of her, his own body flowing with the rhythm of the water. Rachel ran her hands down his back, holding his shoulders and squeezing him between her legs. She crossed her ankles above the low of his back and drew him deeper into her. The fog surrounded them, and the sun dropped from the middle of the sky, now covering their bodies with dappled light, streaking through the limbs and leaves. Their lovemaking sessions always left her satisfied – she was quick to find release, especially when the passion was strong, and the setting swept her away.

This had surpassed every level of spontaneity ever shown by Jake. She had been fully impassioned, by the environment, by the feelings she held for Jake, and by Jake himself, taking her to a lovers' site they had often shared, but never at this level. He was good at surprising her, but over the years of their relationship, there were often spans of time when the passion had seemed to drop. This was a great gesture from him, setting the stage, planning the course of events, and taking Rachel into a sensuous experience that fulfilled her body as well as her heart. She missed her man.

She pulled Jake's jacket up close to her face and breathed in his scent. She drifted off to sleep. •

RACHEL'S STORY
CHAPTER 14: GOOD MORNING

Bang, bang, bang. "Hello. Anybody home?" Bang, bang, bang. Rachel's eyes snapped open and she looked up at the ceiling of the truck cab. It was disorienting with the angled front pillars of the windshield tapering back to the roof above her. It took her a moment to find her bearings. Gus sat up and licked her face.

"Hey, bud," she said, still looking around the interior of the truck, working to sit up in the seat that had been her bed for the night. Gus wagged his tail and gave his usual morning whimper. It was time for the first walk of the day.

"Hey, you okay in there?" the voice came again, and there was another pounding on the door. "Sir, I need you to...."

Rachel sat up and looked out at the police officer who was knocking on her door. Based on the truck and the old Blazer in tow, he wasn't expecting a pretty redhead to pop up and put her face to the window.

"Hi," he said, stepping back to take another look at the truck, trying to fit all of the pieces together. "Is this yours?"

The question seemed a bit unlikely, as she was obviously inside of it, but she knew what he meant. "Yes, I'm sorry, I'll be moving it. This seemed like a safe place for the night." Rachel was pulling her hair back and banding it into a ponytail as she spoke. She snapped Gus's leash to his collar, and the two got down out of the truck.

The officer had begun talking to an older lady walking along the sidewalk. She was wearing a face mask to fight off the dust. He pointed her toward the other end of the building, and she waved a brief "thank you" and walked on down the street. Rachel looked in the direction she was walking and saw a small group had assembled at the doors on the far end of the building. Several were standing, a few had taken seats on a bench. A younger man appeared to give up his seat on the bench to the woman. He took a seat on the ground.

“The library has become popular in the past couple of days,” the officer said, eyeing Rachel and Gus.

Never one for formal greetings, Gus gave the front tire of the truck a morning rinse.

“Why is that?” Rachel asked. She had a lot of other questions in the queue. For instance, is Highway 12 open? Can I take this rig through to Missoula on 12? Does anybody in town have fuel? Where can I find some food? But, if the town was undergoing a piqued interest in literature, she’d bite.

“How-to books, prepper information, gardening tips, history of volcanos... they stopped checking them out. You can only read and reference, take notes and give the book to the next person. It’s old-school Google,” the cop was certainly chatty enough.

“Interesting. Can I get to Missoula on Highway 12 with this?” she asked, nodding to her truck and trailer.

“You can,” he said. “But, wow. Are the brakes good? That’s the first question. And, how good a driver are you? And, I don’t mean any offense. It’s just that 12’s the kind of road the motorcyclists love, you know? Twists and turns. It’s a beautiful drive, if you’ve got the time to look at it.” He was just what she needed, and he was obviously enjoying talking to her.

He continued, “Let me see if that’s open all the way through. We may have some info on that and we might not. Where are you coming from?”

“Texas,” Rachel said, which brought the man to a full stop. “I’m headed to Kalispell, hopefully.”

“I’ve gotta tell ya’, miss, I don’t know what you’re gonna find over those mountains. I’m just bein’ real honest about that. Missoula’s the military’s command post on this whole thing. It’s gonna be a zoo.”

He motioned for Rachel to follow him and they walked toward the police cruisers that were charging on the generators. A very young officer was swapping the plug from one car to another, and the first officer turned Rachel over to him.

"I'll be back out in a minute. I'd usually offer coffee, but...Hey, Wills, give her today's news. Oh, and ma'am, you seem to have a small yellow rearview mirror stuck in your grill." He walked into the dark station house.

Wills was evidently the rookie on the Grangeville police force. Rachel assumed it was a pretty small team as the city wasn't all that large. Maybe a handful of cops patrolled the place.

"I think he meant this," said Wills, offering Rachel a few papers stapled together at the corner. "It came in on the 'fact machine.'"

"'Fax' machine?" Rachel inquired, out of habit. "Did you mean 'fax' machine?"

"Oh, I don't know. Fact. Facts. The printer. We dug it out of the closet, hooked it up, and plugged it into the generator. It's how we get updates."

That made sense to Rachel. The landlines would still be in place. The government would have a communication center linked to the lines and they could power them from a central point to blast out info via fax. She flipped through the pages. No layout, just teletype newsprint. So she started at the top of page 1.

It showed the day's date and the time. It had been sent less than an hour ago, so this was as recent as she would find anywhere. It seemed to be organized by region.

What the pages called "Zone 1" was evidently the area closest to Yellowstone. It was tagged "Classified, see attached." Below that, "Zone 2" had a few paragraphs. The overview said that evacuations were continuing across the entire state of Wyoming. Denver residents were clogging I-80 east and no westbound travel was permitted anywhere in the Plains states. Military supplies were staging into the Zone from a drop point in Minot, North Dakota. Highway 2 was designated as westbound, but for military use only.

Jake had said he was coming on the Dakota route, so maybe he would pass through Minot? They'd been there before, in Minot, to surprise Alex on one of his tours. She knew that area would be marked in some detail on Jake's maps. Or maybe he'd have to go farther up, over the top of it. She wondered if he'd have to cross into Canada. But even if he could get access to a route, where would he find fuel? She'd had a bright spark of hope, but her heart sank as she continued to read the update.

"General U.S." was a section of the report. Beyond the Zone designations, the news wasn't getting any better. The entire electrical grid was down, with some minor exceptions in the far Northeast. A couple of hydroelectric plants and some small offshore wind farms were keeping emergency services alive in Maine, as utilities providers had been able to sever that region from the grid. But officials were working on ways to siphon off power for New York City. Rachel rolled her eyes. Of course, the hoards in the city would be the ones that would suck up the resources, per usual.

The Tennessee Valley Authority, a major hydroelectric producer in the Southeast, was working on system failures and overload issues, but were targeting emergency systems to be running within eight to 10 weeks, once allocation plans had been negotiated by lawmakers in the various states it served. "Eight to ten weeks!" Rachel said out loud. She figured Alex would be on TVA power, so it was a shock to her to read about such a timeline. Two months until any basic emergency access to power was available? How long until services were restored to the public?

She wondered about food mostly. Alex's house would still be intact and the weather would be pretty mild this time of year, so shelter wasn't a big concern. Getting out and about and going places, well, those limitations would be bad for business. The economy would crater, but most financial crises are survivable. Yes, the main issue would be food.

How would you have enough food for a long-term situation?

Spring was here, so it was prime time to start planting – if you had starter plants or seeds. That would be something for her "find" list. Seeds. She'd need to get seeds and starter plants. She'd begin watching for garden centers along her route.

"Ah-hah..." she said again, to herself. That's what the people were doing waiting for the library to open. They're trying to learn how to grow food. That's what the officer meant. She didn't know about Alex's girlfriend or her family. They were all doctors, so they had medical knowledge for sure, but did anybody know how to grow an onion? Rachel had taken part in a small school garden club project with Alex when he was little, but he was more interested in digging up worms than absorbing the teachings of horticulture. And even though Jake's family had been in farming, she doubted he would know how to raise a crop that didn't involve a 20-row planter and other massive equipment.

How was it, with all of the technology and information we had available, that nobody knew the basics. The true basics. Growing a vegetable. Hunting for meat. It had all been lost, cast aside and replaced by nano-theory and IT specialization.

"You can't code a frickin' sandwich," Rachel said, under her breath.

"I'm sorry, what?" The young officer had heard her last comment.

"Oh, no, I'm sorry. I'm just reading this and thinking."

"I chased away some fellas trying to siphon your fuel tank last night," the kid offered. "I didn't even know you were in there."

"Wow, thank you!" she said, surprised at the news, and realizing she needed to be more aware of that risk, even though she hoped to be at the lake by sunset. "How are things? Folks getting desperate?" she asked.

"Two grocery stores were gutted last night," he replied. "We're trying to cover what we can, but I think Walmart's gonna hire militia. You know, contract an armed security force. They'll have to if they want to keep from being overrun." He lifted up a small biscuit sandwich to show her. "We got MRE rations, so we're lucky. They're coming through here, between Boise and Missoula. We're one of the supply stops for first responders."

"Are they coming on Highway 12?" Rachel asked. She wanted to be aware of other traffic on the road, especially big trucks, since it was evidently pretty tight.

"Yeah, it's wild. Can't imagine those big rigs comin' down that road. Scary twists on some of that! And it's a climb from here to there."

Rachel returned to her papers. The overview wasn't encouraging. The West Coast didn't have much ash cover yet, and maybe wouldn't have any unless it made the global trek, which was possible. But they didn't have any power either. Los Angeles had been put in a hardcore lockdown and martial law was going into effect at midnight, according to the brief. The country had basically been split by the ash clouds and sulfuric gas, leaving two distinct areas: everything west of the Rockies and everything east of Nebraska. The Missouri River was referenced as the edge of the impact zone, but the entire nation was in the dark.

Just then, a pair of fighter jets flew overhead, toward Missoula. Rachel and the young officer watched them disappear over the trees.

"High-level security," said the cop. "They're looping 12 to Missoula, then over I-90 to Spokane. Everybody's pretty tense."

Rachel hadn't thought about the national security impacts this would have. She and Jake had talked about the government's push to an all-electric platform. They both felt it was risky and irresponsible, but they were falling into the minority. As more and more people had become influenced by media bias and left-driven political narrative, the voting blocks had continued to shift away from their beliefs. They believed that individuals should have maximum freedom to do whatever they pleased as long as it didn't affect anyone else. Part of that included the responsibility of self-reliance. You had to do smart things and take care of yourselves and your family. It wasn't anybody else's responsibility to take care of you.

But that line of thinking had become unpopular. It seemed that everybody wanted to do whatever they wanted and just take whatever they needed from someone else. Confiscation, redistribution, call it what you like. The politicians were always quick to buy a vote with somebody else's money or effort, so the true working class had been sold out. If you wanted to stay stoned and in storage, you were in luck. They'd make sure you had just enough dope to keep you pliable and just enough money to keep you alive – and voting. In the past few elections, being alive wasn't even a requirement. All of this angered Rachel and she needed to shift her mind back to the work of the day. She needed to find out about fuel and get on the road.

She turned to the last page of the report. "Classified" was stamped at the top with "Zone 1 Update" below. It was a statistical report of casualties and other grim data, along with a couple of photos that were just a maze of gray lines and dots. It was indiscernable what they were. It gave some initial projections of dead and missing, estimated to be between 35,000 to 65,000, but it noted that was entirely an estimate. More than 4.5 million displaced. It said that food supplies would be critically impacted, and distribution solutions were being considered.

A paragraph titled "Energy Sector" said the Gulf Coast refineries were being ramped up, with pipelines coming back into service, but the timeline projections were still in development. The West Coast, where the final refineries had been closed nearly a decade ago, would be waiting for fuel shipments from Russia, which were being negotiated. Historically, crude oil had been shipped around the world, with refinement into consumable fuels taking place more locally. But that had changed. Because of desperation caused by the situation, they were contemplating shipping finished fuels. What would the volatility risks of that entail?

The Army Corps of Engineers was considering a rebuild of the old refineries at Torrence and Manhattan Beach to help get power flowing in Los Angeles. Throughout the report, the time projections said things like "by next spring" or "the following year."

The generator buzzed, kicking off its automatic switch. The light on the charging station turned green. "Gotta roll," said the young cop, reaching for the report Rachel was reading.

"Yeah, thanks," she said, handing it back to him and smiling. "Thank you for your service. Stay safe, okay?" She took a good look at the young man, much younger than Alex. Just a kid, probably 21 or 22.

The first officer came back out of the building, carrying his rationed biscuit and carrying a bottle of water. "I can offer you this," he said, holding up the water. "But trust me, you don't want this." He referenced the biscuit with a bit of a scrunched up facial expression. Not his favorite.

"Our Dunkin' Donuts is closed," he added, winking at her. The age-old cops and donuts stereotype would live on forever, she thought.

Rachel accepted the bottle of water. You never turn that down, especially when you don't know where your next one might be found. The officer looked harshly at his biscuit and motioned toward Gus.

"Sure," Rachel said. "He's not picky." The cop knelt down and held the biscuit for Gus who quickly snapped it up and licked his lips. It was delicious!

"There's a barbecue place, about two blocks down. They're trying to empty their coolers before it's all lost. Started setting up early this morning. You should be able to get a sandwich or something." His radio beeped and a dispatcher said, "Storekeeper shot, Thrifty Mart, all units."

"Shit. Gotta go. Good luck!" He unplugged his car and hung the heavy cord on the hook. With a quick wave, he sped out of the parking lot, hit the strobe lights, and was gone.

Rachel thought about leaving her truck there and walking to the barbecue place, but if somebody had tried to steal her fuel last night, she wasn't going to stray far from it. In fact, she needed to check her gauges and see if they'd gotten any. It didn't sound like Highway 12 was going to be any place to run out of fuel. •

RACHEL'S STORY

CHAPTER 15: BBQ

A couple blocks down, Rachel found Max BBQ. The signage was cool, and it looked like a pretty popular establishment. Or at least, it had been. Two patio grills were smoking outside the front of the building beside a large barrel smoker. Some folding tables made an impromptu buffet line, with a mix of bowls and boxes lined across them. A dead autobot blocked most of the drive, so Rachel parked her truck in the street behind it. One man was tending to the smoker and grills and another sat on the roof of his truck with a rifle. "CASH ONLY" was painted on the back glass. The tailgate was down, and a few people were using it as a bar top for their early brunch.

Rachel locked Gus in the truck and walked up to the tables. "Hi," said a young girl, probably the daughter of the owners. "We're emptying the coolers, so make an offer on what you want."

The selection included tubs of potato salad, macaroni salad, a big aluminum tray loaded with mac'n cheese, heads of lettuce, bottles of dressing, carrots, peppers, potatoes, tomatoes, and rolls. They had a rolling rack of sandwich buns sitting next to the smoker. There were hundreds of them.

Rachel tried to think how to best use the opportunity. She wasn't really all that hungry at the moment. The news she'd just read had pretty much ruined her appetite. She tried to rationalize some logic, hoping to make some grand decision that would solve the pending food crisis. She wondered why they were choosing to sell the food instead of trying to save it. But without refrigeration, most of it would spoil, so they might as well make the most of it.

"I'll take a sliced brisket sandwich and...just a minute." Rachel walked back to the truck and got some more cash from her Critical Box behind the seat. She returned to the young girl standing by the counter.

"Okay, so that was a sliced brisket sandwich, and..." the girl repeated, waiting for the rest of Rachel's order.

Rachel finished the sentence, "And five pounds of sliced brisket, two bags of buns, and I'll take six potatoes, uncooked. The ones with eyes. Along with 10 tomatoes. Lets add a few carrots, plus six peppers. Oh, and that bunch of onions, just as they are, with the stems and roots." She held up her cash, waiting for a reply from the girl.

"Okay." The girl looked at the man next to the smoker and shrugged. There was no cash register, no keyboard, no touchscreen. Just a small metal box with a latch on it. When the girl opened it, Rachel saw it was a tackle box, and the top tray still held a couple of lures and weights in the little compartments.

Rachel gave the girl a $100 bill. "You can keep the change," she said, hoping to quicken any negotiation that may be about to take place.

"Thank you," said the girl, unsure what to do.

Rachel grabbed the bags and started to walk away. "Oh... can I get two more sandwiches?" She pulled out a 20 and handed it to the girl. She ran her groceries and garden starters to the truck and returned for the two sandwiches. The girl gave her a bag with two more of the BBQ briskets, wrapped in foil. She held out some change, but Rachel just smiled at her and turned back toward the truck.

Gus was thrilled to have the smell of fresh barbecue wafting through the cab of the truck, and his tail wagged with delight when Rachel returned with the two extra sandwiches. He was up on his seat, ready and eager.

"No," Rachel said. "Not for you." He looked at her and dipped his head down. He curled his tail and slinked back onto the floor. He looked pitiful. "Really?" Rachel said to him.

She made the block and headed back toward the center of town. Back in front of the police station, she came to a stop. She darted into the dark building and said “hello” to nobody in particular. She found a dispatcher’s office and knocked on the glass.

“Hi,” she said to the lady on the other side of the glass. “This morning a young officer. Wills?...was helping me. An older man, well, not older, but...” Rachel was tripping on her words.

“Chief Riggs, yes, I know who you mean,” the lady nodded.

“Can you give these to them, please? Maybe it’ll be better than this morning’s biscuits.”

“Sure thing. They’ll appreciate it.” She took the foil-wrapped sandwiches and sat them on a desk, starting to write a note. “What’s the name?” the lady asked.

“Just put ‘the redhead and the dog.’ They’ll know.”

Rachel smiled at herself in the rearview mirror as she climbed back into the truck. She enjoyed being nice to people, and she was afraid the world wasn’t going to be very nice for awhile. •

RACHEL'S STORY
CHAPTER 16: UP HILL ALL THE WAY

Back in the truck, Rachel headed for Route 13, the road that would connect her to Highway 12. The long steady climb that would take her to Missoula.

The winding began immediately. Just getting out of town and onto the right road was an exercise in itself. She missed a sign because it wasn't there, and ended up having to back up the truck and trailer. It was a stressful few minutes, making sure nobody was behind her, checking her blind spots – which meant nearly everything behind her – and determining how much bend to put into the rig to miss a fire hydrant, a light pole, and a pine tree. But she did it, with only a slight bump of the back of the trailer into the tree. She rolled back as slowly as possible until she felt it touch, then turned her wheels and went the other way. It was surely an educational trip regarding driving, planning, and patience.

She also pulled the Emergency Box and its assortment of contents up into the cab, most importantly the extra clips of ammo for her 9mm SigSaur pistol. She made some loops of duct tape and stuck three of the clips to the top of the dash, just to the left of the steering wheel. She put the rest in her hunting vest, which she'd decided to wear for this route.

Once she pulled through Lowell, it would be nearly 100 miles of tight mountain road before she hit another town. But she had to make it that far first.

At Kooskia, she intersected Highway 12. She crossed over a rapidly flowing river in the picturesque small town and arrived at the T-intersection she'd been watching for on her map. She had to stop for the stop sign and a small road block, manned by one National Guard troop sitting in what looked like an electric utility truck. A single traffic cone in the middle of the road was the only barricade in place. She certainly could have run the barricade, but thought better of it. If the order was to turn around or that the road was closed, then she'd reconsider.

The soldier waved her to the side of the road, and she pulled to a stop. "What's your destination, ma'am?" he asked, standing back from the truck, looking up at her.

"I'm headed to Missoula," she said, thinking that if she said Kalispell they might make her choose a longer route. "The police chief in Grangeville said this road was open." It was a bit of a stretch, but the facts were right.

"We're running supplies up from Boise on here," he said. "It's usually a tourist road, but now it's semis and haulers. We're running both ways. It's really tight in places. It's your call. I just have to inform you." He was courteous enough but he wasn't a strong persuader. Rachel thanked him for his service, and she was on her way. •

RACHEL'S STORY

CHAPTER 17: THE LONG AND WINDING ROAD

Highway 12 was everything they'd promised. Tight and steep in places, it wound along the river, mirroring every twist and turn. Rachel held a tight grip on the wheel, 'ten and two' was the only way to maintain control of the truck. The pull of the hill would kill her fuel mileage and after just a few miles she realized that making the lake today would be a miracle. She'd always based her travel time on 60 miles per hour. It made the math easy, it was a mile a minute, so converting any map into time had been just simple division.

On the first long grade, she was lucky to get above 20 miles per hour with the rental truck crying out under the load of their furniture and the trailer. And every corner required at least a tap on the brakes, which drove the gear set back into low as the transmission whined under the strain. She'd drop down to 5 or 10 miles per hour and start to accelerate once more, before slowing for the next corner. She recalculated the math in her head. Originally, she'd figured today's route to be eight hours. She now guessed it'd be more than twice that, maybe more.

She couldn't help but remember some of the road trips they'd taken in her Porsche. Winding up through Arkansas was a favorite that they'd done a few times. They'd take the interstate over into Arkansas, then run Highway 7 through Hot Springs and on up to the north. They'd spend the night at a sexy little bed-and-breakfast in Eureka Springs, then either complete the loop or meet Jake's parents in Branson. That little car had been a trophy for Rachel, selected long before as a professional goal. She'd earned it, and she loved driving it. The immediate response of the steering, the firm feel of the road, and the power under her feet gave her quite a thrill. She'd even attended the Bondurant Driving School to build her performance chops. That was a far cry from her Penske truck and trailer setup.

She laughed a bit at that thought. Penske? Hadn't Penske been a racing driver? The name was synonymous with racing. Roger Penske had driven Porsches, just like Rachel in some respects, going on to fame across Formula 1, Indy, and more. The name was legend in the world of racing. And here she was, struggling to make 18 miles per hour on a 5-percent grade carrying a 30-foot billboard emblazoned with the name "Penske."

"Come on, Roger! How about a little more power?" she said, thinking through it all out loud.

Her map had shown dots indicating towns, but as she passed each one they appeared to just be campsites or driveways back into the trees. At Lowell, she noticed a row of fishing cabins. They were quaint and pristine, sitting along the bank of the river, opposite the highway. Maybe they'd come back here and fish one day, just to relax. That's what this type of country was made for – relaxing and enjoying the beauty. With a fly rod and some waders, you could have quite a day, right outside your cabin door. It was ideal. Beyond Lowell, there would be nothing. Maybe some chemical toilets at a rest stop or two, but not much else.

"Okay Gus," she said, looking down at her companion on the floor. "Here we go."

They made another sweeping turn as they passed through Lowell. A couple of truck and trailer rigs had come by, but they'd met at some of the straighter sections of road, and it had gone well. Coming out of the corner from Lowell, two big rigs following close behind one another came around the bend.

Rachel reset her grip on the wheel. "Ten and two," she said to herself. She checked the mirrors, knowing there was nothing behind her. As the first truck passed, she felt her right rear duals run the edge of the pavement. She was giving them as much room as she could. The second truck met her in the center of the corner, and her trailer ran off the pavement. She could feel it pulling her to the right as it ran through the gravel and grass. The river was running right below her and she hadn't seen a guardrail for miles. The few she had seen were marked with recent smears of paint and tire marks.

The two semis were coming down the hill, running nearly three times her speed. She knew they were professional drivers, but damn, it just seemed too fast for the road. As the second one passed, she fully expected to hear contact on either her mirror or back at the trailer. There was only the whoosh of the air compressed between the two surfaces, and then they were gone. Maybe the air pressure had kept the other truck from touching her. Whatever it was, she took a breath, realizing she hadn't breathed or blinked in a long time.

"Hey, bud, why don't you jump up here and join me?" she said to Gus, who decided to stretch and make his way onto the shotgun seat. She'd taken down the bungee cords that had separated them to make her bed the night before. With the twists and turns of this road, it would probably be a good idea to put them back in place. For the safety of both of them. If she did lose control, getting hit by a 100-pound dog flying through the air would not help the situation. Gus probably needed to stretch his legs anyway, so she'd look for the next opportunity to stop and take care of all that.

Thirty minutes later, she found her first opportunity to pull out. It was a tidy little stop with a chemical toilet and room for Gus to walk around. She pulled one of his tennis balls out of the bag and they played a little fetch. He was always eager to chase the ball and bring it back. Getting him to drop it for you, well, that was another story.

She ran him in circles for a few minutes, then refastened the bungee dividers in the cab. He looked sad when she put him back up in his seat.

"Gus, I swear, you are the moodiest dog." He looked at the barrier and back at her. He curled his tail and crawled back down on the floor.

A couple more trucks had gone by, in fact two sets, one running each direction. They were obviously more comfortable with speed than she was, and she was glad that she'd been stopped when the northbound rigs passed by. If they would have come up behind her, they would have been on her tail for a long time. She listened intently for any other traffic coming up the valley before she pulled out onto the road. She had a long way to go.

Three hours of constant turning and slowing and accelerating and braking and watching. She'd had some small antelope cross the road in front of her, but she couldn't do anything about it. Her speed was already so slow, she just enjoyed seeing them run. They were moving at twice her speed. She could feel the tension in her face and her arms and her hands. She'd developed a slight cramp in her left calf muscle and she was working to fend it off.

As she came up on the next blind turn, she saw another guardrail. Somehow it gave her comfort as her rig approached the corner. She looked across it and saw the river below. Probably a 30-foot drop down a rocky bank. A blur of motion to her left drew her attention back to the road, and a white semi blew by her, rounding the corner. She could hear the tires screeching as he was taking the corner far too fast.

Rachel's hands clenched on the wheel and she pushed her rig as far to the right as possible. The increasing grade had slowed her pace and her truck lurched, downshifting to keep momentum. A quick glance out the right side mirror showed the trailer was already skimming the rail. The fender skimmed a couple of bolt heads and sparks flickered into the air.

The screeching continued as the first truck passed. Its trailer kissed the side of her truck, knocking her rear duals into the guardrail. She felt the slight impact and was grateful that the metal barrier was there to keep her out of the river below.

There was more motion to her left as her eyes darted back from her right mirror. She couldn't really do much about what was happening on the road, so her focus returned to the mirror. She was keeping her truck buried in the rail, using it as a bumper to bring her rig around the bend in the road.

There would be a second semi, as it seemed they always traveled in pairs. Rachel worried that the following truck would be even later on its brakes, following too closely behind the first.

Suddenly her trailer lodged, the fender and wheels caught in a pinch between the pavement and the large wooden poles that held the rail in place. She felt a pop as the trailer broke free, separating from the truck. The truck lurched forward, the right wheel going hard into the rail. The front corner of her truck lifted up across the rail and she saw nothing but sky.

The body of her truck was rolling to the left, pushing her into the door as she turned the wheel hard to the left, but there was no reaction from the truck. The white blur on her left consumed her entire field of vision and a wall of blue smoke and chrome shot past her and appeared through the small window in the back of the cab. The screeching of tires and crushing of metal blended into one deafening pitch. The air around her was suddenly full of glass. The impact was tremendous.

She felt herself being lifted up and around. Gus was still on the floor, wide-eyed and looking directly at her, but he seemed to be above her. Her body shot away from the door and there was a sense of weightlessness as the seat belt drew her back into her seat. She saw another flash of sky, a sweep of green, and then it fell dark and silent.

She felt water moving against the side of her face. •

RACHEL'S STORY
CHAPTER 18: CHIEF

"Chief? Chief?" a soft female voice was repeating. Rachel tried to respond but she couldn't find any breath to speak. She felt herself swallow and she opened her eyes into a slight squint. Everything was bright and glowing, too warm she thought. She could feel a tube in her throat. She began to feel dizzy and re-closed her eyes.

"I've got reaction," she heard the voice say. "Let's get her moved." The voice trailed away, and everything was silent again.

Rachel opened her eyes and looked around the room. Where was she? Cloth walls surrounded her, a window, somewhere, was casting light on one of her walls, making the entire cube glow. She could hear chatter and see shadows moving past the curtain that hung at the foot of the bed. Her body was slightly elevated. She looked to her side. Bed rails. "Hospital?" she thought to herself. She was trying to gather her thoughts. She'd been traveling. In the truck.

"GUS!" she cried out. "Gus!" Her throat burned from the tube that had been in her mouth. It seemed to be gone now, but her lips were sore and dry.

A young nurse immediately stepped into the cloth box, "You're okay, Chief, you're okay."

"Where's Gus?" Rachel asked in a frantic whisper.

"I'm not sure. Let me ask. Doctor!" the nurse called out. It was the same voice Rachel had heard before. Earlier maybe, she wasn't sure.

A tall thin man, appearing to be a doctor, stepped in through the curtain.

"Doctor, she's looking for someone named Gus?" the nurse said, with an inquisitive look on her face. "I thought she came in alone," she added quietly.

“Chief, was ‘Gus’ traveling with you?” the doctor asked, stepping closer to the bed.

“Yes, yes!” Rachel replied. “Is he okay?”

“How old is Gus?” the nurse asked.

“About six, I guess,” Rachel answered, not really sure why that was important.

“I’ll check pediatrics!” said the nurse, turning quickly through the slit in the wall.

“He’s a Lab. A yellow Lab.” Rachel struggled to speak loud enough for them to hear. “He’s my dog!” she was finally able to squeak with some distinction.

“I’m sorry, Chief, I don’t know about your dog. If they found him, I’m sure his location will be in the records. Just relax. Let’s just worry about you right now.” And the doctor slid out through the curtain door.

Rachel laid back into the pillow and tried to reassemble her thoughts. She remembered the screeching tires and the impact, being hurled through the air and rolling. She remembered being in the water, but she couldn’t remember Gus. The last time she had seen him, he was above her, as the truck was rolling over the rail. He was confined to his side of the cab with the makeshift crate of bungee cords, which he could have made it through with very little effort. The tethers wouldn’t have trapped him in the truck.

Could he have survived the fall? He wasn’t strapped in, as she had been, but he was down under the dash, so he would have hit the seat, which should have been soft. Rachel began to cry. She could think of how he would have survived the crash and climbed out through the broken glass.

But she could also see how he would have been either killed or gravely injured. The jarring of the trucks, colliding and pushing them over the rail, the tumbling, and the contents of the cab pounding him as everything flew from its place. She remembered her 9mm clips taped to the dash. They would have been like sharp-edged weights, thrown against his body. Her Critical Box would have been heavy as well, crushing down on him as the truck rolled. And there was the stuff from the Emergency Box, and the stuff that was loose behind the seat.

"Oh," Rachel whimpered out loud as she remembered one of the items had been a hatchet. It was in a case, but it would have been heavy and would have fallen out from behind the seat as they rolled. She knew Gus was dead. The more she thought about it, there was no way for him to survive. She pulled the blanket up over her face and sobbed.

"Chief? Are you okay?" a teenage boy came into the space, carrying a small paper tray with some wrapped food. He stood at the end of the bed, waiting for a reply.

After a moment of silence, he spoke again, as Rachel wiped her eyes and cheeks with the seam of the sheet. "I brought you lunch. I'm a volunteer from the Community Church. Were you in the blast?" he asked, a bit shy in his question.

Rachel still hadn't gathered herself. When she tried to speak, her chin quivered and she continued to weep. She couldn't even call Jake to tell him, to hear any of his words of comfort. And he was going to be devastated as well. He complained about Gus's constant shedding, the continuous emptying of the vacuum cleaner, the non-stop walks, and the cost of countless squeaky balls that mostly wound up broken or sunk in a pond or fountain. But he loved Gus, probably as much as Rachel did. He was going to be heartbroken.

"No, honey. I wasn't in the blast. But my dog is missing," Rachel explained.

"Some of my friends are missing," the boy continued. "They were on an end-of-year field trip to see the old mines around Anaconda and Butte.

Then they were going to Mammoth Hot Springs on the north edge of Yellowstone." His voice trailed off as his own tears ran down his face. He blinked a few times and sat the small tray on the edge of Rachel's bed. "I'm sorry," he said. "I'm not suppose to talk about it when I'm here."

"It's okay," Rachel said, patting the bed next to her, inviting him to sit and talk.

He picked up the tray and sat down in its place, handing it to her. She nodded and placed it next to her on the bed.

"What are your friend's names?" she asked, expecting to hear a couple.

"There's Robby and Toby. And Kelly and Beth. Kevin, Gage, Sandy, Kyle, Robin, Russ. Oh, Amber. And Steven."

Rachel was in shock at the length of the list.

"It was my whole class," he said, looking at the floor. "I couldn't go because I got in trouble." His sobs turned into a full cry and he buried his face in his hands.

Rachel put her arms around him and pulled him in close.

"Well I'm really glad you're here," she said, searching for anything that might bring some hope. The young boy's story added more perspective, too much perspective. "And I'm really thankful that you brought me a nice lunch. Thank you."

Rachel was finding her voice. Whatever pain she felt in her throat, she knew it didn't match the pain this kid was feeling inside.

"Alex?" a voice called from beyond the curtain. "Alex?" A nurse stuck her head into the small white room and looked at the boy. She looked at Rachel and gave a sad expression. "We need your help, bud," she said to the boy, placing her hand on his shoulder. "We need to do the rest of the hall."

"Alex," Rachel said softly. "Our son is named Alex too. And I'm so glad to have met you. And I'm so glad that you're okay." She was still reaching for something to say that might lighten the burden on him. "You need to give the rescue teams time, your friends time, to find their way home. I hope you keep your faith through all of this. Please, always keep your faith. Okay?"

Alex nodded and wiped his eyes. His gaze remained on the floor, but he let the nurse guide him through the curtain and he was gone.

Rachel wondered how many more were out there. Lost friends, lost families, lost lives. She thought about her own Alex. Where was he this day, and how was he doing? She heard the short yelp of an ambulance siren outside and decided that she was taking up space needed for somebody else.

"Nurse," she called out softly. "Nurse!"

The lady returned in a few moments, asking how she could help. Rachel asked if she was okay to leave, because she needed to get going, find Gus, and give them the space.

"Under normal circumstances, ma'am, you'd be staying with us for another day or so. But times aren't normal. I'll check with the doctor." And she disappeared once more.

"So, Chief, how do you feel? They tell me you want to be on your way." The doctor was holding a clipboard, marking some notes.

"I feel like I need to find my dog and that I need to go. It sounds like you've got others who need this bed. And why is everybody calling me 'Chief'?" Rachel finally asked.

"Don't know, that's just what they tagged you with when they brought you in. You were evidently on your way here with some sort of rescue rig. Anyway, here's your charts. Concussion, some lacerations, and you'll find some stitches in your left leg. It's wrapped. And, yes, we could use the space."

Rachel slid herself to the edge of the bed. "My clothes?" she asked. "And my truck. Oh, shit. I hadn't even thought about that."

"See the folks at the front table, they'll get you sorted out. Stay safe." The doctor handed her the chart, and she stood up on the floor. She looked down and saw some stripes painted on the smooth gray squares. She picked up her lunch plate and carried it with her, looking around the draped box to see if she was leaving anything behind.

Exiting her 'room,' she found that she was in one of dozens of draped partitions, in some sort of gymnasium or community center. It wasn't a hospital at all, but there were doctors and nurses, all with lanyards she now noticed. Big type with names and locations printed on the cards. "DR Hall – Seattle General, Ortho," "RN Jamison – Portland," "SURG Bates – Spokane, Cardio". She felt overwhelmed as she continued to weave through the maze toward the front of the open hall.

She found the desk at the front door. Paramedics were rolling in a gurney with hanging IV bottles and straps holding a person wrapped in thick blankets.

"Excuse us. Coming through," the medics said as they dropped a stack of papers on the desk and moved deeper into the building. "To the right. Keep to the right," she heard someone direct them as they rolled into the sea of curtains. She looked back across the building. Dozens of rooms, spaces, maybe a hundred.

"Miss? Can I help you?" a lady's voice drew her out of her daze.

Rachel gave the clipboard and file folder to the lady at the desk. "Checking out, I guess," Rachel said. •

RACHEL'S STORY
CHAPTER 19: GUS?

The lady raised up a piece of paper and another young volunteer got up from the bench in the entry and dashed over to her. "318," the lady said as she handed the note to the kid. This girl was even younger than the kid named Alex, who had brought her lunch tray. Rachel wondered if the numbers had started with "1"? Was she the 318th person to go through here?

"Excuse me, ma'am," Rachel approached the lady at the desk once more. "Did the numbers start at 1?"

"Yes, we started at 1. We're probably the least busy unit. Closer to Butte, they'll be in the thousands now. We're mostly overflow for Missoula."

The girl returned with a cart and two large plastic tubs. "318" was taped to the side of each bin. "Here's your things," she said. "There's a dressing area." She pointed to one of the curtained spaces just behind the desk.

"Thank you. Thank you so much," Rachel smiled at the girl. She might have been 10 years old, but not any older. The girl nodded.

Rachel pulled the cart behind the drape and opened the first box. It was her Critical Box and a bunch of the stuff that had been in her Emergency Box. She found the hatchet, nylon cord, her phone, Gus's leash. She began to feel tears well up in her eyes again, but she fought back the emotion. She continued digging through the containers. The second tub held her backpack, her vest, her 9mm and the ammo clips, and her clothes. Her clothes were neatly folded, and as she unwrapped them to redress she smiled. She had grabbed the old fireman's jacket that belonged to Jake's dad from the Family Box a while back in the trip. She'd thought the badge might get her through a tight spot. It was just going to be a prop, but she hadn't found a use for it yet.

"Uh, Chief?" a male voice asked from just outside the curtain.

Rachel had finished getting dressed and she pulled her hair back into a pony tail. The jacket was much too big for her, but she slipped it on and rolled up the sleeves. It made her feel closer to Jake and his family. She stepped back into the open room, pulling her tubs on the cart. “Hi, I’m Rachel,” she said, greeting the uniformed man who was standing there.

“Hi. I wanted to introduce myself. I’m Chief Livingston, Lolo’s volunteer fire chief. Were you headed here?” he had a look of wonder on his face as he looked at the sharp but banged-up red haired lady, wearing her stylishly oversized jacket, sporting a badge that matched his own.

“I’m so sorry, Chief. I’m not really a chief myself. This is my father-in-law’s jacket. It was just in the truck with me. I guess people assumed...” Rachel began to explain.

“Ha, well that does explain some things,” he interjected. “They called me on the radio saying a young woman with some sort of custom rescue rig had been in an accident. Said she had a badge that read “Casey, Iowa,” which didn’t make any sense way out here. But, you were carrying a note from a police captain, and you were pretty well armed.”

He paused for a moment. The confusion was understandable. The man continued, “Then I saw your truck. It’s beautiful. Looks like a ’70. Restored?” He obviously knew his trucks. “I couldn’t see anybody driving that for rescue. Although it is red,” he winked.

“Is the Blazer okay?” Rachel asked. Followed immediately with, “I’m so sorry. There’s so much more going on here. That was a selfish question. I’m sorry.”

“Actually they towed it into our station. It’s over there now. And I’ve got to tell you, it’s brought some smiles to some faces that haven’t smiled in a few days,” he paused and swallowed, setting his jaw. “There’s been a lot of loss. And there’s gonna be more.” He shook his head as he completed his words and swallowed hard.

They walked across to the fire station, its doors open, all of the units gone except an old pumper, probably from the '80s. "They've gone to the Bozeman area. It's pretty rough down there," the Chief said, noticing Rachel's look into the open bays.

There was the Blazer, off the trailer and sitting on the grass next to the fire station. It looked perfect – except for the coating of ash and dust and a long deep scrape that ran down the entire driver's side from the door to the tail. "Ouch," Rachel said out loud.

"Your other truck's a goner though." The Chief helped Rachel lift the tubs into the back of the Blazer. "In fact, the boys in the chopper were surprised you were alive. Everything in the truck was destroyed on impact they said. Pulled the box clean off the frame. Split it in half."

"Oh no!" Rachel reacted. "What about the other driver?"

The Chief just shook his head. It wasn't good.

"But, there is this guy," the Chief drew Rachel's attention back toward the open doors of the station. Gus came running toward her, carrying one front leg, which was wrapped. He was pretty banged up and had some burrs, but he was trying his best to jump on her, his tail wagging fiercely. "He was laying under your little red truck here, refused to leave it. He's been here at the station the past couple days."

Rachel was so excited to see Gus, she was hugging him and rolling him on the ground, checking out his leg.

"Couple of days?" She'd been unconscious for nearly three days? No wonder they seemed shocked by her exit.

Another ambulance pulled up outside the community center, across the street. It said "Boise" on the side. The paramedics pulled two gurneys out of the back and rolled them through the doors. As they were going in, one of the doctors was running out. It was the man she'd seen with the "SURG" tag around his neck.

“Hey, Chief!” the doctor called.

Both Rachel and the man responded, walking quickly in his direction.

“I need to get back up to Missoula. Got a bad one coming in.” The doctor was carrying his backpack and a small duffle bag. “Any ideas?”

The Chief looked a bit blank. While he’d been incredibly friendly and helpful to Rachel, she could tell he was tired and under a lot of stress. All of them were. His momentary silence was all she needed to hear.

“I’m headed for Missoula right now. If I’ve got enough gas,” Rachel said. “You’ll need to give me directions.”

She gave the fire chief a big hug and hobbled back toward the Blazer. She set Gus up in the back, with the stuff from the tubs, and the doctor crawled up in. As always, the engine fired right up. Rachel tapped on the gas gauge to make sure. It read full.

The surgeon was a fairly young guy. “Never seen one of these before,” he said, looking around the interior of the old classic truck. “Is it new?”

•

RACHEL'S STORY
CHAPTER 20: MISSOULA

On the outer edge of Lolo, Rachel saw another of the many green highway signs she'd read throughout this trip. "Missoula 10." Only 10 miles to Missoula. At times, she had thought she'd never be this close. Their furniture was lost, family photos, CDs and albums, clothes, and countless mementos – and she didn't care one bit about any of that right now. Her shoulders were sore, the massive bruise from the seat belt that had saved her life was turning her entire chest purple. The medication on the stitches burned, and her throat was still raw – and she was incredibly happy for where she was right now.

Right now, she was alive, driving her and Jake's classic Blazer, with Gus, who she'd thought was lost, and she was less than 100 miles from the lake house. And, she was helping a young surgeon get to an emergency surgery to hopefully save one of the thousands or millions impacted by this historic disaster. Weighed against what so many others were going through, she felt blessed.

Highway 93 was familiar to Rachel. It was the road they drove every day when she and Jake went into town from the lake. She was looking forward to seeing Missoula, as she was somewhat familiar with the streets and locations. They'd passed by it often and stopped a few times for dinner or lunch. They'd also made a few shopping trips and enjoyed the historic downtown area. It was a neat little city. And being home to the University of Montana, it had a fun, young vibe as well. But that was before. She was curious to see what might have changed.

"I appreciate you driving me up here," said the young doctor, opening up some conversation for the trip.

"Sure. It's the least I can do. Your team looked after me for a couple of days," Rachel replied. Her leg was really starting to burn, probably from the stitches, and she realized that the motion of the Blazer was also making her head throb.

"Hey Doc, I know you're thanking for me for driving you, but could you drive? I think I might have jumped back in the saddle a bit too early."

"Actually, I don't know how to drive," the young man responded. "My parents used public transportation, and I have an autobot. I've never driven a car."

"No way! Not a go-cart, a dune buggy? A golf cart? No offense, but you're a doctor!" Rachel's take may have been a little too direct. "I'm sorry. What I'm saying is, you're obviously super-smart, so it seems like a pretty basic skill."

"Nice recovery," the doctor laughed. "No, I've just never done it. And none of my friends drive. I mean, why? The services are so easy to use."

"I guess," she said. "But it gives you so much freedom, so much independence. And, it's time for you to learn, if you really want to get to your appointment." Rachel's head was really spinning.

She stopped on the edge of the road and coaxed him into the driver's seat. Gus made a whimpering sound and curled up down on the floor. "Come on, Gus," Rachel said. "Have a little faith."

"Okay, Doc," Rachel said. "This is the steering wheel. It connects to the front wheels with a rod that rotates a gear set. The more you turn the wheel, the more the vehicle changes direction. It's proportional." Her instructions were a little heady, but she figured that, as a smart man, he might grasp it all at a higher level. "Does that make sense, or am I sounding silly?"

"No, no. That's perfect. I get it. And my name is Steven," he added.

Rachel ran through all of the controls – the gear shift, the accelerator, the brakes, really just the basic items he'd need. The little truck had been originally built in 1970, so it didn't offer a lot of features. She also told him about "feel," which he would develop pretty quickly, she believed. And distance planning. Knowing how long it would take to stop and not turning too sharply at speed. Slow. Easy.

Steven pulled the shifter down into drive. The little truck answered with a feel of engagement. He eased off the brakes and they began to roll forward. Looking over his shoulder, he eased out onto the road. As he pushed the accelerator, he smiled.

"This is awesome!" he giggled. "It does exactly what I want it to do! I could go anywhere!" He was acting like a kid, laughing and checking out the blinkers and talking to himself as he drove along. He was thrilled as they drove down the highway.

"Steven, you're doing great. But you've got to go faster than 20 miles per hour," Rachel hinted.

"Oh, right," he quipped, as he pushed the accelerator a bit deeper and moved the needle up to around 50. "Wow. This. Is. Just. Awesome."

By the time they reached the Missoula City Limits sign, Steven was right at home. He was an avid bike rider, so he understood all of the pieces of road awareness, keeping a line of tack, looking ahead – this was just different from what he was used to. He was a natural, attentive and aware of the road and the machine.

Rachel's headache was better, probably, she thought, because her mind was focused on teaching Steven to drive. And her leg was more comfortable as well. Maybe this was just something that she needed to do. Maybe deep down, she just needed to bring some awareness to this bright young surgeon.

Rolling through the streets of Missoula, Steven was driving like a pro. He even had his arm on the edge of the window, driving with one hand and talking. It made her proud. Even Gus had climbed up off of the floor to look around.

Like every other town she'd been through lately, the streets were littered with dead autobots and rows of EVs, all in line at the charging stations, vacant. Some of them had phone numbers written on the windows. "Call to move." How would anybody call? The cells were down, with no electricity to run them.

Even though Flathead Lake, where Rachel was heading, had a large hydroelectric dam, it would only generate so much power until the water levels dropped too far. And where would the power go? That was all being hashed out in Washington, no doubt. The power would go to the highest bidder, which meant California. But there was no system in operation to carry it. She hoped they wouldn't drain her beautiful lake. The water was so clear you could drink it. And she believed that they may need to drink it. It would certainly be a major source of food for many while this was being resolved. She was wondering about a lot of things, and so were many others.

Navigating the stalled cars, they weaved their way through Missoula. They both watched for signs for the airport, where one of the large medevac units had been placed. Steven had been there before, but of course, he hadn't been driving.

As they got closer to the airport, she noticed more National Guard troops as well as other armed people standing in front of businesses and at intersections. Barricades had been placed to block a number of the commercial parking lots and a line of people flowed across the Walmart property. Rachel looked closer toward the entrance and saw what appeared to be armed guards, standing on each side of the doors. A small generator was shooting light through the store's windows.

"Walmart has armed guards?" Rachel asked.

The doctor tilted his head and nodded. "Wait 'til you see Costco," he said.

They passed by Target, which also had guards and a long line. A number of semitrucks were sitting in the parking lot, but Rachel noticed their rear doors were open, and they stood empty. "EMPTY" was spray-painted on one of the fuel tanks.

At the next intersection, they turned toward the airport. There was Costco. Red boards had been fastened across the entrance in the shape of an "X" and what looked like a pair of snipers stood on the roof. "Are those...?" she pondered.

"I think so, yes," the doctor said. "It's going to get pretty shaky before this is all over. I don't know what your plans are, but I hope you have some." He looked back out the windshield and continued his thoughts.

"I'm glad I'm here. Kind of inside the system," he stated, seeming to speak more to himself than Rachel. "I wouldn't have been prepared. My fridge has a few energy drinks. My pantry? It's where I keep my workout gear. I'm really worried about my family."

He looked pretty vulnerable at the moment.

"Where is your family?" Rachel inquired, hoping it would be a positive answer.

"Denver," he replied softly. He started to say something else, but he stopped. A couple of silent moments passed. "Here's our gate," he said.

They turned into the complex at the first set of barriers.

He handed his lanyard and some other papers to the guards.

Rachel could hear the beat of choppers in the air. A large transport plane crossed over them and touched down on the runway. This was a serious checkpoint with full-auto weapons and large metal crossbucks blocking the passage. They had to make three consecutive 90-degree turns to make it through the gauntlet after the guards approved their entrance.

Steven pulled the little red truck up to the row of temporary buildings sitting next to one of the main hangers. The doctor grabbed his bags. "This is my stop," he said, searching for anything to say that might be recognized as a bit lighthearted. "I wish I could..." his emotions started to show.

"You're doing everything you can," Rachel said. "Thank you so much. From all of us, thank you. Stay safe, okay? And keep driving!"

He pulled it together and smiled, closing the door with his hip. Gus whimpered from the back and Rachel said. "Alright. Come on up."

Rachel moved around to the driver's position. Gus moved gingerly to the front seat and made himself comfortable. He'd never been allowed in the classic cars before, but it seemed a lot of rules had changed. Rachel was just glad to have him with her. She made her way back to Highway 93 and turned north. They would be at the lake in a couple of hours. •

• • • • • • • • END OF "RACHEL'S STORY" • • • • • • • •

Gus and the Blazer at Lolo, Montana.

"...our world has fallen
into darkness, but I know
each day he is closer. We will
be together again soon..."
– Rachel, waiting for Jake

CHAPTER 49: CANADA, OH CANADA

I slid to a stop just outside the modern metal and glass structure, physically exhausted but emotionally wound. I got out of the truck and paced in a small circle for a few seconds.

The dam! I needed to tell them about the dam. I ran to the side window, next to the lanes where incoming traffic would have stopped. I knocked on the frame and caught the man's attention.

"Hey, what's the deal? Are you okay?" a man called out from the back of the guard station. There was only one vehicle in sight, a little pastel autobot with a government sticker on the side. I assumed he was alone.

"Yeah, I'm okay." I answered. I probably looked a bit crazed. I certainly felt that way.

"Do you have a radio?" I pleaded. "The dam broke. Down at Wolf Point. From the earthquakes," I exclaimed. I was shouting through the thickness of the glass.

"Wolf Point? You mean Fort Peck Lake?" his voice moved from standard questioning to a higher level of intensity. "Ah hell, what's next? No, our radios are out. Went down with the power. I've got my solar stuff here, but nobody's in range."

He moved over to a map on the wall. He turned back towards me, perhaps hopeful, and his voice became more normal again, although shouting for me to hear.

“How bad? You mean, it flooded the road?” His gaze returned to the map.

“No. Really bad. The towns down river are probably gone.”

“SHIT!” he slammed his hand on the map. “Goddamn it. I’ve got to...I need to...” He began staggering around the area behind the counter, looking at his radio set, looking at the map. It looked like he wanted to leave but was conflicted with manning his post. I guessed it was his family. We were only about 60 miles from Wolf Point. It was the closest town of any size.

“Is there anything I can do to help you?” I asked, as he appeared to become more and more frantic.

“Are you sure?” he stopped and asked, returning to the wall map. “Frazer. Right there. The town of Frazer?” He held his hand up to the wall, pointing at the map. His eyes were locked on me.

I looked at the detail of the road. That’s probably about where I had stopped, maybe a mile or two in either direction, but that’s where I had been. I nodded.

“I’m sorry,” I said.

“I gotta go!” He grabbed his walkie-talkie and ran out the side door. He jumped into the government-issue autobot. I watched him fumble with the control pod, trying to get it into some form of manual mode, but it wouldn’t let him override the programmed setup. He pounded on the little dash panel as the tiny car hummed slowly onto the road and pulled away, maintaining a safe and steady speed. It looked surreal.

In your mind, the frantic person jumps into their car and speeds away, throwing gravel and squealing tires as they fishtail down the road, shifting through the gears, the roar of the exhaust trailing off into the distance. That’s the vision that we all see in that situation. Instead, what I witnessed was a guy the size of a linebacker, crammed into a light blue plastic egg, pulling away slowly and peacefully, with only a slight buzzing sound that quickly diminished to silence. The visual was more like an Easter parade than a desperate man's flight to save someone's life.

I should have cared more. I really should have. But I wondered what his choices had been. Was he, in his heart, against all of this crap that was trapping us all without any options in this situation? Had he stood up to his superiors when they replaced his pickup truck or Tahoe with a glamorized golf cart? If I had been a truly dangerous felon, what could he have done? Would he have tasered me? What if the charging port for the taser was dead? Would he have asked me nicely to stay on this side of the imaginary line that blocked my passage into Canada?

I didn't know who he was going to save, but I knew it was probably too late. I wasn't happy with myself for being so cold and bitter, but I'd nearly died twice, and I was understanding the logic of being a wolf instead of a sheep.

I got back in the truck and continued north, driving under the gantry of electronic sensors and cameras that were put in place to scan and record every vehicle that passed through the checkpoint. Undoubtedly the best and latest in tech and hardware, linked to the national grid, featuring facial recognition, license plate readers, infrared heat and chemical detectors, high-definition visual and audio recorders, and probably even more stuff than I could imagine. Designed, developed, delivered, and connected to the NSA's data bank of images and records, for indepth, real-time acquisition of archived information and cross-reference of who, what, and where was associated with anyone passing through the array.

There was only one small problem. It was off.

Unimpeded by the million-dollar investment in security apparatus, I simply drove through and stopped on the Canadian side of the line. The two stations were about a quarter-mile apart. A slight-build kid, handsome and clean cut, greeted me at the passenger window of the truck.

I thought about how this was going to go. I had my passport in my Critical Box as well as my driver's license, so my ID was going to be covered. But my truck had no plates. I still had them, stuck in the back, along side the big fuel tank, and I could screw them back on, but right here, in front of border patrol? That would look a little odd. And then what do I tell them when they take a look around the vehicle? "Here's my secondary fuel tank, a bunch of gas cans, a few thousand rounds of ammo, oh, and a few guns. There's a police light, but it's my dad's." I could already feel the handcuffs on my wrists.

Maybe this was another time to ask forgiveness instead of permission. Since he appeared to be the only one there, and with everything that was going on, maybe he didn't have communication with anyone either. That was likely. We were a long trek away from anybody on either side of the line, certainly too far for a standard two-way radio. I considered hammering the accelerator and just going. I wondered if those might be the best odds. If they stop me further into Canada, I'd beg forgiveness. It's not like anybody's going to give me permission.

Permission? Geez. I had permission. I dug around in my backpack and grabbed the envelope from the sergeant. I pulled out just the second page. "Nobody was to delay my mission." That's what the letter said, on official government paper, stamped and signed.

I was clear and direct. I handed the young guard my passport and license, along with the second page of the letter. I put both hands on top of the steering wheel and looked straight ahead. I said, "I was traveling Highway 2, en route to Kalispell. An earthquake broke the dam at Fort Peck Lake and blocked the road. I need your permission to use Canada 1 to get to Glacier National Park." I took a deep breath and waited.

"The dam broke?" he asked.

"Yes sir, not an hour ago. I barely escaped. I was below it when it happened. I really need to get going. Did you see the letter?" I played as serious as I could.

He was standing just outside the passenger window, where a tuft of buffalo hair still adorned the broken mount where my rearview mirror used to sit.

I added, "For what it's worth, I've got a big red 'C' spray painted on my hood from the last checkpoint." It wasn't completely true, but it wasn't necessarily false.

He walked around to the front of the truck and pulled a color card out of his pocket. He laid it on the hood and checked the color on the "C".

"The color's gotta match," he said flatly, explaining what he was doing.

"Yes. Correct color is important. Canada has good branding." I don't remember whether I was being sarcastic or ironic or simply stating fact. But I thought it was an interesting detail that a specific red had been designated, as some base-level security device.

He stood there for another moment, looking at my crimson C and reading back over the letter. He took another check through my passport. Then he handed me my credentials and waved me through. "Good luck, sir," he said.

"Thank you. Thank you so much." •

CHAPTER 50: UNCHARTED TERRITORY

I had no maps for Canada, just the thin strip of territories that appeared above the U.S. highway layout on the front spread of my atlas, along with an even thinner strip at the top of the Montana page. I'd never anticipated utilizing Canada in any part of my plan. Perhaps I was too limited in my thinking. But that was the information I had, so I made the best choice I could. I chose the big, main route – the Trans-Canada Highway, Canada 1. It would require extra time and fuel to reach, as it lie almost 100 miles north of the border. But once on it, I could run nonstop, dropping onto Highway 3 at Medicine Hat, and on to Fort MacLeod.

That's where I'd turn south and begin winding my way back into the United States. Then on to the lake. I decided it would be the most efficient pathway overall. And hopefully it would provide the least risk and drama. Frankly, I liked the names, too: Moose Jaw, Medicine Hat. They sounded authentic. And I was hoping less encumbered.

As long as I kept my truck pointed north I would run into Canada 1. Through the name, I pictured a wide, smooth superhighway. "Trans-Canada" sounded very modern and 1970s futuristic. "Canada 1" had to be the ultimate, top-notch road in the country. I'd see when I got there.

I supposed that if I ran north long enough, eventually Santa could help me get back home if necessary, like he did with Karen and Frosty – in a time when life was simple. But we grow from those childhood tales and chart our long-term paths. Some people stay on track forever, enjoying the continuity and repetition. Some wear it into a deep groove, trapped by walls that limit their vision and drag them down. Some skip around on the record, jumping from path to path, sampling a variety of lives.

Some pick a path, but the road changes. Detours are placed by others, and routes are put off course.

I realized on this journey that my life's path had been a mix of these. Mostly I'd charted my own way, but there had been obstacles, hills, and ravines. Across the course of life, I'd been trapped in ruts and managed to either climb out or be helped out by others. Along the way, I'd been fortunate in those I'd met and befriended. That had been the spice of my life's flavors. I always seemed to find exceptional people around me. The ride had been a good ride, and I hoped that it continued.

Reconnecting with Rachel would be the pinnacle for me. I knew that we could work around whatever was in front of us. We could grow food, rebuild our lives.

We had a beautiful little cabin that held everything we needed. Alex would be safe in Tennessee as he rebuilt, and the country rebuilt around him. I still wondered about my folks and about Rachel's family. But just getting out of the ash and hysteria was calming my thoughts and giving me a renewed sense of hope for everyone.

Driving north, breathing clean air, and seeing some clear sky, I was invigorated and excited about where life would lead. But first I needed to finish my plan. Just as my maps had run out, so had my plan for the rest of my journey – arriving, continuing. •

CHAPTER 51: PLUG ME IN

Driving in Canada was like returning to Kansas a few years prior. The sunset in the west was casting beautiful light across the plains, saturating the green and yellow colors of spring. If you were looking to make brilliant photographs, this was the time of day for it. "God's light" is what we used to call it back in the day, when you could still use terms like that in a professional setting. And it was true.

The sun's warm pre-evening rays coming straight in from the side, warming every surface and enhancing every hue. The shadows were rich and blue with reflected sky light filling in the details of every crevice, line, and wrinkle. It was spectacular, and driving north, it filled my windshield with the beauty I'd always enjoyed crossing the plains in America. Oklahoma, Kansas, Nebraska, the Dakotas, the eastern edge of Colorado, and Wyoming. I wondered what those places would look like in a year, five years, beyond.

There would always be the contrast now. The difference between what was and what is. The difference between here and there. The clash of what we had become and what we would become. I had looked forward to unplugging from everything, the emails, the social media circus, the game. I had asked for a more simple life, and evidently, God was going to provide just that.

Perhaps I shouldn't have wished so hard, or maybe I should have been more deliberate in my prayers. Specificity is always a good thing. I needed to remember that, although most people were probably tired of my overly detailed analytics. So maybe I just needed to be more direct in my daily life, but more refined in my faith. I could do that. I'd work on it.

I chose not to stop in Moose Jaw, although I really wanted to. It had such a unique appeal, but I still had no license plates mounted to the truck, and I was carrying a lot of weaponry. Again, best to opt for the smaller places.

Swift Current had an appealing name as well, and the sun would be lower in the sky. It would be nearly dusk when I rolled through there, and my lights were all still covered in black gaff tape. I'd need to unwrap those, if I was going to be driving at night. I made a Sharpie circle on the map. Swift Current. It would probably be about 7 p.m. when I arrived.

The trek along Canada 1, the Trans-Canada Highway, was almost relaxing. If it hadn't been for the horrible surface conditions caused by relentless severe weather and freezing and thawing subsoils, I may have been able to take one hand off of the steering wheel. Some of the miles were as smooth as silk. Others were cratered with potholes rivaled only by the state of New York's highway system. Those parts, which were actually most of it, were brutal, to both body and machine, but I should harbor no complaints. It wasn't the big, wide super-slab I'd hoped for, but it was taking me where I needed to go.

Rolling toward Swift Current, I saw signs for all of the major fuel and electric stations. I wanted to see if any were actually open for business. It hadn't dawned on me whether or not Canada would be in the same power fix as the U.S. Were our systems connected? It would have made sense, logistically, especially in the remote areas that made up most of the border along my route. But I had no idea. I looked around the landscape. I saw a few farm lights coming on as the sky darkened. They could be generators, or personal solar units, but the answers I'd find in town would fill in the blanks.

Swift Current appeared to have power, so I selected one of the larger stations. No surprise, I picked the one with the signage I was most familiar with. My big tank still had their brand of fuel in it anyway, so I might as well be consistent. As Dad always said, "You dance with those who brung ya." What he meant was, you show loyalty and preference for those who show the same toward you.

I remembered as a young boy, maybe 10 years old, I was standing next to Dad at the grocery store. He was working behind the meat counter helping a customer. It was nearly lunchtime. I tugged on his pant leg or apron and asked for some lunch money. "Can I go get a hamburger?" I had said.

"In a minute," he said, referencing the customer standing on the other side of the case. So I stood and waited. I was always pretty well-behaved, as far as my parents knew.

When he was finished wrapping some meat for the man, he turned to me and knelt down. "Here's a dollar," he said. "Today, you're eating lunch down at Jerry's Cafe."

"Ah, I don't like the hamburgers at Jerry's," I replied. "They have too much stuff on 'em." Jerry's place stacked lettuce and tomato and pickles and onions on their burgers. And they toasted the buns and made them too crispy. I preferred the basic meat and cheese burger on a big soft roll, the kind that was served at one of the other cafes in town. My taste in cuisine had always been pretty simple.

"No. Today, you're going to Jerry's."

"Why?"

"Because the customer at the counter, the man I was helping, was Jerry. He's doing business here, so we're going to do business there." It was a point that obviously stuck with me to this day. "Do you understand?" he asked.

I nodded. I understood.

"Ya dance with those who brung ya."

"Thanks, Dad!" And truly, "Thanks, Dad" for all that you ever taught me about the nuances of life and business. I missed my Dad a lot.

But that is what lead me to that particular fuel and charging station. Sure, I'd lifted a tanker's worth of fuel from them a few days ago, but I wouldn't be sending a bill for my time. The time that had set much of this in motion. I was calling it even. So now, we'd move forward.

I parked the truck next to the far queue at the charging ports. It was away from the door, away from the handful of other vehicles that dotted the lot. I locked the doors and walked toward the entrance. An attendant was coming out to the pumps and chargers.

"Do you have any fuel?" I asked as he passed by.

"Sure," he seemed a little surprised by the question. "Gasoline, diesel... for now."

"For now?" I puzzled.

"Well, you know, until they screw us like they did down in the States. So, yeah. For now."

That was all I needed to hear. I returned to my truck and pulled to the pumps. I filled everything I had. The truck tank and the spare cans. I had forgotten that I'd lost the two looter's bait cans that had been tied to the back. That was disappointing, as that was 10 more gallons I could have added.

I loved the old pumps that they had, the kind with the flip-up handle and no digital keypads. Probably the last station on the planet to use them. They even had a dumping station, so I was able to refresh the questionable supply I'd picked up in Nebraska. This would get me to the lake with plenty to spare.

I walked inside to pay.

"It's cash only," said the lady behind the counter. "All of the credit systems are down 'cause of that blackout."

“No worries,” I said, pulling out the cash in my pocket.

“And we can’t do the loyalty card discount either. Do you use this brand often? I can get you a loyalty card if you don’t have one. You just can’t use it now.”

“That’s okay,” I quipped. “I’ve had mixed success with this company and its loyalty lately.” I was pretty amused at myself for getting in a little jab at the corporate structure, even if I was the only one to appreciate it.

I handed her the cash and she winced. “Dollars?” she said.

“Oh, I’m sorry.” Obviously I hadn’t planned on needing different currency.

“Yeah, I don’t know what the value of this is going to be anymore,” she stated, fanning through the bills, talking mostly to herself. And she was right. A lot of the heritage of certainty, the premise of strength and value that had long been related to the U.S. dollar, was certainly on the chopping block right then. We’d been in trouble before, economically, back during the whole COVID fiasco, but that was a worldwide downturn. It made a deep impact, but everybody was in the same boat. The whole globe had shut down, taking everyone down with it. But this was different. This would be a U.S. issue. The rest of the world would keep on chugging along. Would we be the shutouts? Would the open borders concept work both ways?

“Are your cell phones working?” I asked. Hoping that I could get in a call to Alex. In reality, it had only been a few days, but in my mind, it had been forever.

“You can give it a try. I don’t think the U.S. cells are working. Maybe if its an old landline?” she shrugged.

Sure enough, I couldn’t get anything except a fast busy signal. I tried Alex, Mom and Dad, and Rachel. I also tried Rachel’s family, the ones I had numbers for. No response from any of them. It was still dark down there.

"What do you hear about all of that?" I asked, hoping they might have some untainted information or news that hadn't been spun and politicized.

"Sounds like a bad deal. They're saying at least a year, probably more. I think they're gonna divide the country into sections. Mostly focused on the coasts, you know. They've got to bring the pipelines back on, the refineries. It's going to be bad for a lot of people. You American?" she finally asked.

"Yeah," I nodded.

"I'm not sure how you got here, 'cause the border's shut down. At least that's what I heard. We can't take them all in. We've gotta look after ourselves."

She went on to talk about Canada's energy supplies, even the heavy oil that's plentiful in northern Canada. It's incredibly expensive to produce and refine, but at least they've got a variety of resources in play. Canada had remained welcoming to nuclear energy as well, and they had added solar and wind to give them a broad range of options. And they had never stopped using a particular source or placed a restriction on usage due to political pressure. Given their long harsh winters and wide open spaces, liquid fuels and natural gas were a necessity and would remain so for the foreseeable future. She summed it up pretty well in her final comment to me.

"I think the States got ahead of themselves. And it's sad. The people are going to pay a big price for that."

I thanked her for the updates and the currency conversion, as well as sharing her perspective.

"Oh," I asked. "Are your charging stations open for EVs?"

“Yeah, but not many here have moved beyond hybrids. Across the longer distances, you know, people don’t trust ’em. It’s like those little pod things that drive by themselves. That’s just crazy. I can’t imagine people who are incapable of driving.”

“Well said. Thanks.”

I was excited to have a full supply of fuel and to be on my way home. To our new home. With Rachel, at the lake. •

CHAPTER 52: RETURN TO AMERICA

The road to Medicine Hat was more of the same bouncing and banging across uneven asphalt and rugged cement. A smattering of lights dotted the world around me, but I had no reference. Was this a normal night? Were half the lights off? Most? A few? Either way, they had electricity here, at least some. And I'd been able to get fuel. If everything went bad at the lake, we could always escape to Canada, although the lady at the fuel stop was in favor of a closed border. I understood her position, and I felt the same about our own. But the reality was, if enough pressure was applied, we'd cross, just as others had crossed ours.

And Canada was close enough that we might be able to make fuel runs into the northland for a refill on tanks and barrels. It was still unknown. We'd see in the coming days and months how that would play out. We might be close enough to work some blackmarket fuel if it came to that.

It was getting late when I crossed onto Highway 3 at Medicine Hat. I'd run it to Fort MacLeod, then come straight down into the top of Montana, crossing the border back into the U.S. I assumed the border station would be open at night. I'd never known a country to be "closed," but maybe, following this event, America would be.

I followed the signs and drove by sheer rote practice. I was exhausted and wondered if I should just stop and sleep. I couldn't risk falling asleep behind the wheel – the one thing the autobots had on me. It didn't matter whether their driver was awake, sleeping, stoned, or not even there. I recalled the sight of my first empty autobot, driving down the street, taking itself to its driver. That had been a moment to remember.

It would be around midnight when I crossed over the border. Another pair of guard houses, one on each side. The Canadians would probably be glad to see me go. The Americans, I hoped, would welcome me home.

And that's about how it went. The checkpoint on the Canada side took a cursory look at my papers and waved me on. I'd only been there a few hours, and I made sure that my special letter was on top of the stack.

Pulling into the U.S. side, the facility nearly matched the one I'd seen earlier in the day. "Anything to declare?" was the standard question.

What would I say? "Well, my son and I stole a rack of garden seeds from a Walmart in Missouri. Oh, and I hijacked a tanker truck from a fuel terminal in southern Iowa, trashed a few blocks of Blair, Nebraska, and shot a man in North Dakota. On the bright side, however, I donated two hundred gallons of fuel to my local volunteer fire department, helped the Army position a charging station in western Montana, and alerted authorities to a dam break near Wolf Point. Oh, and I bought some roasted peanuts and a case of Coke in Swift Current."

"So, anything to declare?" the border agent asked again, bringing me out of my day dream.

"Not really. Some peanuts and soda," I replied.

I was tired, but the conversation was waking me up. My adrenaline was beginning to kick in. I'd need it to get the finish line.

I remembered all of the fuel, the ammo. I handed him the letter.

"This should cover it." I looked him in the eye, and his gaze dropped to the letter.

He read through it and turned it over, looking at the back. The government seal was actually stamped into the paper. He flipped through the rest of my documents and handed them back to me. He walked around the truck and checked out the random damage.

"Looks like you've had quite a trip," he added.

I nodded and put my papers back in the console. My pistol and shotgun were still there, in plain sight. I'd completely forgotten about them. Maybe after seeing the letter, he decided not to question them. Or maybe he just understood their purpose.

I pulled ahead, again passing below the dead electronic arch of security intended to keep me safe. So much of it was illusion. Like the shoe check at the airport, scanning my 80-year old mother's purse, and the fences that ran from the checkpoint where I sat. Solid and secure, they ran out a few hundred feet into the trees then just stopped.

But I was glad to be back. I was proud of my country and all of its problems. It was still the best place in the world. I hit the high beams and headed toward Glacier. •

CHAPTER 53: GLACIER

Bordering Glacier, I thought about all of the years we had bordered Yellowstone, failing to stop and appreciate its grandeur. Had people traveled this same road for years, never turning in to explore the trails and beauty the park offered? I guessed it was possible. We had done just that.

Although it was completely dark now, winding down the eastern edge, I could imagine all of the white caps, christening the peaks across the entire range. Most of the snow had melted down here along the main road, but above, "Going to the Sun Road," the scenic drive that wound up and over the pass in the park, would still be closed. Most years, that road didn't open end to end until late June. And I'd seen it still closed on the Fourth of July. Cutting the deep path through the banks of snow required a host of patience and technical skill. Avalanches were always a possibility. Then, after all of that annual effort, it might stay open for four months at the most. The snow would close it down again by mid-October. That's probably what kept it beautiful – keeping humanity out for most of the year.

I was at the point in the drive where the "snow sheds" over the train tracks had always interested me. Where the railroad tracks have been cut from the edge of the mountain, long structures of wooden truss and metal roofs create an open tunnel-like building, running for incredible distances, keeping snow and falling rock from blocking the rails. This had been the first place I'd ever seen them, and I had been impressed with not only the engineering and construction, but the original concept. Somebody had walked into a room and said, "I have an idea!" I loved those moments, and I loved those people. Original thoughts have lost a lot of value in recent times, so I will always champion those who will risk sharing their visions and ideas with others. There are always those who will ridicule and naysay, but those who take the chance, they are the ones who catch my attention.

So did a mule deer, standing in the middle of the road. I was glad that I no longer had a 170-foot road train behind me, as I couldn't have stopped in time. I braked to a stop and watched him. A lone bull, taking a late-night stroll through his territory. He stood in profile to me, turning his head slowly to size me up, weighing his choices. Unafraid, he stood there for a minute or so, finally taking a couple of graceful steps to the side of the road and into the trees.

I'd met mule deer before. My favorite was another lone male, crossing my path. I had been out on a hike, by myself, to gather my senses and ponder the questions of life. That's code for "me time" – we all need that on occasion. I was hiking up the trail to Avalanche Lake, above the main road by Lake McDonald. It was early in the season and not many others were out yet on that morning. Cruising along, my head down, watching the rocks and roots that formed the trail on that particular hillside, I suddenly caught a glimpse of fuzzy tan hair. I stopped on a dime. And so did he.

We were face-to-face, standing on the trail. He'd been coming down, I was going up. Our noses were about 18 inches apart, and we just looked at each other. Realizing he was a deer, I said, "Well, hello. How are you this morning?" Although he didn't answer me, he did simply step around a tree that bordered the path, and we each continued on our way. We were just two animals, passing each other on the road of life. He respected me. I respected him. We both carried on.

Had that been a mama grizzly, with me between her and her cubs, it would have been a different story. One that I would likely not be here to tell. Again, simply two animals on a path, but an entirely different outcome. Even though I would have meant her no harm, she would not have known that or cared. Her responsibility was to her kiddos and she would respond in an all-out assault on me to defend them. I was lucky it was a lonely deer, just looking for someone to talk to.

And that's the road of life as well. We try to pay attention; we must pay attention. We must determine if those we are meeting are friend or foe. And we must be willing and able to defend ourselves in a manner superior to who or what we cross. That's how mutual respect is forged. That's how we survive to tell the tale.

Rounding the bend, I passed the entrance to West Glacier. The roads were empty, the buildings dark. I could see the light from the fireplace in a couple of homes I passed. I'd never noticed that before, as the yard lights and porch lights, and other lights left on in the houses had always outshone the flickering yellow glow. It looked welcoming.

The road was familiar to me now, having driven this particular stretch many times, returning from hikes with Rachel, day-long sightseeing tours with friends and family members, and a few of my own personal escapes into nature.

It had been the longest day of my life. Not in hours, as I'd turned a significant number of 24-hour days in college and the career. All-night road trips had always been a part of keeping up with Alex's schedules for games and events.

The day had started in Minot, in a gigantic road-train contraption, the likes of which I'd never seen in person. Taking it across the ash-washed plains, and seeing the sea of medevac choppers coming in, also, unlike anything I'd ever witnessed. The tumbling wall of water, chasing me through the valley – the curious man in the red truck, whom I'd watched die, buried beneath thousands of tons of rolling mud.

That was followed by the drive into Canada. The near normalcy of the fuel stop had been a mental oasis for the past few days. And now, I was close, so close to Rachel and the cabin. I knew the road. I hoped for her safety. I prayed she'd be there. I didn't know what I'd do if I arrived and the cabin was empty. •

CHAPTER 54: THE LAKE

Seeing the lake, as I made the approach down Highway 93, brought both a warm sense of hope and a cold shudder of nerves. What would I find at the cabin?

I was hoping to find Rachel already there, safe and sound. When I found her there, what would I do? Grab her and hold her, or bombard her with a hundred questions?

Was she okay? Did she make any choices that would haunt her for the rest of her days? What was the impact of the trip on her faith and the other things she believed in? Did it alter her core values or reinforce them? And how did Gus manage the trip?

There would be the personal and emotional sides, and there would be the logistics. Exactly how did she get there? Had someone helped her? Had she helped others?

We would have time to share our stories, tell our tales, and repent for our misdeeds. If she were there.

She had to be there, or my mad journey would begin again. To Newport, where she'd said she'd go if she couldn't get to the cabin. She'd told me the route she was taking, so I'd simply track it. I'd search for her along the way, then I'd go to Newport. To find the redhead and the dog. Everybody would know them.

Just seeing the lake, I knew I'd see her again. Then I wondered, how soon?

I saw some flickering glows in a few of the houses that lined the lake.

All of the electric lights were off, giving the appearance of an earlier time in history, a simpler time. I could see the soft waves of smoke coming from a chimney, like a painting I'd seen.

"Bang!" I had missed seeing the rock that had tumbled into the road. The right front corner of the truck dropped down and pulled me to the edge of the highway. I couldn't believe it. I was less than 5 miles from the house.

Grabbing my flashlight, I got out of the truck and walked to the other side. The tire was completely flat, punctured by the edge of the rock. I was so close! And I was so tired.

I pulled the truck off of the road into the trees behind the Church Camp sign. Nobody would use that road for another month at least. I'd take care of the truck in the morning. I would return and change the tire, then finish the drive to the cabin. I hadn't seen anyone in hours, so the truck would be safe. Even with the world physically and literally collapsing around us, I trusted my neighbors up here.

I only had a few miles to go. Around the sweeping bend, down the gravel lane, and around the point road to the cabin. I knew it like the back of my hand. I knew I'd get there.

Alex's bike was pulled from the rack and placed on the ground. Like the old man in Missouri, I was a bit wobbly at first, but it came back to me. My 18-speed trail bike was a bit more suited to my size than Alex's little banana-seat Schwinn, but I made it work.

I had my backpack strapped across my shoulders and nothing else when I coasted into the foot of the driveway. I could see the glow of the fireplace, lighting the main room of the cabin. The Blazer was parked near the steps – scratched! In another place and time, I would have been upset. On that day, I smiled.

"Rachel!" I called out. "Rachel!" •

CHAPTER 55: THE TALE ENDS

We held each other for a very long time. Tears streamed down our faces, and we laughed. We really didn't say anything for the first few minutes. I remember lying in our bed that first night, listening to the wood pop in the fireplace and holding onto my beautiful lady. My world had been renewed.

In the morning, we walked back to the truck and changed the tire. We brought it home and parked it next to the Blazer. They were both battle-scarred and dirty, but they made a fine pair. They'd toughed it out. They held together and they helped see us through. They both deserved a bath and a fresh coat of wax.

We took a deep breath and looked out over the beautiful clear lake. The sky to the southeast was still dark and clouded with ash. We knew that thousands were out there, still suffering, still looking. Maybe they'd never find who they were looking for. We said a prayer for them and held them in our hearts.

We didn't really know where life would take us beyond that moment, but the important things would be managed. We had each other, and we had faith in our family members. We believed that they were living their lives, following their faith and values in different places, under different circumstances.

So we decided that in the big picture, we should follow our own doctrine. To let others live as they wish to live, but not allow them to impact our lives. To be self-reliant and take care of ourselves first, because that allows us to then reach out to help others. We didn't need the obstacles and guidance of all of the rules and regulations that didn't serve any of our own objectives. Like the mule deer on the trail, I'll respect your path, and you'll respect mine.

Over time, we planted our seeds and tended our garden. We fished and hunted and gathered. We fully appreciate what it means to truly and deeply love each other, our family, and the land on which we live.

So now, the light is back on. Will we ignore its allure, or will we again fall to our dependency on what it offers? There are benefits, but there are costs. Will we forget how to navigate by map, by compass, by the stars, as we did before? Will we learn anything from the sacrifices paid by our friends and families for these invaluable lessons?

What else comes with the light, as it flickers back to life?

It means that the outside world is beginning to return to its former self. What will we find there? What happened to the masses? What happened to our family members, our parents, Alex, Holly, her family? We will eventually learn what happened to everyone, including our parents. Have they survived? Have they endured? The light means communication will be close behind. Will we share cards through the mail? How will we reconnect our lives?

The new questions are almost endless.

What about food? Was the food supply sufficient to sustain everyone, or had there been incredible suffering or violence across the country? What about the grid and technology? Had futuristic ideals been traded for near-term realities? How was the power back on? Had the energy sector returned to a broad-based solution?

Most critically, had the political set realized that they could control us to the point of demise? If so, would they see that as something to avoid or to abuse?

It's a lot to ponder. A lot to consider.

I've stood in my garden for a few long years now. I've watched the bulb. I've wondered if I wanted it to come back on at all. But I've never waited for it.

I've moved ahead, learning to live without it and everything else it brings. Because, with it will come the desire to become reliant upon it once more, abandoning our candles and lanterns, riding instead of walking, sending each other words instead of communicating, and devolving into a culture that expects someone else to provide us with what we need, just because we want it, simply because we pressed a button.

I'm not sure what I think about all of it just yet. But the light is back on, so...

••••••••••••••••

Eric Whetstone

A professional designer and communicator, Whetstone lives in north Texas. He's also experienced in song writing and automotive restoration, and he loves to drive. If you're looking for a creative thinker who can perform evasive maneuvers at high speed, this is your guy.

A small town boy with an authentic farm background, he's also shared the conference tables of some of the nation's top CEOs. And he's logged miles in the tour buses of top entertainers. His life experiences are about as diverse as they get.

"It's been a good ride," he says. He's produced projects for Fortune level companies and seen his vehicles in automotive magazines. Whetstone has also written a music album ("Rocket Fuel"), played sessions as a drummer with his son – Zach Stone, a Nashville writer, recording and performing artist (ZachStoneCountry.com) – and performed stand-up comedy in local clubs. Now, he's written his first novel ("Gridless"). Everyone should chase their dreams with passion, he believes, and he certainly has done that.

Growing up at his parent's grocery store, his dad was also a farmer and the local volunteer fire chief. "As a kid, I got to run the siren on the way to actual fires! At the store, I stocked shelves and ran the cash register. At the farm, I picked up rocks, put up hay, pulled weeds, and cut thistles, along with running big machinery, mending fence, and working cattle." It was the perfect childhood: Maximum freedom, restricted by maximum responsibility.

Whetstone also works alongside his beautiful wife, a former fashion model, on a number of ventures, including her patented sports bra, designed for high-impact motion reduction (SugarSports.com).

Currently, they're renovating a home in the historic district of Grapevine, Texas. And, they do have a cabin in Montana, where she catches fish much larger than the ones he catches. •

CPSIA information can be obtained
at www.ICGtesting.com
Printed in the USA
LVHW031044031220
673098LV00004B/48